WITCHOPPER

DAN SOULE

For Mum and Dad
and for my hometown

FREE BOOKS

NIGHT TERRORS

Sweet dreams aren't made of these. Something more than ghosts pursues a family through a desert war zone. A slaughterman says goodbye to his job, but a place of death opens many doorways to darkness. From a father with a dark past, a young woman's inheritance passes on more than she thinks. And a mother's coffee shop daydream could unleash her worst nightmare. These are just some of the dark imaginings that will infect your dreams and rip you from sleep with a cold sweat because you've got NIGHT TERRORS.

Editor of *The Ghost Story*, Paul Guernesy, says: "Dan is a cinematic writer... he steadily builds the mood of his narrative from a whisper of uneasiness to a crescendo of full-blown cosmic horror."

So, grab this collection today from the pen of breakthrough horror author Dan Soule. Join the growing horde of insomniacs who've said goodbye to sleep and hello to NIGHT TERRORS. Download it for free at www.dansoule.com

PROLOGUE

SCHOOL CHILDREN from the Nottinghamshire town of Southwell have a playground game similar to *What's the Time Mr Wolf* and *Blind Man Buff* that is peculiar to the town. The game is called *Witchopper*. One child plays the Witchopper with their back turned to all the other children, who must sneak up on the Witchopper as they sing the following song:

> If you see the Witchopper
> Then you'll come a cropper
> Never mind how hard you try
> If you look in her cold black eyes
> When it's time to go to bed
> You'll be sure to wake up dead.

The sneaking children must close their eyes when the Witchopper turns, for if they make eye contact, they are out of the game, along with much screaming in a mix of delight and mock terror. Then the song starts again in a never-ending childish pantomime of death.

(From S. Lovegrove, 2012, *The Witchopper, Nottinghamshire Folk and Pagan Religious Practices at the Cusp of Modernity.* PhD Thesis, University of Nottingham.)

1

Facsimile from the notebook of Richard Peters

30th May 1820: Final entry from the diary of Reverend Gordon Moseley, vicar in the diocese of Southwell

Great sins have been perpetrated in this town. Sins that have snaked and entwined into one another to become a thicket of hate. It is a briar of her making and our immortal souls will bear the scars of our entanglement with her, as God is my witness.

I dreamt that none of us shall ever look upon his heavenly face because of that witch. When I close my eyes, I see only tortured images with the writhing worms and dark things of the earth.

It is three weeks since we dragged the witch from the Burgage gaol and meted her unspeakable crimes with the fury of good Christian men.

Three weeks and the town is quiet. People dare not look one another in the eye and all pass quickly about their business. Each and every face looks as tired as mine, for if my fellow man is like myself, the vision of that wretched woman has denied them any reprieve from their sins in slumber.

At the end, she uttered something, an ancient superstition in the old tongue, like one of Cromwell's witches. At first it meant nothing, nonsense from a bride of Satan. Yet last night once more I could not sleep. I rose finally with the sun and opened the Minster, my thoughts crowding in on me. I sought sanctuary in the Chapter House. It has always been a place to think, a refuge for the mind. But there, on every wall, he stared back at me, branches and leaves creeping from his mouth and ears. He was everywhere, in the ground of every street, in the stone, wood, and brick of every building, and in the grass and the trees and the plants of all else. That old god, whose name she invoked, laying his hex upon us.

I think too much. I am so awfully tired, and despite that I drink, I am so terribly and insatiably thirsty.

THE SPIDERY IDIOSYNCRASIES of the Reverend Moseley's copperplate handwriting became ever more erratic. He dipped his pen hurriedly into the inkwell on his writing desk, splashing uncharacteristically careless spots. The letters had degenerated into an almost illegible scratch as his hand shook, either from fear, fatigue, or both.

He struggled to replace the pen in its resting place on the desk. A flickering orb of light from his bedchamber candle illuminated his late night penmanship, while outside a cold moon, nearly full, shone down from an almost cloudless sky.

Swallowing hard, the Reverend felt the acid bite of dehydration and quickly poured himself another drink. He'd had the housekeeper place a jug in his room every night for three weeks now. A meagre splash of water fell into his glass. He drank it like a castaway on a raft, in the midst of a bleak ocean, might drink a puddle of rainwater on his leaky deck. It was never enough. Every morning the jug was drained, but still his thirst grew.

The slight man rose from his writing desk. Dressed in his nightgown, his cheeks drawn and eyes sunken, Moseley passed the mirror above his dying fire. The priest saw the image of a wraith staring back at him in the mottled glass. It was a true image, he thought briefly, before sniffing haughtily at the idea and burying it down, just as he had with the acid bile of his sickness. He wrote thoughts on paper to distance himself from them. It was silliness. All would pass.

The fact that only the Reverend saw the wraith in the mirror had also been playing on his mind. The gentle Doctor Goodyear hadn't detected any malady, unable to meet the Reverend in the eye throughout their consultation down in the parlour four days since. Picking off the leeches, the doctor had recommended brisk walks to fortify the constitution and a nip of brandy with milk at night.

The Reverend smirked at the idea of his enfeeblement. He poked the fire and the wraith smiled back with hell-cast shadows wrought across its haggard complexion. Moseley's own smile uncorked itself on seeing the happiness of his dark twin. He had to scrunch his eyes tightly and open them again to be sure that the wraith wasn't still smirking back at him. Sure enough, the smile had gone, and Moseley hurried from the mottled mirror to his bed.

Placing the candle on his bedside table, Moseley hoisted up his nightgown in one hand, while he readied the bed pan in the other. He held his nub of a penis between thumb and forefinger, trying to stifle his grunts and gasps, a cold sweat beading over his pallid skin as fire slowly melted its way from his bladder to his urethra. Muffling his cries, Moseley bit his lip so hard that he tasted blood, and a thin trickle of molten urine trilled against the porcelain bowl. Sweat ran down his face, and he panted with his eyes shut, upper body hunched, his penis gripped tightly in his shaking hand.

When he opened his eyes, the bedpan fell, smashing on the threadbare rug. A silent scream opened Moseley's jaws while his eyes glared wildly. It wasn't that his urine appeared as a dark porter ale in the gloom, or that the pan was speckled with blood. It was that the nub of his penis was black and necrotic and, far worse, it was no longer attached to his groin. The dead nub fell to the floor, as a pathetic whimper escaped his lips.

Moseley moved frantically, grabbing at the candle, knocking it over. Only luck, if it could be called that, meant that it did not fall on the bed clothes. Snatching it up, the Reverend blundered from his bedchamber, cutting his feet on the porcelain shards of the broken bedpan.

The vicarage didn't wake when he tumbled into the walls and hurried down the stairs. The door was left wide open to the night and would be found that way in the morning. Moseley, whimpering and chuntering incomprehensibly all the while, stumbled into the moonlight, bare feet slapping on the garden path that led into the graveyard surrounding the Minster, a monolith rising over the town.

In the moonlight, the shadows of the graves followed the priest's futile haste. He carried the heavy iron keys, which jangled. Blood rushed in his ears only to be joined by a susurrant sound of something, perhaps everything, moving, growing, watching the priest try to outrun his fate. Or perhaps it was the sound of Fate herself, sister to the Reaper, come to meet her brother for the collection of another damned soul.

The key butted ineffectually against the lock, like a panicked fly trapped under an upturned glass. There was a hissing noise, as something serpentine drawing closer and closer, as if the ivy was winding snake-like over the gravestones and the sycamore roots burrowed and churned beneath the earth towards him.

Finally, Moseley's trembling hand found its mark. The key lurched into the lock and muscles contorted in his twisting wrist. Straining to open the door, the Reverend fell through the portal. Scrabbling on his backside, bloody feet slipping as he backed away from the sounds that pursued him, Moseley withdrew into the church. *It,* whatever it was, stopped, halting in the night beyond the porch of the north door to the Minster's nave.

Moseley stared wild-eyed into the dark, paralysed for a moment, before hurrying on his knees to the open door, to shut out the things in the night.

Reprieve. Sanctuary. The hallowed space of the Minster would protect him, the Reverend thought, gathering himself. He was cold, dressed only in his nightshirt, and still shook with fear as he padded into the middle of the vaulted nave, leaving a trail of bloody footprints.

The great font lay on the other side of the cathedral between two thick sandstone pillars near the huge oak front doors. The Reverend had no chalice for his sacrilege, lifting the wooden cap from the font with the help of a pulley system at the nearest pillar. He fell on the font like a child's toy soldier drinking from an eggcup at the breakfast table. Scooping handfuls of water, Moseley drank and drank. The water sloshed into his belly, causing it to distend, and still he drank. But it was never enough. Eventually, with his nightshirt soaking from the holy water, he slumped to the floor, sobbing.

The serpentine noises from outside rose up once more, interrupting Moseley's self-pity. He sniffed, inhaling the snot dripping from the tip of his nose and listened, unsure. The rustling, hissing sounds had amplified in the vaulted echo chamber of belief in which the Reverend had sought safety.

But it... her curse... no, *she*... had found him. Just as he had been unable to hide in sleep, she was coming for him as the irrational part of his mind feared she would. Moseley put his trembling hands to his ears as the noise grew to a crescendo. Like the terrible rumbling of an avalanche, the sound grew so intense it became a vibration, penetrating every ounce of his flesh until it rattled his soul.

"No!" the Reverend screamed with defiant terror.

Shadows in the great nave began to move. From where they lurked, hulking in corners, they thinned, growing longer, solidifying, joining each other. A thousand tendrils of different sizes, from every corner, crack and crevice, slithered out toward him, entwining like a thicket of briars, a churning chaos of life. With it came the potent smell of woodland decay, sweet and earthy. From the loam of nourishing death, the perfume of existence blew through the church, a building which had been planted a millennium ago on *its* land, built from *its* rock and wood and transmuted ores by the sweat of *its* people.

The Reverend shook his head, tossing it from side to side, hands still covering his ears refusing to accept. "N-n-n-n-no..." he stuttered. A small trickle of dark brown urine oozed from the scab encrusted hole at his groin, hidden like a woman's private parts beneath a mat of pubic hair.

Moseley turned his head left and right at the faint sound of giggling children playing among the pews and hiding in the dark. And with them in the shadows there was something else watching, something great and towering and powerful. *God!* Could it be God had come to deliver his faithful servant? Moseley hoped in vain.

From that dark she emerged.

There were screams of a tortured death, which echoed through the great nave. The terror bounced from the walls, repeating itself as the faithful might chant their psalms in the learning of a hallowed lesson.

2

SHE SMELT OF SPRING FLOWERS, sweet and new. Her touch was soft, her lips like velveteen down, skin warm like yielding mosses. Her hands ran through Rob's hair. Her fingers, with nails of bark, and a hundred exploring tendrils, sent electricity from the nape of his neck to the tips of his toes, which curled in spasm, lost in a sublime warmth of no fixed location but omnipresent. Back arching, pressing into a heat that would consume him entirely, folding him in on himself until he no longer remained. A writhing mass of sweating skin and lush dew-covered forest, touching the divide in an ecstasy of oneness. Sweat and sap, pollen and...

Rob woke. The touch of his boxer-shorts on his crotch rubbed him as on a tender, barely healed wound. The wetness of his dream was already growing cool over the skin of his belly, and the material of his underwear felt sticky and unclean. Trying to wipe the clamminess from his face, Rob hit the screen of his phone. Midnight. He'd been asleep barely an hour.

Rob changed his underwear, hiding them at the bottom of his pile of washing. His new pair of shorts pressed just as sensitively on his

9

privates, which still throbbed painfully, jutting out preposterously, like a small demon Rob had little to no control over. In the dark of his room, sweat cooled on his bare torso. Rob pulled on a dressing gown from a hook with a racing car back plate. The room was decorated for a boy at least half his age, with race cars on the carpet and superheroes on the wallpaper. His parents had promised to let Rob redecorate as he wanted. Childish though it was, in the dark, the superheroes were lunging silhouettes, the racing cars the shadows of a rocky, broken path. Rob shivered, pulling the dressing gown around him, closing his eyes, trying to pull the dream of the woodland goddess back into his mind. His shorts twitched, and then he heard something.

In the sleeping house, there were noises. Rob strained to hear. The shadowy, broken floor did not feel like a child's fun space. Rob tiptoed as quickly as he dared across it, the throbbing in his boxer shorts shrinking away. The sound of the turning door knob felt as though it was giving away his location. Rob slipped onto the landing, a floorboard creaked, and he took his weight from it, stopping to listen in the hallway. There were those noises again. A low mournful groan. Rob swallowed, thinking even that sounded like a twig snapping underfoot in a dark wood. A squeak, and then another. Rob thought about going back in his room and putting something up against his door, climbing into bed, and curling the duvet around his feet, but he knew he'd seen rats above him in the attic when they'd moved in, and his father, Richard, had sent him up into the eaves to store boxes. The rodents could be scuttling above his room or in the walls or beneath the floorboards. He needed to get close enough to locate the sound.

Three steps farther down the hall and Rob heard the moan again followed by the squeaking. He stopped dead, blood rushing in his ears. The squeaking continued, like a door with a rusty hinge caught in a draught. His dream of moments ago now forgotten, Rob's legs were lead-heavy, each step a clumsy placement in the dark of a house that felt foreign and strange.

The noises stopped.

Rob listened.

He was nearly at the top of the stairs. Inkish night cast a Rorschach of dark shapes on the landing. The house lay silent, listening for Rob as much as Rob listened for it. A ladder climbed to the black attic. Rob resisted the urge to look into the abyss above, sensing eyes on him. The light switch was only a few feet away. Its illumination would banish the dark and those things which hid behind its veil. But even though the house was still a strange new thing to him, Rob remembered the loose floorboards at the top of the stairs. He hesitated. Forward or back?

Rob jumped as two cats screeched outside. His heart lurched at first and then, getting past the initial shock as the caterwauling continued, Rob calmed, realising his foolish mistake. Knowing his nerves in this new place were getting the better of him, he decided to go back to bed, hoping his dream would return. He was beginning to turn back when he heard something that truly terrified his teenage mind.

The rhythmic squeaking started up again, as if it had paused, listening, just as Rob had, and decided there was nothing there, only cats fighting over their garden territories for the night hunt. With the squeaking came the moaning, and Rob felt revulsion. The squeaking got faster and the moans of his parents louder as Rob retreated to his bedroom, shutting the door tight against the horror.

3

———————

"Yes, I suppose. Sex can be quite funny," the Reverend Lovegrove said. He was completely unfazed by the class of almost thirty teenagers sat snickering before him. "There's an awful lot of humour based on sex, so it's quite natural that you should find it funny. The best humour is based on taboos, and with sex there's so much we don't talk about. The whole biology of it is by far the most simple part, wouldn't you agree?"

The class said nothing, but neither was it laughing now.

"When you think about it, sex is really the heart of most things, isn't it? Charles Darwin certainly thought so. Competition pressures on natural selection in mate choice. That's not just for animals, is it?"

Mr Bryce, the form tutor, lurked in the corner pretending to read a book, peering periodically over the pages with a hard stare to silence the group.

Rob Peters, as was his habit, let his pen mediate between his subconscious and the world around him, doodling on a page at the back of his notebook, while he tried not to snicker like the rest of the class. He had captured perfectly the shiny forehead of the prematurely balding Reverend Lovegrove in his caricature. He had exaggerated the man's slight foppishness by the expression he had given him. Like all caricatures, it was an unkindness edged with the cut truth.

Ally Strachan, a small Northern Irish boy originally from Belfast, sat next to Rob. "Not bad," Ally whispered. Ally and his small gang had become Rob's friends. They were in the same form group and shared enough classes with Rob, who was looking for anything to hold onto in the new school, to be pulled into their circle.

The searching eyes of Mr Bryce fixed on Rob and Ally. Rob quenched the small smile he had on his face and tried to surreptitiously close his notebook and make like he was listening. Mr. Bryce's eyes lowered back to his paperback.

While the painful lecture droned on about responsibility, love, and respect, Rob's eyes wandered to the side of the class. Sat at a table, biting her lip trying to ignore the hushed comments of her friend Effie, was Julie Brennan. She was quite possibly the most beautiful thing Rob had ever seen. He sat behind her and across the aisle between the desks. From that position Rob could see the languorous line of her neck, the curve of her jaw, the delicate folds of her ear, behind which she occasionally tucked her curly hair. Without thought, his fingers pressed the pencil down, ready to commit those lines to an imaginary page and mark with his artist's embellishment what he perceived.

"She's not for the likes of mere mortals as us, Robbo," Ally whispered in Rob's ear.

"Ally Strachan, have you something you'd like to share with the whole class?" Mr Bryce's voice cut across the Reverend.

The restlessness of the teenagers stilled in anticipation. Along with the rest of the class, Julie and Effie turned to look at Ally. Rob blushed.

Without missing a beat Ally said, "Thanks for asking, sir. I was wondering if the Reverend would cover the sticky issue of internet porn?"

Several of the class were unable to contain their laughter.

"Black, Johnson, Sims, that will do." Mr Bryce narrowed his eyes on Ally.

For his part, Ally projected a face of naive, honest interest in his question.

"You think about internet porn a lot, do you, Ally?" Mr Bryce countered. There were more titters immediately swatted down by a rapier sweep of Mr Bryce's glare.

Ally replied, "I wouldn't know anything about that, sir. But I read something on the BBC website about how porn," there was more tittering at the legitimate use of the word porn, "was warping young minds, sir. It seemed relevant and pressing, sir."

Mr Bryce couldn't narrow his eyes any further, and Rob thought if he was to caricature him right then, he'd draw a pile of dynamite sticks piled into his skull with a short fuse fizzing away to impending ignition.

"If I may, Mr Bryce," the Reverend Lovegrove said, still as sanguine as ever. "I think this is a most excellent topic to address."

The school bell rang like a referee's whistle. Chairs scraped back as teenagers reached under desks to stuff them with notebooks. The Reverend Lovegrove perched casually on the edge of the desk, and Rob thought his caricature had done the man a disservice. He really did look kind and intelligent, but neither of those things were particularly funny.

"We'll save it for next time," the Reverend said, his words barely audible under the rush to leave.

"Football," Ally said. It was a question, command, and statement, all at once. And in the rush of bodies, Rob allowed himself to be swept along. The school still had an unfamiliar edge. He had to think about where he needed to go in the transitions between lessons. At least at break times the crowd surged like storm water down centuries-worn gullies, depositing them in the cafeteria or out to the concrete play areas. Rob found the organic automation of the herd to be a place to hide while he found his bearings in its mass.

Outside, Rob took up position between two piles of deposited school bags standing in for goalposts on the concrete. He liked football well enough, and as the new boy he was content to serve his time in the nets. Besides, it gave him a break and a chance to sit back and watch.

A dozen or more games pin-balled around the playground, overlapping and navigating invisible lines of hierarchy, age, and friendship groups in a lived chaos between the order of lessons.

The ball was downfield when suddenly more than half the players lost concentration. The opposition made a break for it. A boy Rob thought was called Johnny saw his chance and thundered the ball at Rob. He struck it too hard and the ball sailed over Rob's head, hit a post holding up the wire fence and pinged off to the side. A chorus of "over!" rang out, to confirm by consensus that the ball had missed the half-imaginary goal. Ally jogged over to Rob.

"Oi, Potty, get your head out of your arse and chuck us the ball back, would you?" Ally shouted. A boy in Rob's year was sat writing in a notebook on a bench as Julie and her friends, Sally and Effie, walked past. Rob had his back to the girls' appearance on the pitch and realised *they* had been the distraction. "Come on, Potty. You don't need to fix your make-up," Ally shouted. Rob heard some of the boys laugh. As Julie and her friends sat on a bench and began to talk. The boy Ally called Potty visibly sighed and put down his notebook. He had black hair that didn't match the pale colouring of his skin and freckles. Rob suspected he was naturally a redhead. Potty picked up the ball and spun it in his hands.

"Fuck me, Potty. Actually, I'd rather you didn't. Just kick it back," Ally shouted.

Potty gave the ball a small toss in front of him and punted it high and down the playground.

"Thanks, you wanker," Ally shouted with disgust and ran back to the game as someone on the other team went to collect the ball.

Rob barely noticed the boy sitting back down to carry on writing, because his eyes met Julie Brennan's. She'd looked his way, and for a brief moment, she'd actually looked *at* him. She smiled and laughed when Sally Watts said something in her ear. Rob flushed. Were they talking about him? Were they laughing at Ally? Or was it some other impenetrable mystery he'd never fathom the answer to?

"Rob, man on," came the shout from his team, right before the ball whistled past him through the goal, followed by groans as the school bell rang.

"Nice one, Rob," Chris Ward, one of Ally's gang, said.

"Sorry, Wardy, I wasn't looking."

"Don't be hard on Robbo," Ally said, shouldering his bag and putting an arm around Rob's shoulders. "He was admiring the goddess that is Julie Brennan."

Henry Willits laughed. "Don't blame him. I admire her every night, when the lights are out."

"And your sports socks thank you for your donations," Wardy said.

"A boy's got to dream," Ally said.

"Wet dream, more like," Chris said.

"Aye, a wet dream she is." Ally looked wistfully in the middle distance.

"Better just keep it a dream, unless you want to lose your teeth," Chris said as the boys moved off.

Rob didn't get it. "Teeth? What does that mean?"

"Well, Robbo, me lad," Ally said, releasing him from his shoulder hug. "Our resident goddess there doesn't mix with mere mortals such as us. She only favours the company of older gentlemen. And this particular one is called Danny Broad. He is an especially large fellow, like a titan of old."

"Is he at our school?" Rob asked.

"No, no, Robbo. Only the best for our Julie. Danny goes to a private school in Nottingham."

"His dad is the chief constable," Henry added.

Ally grinned. "So he could smash your teeth in and get away with it."

4

"HAIRY HANDS."

There was a titter around the table. It was funny, but the titter had an edge of nerves. Most of them had not met Richard Peters before, and he was something of a minor journalistic celebrity, brought low from the pantheon of London's Fleet Street to the plebiscite of the regional press at *The Newark Advertiser*. And now he was their editor. He knew they probably had questions. Many of them would have dreams of working for a big newspaper or media outlet. They wouldn't be journalists if they weren't curious as to why he'd given it all up.

In fact, Richard would think about firing them if they *weren't* suspicious about his claim that it was for a more comfortable family life. That's exactly what every public figure says when they are covering something up. Of course, for Richard it was true on both counts. He was doing it for his family and there was an ulterior reason for it. But he didn't want to share it with this lot.

Tim Smith, the sub-editor, was taking shotgun on the meeting, whilst Richard got his bearings. He seemed like a good guy. Actually, he seemed like *too much* of a good guy to be a journalist. Richard understood that Tim had gone for the job as well, and he'd served his time at the local rag for the last fifteen years. Richard swanned in at the last minute. The owners had gobbled up the chance to have such a premier league journalist as the new editor. Richard's appointment had produced a bump in advertising revenue. None of this seemed to faze Tim. He was about the same age as Richard, with straight black hair as thick as the black rimmed spectacles of the Clark Kent variety he wore. Tim came across as bookish and kind, and if it was an act, it was a very good one.

Tim was looking to Richard, while Richard scanned the faces of his staff. The youngish female journalist, in the far corner of the table of the meeting room, came out with the hairy hands suggestion. A few colleagues still had small nervous grins, but the young journalist had put her head down and suddenly looked as though she needed to make notes on the pad in front of her.

"Sorry?" Richard looked at Tim for the name.

"Izzy," Tim provided.

"Sorry, Izzy, could you say that again for me?"

Izzy shifted uncomfortably in her seat. She was pretty, petite and blonde, and Richard thought she'd look good on camera. "I said..." Now she didn't seem half as confident. "...hairy hands."

No one laughed this time. The words were greeted with stony silence.

"Go on," Richard encouraged. Izzy seemed to bloom in confidence at his encouragement, and Richard liked that look on her. She was even more attractive when she smiled, so much so Richard wondered whether small time print journalism was merely a stepping stone for her.

Izzy glanced at her notes and then at the faces of the colleagues and cleared her throat. "Does anyone else remember hairy hands?" Again, she looked around at her colleagues for some support. Most of them looked away but one or two nodded. That seemed enough to encourage Izzy.

"I was thinking about old regional ghost stories and the supernatural. Things like that. You wanted something a bit different and of local interest. Well, there's loads of those ghost stories all over, aren't there?" This produced a few more subtle nods of agreement. "I grew up on the moors. And it was one of those Yorkshire things, you know about the invisible hairy hands and how they would grab the steering wheel of a car and drive people off the road. I mean, they were probably all pissed. How could they tell the hands were hairy if they were invisible? But the story had some traction for quite a few years. And I remember being a kid and it featured on early morning Saturday TV. And then there were those hell hounds..." Izzy trailed off, sounding as though the more she talked about the idea the more ridiculous it seemed.

"I like it, Izzy," Richard said, looking into the middle distance above Izzy's head and then back at her. Suddenly, the other staff around the table brightened to Izzy's idea.

"That's a good angle," Richard went on. "There are lots of local ghost stories, and we are in the business of telling local stories. I think there's a ton of ideas we could spin off from that. Okay, give me some more," Richard gestured with his hand for the staff to come on. "I want local ghost stories or other supernatural things you know about and potential ideas about how we might use them. Go!"

"White ladies," someone called out.

"Thanks, er..." Richard looked at him.

"John Cleese," Tim said with a twinkle in his eye.

Richard gave him a 'seriously, that's his name?' look, and Tim answered with a bright smile and a nod of his head.

"Good, John. Anything else?"

"No, it's grey ladies, isn't it? I grew up in Sutton-on-Trent, and we had a grey lady who haunted the village pond. She was supposed to have died in some horse and cart accident back in the... I don't know, ages ago."

"Karen Wilton," Tim put in, speaking quietly into Richard's ear.

"Footprints in the snow that went up over rooftops," another journalist said.

"That was in Germany, not here," another corrected.

"The hanged man, out at Thoresby."

"Oh yeah," someone almost gasped. "That one used to freak me out as a kid."

"The beast of Bodmin Moor."

"That's Yorkshire though."

"No, it's in Cornwall."

"Oh yeah, right."

"Rolleston Station is well known for being haunted."

"There is the black-hooded phantom in Calverton. Lots of taxi drivers won't go there after dark."

"What, even an Uber?"

"God, Uber! I can tell you a horror story about my last Uber." Several around the table groaned.

More suggestions were batted around, everyone knew at least one ghost story or strange supernatural event was somehow part of the local town or village's mythology. And then it came:

"The Witchopper. That's the creepiest of the lot. It's got its own nursery rhyme and everything. Right in the middle of our patch too. My fiancé grew up in Southwell. She still scares the living daylights out of the children when they're playing up."

Tim leant in again: "Simon Farley."

"Thanks, Simon. I'm from Southwell," Richard said. It was such a mundane thing to say but had the effect of stopping everyone's chatting. They looked at their boss as if finding out this minor piece of information about this strange new being in their midst was some important revelation. Really, they were just journalists who were starved of information, and so anything seemed that it might be important. Again, Richard thought, this is probably a good sign, they were the breed of newshound that he knew and loved. "Right, we've plenty of ideas to play with, but we need some other element of the hook. Ghost stories are good. Everyone loves them. But how do we develop them?"

They began to bat around ideas, talking about linking it to local fêtes or the tourist industry. In truth, this was never going to be a big segment, but Richard could maybe see it becoming a regular little thing for a few months where they went through local ghost stories as a fun interest piece. More importantly, it had broken the ice, and he didn't want to start by busting their balls. He let them talk it over for five minutes before moving them on to the more important business, not least advertising revenue, fluff pieces on local businesses who take out advertising. Tim had already told him the preparation for the local May Day fair was a big part of their year, as were school photographs in the spring, which always featured in *The Newark Advertiser*. All those mums, dads, grannies and grandads buying multiple copies to have little Katie's picture in the paper always boosted sales for that month.

How the mighty have fallen, Richard thought. From ending politicians' careers to head shots of schoolchildren bought by a dozen family members. *Stop moaning. No more excuses, no more lying. You've got to make this work.*

"Right you lot," Richard raised his voice above the hubbub. "Fun bit's over, now down to advertising revenue. Tim, you'd better take it from here and fill me in as much as everybody else."

5

JANE WALKED into the bedroom wearing only a dressing gown and drying her hair with a towel. Richard sat on the bed tying his laces. His wife was smiling to herself as she passed, and not just because she'd just had a hot shower.

Richard playfully grabbed her around the hips, pulling Jane onto his lap. She gave a mock cry of surprise and laughed. Richard looked into those beautiful grey eyes and felt lucky, really lucky, considering everything. He kissed her on the lips. She kissed him back. Their lips moved like old dance partners remembering each other's rhythms. His tongue found hers, lightly touching before withdrawing. Their lips coming together was more than enough to get Richard aroused. Their marriage had been reborn, and with it, their desire for each other. Their mouths closed again, but they were halted by a creak at the top of the stairs.

"Rob?" Jane called, craning to see. The bedroom door was wide open and Rob's shadow disappeared from the door frame, moving across to the top of the stairs. Then, the sound of his feet trudging down the stairs.

Jane rose from Richard's lap, still smiling, returning to dry her hair. Richard tapped the flesh of her bum, and lightly she batted away his hand.

"Not now, you cheeky bugger."

"What time is your interview?" Richard asked, coming up behind her to fix his tie.

"Eleven." She nudged her bottom back to push him away.

"Nervous?"

Jane gave a small shrug. "What will be will be. It's not as if I haven't done the job before."

Jane had been a medical secretary when she returned to work after Rob was born. She had studied graphic design at university, which was where Rob had got his talent for illustration from, although he eclipsed her ability by the time he was twelve and now, she knew, his talent was something very special. After university, struggling to find a graphic designer's job, Jane had trained to be a copywriter, but she'd never enjoyed the work. Having Rob hammered that home, gave her a new perspective. The hours working as a copywriter in London were long and unfulfilling: helping to sell sugar to kids or debt to the poor. Well, now she had her own kid, and her own debt. Things had to change.

A medical secretary's post came up at the local GP's practice. It suited their childcare needs, plus Richard's job was really taking off, and so Jane left the job when they decided they must leave London.

The front door closed heavily.

"Rob?" Richard called, dropping his tie, looking at his wife through the mirror. They both listened for an answer that didn't come. Jane went to the window looking out from their bedroom and pulled back the edge of the curtain to see Rob reaching the bottom of the drive, his old school bag slung over his shoulder, headphones in his ears.

"Weren't you supposed to be taking him to school today?" Jane said.

Richard leaned over, kissing his wife quickly on the side of the mouth. "Yep," he said hurrying for the bedroom door. "I'll catch up with him."

"What about breakfast?"

"I'll grab something on the way to work."

With Richard's feet thundering down the stairs, Jane called after him. "Have a good day too."

"Thanks," he called back, the door slamming behind them, rattling the brass letterbox.

"Can I not walk in by myself? I'll look like a right tool if my dad brings me into school."

Rob sat in the passenger seat, both headphones still in. Richard couldn't tell whether the music was on or off over the hum of the engine. They turned right at the crossroads, the bottom of the common called the Burgage. They drove past the museum of the old jailhouse and a local landmark called the Hanging Tree, which stood dying at the edge of the common. When Richard was a child, it still burst into green during spring. Now its bare branches creaked and knocked.

"We spoke about this. This is a chance to spend more time together."

Rob tutted loudly, turning to look out of his window, the rows of quaint, Arcadian, Georgian, and red brick Victorian houses sliding by outside. The town looked like the quintessential English country idyll, the kind of place that would have been put on promotional material to attract American tourists. Which is exactly what the tourist board had done.

"Tell you what, I'll drop you at the top of the lane off Westgate. It cuts straight down to the school. You can walk in by yourself. Come to the main reception and I'll be waiting for you in the headmaster's office. How's that sound?"

To this gave Rob an ambivalent movement of his shoulders. He fished his phone from the inside breast pocket of his school blazer and started to check through his apps.

"Come on, mate. I'm trying," Richard said, with a slight edge on his voice that he didn't intend.

Rob's face hardened. "You're trying?" His tone was already harder than his father's. "You're not the one who's been dragged out of

London against your will to the back arse of nowhere, away from all your friends."

"Don't take that tone with me, Rob. I'm still your dad." Richard had matched his son's tone and volume.

"Really?" Rob retorted, adding in a heavy helping of sarcasm. "You have a funny way of showing it."

Richard felt his blood pressure rising. "What's that supposed to mean?" He'd had just about enough of his son's sullenness, his constant talking back, when he could be bothered to speak at all, that was. Rob couldn't see the bigger picture and what they were trying to do.

A derisory snort came from Rob's side of the car, and he turned up the music on this phone. "Yeah, right!"

This wasn't an end to it, as far as Richard was concerned. The snort did not have a calming effect. Rob was acting as though he'd just won the confrontation. In truth, Richard had never been very good at losing an argument. It didn't suit the high-flying acerbic political pundit he'd become at *The Telegraph*. He didn't respond passively to people's challenges. He hit the brakes hard. They skidded to a halt, throwing them forward before jolting them back into their seats. Rob looked up in surprise into the dark countenance of his father's face. Richard slapped the phone from Rob's hand; and it fell between Rob's legs. He pulled his headphones out of his ears.

"What the fuck did you do that for?"

Rob was shocked and taken aback. He'd heard his father shout before, but he'd never known him to use physical force. He'd always been so absent. The shouting matches were normally with his mother, always muffled through walls, never far away in their apartment in London. However, those arguments had stopped a few months ago when everything changed.

"I'm still your dad," Richard spat every word. "Show me some respect." He was saying the words, but even he was thinking they were ridiculous, as though some other prat was saying them, the idiot who'd cheated on his wife and barely been there for his son. "...and try not to be such a selfish prick, Rob. We're doing this for you. We're doing this for all of us."

A car beeped its horn, pulling out around their stationary vehicle which blocked the road.

"Yeah? No one bothered to ask me though, did they?" Rob snatched up his phone from between his legs, along with his bag, and opened the door, jumping out. "And I'm not the one who has been a prick, am I, my dad?" He spat it with venom and the sting sobered Richard for a moment. His son slammed the car door and set off apace, striding along the pavement onto Main Street. Another car blared its horn passing Richard.

"Fuck!" he hissed the initial fricative, gritting his teeth after the hard-ending consonant, hitting the steering wheel with the palm of his hand. "Fuck, Fuck, Fuck!" he shouted, punctuating each expletive with a strike on the steering wheel.

The worst of it was that his son was right. Richard was the one who had been a prick, a world-class prick, a prick to end all pricks, and still Jane stayed with him to try to rebuild their marriage. Richard took a deep breath, put the stalled car back into neutral, and started her up again. Rob was already becoming smaller and smaller, a young man in the distance travelling away from him, becoming a stranger, and he didn't want that. He'd make it up to him. They would do something together. He had to fix it.

6

JANE GAVE her notes one more quick look-over before taking a final swig of tea from a mug she'd forgotten they had, only finding it now they were unpacking their old life into their new. It was a chipped souvenir of a trip to Tenerife she and Richard had taken after graduating. They had been poor. The apartment was crap and Richard got sunburnt badly on the third day, but it was a great holiday. It existed at some last stop before the final destination of adulthood, where all life's possibilities shrank before the realities of the real world. They lived in a series of long days, all of which felt like endless lazy afternoons, empty of commitments but full of wine, long wet kisses and sex, so much sex: between old sheets, in the shower, on the kitchen counter, the sofa, even a blow job on the balcony, while a pot-bellied Spanish man had a cigarette next door behind a flaking whitewashed partition, hocking phlegm as Richard tried not to cry out through the convulsions of his orgasm. When they arrived home, England was a tepid summer of sullen greys, but it felt like they carried the endless sun of the Canary Islands back with them into the seriousness of adulthood. But slowly, inevitably perhaps, the heat of that glow had faded until it was a chipped memory forgotten at the back of a cupboard.

The mug was placed on the kitchen counter. Jane had no time for regrets this morning. She had a job interview to take, then a house to finish unpacking, and a family to organise. Scooping up her handbag and checking herself in the back door's glass, Jane straightened her jacket. The glass had six small panels, fracturing her reflection and presenting her with multiple versions of herself, each subtly different. Trying to ignore her tiredness, Jane put on her best smile in defiance of the six middle-aged women who stared back at her. The past was just that. She practised her best 'how do you do?' face and swallowed her nerves.

"They'd be lucky to have you," she told her six selves, who despite their differences all said the same.

Thrown off by the lack of order in the house, Jane had her head in her handbag, checking she had everything. She opened the front door with one hand, while her other riffled through the bag, looking for keys. They were under her purse. She stepped down onto the rough welcome mat the previous owners had left. Still half-in, half-out, Jane threaded the mortise key into the lock. A fluttering at the corner of her eye made her pause, becoming aware that she was being watched. Slowing, making no sudden movements, Jane looked up. They were *everywhere*.

Hundreds of starlings roosted on Jane's car. A living blanket. The birds flowed from the car all over the short driveway to the low garden wall and, sure enough, the patch of grass that was the front garden, lying beneath two cherry trees at the front wall. The trees were in full bloom of soft pinks that had begun to snow petals in the gentle breeze. Starlings roosted there too and on the wall beneath and on their window sills and the roof of the porch above Jane's head. But only here, on their property. The birds had congregated in this small patch and not on any of their neighbours or the pavement or road.

The birds' small heads moved in furtive twitches, looking at Jane through each of their small black eyes in turn. They were beautiful. The sun reflected from their feathers in miniature cosmic rainbows. For the first time, Jane understood why they were called starlings. The white spots of their feathers were pricks of starlight, and in their multitudes, they were a blanket of the heavens resting on her family's property.

Something deep had been churning in Jane's stomach, a yearning hope for a sign, for something, for anything, to let her know she was doing the right thing, that they were going to be alright. And as silly as it was, this piece of utter random chance felt like this was it. The sign. Even if it was a placebo and not the real thing. *Because the real thing doesn't actually exist.* God, the world, whatever, doesn't *give* signs. Jane knew that. She also knew in her life as a medical secretary and as a copywriter selling pharmaceuticals that placebos were real, with real effects conjured by the subconscious mind. And she would take it, take with both hands.

The keys slipped from her hand, rattling when they landed. The starlings took flight, the flutter of their wings burring into the sky. Jane followed their flight as they came together as one, undulating, pitching one way and then oscillating the other until they disappeared, like some being from another world, bizarre in its beauty, here to observe from the stars and then gone at the speed of starlight.

Jane checked her watch. There was plenty of time. A short walk around the corner and up the road named the Ropewalk to the medical practice would take no more than five minutes. Perfect, she thought, locking the house. When she hit the pavement, Jane looked for the birds. She did not see them but, for the first time in a long time, there were possibilities ahead, like the spring sun signalling new life.

7

THE CLASS HAD BEEN SHEPHERDED by Miss Longman, their art teacher, along the paths skirting the playfields and Southwell's park. The park was stepped with two football pitches and edged with grand chestnut trees and Victorian red brick walls. A tennis club, surrounded by wire fencing, sat at the edge of the park, where retired folk cantered stiffly around the courts, swiping at yellow balls. Tucked in a corner, out of sight, near the footbridge over Potwell Dyke, was a small, secluded cemetery.

Excited by the change of scene, the teenagers were a hubbub of conversation, except Rob, who was without his new group of friends in art class. He followed quietly at the back, glancing at Julie Brennan when he thought he wasn't being observed. Art would have been Rob's favourite class, even without Julie. Miss Longman had been quite literally speechless when she reviewed the portfolio Rob had brought with him from London. Rob had blushed. It wasn't false modesty but embarrassment at the attention it drew from the rest of the class.

They reached the Minster, threading through a short, winding alley leading away from the playing fields. The cathedral towered above them, and the teenagers quieted without having to be told when entering the august building.

The Reverend Lovegrove was waiting for them in the circular Chapter House that branched off from the main nave, where a modern twenty foot statue of Jesus, made of gold, looked down on the great space. The Reverend welcomed them with a warm smile and beckoned them in.

"Come in, come in. You are all welcome. Make yourselves at home," he said, as if this was his own home and he was keen for them to come and visit again.

They'd filtered in, with Rob at the back and Miss Longman at his side urging the group on. The teenage class approached the space more like cattle entering an abattoir than a GCSE art class on their final excursion before exams. Rob found himself standing behind Julie, who stood next to Effie. He tried not to stare at her, fixing his eyes on the Reverend, but she smelled *so good*. Like an apple orchard after rain and honeysuckle in the breeze. It was a smell with its own glamour, and it swirled around in Rob's head, enchanting the space between them.

The Reverend clapped his hands together with relish. "The Greenman, sometimes known as Jack in the Green," he began. "Miss Longman asked me to set the scene. The Chapter House, as many of you will have heard before, has some of the finest examples of medieval carvings of this mysterious chap."

The Reverend walked over to one such example nestling in the intricate sandstone carvings, adorning wooden seats which ringed the room.

"Come closer and see," Lovegrove encouraged. "He was part of my PhD thesis, and I have been wrestling to turn it into a book for too long now. Some say the Greenman was a pagan god, only half remembered in folk tales and carvings such as these. Others say the church used these folk memories as symbols for the Christian calendar along with its other stories of life and death, birth and rebirth, winter and spring, Christmas and Easter. The Greenman is a forest demon for others, like Pan of Greek mythology. Sometimes he is a trickster, sometimes he represents the outlaws of the wild wood, like our famous Robin Hood. He is a metaphor for the wildness within us all. In short, he is an enigma. We do not know who or what he really was. But like any great symbol, his truth is not contained within the image itself."

The Reverend's voice grew quiet and self-reflective at this, his face close to one of the carvings. "It is what we bring to it. It is what lies in *our* imaginations and in our hearts that counts." He drew in a breath, as if surfacing from a deep pool of thought, whose depths remained murky to him no matter how many times he dove into them searching for answers.

His voice brightened. "An excellent subject for a group of talented artists, I think." The Reverend raised his eyes to Miss Longman.

"Thank you, vicar. Right class, get out your sketch pads. You also have special permission to use your phones to take pictures for later reference. Let your imaginations run wild. The carvings are only your starting point. You have nearly two hours." From within her stripy woollen jumper, at least four sizes too big, Miss Longman spread her arms wide like the giant Jesus in the nave. "Begin," she announced theatrically.

Sketch pads and pencils in hand, the herd of children tentatively separated from each other to explore the room.

Rob approached a carving as the Reverend Lovegrove said his goodbyes. It was of a man with branches growing from his mouth and foliage for hair. He didn't hear her approach, feeling himself already pulled into his imaginative inner world.

"Do you have any spare soft pencils, Rob?"

The Chapter House could have dissolved into a dew wet apple orchard. His mouth dried, and suddenly speaking had become a forgotten memory of a more advanced civilisation, lost in a flood created by its own hubris. He was but an inarticulate descendant of once great beings, one who could now barely oppose his thumbs. Julie Brennan was standing next to him, tucking a lock of hair behind her ear.

Rob searched for words, but his tongue lolled in his mouth, a floundering whale crushed under its own bulk. He made a small dry noise, as though the whale was dying, coughed to clear his throat, and still found no words. A smile kinked the edges of her lips. Julie waited patiently, flecks of polished walnut lucent in her eyes.

Finally, mercifully, she said: "A B2 or 3 pencil would be great."

Rob nodded wordlessly and fumbled for his pencil case, dropping his large sketch pad so that it slapped loudly on the Chapter House floor. Everyone looked around at the noise. Rob's fingers had lost all of their artist's dexterity. He grabbed a fist full of pencils, a mix hard and soft, and thrust them forward, presenting them to the glamorous creature which had cast her spell upon him.

Effie Black laughed behind her hand and rolled her eyes.

Inspecting the fistful of pencils, Julie reached out and plucked one from the chaotic sheaf of sticks. "Thanks," she said, and left him with his arm still outstretched.

After a short delay, Rob almost shouted: "You're welcome!"

Julie gave him another smile over her shoulder, while Effie tried not to laugh out loud.

She knows my name, Rob thought, heart pounding in his chest, and then he finally lowered his arm. And with an act of will, he pulled his eyes from Julie, who had begun to put initial marks on her sheet of paper.

Rob picked up his pad, still whirling from the revelation that Julie had said his name.

"Tick tock, Rob," Miss Longman was tapping her wrist from across the room.

Rob found the carving again. He let himself see it, really see it, the texture of the stone, the hand of the mason still present in the faint lines of his chisel, even centuries later. The foliage of different trees suggested the forest. Rob's hand began to move across the page, and he was gone. Time compressed. He wasn't himself anymore. He had become a channel, or that is how it always felt once it was over. There were moments of his own consciousness and ego in there making decisions. But as often as not, when Rob stopped to think about it, that feeling of self-control was something of an artifice. It was added on after the fact to explain what came out of his fingers. It had been this way since Rob was a small child and had shown a talent for drawing, a talent which his mother, her own artistic life stifled, was happy to encourage. She'd shown her son what she knew, and he'd picked it up so quickly and effortlessly. He would sit for hours, even aged five and six, lost in his creations.

Rob was lost again now, this time in the wild wood. His fingers moved quickly but surely over the paper, capturing what he saw in his imagination. An ancient oak tree, preternaturally large, with thick, gnarled bark winding around its trunk like corded muscles beneath a shaggy growth of moss and lichen. Mistletoe and ivy wound around its trunk and boughs, like rags threadbare with age. The thick canopy of the forest allowed only a dappling of light, cast faintly upon the throng of life that watched from the shadows, only hinted at by pencil marks suggesting shapes and tone. At the foot of the great oak was another figure, flitting through the wood: a nymph conjured from the nothingness of the page. The graceful line of her neck swept down to supple shoulders. Breasts, small and nubile, were hidden by moss; her flesh was leaves and the texture of bark, sweeping down to a thin waist that flared out sensuously at the hips. Small flowers grew from the bark of her skin, covering her legs. She looked at home, a creature of the wild wood. No, not a creature, a Goddess. And the oak was her temple.

The clap could have been the click of a hypnotist's fingers, waking Rob from his trance. He stood in the same position he had been in for nearly two hours, working in a kind of complete focused ecstasy. Rob became aware of the pain in his hand. He hadn't noticed Miss Longman observing him during that time, marvelling at his intensity. Nor had he noticed how the others in the class had been drawn to look at the oddity of a boy so engrossed in his work. Some looked startled, afraid even, at this boy and what he could create. They would return to their own mundane efforts a little less confident in whatever ability they might have had.

"That's it, everyone. You can put your pencils and equipment away. It'll be part of your homework to finish your composition for next week." Miss Longman began to walk around the building, giving one final look at her class's creations. Like most of the class, she had given Rob his distance, not wanting to break a concentration that seemed absolute. She looked over his shoulder.

"Amazing!" The word came out as a breathless whisper.

Rob felt the teacher approach closer, feeling her presence over his shoulder, entering the rarefied space around him tentatively, as if not wanting to risk startling a strange creature. Her hand reached out, seemingly wanting to snatch the picture and being too afraid, in case it would prove to be a mirage. Finally, her fingers lightly touched the edge of the sketchpad.

"May I?" She was not being polite. Miss Longman was asking permission from some greater power. Rob inclined his head to her and released his grip. She took his work in both hands and held it before her. Her eyes danced over the page. Rob could tell, disturbingly, her heart had quickened, her chest visibly rising and falling. Rob's mouth went dry. He was aware he had talent, but whenever a teacher wanted to inspect his work he always had the feeling that it wouldn't be good enough, or that he would be found out as a fraud, despite the fact that over the years the reaction to his gift had only ever been of one kind. Miss Longman lifted her right hand and traced it over the page.

Miss Longman swallowed and cleared her throat not once but twice. "This is beautiful work, Robert."

Rob shifted nervously, realising he was in the middle of the room and the centre of attention. All his classmates around the edge visibly perked to take an interest in their teacher, even those not interested in art. He saw that Julie, too, was looking at him, waiting to see what the strange new boy had done.

"You have a rare talent," Miss Longman said, almost dreamily to herself, but the acoustics of the Chapter House carried the compliment to everyone in the room.

Wanting to hide, Rob blushed. The pupils moved furtively again, necks craning to see, some shuffling closer.

"Such interpretation; such draftsmanship." Suddenly, her face brightened, snapping from her reverie. She beamed at Rob and flipped the large sketchpad around in her hands to present it to the class, turning slowly to let everyone gaze at what Rob had drawn. Some eyes grew wide. Some mouthed "wow," but more troubling to Rob, several smirked, whispering behind their hands to each other. Even Miss Longman picked up on this. It was not the reaction she was expecting. When she had completed her circle, she turned the drawing back towards herself.

Was it the erotic nature of the picture? The breasts perhaps? He had covered them with artistic modesty. The class had done life drawing before. No, it wasn't that. Was it the curve of the hips or the taut but gentle line of the nymph's bare body? No, there was nothing pornographic in this composition. Eventually, it dawned on her as the whispers of the class scythed through the quiet of the room. It was the face. How could she not have seen this immediately? She looked from the page to Julie and then back to the page and then once more up to Julie, before fixing a smile and quickly handing the sketchbook back to Rob and clapping her hands.

"Gather your things now and pack your bags. Back to campus we go."

The class hurried to pack, many of them giggling and nudging each other.

Rob stood alone, staring at the picture in his hands and then, just as it hit Miss Longman, he saw it for the first time. He looked from his picture to Julie. Effie cast glances back at Rob and then whispered behind her hand to Julie as she finished stuffing away her things. But Rob could see that Julie had flushed red, just as he was.

The nymph in his picture bore more than an uncanny resemblance to Julie, not only in her face, but also in every detail and proportion of her form. The size of her breasts. The ratio of waist to hips. Her ribcage and the length of her torso to her legs. the width of the shoulder. The line of her neck. Her jaw. The slope of her nose. The fullness of her lips and the shape of her eyes. Julie's entire beauty Rob had captured on the page as good as naked and turned her into a woodland goddess.

Rob's mouth felt like sand as Miss Longman called back: "Come on, Robert, keep up."

The class bustled in a chattering horde up the corridor, their laughter echoing hollowly as they left him behind.

8

THE BATHROOM MIRROR squeaked as Julie Brennan wiped a thick arc of clarity through the steam. She rolled on deodorant, which stung after shaving her armpits, and gave herself a few sprits of her mother's Dior perfume, rather than the sweet girlish one she got from her parents for Christmas. She wanted to smell like a woman, not some little girl. She pulled up her knickers, fresh from a pack of three she acquired in secret on a trip to Nottingham with her friends. Acquired was the word, because she didn't purchase them. They were slipped into another shopping bag while she and her friends tried to appear comfortable looking at such sophisticated underwear.

"They'll barely cover your bum, Jules, and you've hardly got one in the first place," Sally said on the bus home.

"Are those for you or Danny?" Effie asked, causing Julie to turn red.

She didn't dare put the new underwear in the wash in case her mother, or worse, her father, noticed. She'd hand-wash them in the bathroom sink and hide the pack at the bottom of an old box of teddies and her Barbie and Ken dolls, stuffed at the bottom of her wardrobe. She couldn't bring herself to get rid of the toys. It would be like throwing out old friends she used to have endless parties and conversations with.

Rocking from side to side, Julie inspected how the knickers made her figure look. They were yellow, with faux lace around the waist and a tiny satin bow. She rubbed her hand over her flat stomach, sucking it in despite the fact that her pelvis bones poked out at either side of her hips, like the small nubs of newly growing horns on a kid goat. Twisting around to see how they made her bum look, and then back to the front, Julie gave a deep sigh which fogged the mirror again. When she wiped it clear, her breasts were still disappointingly small, her belly not flat enough and her bum not... well, she couldn't decide whether it was supposed to be small and pert or big and round.

Julie's phone vibrated on the shelf above the sink. She snatched it up, gazing into its bright light.

"B there in 10 xo" the message read.

She messaged back a double X.

Julie's heart pounded in her chest so hard she thought she'd be able to see it pulsing between her ribs. Her fingers almost trembled when she fished out her other secret acquisition: a padded bra to counter her small breasts. It matched the skimpy yellow knickers, and it took three goes to fasten it, either because it was new or because her fingers shook.

This time, Julie looked at the girl in the mirror and tried to work out who she was. Was she trying too hard? Was she ready? What did she think she was getting herself ready *for*? She inspected the new, improved breasts, larger and fuller, the bra pushing what flesh she had up and together. They're not real, though, are they? Julie thought.

A knock came at the door. "Will you be much longer, duck?"

"Just drying my hair, Mum," Julie said, as a shock of adrenaline surged through her body, making her legs feel like deadweights. Grabbing a pair of jeans, the ones Effie said made her bum look nice, Julie's fingers tingled and so too did another part of her body. She tugged the tight jeans up over her boney hips.

The deodorant stick tumbled from the glass shelf below the mirror into the sink even though Julie hadn't touched it.

Pulling on her tight T-shirt, there was a pang of doubt, seeing the exact effect she planned for. The hairdryer screamed into the curls of her brown hair, which she then tied up in a ponytail. Make-up was one thing she couldn't risk, not even a little eyeliner, but she'd secreted lip gloss in the pocket of her jeans as she ran down the stairs, grabbing her jacket from the coat hook beside the door.

"You haven't had any lunch," Julie's mother called after her, just as Julie got to the bottom of their drive. Her father's broken taxi was parked there, waiting for money to repair it that would never come.

"Meeting Sal and Eff for something in town," Julie called back, hugging her coat over her chest until she was out of view.

"Do you need some..." But Julie was gone.

JULIE COULD HEAR the thumping bass spilling from Danny's car even before she rounded the corner. The pulsing vibrations magnified the pounding in her chest. She paused at the back wheel, quickly applied the lip gloss, and checked how she looked.

The music blasted when Julie opened the passenger side door. Danny gave her a nonchalant look then went back to typing on his phone. He swept a hand across the passenger seat, knocking crumpled wrappers onto the floor. Julie got in and sat while Danny finished on his phone. When he had, he threw the phone onto the dashboard, giving Julie a wink. Leaning over, he put his hand on Julie's upper thigh and they kissed, their tongues entwining. Danny pressed his mouth hard into hers, and his hand began to move up her leg.

Danny pulled away just when she thought he was going to move his hand a little *too* high. He grinned at her and hit the accelerator.

They sped down country roads, taking blind corners at speed as the hedgerows whipped by. She gripped the door handle tightly. Danny slowed, turning onto a single track country lane and parking under a chestnut tree in one of the passing points farmers. It was private and secluded, and the trees and hedgerows in spring bloom put the car into the shade.

When Danny turned off the engine, Julie was sure he'd be able to hear the thumping of her heart. A confident smile cracking through his stubble, he looked her up and down. Danny was three years older than Julie. Nineteen but could probably pass for several years older than that, but then, so could she.

The car smelled new. Julie had never been in a brand-new car before. And she had never smelt someone as intoxicating as Danny. His cologne was expensive, just like his car and clothes. He reached over and put his hand around the back of Julie's neck. His hands were soft and warm, pulling her towards him, leaning in. The smell of cologne this close was even more hypnotic. The leather trim of the seats creaked, still too new and unsubtle. Julie could taste his mint chewing gum, and the roughness of his stubble scratched the soft skin of her face.

If her heart had been pounding before, that was nothing compared to now. The sound of pumping blood rushed in her ears. He put a hand on her hip, but it did not stay there. She mirrored him at first, placing a hand on his chest but also pressing her knees together. Danny's hand strayed first to Julie's belly under her T-shirt. She flinched reflexively at how the graze of his fingers tickled. She laughed lightly, her full lips pulling back into a smile both sheepish and amused. He gave a dissatisfied grunt. His hand never made it up past her ribs as Julie kept her arm unyieldingly in the way. Danny then tried to come over the top, and Julie had pulled her hand up to his face to close the gap. After that he kissed her more insistently, pressing his tongue further into her mouth. Julie's face was getting wet with saliva, and Danny's stubble was rubbing so much she thought she'd end up with a rash around her mouth, but she didn't want to disappoint him. All her friends had cooed with jealousy when Danny had started taking an interest, sending her flirty messages and tagging her in his Instagram posts. He was older, tall and handsome, everyone thought so, and he was interested in Julie, really interested, and she had shoplifted the sexy underwear to... to what?

The wandering hand was back on Julie's hip, considering it's plan of attack. It slid down her thigh and then across to her other leg, rubbing up and down, making small advances with every upward stroke. Closer and closer his fingers moved. Julie tensed as he reached the top of her thigh.

"No!" Julie meant to whisper it, but it came out as something more insistent, her hand closing around Danny's wrist, pushing him away. He resisted, pressing his fingers into the crotch of her jeans as if that would persuade her otherwise. When she did not capitulate, attempting to scoot away towards the passenger door while her hand continued to hold back his wrist, he lunged forward with his face, covering her mouth, pulling Julie by the neck. She tried to pull away but there was nowhere else to go. She was backed against the door. Danny pulled her head towards his. She pushed on his chest with one hand as the other tried to deal with Danny's grinding fingers.

"No!" she tried again, as the hand she'd placed on his chest folded against his pressure. Suddenly those things which had seemed so attractive, his height and muscles, were now scary and overwhelming. He did not listen to her. Instead, Danny moved from his own seat, looming over Julie, pressing her down, his hand gripping her thigh roughly, forcing her legs apart.

"No!" Julie said a third time, almost a shout, turning her face away from him and pushing a palm against his mouth.

Finally, Danny stopped. He drew away to his side of the car. He put his hand on the wheel, casting her a withering sideways glance that made Julie want to shrink even further into the small space between her seat and the door.

"I'm sorry," she said quietly, hugging herself.

"Whatever." Danny tapped the wheel with his third finger in a hard metronome, glowering out of the window into the rain.

Julie sniffed.

"There's no point being sorry. You know, you come out with me looking like..." He didn't finish the sentence. It faded into the whine of an ignition and the throaty grunt of the revving engine. Danny pumped the accelerator twice, the needle on the rev counter twitching up and down, up and down, before he punched the gear stick into first and floored the pedal. The wheels spun, found traction, and Julie was pinned into her seat, fumbling for her belt.

THE CAR SKIDDED TO A HALT, and the seat belt tightened across Julie's chest. Danny didn't say anything. Julie freed herself and opened the door ajar but stopped. "I'm sorry. I... I really like you, Danny."

He let the silence hang in the air. "Really?" he said flatly. "Look Jules, you're really fit, but you're not the only girl around here. I thought I'd take a chance on you being younger. I thought you were more mature. Guess I was wrong."

"I'm sorry."

"You said that already. Let me know when you've grown up." He didn't say anything else. He sat waiting, staring through the wipers brushing away rain like inconsequential tears. She got out, and the door had only just clicked shut when the tires spun and the car sped off, throwing up spray. Julie watched him go, holding herself, wishing she'd brought a coat, wishing she didn't feel so stupid in a push-up bra she'd stolen to impress a boy who'd left her in the rain.

But even then, Julie still wished he'd come back.

9

MILLICENT PULLED on her Wellington boots with excitement. "The flowers will have loved the rain," she told the man. She was sure she knew him, but just couldn't quite remember his name. He knew hers and acted like they were old...? Milly couldn't remember the word. He had a nice smile, when he did smile. Today Milly thought he was sad and the smile was heavy on his old face. She hadn't enjoyed the morning, nor the night for that matter. The rain had kept her up fretting more than usual, not that she was sure what she was so anxious about. When the sun had finally chased away the rain, Milly put her coat on and was about to go into the garden in her bare fect. Luckily, the man - what *was* his name? - had tapped her on the shoulder, holding up a pair of wellies with that heavy smile. He'd helped her put them on and opened the French doors to her friends outside. Giggling, she'd waved back at him, looking at her from behind the double glazed glass, as if from another world. All her friends looked so beautiful after a downpour. Milly didn't know why she got so worried by the rain. Maybe it was because she wasn't allowed outside, or perhaps it was because the falling drops of water sounded like whispers she couldn't understand.

Brian turned away as Millicent reached the edge of the flowerbeds. Her trowel and fork still lay at the edge of the lawn. She picked them up and disappeared among the plants and shrubs, which had thrown off the shyness of winter weeks ago and now positively buzzed with life, showing off their colours, stretching their limbs in the sunshine.

Brian picked up the neat pile of clothes he'd got ready for Millicent the night before and moved them from the arm of the sofa to the dining table. There was no reason to move them other than because it gave him something to do. She wouldn't put them on anyway. Perhaps, once she was wet and muddy from the garden, she might consent to get dressed. Or perhaps not. He'd probably move the clothes back again before she came in and refused to put them on, complaining that they were old woman's clothes. He felt tired and wanted to take a nap and let out a short hollow laugh at himself. He wouldn't. He couldn't risk a nap.

The doorbell rang and Brian grunted. His right knee always acted up more after the rain or when he was tired, so today it was doubly sore.

The chain slid metallically and then fell with a rattle and a tick-ticking against the door.

"Oh Jesus!" Brian muttered to himself.

The Reverend Lovegrove stood on the doorstep, his forehead shining underneath a drastically receding hairline that had long ago fled behind the crown of his head.

"Brian!" the churchman said with unwavering cheerfulness. "Is it a bad time?"

Brian put on his heavy smile once more. "Not at all, Reverend. Millicent has just popped outside into the garden though. Can I get you a cup of tea?"

Reverend Lovegrove stepped inside, wiping his feet. "How is she today?" He followed Brian into the kitchen.

The kettle grumbled and Brian took two mugs out of the cupboards. He rubbed his face, wiping away the tired smile. "I don't think she knows who I am again today. We didn't sleep well." There was no anger in his voice, only sadness.

"The rain?"

44

Brian nodded weakly.

"Do you need anything? Have you thought any more about respite? You'll need a break too."

Brian stared out of the serving hatch from his galley kitchen and over the dining area in the living room through the French doors. He could see his wife kneeling in the mud of the flowerbed, tending her beloved plants. His heart ached.

"How can it be that most days she can't even remember my name? How can it be that some days she can't even remember her *own* name, and yet she remembers every single Latin name of each of those plants out there?" These weren't angry questions. They were flat and exhausted. "Why would God do something like that?"

The kettle kicked off from its growling boil and descended into a chuntering grumble.

"I'd be lying, Brian, if I said I had any idea. It's a cruel disease. But if you need anything, I'm here, and so are your friends. We're all here for you and Millicent. Don't be afraid to ask."

"She should have a better afternoon. She always perks up after a good session in the garden." Brian stirred the teapot and added milk to the mugs.

"Oh, that reminds me." The Reverend put down the notebook and Bible he was carrying. The Bible was more of a prop than anything, a thing that people expected to see. Hardly any of them actually wanted a reading or a blessing anymore. Chats and cups of tea were the order of the day. Or coffee. Coffee had become very important in the last fifteen years or so. Hardly anyone drank the stuff before, now one couldn't move for coffee shops. The Reverend produced several packets of seeds from his pocket. "I saw these in the garden centre and thought Millicent would enjoy them."

MILLICENT DIDN'T FEEL the cold, muddy ground soaking through the nightdress to her knees. "Now, now, you wait your turn," her voice tittered gently as she unpicked the tendrils of the *Atropa Belladonna*. The plant's stems entwined possessively around her wrist. She freed herself, passing her hand through the plant's leaves by way of recompense, like petting one of many eager puppies. Her *Mandragoras* wanted some attention too, and so did the *Campanula Glomerata*. "Yes, I missed you too. What have you been up to? Ah, is that so? Is she really?" Millicent gave her touch to each of her plants, listening to their stories. "But why now? Hmm!" she said doubtfully. "Oh, don't get upset with me. There have been too many chances. It has never worked. Really? Why is he so sure? Well, tell him from me, I think it's unlikely. I know he knows what I think."

The soil around the plants at the back of the bed began to undulate, and up from somewhere beneath the thick mud emerged fronds and tendrils, but not from any of Millicent's plants, and with them came a smell of sweet and earthy decay. "Hello, Jack!" Millicent said, face brightening even further. The fronds and tendrils unfurled, reaching out to the old woman. She gave them her hand and they tenderly entwined around it. "I'm just fine, you silly old fool. Thank you for asking." Her plants fell still, and the fronds and tendrils which appeared from the earth retreated beneath the surface. "Oh, don't go."

There was a small rumble of thunder far off. Millicent gasped, suddenly feeling alone and afraid. A shadow fell over her.

"Hello, Millicent, you remember me? I'm Reverend Lovegrove. I brought you some seeds."

Millicent clutched the muddy trowel to her nightdress, smearing it with dirt. She struggled to her feet, cowering like a frightened animal, her eyes darting furtively around at anything but the Reverend.

"Here you are." Reverend Lovegrove held out the packs of seeds. The thunder rumbled again, only quietly. Millicent flinched.

"A storm is coming. No, no, no. It can't. No, no, no." She bustled past the Reverend, knocking the packet of seeds from his hand, and scurried across the lawn toward Brian, who stood waiting as he always did at the French windows, hoping his wife would come back to him.

10

CHARLES WINDSOR -- "NO RELATION" he would always joke -- had been a farmer all his life. It was what Windsors did in this part of the world. Just like his father before him, and his great grandfather before *him*, and so on. The Windsor family had been farming on the edge of Southwell for more generations than could actually be remembered. Over the years, they'd had more luck than most other farmers. And through the good fortune of surplus money and canny marriages they had been able to acquire ever more land. They were by no means a large farming conglomerate, but theirs was still one of the most sizeable and profitable farms in all of Nottinghamshire. While such success might cause jealousy in small communities such as theirs, that was not the case with regards to the Windsors, or at least as far as Charles was aware.

Charles was a member of the local Chamber of Commerce, the Federation of Small Business, and of the Country Landowners Association, as well as the Rotary Club and the Masons. Although, his true pleasure lay in having a pint down at the pub with the other chaps from the town. He favoured the *Saracen's Head* for its red leather chairs and open fire, but he also made a point of drinking in the *Wheatsheaf* and the *Hearty Goodfellow* from time to time, where more of his farmhands and local tradesmen were likely to enjoy a drink.

He had even had a student from the agricultural college in Brackenhurst come to study his farm for their dissertation, interested in procurement, field layout, resource allocation and financial budgeting, and all the other usual stuff that goes with running a large successful farm.

But Charles would tease the student that what really mattered was having a traditional mindset. Respecting the ways of the country. Farming was about the ebb and flow of the seasons and the feeling of the land and the sacrifice and the toil that man and beast put into the soil. It was the *earth* that gave back. The young student, Mandy, humoured him with pleasant smiles. Like so many of the young, she thought she knew better. Machines, numbers and systems, order and predictability were their new gods, the things that they worshipped. Though Charles would acknowledge part of the success of the Windsors had been learning to move with the times, taking on new technology and ways of doing things when they seemed appropriate, he also knew, just as his father, his grandfather and his great-great-grandfather, and so on had all known, they were *country* folk and would keep its traditional ways.

It was a fine spring day as Charles pulled on his Wellington boots, grunting slightly with the effort. He was a man for whom middle age was something of a waning season. Still, he was full of life and ready to go. The birds were singing, plants were coming into bloom, and they were already beginning the process of selecting which of their winter lambs to slaughter to fill the shelves of the local supermarkets and butchers.

His boots made a rhythmical crunching across the farmhouse gravel before he met the patchwork of compacted earth and concrete drives that made up the passageways and courtyards between his many farm buildings and barns. He felt in the pocket of his green waxed Barbour jacket to check that he had everything he needed for this morning's work. In his other hand he had a short length of rope, its loop tied with a sheaf knot his grandfather had taught him as a boy, and which he had never forgotten.

"Morning, Charles!" Eddie Grimshaw waved as he sprang down from a tractor.

"Morning, Eddie!" Charles waved back cheerily, and the whisper of a breeze blew in his silver and orange hair.

"Where you going off to?" Eddie fiddled with the power-hose to wash down the tractor.

"I noticed a sick lamb last night. Just going to separate him from the others. Vet's going to come later. Are you up in the top field today working on hedgerows?"

"Just heading there in a minute. Shall we talk about tomorrow's market?"

The best of the lambs needed taking and selling at the market. Prices weren't great right now. There was so much lamb coming in from New Zealand and other areas: cheaper, nasty lamb from Eastern Europe. However, they would endure, that was one thing that Charles Windsor was certain of. "Good idea, we can chat about it after lunch. How's that?"

"Righto, boss." Eddie turned back to his hose. Its pump whirred and then the water shot forth in a great hiss.

Charles unlocked the wide steel gate to the field and shut it behind himself. Like every good country boy knows, one cannot pass through a gate without also closing it. It was the natural order of things and the respectful thing to do. Charles had no problem with people walking on his land, it was the way of the country. He was merely the custodian. He made it fertile and profitable, with help. But as it had been as far back as the Middle Ages, people were allowed to wander the fields as long as they respected it by closing gates and minding the crops and animals there.

The lambs huddled around their mothers in twos and threes. Some suckled at their mother's teat. The more adventurous ones were frolicking and playing, running and jumping with surprising agility. Charles stopped for a moment and surveyed his flock like the Good Shepherd, checking on each of them. He passed an experienced eye over them, noting potential problems, which ones might need a little more feeding or if there were sickly ones. They were just as they had been last night: all in fine fettle and ready for slaughter. He had great bloodlines, the best pasture, and the sun shone down on. People might buy cheap lamb, pumped full of hormones and God knew what else, but they wouldn't taste like these ones. The French have a word for their wine that so perfectly encapsulates Charles's philosophy: *terroir*. That is what his lamb had. They took on the flavour of their environment. They quite literally embodied it. The lamb was the land, and the land was the lamb. This was another one of Charles's little adages, one he got from his father, who probably got it from his grandfather, and so on.

He spotted the robust one that he had marked out last night. A twin, good natured with its mother and sibling. The healthiest of the whole flock. It would make the finest eating. It had the perfect amount of fat, perhaps a touch more than modern tastes preferred. That had been out of fashion for the last few decades, but Charles had noted in *Farmers Monthly* that fat was making something of a comeback. The lamb did not flee from Charles as he approached. He was a benevolent figure, their Shepherd, who kept them safe, fed and sheltered. He was as their God, and the most benevolent God was he. So when he approached, they came toward him. He chuckled and spoke gentle approbations, patting them on the head and rubbing their flanks, both in affection and also feeling the density of the muscle and the layers of fat and the quality of the wool. And then to the healthiest of all the lambs, the finest of specimen that he had bred this year, or perhaps for several years, he took the short length of rope and looped it over the lamb's neck as a leash.With a double-click of his tongue onto the hard palate of his mouth, he said, "Come on boy, let's go for a little walk."

Dutifully, the lamb followed Charles like a well-trained dog at heel. Occasionally, it would stop to feed and ruminate on the grass. Charles would give a little tug on the rope and the lamb would follow on. Charles mused that this really was the finest of mornings, and mornings were the choicest part of the day. Farmers work unsociable hours. But they see more sunrises and sunsets than anybody, and in the spring there are moments like this, when life is full of teeming effervescence and the sun shines in such a way to make a man think that there really was something mystical about the world, that life in all creation was undoubtedly a form of magic.

They left the field with the other sheep, entered another, down the hill towards a stream at the bottom. Halfway down this second field, the lamb became skittish, tugging at the rope. Soon after he heard a barking, and Charles spotted the dog immediately. Its ears were back, and Charles could tell the animal was not trained to be around livestock. He gave a heavy sigh, experience telling him what was coming. The dog seemed oblivious to all else apart from the lamb, trying to come up behind them and follow the wolfish instincts Charles engendered in his own sheepdogs. This dog, however, appeared to be some sort of cross. Definitely part Labrador. That was good. They had a soft jaw, clever enough and kind dispositions, but a weakness for food. The other half, though, was probably Alsatian. That could go either way. Frightfully bright with incredible protective urges. But worst of all, they were bred for their bite.

Charles shortened the leash as the dog lowered its body, skulking after them. Its owner was now in earshot, shouting and running up the hill out of breath. "Timmy! Timmy, no! Come back, Timmy!"

Charles didn't worry. He knew what was coming. He moved the lamb behind his legs. It tried to tug, wanting to run, which was the last thing it should do.

Here it came, the charge.

The dog's wolfish instinct had taken over. It lurched from its skulking position and came pell-mell for the lamb. The lamb attempted to bolt. Charles knew the knot would probably constrict its neck, but he would loosen it soon enough. The dog would have to run around him, so Charles pulled the bucking lamb out from behind him to show it to the dog, giving it a clear target. The dog's eyes had a wild glaze; its genes telling it that soon it would taste blood. In one fluid movement, the moment before the dog was about to strike, Charles whipped the lamb behind his legs again and stepped forward, grabbing the Labrador-cross by the scruff of its neck. His shin connected with the dog's chest and lifted its front paws from the ground. It was a big enough dog and its momentum caused them to waltz in a threesome. As the momentum lessened,

Charles let the dog drop back to the earth. He'd broken its initial concentration, but it could still smell the sheep. Its gaze began to flick back to its prey, and Charles, in a commanding voice, shouted: "No, Timmy!" As he did this, he butted the dog with his shin again, invading its personal space as the alpha would dominate the beta. It had the desired effect. The dog's attention was broken again and each time it looked back to the lamb Charles repeated the call and the action.

"I'm sorry. Timmy, no!" The dog's owner had caught up at last. A thin man with glasses and even thinner hair. Probably a similar age to Charles. Charles didn't recognise him, but then, the town had grown quite significantly recently. Perhaps he was new to the area? He looked more sheepish than the lamb.

"I'm so sorry, he's never done that before," the balding man said, reaching out to take the dog by the collar and affix its lead once more. Only once it was attached did Charles let Timmy go, who immediately lurched, nearly pulling its owner to the ground. The owner pulled it back like a fisherman fighting a titanic battle with a leviathan rainbow trout.

"No harm done," Charles said. "He was just being a dog. It is a hard instinct to train out of them. We do have some lambs in the upper field, so perhaps stay clear of those for the next week."

The balding man was still panting with the effort. "Absolutely. So sorry, again. I'll keep to the nature trail from now on."

"Think nothing of it," Charles said, waving them off. "Have a good day, sir." The man looked ashen-faced and nodded, hauling his unruly hound with him and muttering admonishments Timmy would never understand.

Charles and his best lamb continued their walk down the field. He circled his left shoulder, now sore from his entanglement with Timmy. Quite soon after, they came to the bottom of the field which lowered almost down to the level of the stream, running along the edge of Southwell. In the Industrial Revolution, there had been a mill that utilised the stream. It had been derelict for many years, but then twenty years ago a developer turned it into a set of luxury apartments. They looked quite impressive now. In fact, Charles owned four of them and rented them out. They'd proved to be rather a good investment.

They reached the corner of the field and walked into the middle of the hedge. There was a large, broad hawthorn with spaces in between. They threaded their way through as though exploring a maze. Eventually, they emerged into a covered space the size of a large room, seemingly held up by a central pillar.

It wasn't a room. They stood under the canopy of an old weeping willow. The morning light refracted through the gossamer canopy as if through stained glass, giving the space the feeling of a holy place. Local teenagers and children all found their way out to this spot. The young ones played and the older ones left behind the detritus of their bacchanals: cigarette butts, joint ends, discarded cans and bottles of beer, cider, and wine, and it wasn't unusual to find the occasional condom. Charles produced a black bin bag. He tethered the lamb to the trunk of the willow and filled the bin bag with the bottles and cans. Thankfully, there were no condoms today. With the bin bag three-quarters full, he tied it and placed it at the edge of the circular area where the branches touched ground. Then he untied the lamb and patted the trunk and rubbed the lamb's flank, marvelling again at the quality of fat and meat.

"You are the best of them," he told the lamb, and it gave a small bleat in response to its benevolent God. Charles shortened the leash in his hand by wrapping it around his forearm and then reached inside his pocket and produced the other length of rope he brought with him. This was longer and more durable and already had a ready-made noose tied at one end. He pulled the lamb close, holding it around the flank, and then looped the noose over the animal's hind legs. The lamb kicked a little and bleated in protest, but it did not fight. Then Charles pulled the rope around. It closed tightly around the beast's ankles, causing it to topple to the ground. The lamb panicked and tried to rise, crying out.

Charles lifted the rope so that the lamb had only its forelegs on the ground. It twisted, tweaking Charles' shoulder somewhat, but he ignored the pain. Looking up, he saw the old bough that he and his father had always used, and that his great-grandfather had used, back in the long tradition. He threw the rope over the bough and caught the other end, then hoisted the lamb up until it hung upside down, its head swinging approximately a foot from the ground. Charles tied off the rope around the trunk, utilising another of the knots he learnt as a boy. He knelt down, calming the lamb with softly spoken words. It still bucked and swayed. He took it by the scruff of the neck. "There now. There now. Easy. Easy." He continued to soothe it as he put his hand in his pocket and took out an old knife, which had been sharpened so many times that the previously convex blade had started to become concave in the middle. Its edge had not been dulled, however. The family had kept it sharp for many generations with diligent applications of the whetstone. Many hands of the Windsors had wrapped around its handle over the centuries. As far back before they *were* Windsors and the name was the Old English: Wenban.

Charles pulled back the lamb's head, exposing its throat. "There now. There now."

Plunging the knife three inches into the animal's neck, he sliced from one side to the other, opening up both jugular veins. The flesh peeled apart at the touch of the razor-sharp blade and the strong heart of the lamb pumped powerful jets from its open veins, spraying Charles's wax jacket. It would wipe off easily in the water of the stream. The lamb bucked, but with the effort only made its heart pump faster, expelling more precious blood, which splashed on the roots of the willow tree, pooling there. Eventually, the lamb ceased twitching.

Charles held back its neck until all its blood had been rendered, then he placed the tip of the blade at the animal's groin and, in one swift action, sliced it open to the rib cage. Out tumbled the purplish-blue offal: stomach, intestines, kidneys and liver. Charles sawed through the oesophagus, and the entrails tumbled wetly to the floor. He let the lamb hang for a moment while he ambled down to the stream beyond and washed the knife with dock leaves and water from the stream. He splashed the blood from his jacket. The weather was warm now, and he would not wear the coat back up to the farm. Instead, he'd carry it over his shoulder folded inside out.

When he returned to the lamb, still gently swinging upside down, birds chirped. In the distance, he could hear cars from the town and the oblivious bleating of lambs in the field above them.

Charles untied the offering and gently let the body come to rest on the roots of the willow tree. He reversed the procedure, unthreading the rope from the bough and untying the lamb's legs. Folding up the lengths of rope, he put them back in his jacket and then slung the coat over his shoulder. His offering made, Charles left, picking up the plastic bag of rubbish as he went.

The lamb lay still. It's eyes open with a blank stare. Its white wool was soaked pink around the neck and over its face and muzzle.

Steadily, like the rustling of leaves or the squirming of countless bugs beneath the earth, a sound rose. The ground beneath the lamb moved as the languid weeping branches of the willow swayed and whispered. From the earth grew glowing fronds and tendrils. The roots jiggled free from the earth. They rose around the dead body of the lamb lying in a pool of its own blood. They grew like grey swaths of grass in a lush meadow until they towered over the lamb, before folding over it, wrapping the lamb in a death shroud, until it was cocooned within a mass of organic wrapping like a chrysalis. The larger roots at the base of the tree shook apart, creating an orifice. The hissing and rustling grew louder still. Once the hole was large enough, fronds and tendrils took the body of the lamb beneath the earth. The roots moved back into place. The soil, once soaked in blood, settled back to its usual rich brown. The swaying boughs of the willow fell still, while the birds sang, and life continued.

11

THERE WAS a knock at the door.

"Come in," Richard said.

Izzy slipped inside and closed the door behind her.

"Izzy, what can I do you for?" Richard said, looking up from a spreadsheet of numbers, wondering if this is what his life had become, a punishment of balancing the books with parochial stories and ads for local butchers.

She came over to his desk, young and blonde like Jane. Richard had noticed her small waist and curves. *Stop it*, he thought. But it was like telling himself not to think of pink elephants.

"I've put something together for you on the ghost stories." Izzy came around the desk and put her laptop in front of him.

Her perfume wafted over Richard as she leant over his shoulder. An extra button on her blouse seemed to have come undone so that Richard caught a glimpse of the taut flesh of her breasts.

"I focused mainly on the Witchopper story for you, digging up stories in the archive, looking through local records. I also put a list of references together. Some of the books are out of print, but I've ordered them into the library for you."

Richard traced his finger across the track-pad of the laptop to reveal more and more data. Izzy was so close he could feel her body heat, and her thigh would occasionally brush against his hand.

"Great initiative, Izzy." Richard wanted to encourage her. As her editor, of course. "I'm a little snowed under at the moment." Richard glanced back at the spreadsheet and was reminded as to exactly why he was here giving a shit about the ad spend on sausages. "Maybe we could go through it later?"

"How about just after five? I could walk you through it all. You could tell me what to do next. I'd really appreciate learning from all your experience." Izzy had dropped to her haunches, closing up the laptop so that she was looking up at him, white teeth sparkling.

God, she was pretty, and young, too young, and a member of staff, Richard's brain told him. Then her hand rested on his knee as she steadied herself to stand.

"Sure," Richard found himself saying, his heart beating just a little faster than it should.

"That's a date," Izzy said, leaving.

"How are you settling in?" Dr Ken Bishop was one of the senior partners at the GP practice. He was tall and lean, and with his hair declining in middle age, he'd taken the proactive decision to shave it all off and be done with it.

"Everyone has been lovely," Jane said, leaning against the counter in the staff coffee room, more of a cupboard than a communal space.

Ken checked no one was around and said, "What, even Miss Wainwright?"

Jane nearly spat out her coffee, and they shared a conspiratorial laugh. Miss Wainwright was the grande dame of the administrative staff, or so she liked to think.

"Okay, *nearly* everyone," she agreed.

"She's very good at her job," Ken admitted. "And she's not so bad once you get used to her."

"Really? How long does that take?"

"I don't know. She's worked here for nine years, and I'm still waiting. It'll be any day now," Ken said, and they laughed again.

"How are you finding our town? You've a boy, don't you? Is he settling in? I'm sorry, too many questions," Ken apologised. "More coffee?" He offered Jane the glass jug.

Jane smiled and held out her mug. Ken was nice, easy to talk to. She already knew a lot of the patients adored him. He was the one they all wanted to see, the older ladies especially.

"We're good, I think. Rob is settling into school. Richard's job is a bit of a step down, but life here isn't as fast as London. It all seems to be going great," Jane concluded.

"I'm glad to hear it. Moving to a new town can be hard," Ken said, polishing off his coffee. "But remember it'll never be as hard as old Miss Wainwright." He smiled. "Best get back to it, in case she catches me slacking. I'll see you later."

A brightness still lingered on Jane's face as her phone sounded in her bag. She pulled it out, checked the message, and the brightness disappeared. The message was from Richard.

"Got to work late. Bloody nightmare! Eat without me. Tell you about it later. x"

They were going to get a take away. At least Jane would have Rob to eat it with. She put her phone to sleep and tried to push away the thoughts of a familiar ring to that message - and the reason why they moved from London.

"THAT'S AMAZING."

Rob's pencil paused. He'd been shading the enlarged chin in the caricature of Mr Bryce, who was yet to enter the form room. Ally, sat next to Rob, desisted in taking the piss out of Henry. All three boys stared up at Julie Brennan, who was looking over Rob's shoulder at his drawing.

"That's hilarious. You totally got Mr Bryce."

Words failed Rob.

"He does have a talent for capturing things on paper. How *is* your latest art project from the Minster coming, Rob?" Ally said.

Rob blushed.

Julie ignored Ally.

Curious about what was going on, Effie and Sally had appeared at Julie's side. Effie snorted. "Christ, that's hilarious."

"That's what I thought too," Julie agreed.

"Great minds, Jules," Effie said.

More of the class was becoming interested in Julie giving her attention to someone other than Effie and Sally, when Mr Bryce strode into the room. "Right, you lot. Quiet down. Johnathan Rose, stop punching Wallace in the arm, thank you. Julie, Effie, Sally, take your seats and leave Mr Peters alone."

Chairs scraped. Notebooks were shoved back into backpacks and the hubbub quietened. The register was taken, instructions for the day given, and the form was dismissed with more scraping of chairs and a renewal of the hubbub. Henry was pushing Ally into Rob as they crammed to get out of the door, and he stumbled into Julie. She began to fall, and without thinking he caught her by the hand, helping her get her balance.

"Sorry," Rob said as they came face to face.

"It's okay," she said, their eyes meeting.

"Ally, you are such a dick," Effie said.

"What? It wasn't me. Blame Henry."

"Chris started it," Henry complained.

"Hmm, what?" Chris said, utterly bemused by how they were in a conversation with these three girls, with whom conversation had previously seemed like an impossible dream.

Rob and Julie stood looking at each other.

Effie grinned. "What you doing tonight, Rob?"

"Huh? What?" He was as bemused as Chris.

"Tonight, it's Friday. Are you going out?"

"I..." he stuttered, still trapped by Julie's brown eyes. "I don't..."

"Yeah, of course we are," Ally butted in, shoving Rob in the shoulder and breaking the spell. Julie lowered her gaze and took her hand from his to retrieve her bag.

"Maybe we'll see you at the old willow tree tonight then?" Effie said.

"Yeah," Rob's voice wavered on the edge of cracking embarrassingly.

"We'll be there," Ally said, throwing an arm around Rob's shoulders.

Rob stood dumbly as the girls walked away.

"Well, Robbo, it looks like we've got a date with destiny tonight," Ally said, still draped over his shoulder.

12

Rob let Jane kiss him goodbye, enduring the usual requests for him not to "get in any trouble". Jane knew London presented far more threats for a teenage boy than this sleepy little town could in a thousand lifetimes, but still she worried. She was his mother. It was her job.

In the empty house, Jane poured herself a glass of wine, made and dressed a salad in a bowl for her dinner and checked her phone. There were no messages.

Dark was beginning to fall and the house still felt a little strange. Jane had to think twice about where everything was. Tucking her feet under herself on the sofa, she picked at the salad and drank the wine to the banal musings of an early evening magazine show, and then checked her phone again.

Izzy's seat was pulled close to Richard's behind his desk. Her laptop and various papers were laid out.

"I tracked down the parish records for Mary Hooper, the Witchopper, and local magistrates documents from the library archives record the date of her death."

She leaned across Richard to get the file, and her breast brushed over the back of his hand which was scrolling through the *Newark Advertisers'* own records.

"Here," she said. "The magistrates state she died in the Burgage gaol, which of course contradicts the local folktale that she was hanged by a mob from the Hanging Tree on the Burgage green *outside* the gaol."

Richard nodded along. Izzy flicked her hair back, pulling her seat closer so that their thighs touched. Her hand took over from his at the mouse, gently nudging him aside.

"I've pulled all the *Advertiser's* stories into one file and put them in chronological order from the 1860s to present. There are twenty-three stories about a local person's death attributed or linked to the Witchopper. And a further thirty articles in which she is mentioned, usually in a Halloween editorial. She's also been discussed in a number of books over the years."

"Books?" Richard asked, noticing the muscles in Izzy's neck rippling subtly under her firm skin as she cocked her head.

She let her hand fall to his knee for a moment before she rustled through a file. "The Witchopper is an entry in a number of older books, now out of print, about local folktales and ghost stories. The library is tracking them down for us."

"How do you know she's in them if you've not seen the books yourself?"

"This," she said, beckoning Richard to look at a piece of paper on the desk.

She smelt intoxicating, a light musk with notes of cinnamon.

"It's the PhD thesis from...?" Izzy pointed at the name.

"James T. Lovegrove? Who's he?"

Izzy put her hand on Richard's forearm. "Your local vicar. He wrote his thesis about her and religious beliefs of the 1800s. These books are from his bibliography, and the thesis is online in the British Library."

"This is great work, Izzy."

Her hand was still on Richard's arm.

"Really?" she said, their eyes meeting.

"Really."

Izzy's fingers slowly traced down Richard's arm to his hand.

ROB MET ALLY, Henry, and Chris at the bottom of the Burgage green at the Hanging Tree. Its bare branches formed a dark cobweb against the gloaming sky. From there, they headed down to the Victorian mill, converted to upmarket apartments at the turn of the millennium. A stream ran along the back of the mill, which was at the edge of town. Rob had only a rough idea of where he was. The light was failing. Ally led them along the bank of the stream to a point at which they could cross, jumping from stone to stone. On the other bank, they followed a path through the hedgerow. The sounds of voices and tinny music, played through mobile phones, was growing louder. Chris had purloined a couple of bottles of wine from his parents' stash in their garage.

"They won't miss it. They got cases of the stuff for dad's fiftieth," Chris said.

Rob looked at one of the bottles. "Did you bring a corkscrew?"

"Oh, crap!" Chris's face fell.

"Dumb ass," Henry said.

"I didn't see you lot bringing anything,"

They'd reached a change in the hedge as Ally pulled back the weeping branches of the willow tree and said, "What do you mean? I brought my sparkling personality." And they entered another world.

JANE FLUNG down her phone after checking it for the umpteenth time.

"For God's sake, Jane, he's only working late. It's a new job. He's just finding his bearings. It's not the same," she told herself, pouring another glass of wine.

But her heart was telling her something else. She could feel the tears threatening.

"No!" she said defiantly. But then she was standing in the middle of her living room with a glass of wine in her hand feeling incongruous, while on the TV the clean cut presenter asked a movie star if they've ever delivered a sheep. For a flashing moment, the movie star looked like Jane felt, but then recovered with a quip in the twinkle of a laser-white smile. Suddenly the new house, with their things still not completely unpacked, seemed like a giant 'told you so' from that part of her which had pleaded with her to leave Richard after his affair in London. *But he changed. He made amends. He'd given up everything* for them moving to a new life here. He wouldn't throw all that away.

IT FELT LIKE A DREAM, sitting next to Julie Brennan under the canopy of the old willow tree.

Both he and Julie seemed tongue-tied. Effie and Ally, however, made up for that, bantering across the space in a verbal joust. Effie seemed interested in Ally, but his eyes kept moving to Julie. Effie, for her part, was undeterred, as if this was an occupational hazard of being friends with Julie. And besides, Rob had noticed Effie looking at him more than once.

Luckily, Sally had the initiative to bring a bottle opener for the white wine she had taken from her parents' stash. Other groups of teenagers were there from their year and the sixth forms above them. The woody smoke of cigarettes mixed with cannabis misted the air. Couples french kissed, groups talked, some danced to the music from phones. A little bacchanal on the fringes of town. As the three bottles they had between them circulated, Rob began to relax, and so did Julie.

"What about Lovegrove's sex education talks?" Rob said, and then blushed in the dark, having gone straight for the topic on his mind. *Could I be more blatant?* he thought. Luckily, Julie laughed.

"I know, right. So awkward, and he barely notices. Nothing embarrasses that man," she said.

"It's like a superpower, if you think about it," Rob said, and felt stupid immediately. But Julie cocked her head at this, considering it seriously and looking right at Rob, right into his soul. Suddenly Rob felt naked and ridiculous on top of stupid.

"Yeah, it would be pretty amazing to be able to go through life without being embarrassed. Think of all the things we never do because we're afraid of what people will think."

"Hey, Rob," Ally butted in. "Speaking of superpowers, let's see your phone. Effie wants to see the picture you drew of Julie."

Rob gritted his teeth but was already fishing his phone from his pocket and opening it up. "It's not Julie," he said, passing it over with the pictures open at his art portfolio.

"Okay, Robbo. I'm only teasing, mate," Ally said and snatched the phone.

"That's *your* superpower," Julie said quietly, leaning in so only Rob could hear. Every nerve in his body tingled as her warm breath brushed his ear.

"What's yours?" Rob said. They were close now. He could make out the tiny flecks of darker walnut brown in her hazel eyes. Or maybe that was his artist's imagination conjuring an even more mystical version of her out of the darkening evening.

"I don't have one," she said with genuine modesty.

Oh my God, Rob thought. How can she think she doesn't have a superpower? She was gorgeous. Dazzling. It was an act of will for Rob just to form sentences around her. His picture of the wood nymph wasn't Julie. Not even close. In the flesh, she was something he couldn't hope to capture on the page.

There were only inches between them. The party had faded away. They were the only two bodies in their universe, being drawn together by their mutual attraction. If he leaned in, Rob's lips would meet Julie's, and they'd be one.

"Cops!" the shout went up, followed by girlish screams and a bedlam of movement.

"Stop!" Rob heard one of the policemen call as they blundered their way along the bank towards the willow.

Julie's hand grabbed Rob's, and they were on their feet running in the dark. They broke through hedgerows and then cut across a field. Teenagers ran in multiple directions as two flashlights cut haphazardly through the night looking for them. Excitement and danger blended into a heady cocktail. Rob tried to go up the field in the direction he saw some other shadows run.

"No, this way," Julie said.

They found the corner of the field and slipped through a hole in the hedge and onto the old train track that had long since become a nature trail skirting the bottom of the town. Gravel crunched underfoot. The cries and shouts grew quieter and quieter and eventually Julie slowed. They stood, holding hands and panting, their breath frosting faintly.

She turned to look over Rob's shoulder, back down the trail to check if they were safe. A muted giggle left her mouth, and Rob liked the sound of it very much. It was coloured with exhilaration, like birdsong in the safety of the canopy, while hawks circled unseen above.

When Julie looked back to Rob, their bodies were pressed together, hearts drumming. She smiled, a flash of moonbeams in the space between them. The warmth of their breath bathed each other's face in sweet alcoholic vapours. Julie's smile flickered. Rob leant in as if to see where the moonlight had gone. Julie did not pull away. She looked into his eyes, and suddenly they were both serious, under the sway of forces that felt beyond their control. If he had been sober Rob would never have dared to kiss her, but he wasn't sober.

Their lips touched and parted. Tongues touched, explored, tasting each other.

An excited call far off broke their tender kiss. Rob felt the nervous weight of his legs, lost in this strange new place. Julie looked over his shoulder again and then pulled Rob from the track by his hand. Like the nymph from his picture, Julie disappeared into the hedge, and he followed.

Izzy PULLED her knickers up and her skirt down. The numbing fog of the orgasm was clearing from Richard's head, replaced by realisation of what he had done (again). Now that it was over, that her youth, the eagerness of her firm body, and the enveloping heat of her was gone, their fleeting act of love making - no, it wasn't that - their *fucking*, stood in the cold, shameful shadow cast by his marriage, his family.

Izzy looked down on him, slumped in his editor's chair, buttoning her blouse, this time all the way to the collar, then bent over him and kissed him. It was like a full stop, clear and definitive.

"I better get going," she said.

"What time is it?"

"Quarter to ten," she said, with a glance at her watch.

"Shit! Really?" Richard said, standing and fastening his trousers.

"Really." Izzy was picking up some of the papers that had fallen on the floor.

"Shit!"

"Richard."

"Shit!" He was frantically picking up papers too.

"Richard," Izzy said again, calm but firm.

"What?" Richard looked at her, padding his jacket down for his keys and phone.

"It's okay. Just a little fun. I've a boyfriend too."

"You do?"

"Yes," Izzy said. "Don't look so hurt."

"I wasn't... I didn't mean..."

Izzy laughed and grabbed him by his collar. Her tongue found his, and she finished the kiss with a little bite of his bottom lip, causing Richard to grow hard again against her.

"Down boy. I'll see you Monday. You've all you need here." She tipped her head to the documents on his desk. "And remember, the interview with the landlord at the Witches Brew is set up for tomorrow morning. You want me to do it?"

"No, no, I will. I'm going to take Rob." When he said it, another wave of guilt hit him.

"Have fun," Izzy said, and left Richard to sort himself out.

TWO-THIRDS OF A BOTTLE of wine had done little to calm the argument in her head. Phone him. Don't phone him. Text. No, don't. Where is he? Stop being so suspicious.

Ultimately, Jane's darker side was a bad drunk and won the argument.

But just as she snatched up her phone, about to write a sniping text, the phone buzzed and lit up in her palm.

"Sorry. Heading back now. Nightmare meeting with Tim and one of our biggest advertisers. Tell you about it later. Hope you ate without me. Home in 30. xxx"

It was work. That's all it was, Jane thought, pouring another glass of wine.

THEY HAD to stoop to get through the small opening in the hedge, dropping to their knees. Rob and Julie's lips drew them together more familiarly, tongues exploring ever more confidently. Hands found skin beneath clothes. Smiles at the tickling touch pulled back from kissing lips. From knees, they slunk to the cold, dry ground, covered in a desiccation of leaves, clumsily pulling apart and coming back together searching for syncopation in a new world of sensation.

In the heady whirl of drunkeness, they became each other's fantasy made flesh, with warm skin beneath soft hands, mouths eagerly mirroring. And Julie found herself thinking how nice this was and how Rob was not Danny. His hands didn't grope, his tongue didn't force its way roughly into her mouth. Julie thought of Danny and his chides that she wasn't "mature" enough. Their argument and break up days ago, along with the alcohol, worked their influence upon Julie's desires. To *be* a woman. To *be* older. To be *wanted*. To be those things Danny told her to be, and which she thought others expected of her in the way she drew their looks. In Rob's arms, in that moment, maybe she could be those things and try them on like an actress dressing up and playing the part. She let herself fall back, bringing Rob with her, running fingers through the hair at the back of his head. In the gentle play of her nails against his skin, Julie thought she could feel the electricity through Rob as he leant over her.

Perfervid moans hung softly in the air as hands strayed beneath clothing, lingered at hems, delving tentatively further, finding in each other a contrast of hard and soft. They pushed into the other, breathing quickening. A rustling too, maybe of the wind in the trees, but it felt like she was connected to him and everything else; the ground, the hawthorn, the grass in the field swaying and pulsing.

Julie rolled them over, pushing Rob to his back, giving them respite in which their heads swirled. She rubbed his chest with her hands, breaking their kiss to look at him and the effect she had on him. His brow creased, and Julie thought she had hurt him and paused until he raised his hips, and she lowered her lips back to Rob's reposeful kiss. In the stolen underwear, Julie played the woman she thought she needed to be, feeling its power. The rustling of the leaves seemed to grow, and yet Julie felt no breeze on her skin.

When she kissed the flesh of Rob's belly he gasped with each touch of her lips. The musk of their excitement seemed natural in the earthiness of their bed. She lingered there, on her knees, letting her tongue and lips kiss and lap at the skin beneath his belly button. Rob stroked her hair, lost in pleasure. Julie was about to kiss her way back up to Rob's mouth, missing his lips, having flirted with the edge of something, when they heard a snigger, aware of a light illuminating their enclave within the hawthorn hedge.

Rob opened his eyes in horror, his hand still resting on Julie's head as she finished circling her tongue with a lingering kiss. She felt him tense and say something in a taut exclamation.

"Hey! Wha...!

When Julie opened her eyes and looked up to Rob, he was shielding his face from the sudden white light. The three boys, shrouded behind the light, burst into laughter, and in a scuffle of feet and the brushing of branches, they disappeared back through the hedge wall.

"MA-RY! Julie is a right MA-RY. Nice one Rob!"

Julie sat up. Even in the dark, Rob could see she was hunched over, the womanly act tossed away with hot embarrassment. Rob sat up and reached out a hand to her and, flinching from his touch, she scrambled to her feet.

"How could you?" Julie sobbed, disappearing through the hole in the hedge. The words made Rob's heart fall away with a lurch, and he sat there in the dark, not knowing where he was, feeling embarrassed and utterly alone.

Rob was lost on the nature trail. Julie and whomever the boys were - although it must have been Ally, Henry, and Chris - had run off into the dark. He eventually found his way off the trail and into a housing estate, and from there he managed to find Lower Kirklington Road, although it was a cold ten minute walk away in the dark.

His mobile phone was waiting for him when he finally made it home. It lay on the front doormat. The dread that Rob had felt when the laughter had interrupted him and Julie, moved from his stomach into his throat as he bent down to pick up the phone. The front door opened. His mother looked at him, worry on her face, but then he realised it wasn't for him. She looked surprised to see him. A moment later, his father's car then rolled into the driveway, and Rob could tell it was Richard she'd been concerned about. He knew that look. It was why they moved here. Yet another layer of dread added to the woes Rob held in his hand.

"Sorry, I'm late," Richard said, as Rob slipped past his mother.

"Everything alright?" he heard her say at the bottom of the stairs.

The phone buzzed continuously in his hand as Rob ascended the stairs, seeking solace in his bedroom. When he swiped the phone on, it was full of messages and a cold horror peeled over his scalp and down his spine, the dread maturing into nausea.

The first message was from Tom, one of his old friends from London. "What the fuck Rob!" Rob checked all his apps quickly, tapping and finding each full of notifications and messages, all of them pointing to one thing. The video clip stood frozen beneath his thumb and he tapped it despite knowing exactly what it would show, or rather seem to show: a video of Julie performing oral sex on him uploaded and shared to all his apps through his profiles.

"You sick fuck," one message read from a girl he knew in London. Rob checked and she had unfriended him from all her accounts.

This was only the beginning.

13

ROB FINALLY FELL ASLEEP ONCE the teenagers berating him had too. No matter how many times Rob tried to delete the video from his apps, it would immediately reappear. In desperation, he began to delete his accounts, one by one, but they wouldn't go away. Finally, they were being suspended by the platforms themselves only for new accounts, apparently in Rob's name, to spring up and start sharing the video again. At last, through a combination of stress and tiredness, Rob had dozed off, the phone still in his hand. When it slipped from his grip and fell on the floor it did not wake him. The sun would be up in a matter of hours.

Rob woke when his dad knocked at his bedroom door and entered. Rob was confused and bleary-eyed.

"We're going to do something together today. I'm writing a piece on the local Witchopper legend at the *Witch's Brew*. It'll be a good chance for you to get to know the town, and well..." And *him*, Richard wanted to say.

Rob protested with a pained exhale, but then his dad handed him one of the newspaper's expensive digital SLR cameras he'd hidden behind his back.

"Come on, mate, I could use your artistic eye."

Rob wanted to say no, but then the phone caught his eye, still laying on the floor between two-dimensional race cars where it had fallen from his sleeping hand. It was undoubtedly full of the nightmare reaction to the deceptive video of him and Julie. Kissing Julie was a dream come true which had now become a nightmare, and not just for him but Julie too. What must she be thinking right now? What was she feeling? And all of it was out of Rob's control. Why had Ally and the guys done that to him? He'd messaged them, but they had not responded. In fact, they had been conspicuously silent when the video went up. And Ally, Rob knew, was good with tech and programming, but why this? Why him? And why Julie?

The SLR camera and an excursion with his dad to investigate some stupid legend would at least take his mind off things. Bonding with his father, while a tortuous idea, couldn't possibly be worse than what was happening online. "Fine," Rob agreed.

The tired capitulation in Rob's voice, so out of character for their interactions, made Richard hesitate for a moment. "Great. I'll see you downstairs in fifteen then."

Over tea and toast, which Rob picked at, Richard explained that every child and adult from the town knew a version of the story, and that there was a playground game with its own song called Witchopper. In the 1800s the *Witch's Brew*, now a pub and hotel, had been a foundling house, where the unwanted newborns and children "washed up by the tide of progress in the new industrial age" were discarded, or at least that was the dramatic note Richard had scribbled in his notebook, showing Rob, who struggled to feign interest.

Richard got a message on his phone then. He fished the device from his pocket, read it, and put it away as if it hadn't happened. Rob noticed his mother look up from doing the dishes with an expression that unnerved him because it was so familiar. As was the shouting coming from his parents' bedroom last night. Richard didn't notice her look and carried on.

"Mary Hooper ran the foundling house. She was a spinster with no children of her own. One night, midnight in most of the stories, she was discovered burying a child somewhere on the edge of town. A rumour of witchcraft spread quickly and hysteria erupted in the town. A mob descended on the small gaol housing her on the

Burgage green. It's a museum now. Anyway, Mary was given up to the mob. The details about what exactly happened are practically nonexistent, but they strung her up on the Hanging Tree. All the stories agree on that. As does the Magistrate's report." He tapped a pile of notes encased in a manila folder.

They got in the car to drive up to the *Witches Brew*. The pub was located at the edge of the shops and businesses of the town centre and in the shadow of the Minster. As he climbed into the car, Rob asked: "But if her name was Mary Hooper, why is she called the Witchopper?"

"Ah," Richard said conspiratorially, starting up the engine. This enthusiasm was new to Rob, and he found he quite liked it. "The story didn't end there. A few years after her death, the new warden at the foundling house reported seeing Mary. More children died in mysterious circumstances and then so did the warden. Mary Hooper was blamed again, back from the grave to wreak her revenge, so the locals said. Eventually the foundling house was closed. Other sightings were reported over the years, always associated with the building and a mysterious death. And so the ghost story developed of Mary Hooper, which became 'the Witch Hooper' story, then 'Witch Hopper,' and finally just 'Witchopper'. If you saw her then you would soon be dead. Parents still tell their children if they're not good the Witchopper will get them. A playground game grew up in which the children sing a nursery rhyme about Mary Hooper:

> *If you see the Witchopper*
> *Then you'll come a cropper*
> *Never mind how hard you try*
> *If you look in her cold black eyes*
> *When it's time to go to bed*
> *You'll be sure to wake up dead*

"Children have sung that for more than a hundred years while they play the game. One child, who plays the Witchopper, sings the song with their back to their friends as the group try to creep up and touch them, but if the Witchopper turns around while they are moving with their eyes open, then they're dead. Much screaming is involved."

They had reached the *Witch's Brew*. It was a very different car journey than their disastrous one last week, which ended in Rob storming off.

"What do you think?" Richard said, pulling on the handbrake.

Rob fiddled with the camera. "Weird," he said, aiming the lens and taking a picture through the car window, trying out the settings. *And kind of interesting*, which he wasn't going to tell his dad, although his tone might have communicated as much.

"It's all just a load of superstitious nonsense," Richard said, immediately undermining his enthusiastic telling. "Remember though, behind the prejudice is a *real* human story. That's the angle we're taking. Journalism is all about angles, well, angles and getting the bloody stories finished on time. You get as many shots of the pub as you can, and if they're any good we'll put them with the story and credit you. How does that sound?"

Rob looked away from the viewfinder and even managed a smile. "Cool," he said.

"Now remember, try not to be too scared," Richard said, opening the car door.

Rob replied sarcastically. "Okay, I'll try." Richard laughed.

They got out of the car and crossed the road to the *Witch's Brew*. The landlord was expecting Richard, and was happy to have *The Newark Advertiser*'s editor in chief in his establishment. Izzy had promised him a nice puff-piece on the hotel pub in exchange for a nosy around the old place. The landlord was called Amos Blessing, a short stumpy man whose shirt stretched tautly over the puffy flesh of his thick arms and belly, stretching open gaps between the fastened buttons. He had a thick, squat neck that continued the parallel creases separating his two chins, and he had a habit of constantly hitching up his trousers, which struggled to find purchase around his wide middle. Rob noticed that his shoes were far from new, but had a matte sheen from being regularly cleaned and polished, and while he had both nose and ear hair, it showed signs of being evenly trimmed. In all, Rob got a sense of well groomed grossness, and a caricature as bawdy as one of George Cruikshank's satires of Georgian England formed in Rob's mind. He snapped a photograph of Amos Blessing, who smiled broadly.

They followed the stumpy man through to the back of the pub where the ladies and gents toilets sat and then down a narrow flight of stairs where the temperature noticeably cooled. The door at the bottom was newly painted white and stuck a little as Amos gave it a shove with his shoulder.

"Need to sand that down," the landlord said to himself and turned to Richard and Rob. "This is the cellar where the dastardly deed was done. We keep the barrels down here now." He palmed his thinning hair flat. "The girls hate coming down here to change the barrels. I have to say, even I get a chill now and again, like something evil is looking at me from behind." He was a man used to spinning yarns across the bar and directed his dramatic delivery towards Rob, whom perhaps he thought more susceptible.

"That's it, Rob. A shot from the doorway. Yeah, this is where some of the bodies were found a day or so after her death. This was the old kitchen. She probably used the large fireplace to heat the water for the tub," explained Richard, scribbling as he did. It was cold enough to make Rob shiver, and the air was musty with mould.

"Or to boil up the children's bones and feed them back to the ones still alive," Amos added with relish.

Richard rolled his eyes and gestured with his pencil. "Take a shot of the old fireplace. Most likely it was just a peasant broth made with animal bones no one wanted. Of course, in the stories, it's always the children's bones, but the magistrates' and the doctor's diaries never mention it."

"Doesn't mean it didn't happen," countered Amos.

"Why would they lie?" Richard didn't look up from his writing.

"Witchcraft, killing a woman without a trial, a baby killer employed by the church. Take your pick. There's plenty of reasons for them to cover up what happened here. Folks back then were more prudish than today."

Richard conceded a shrug. "Maybe."

Amos scrunched his brow together behind Richard's back, his

small eyes looking hard at Richard from under what Rob thought looked like fat, hairy caterpillars. He added it to the mental sketch in his mind.

They left the basement, and Rob wasn't sorry to see it go. It was probably the cold and mould but he couldn't help shiver involuntarily while he snapped pictures and the adults talked.

"There's been a few sightings of her up here," the landlord told them, huffing as they reached the top of the stairs to the first floor. They stood in front of a slightly crooked window at the end of a long forbidding corridor, weakly lit by daylight. Amos hit a light switch with a thick, hairy finger, and the corridor came to light under the glare of harsh phosphorus strip lights. "Her bedroom was the second one down. Tourists love that one. They never sleep though. You can always see it at breakfast. I tell them to take a walk down to the Hanging Tree on the Burgage. They wouldn't be the first people to say they've seen her hanging from one of the branches, tongue black and swollen, sticking out of her twisted mouth like a giant dead slug." The landlord clearly revelled in the gruesomeness.

"No fair trial for Mary," said Richard, and Rob took a shot of the corridor, uneven with the lines of an old building.

"She got off lightly, if you ask me," said the landlord.

"Perhaps the children died of an unknown disease, and in the ignorance of the day they blamed a woman with little social standing, no family ties, an outsider taking care of foundlings which the town's own people disowned."

Amos shuffled irritably and the caterpillars tensed on his brow again. A solidity came over the landlord. "That's an interesting idea, Mr Peters, one for a more educated man than myself." Amos knew the power of self-deprecation. "But in my line of work, as in yours, I've seen a lot. We make a study of people, you and me. It's the way of our professions, is it not?"

Rob shuffled and played with the camera. He was in the middle of something. He'd felt a similar 'betweenness' with his parents when they were still in London, as if something was not quite right, but the adults wouldn't speak its name, and in truth some of that had followed them to Southwell.

"There are," the landlord went on, "I'm quite sure, people who are pure evil, bad to the bone. You can dress it up in psycho-babble or bleed on about how their daddies used to hit them and their mothers didn't love them, or that it was society molded them into a pervert, but the end result is the same: evil things are done by evil people."

Ignoring the tubby man's monologue, Richard asked: "Her bedroom was down here, you said?"

"That's right. Could I leave you to it? I've got some things to get on with before the lunchtime rush." Amos hitched up his trousers as he waddled off.

Rob took another photograph of the corridor and another of the crooked window. The old floorboards and walls undulated organically. It felt cold up there too, even though the radiator under the landing window pushed heat onto the back of his legs.

"Shall we check out where she slept?" Richard said, fun returning to his face now the landlord was gone.

The floorboards creaked under foot almost as comically loud as a sound effect in a travelling funfair's house of horrors. They both stopped, looked at each other, and broke into grins.

"Boo! She's coming to get us," Richard said, giving Rob a push on the shoulder.

They creaked halfway down the corridor to a door with an old Formica handle splattered with minuscule spots of white gloss paint, giving the impression of liver spots on an ancient gnarled hand. Richard tried the handle, twisting it in his grip, his knuckles whitening. But nothing happened. He tried it again.

"Stuck," he told Rob, putting his shoulder against it. "Always happens with these ol..."

The door suddenly flew in, and Richard cried out. Rob jumped at the bang as the door hit the wall of Mary Hooper's bedroom. Richard disappeared from Rob's view, and his heart leapt, the camera slipping from his hands in the confusion, and he fumbled to catch it before the lanyard around his neck saved it for him.

Richard sat on his backside, hair over his face, guffawing. Rob, in the doorway, caught the camera swinging around his neck and took a quick shot of his old man.

"You cheeky sod," Richard said, picking himself off the floor.

They checked out the room, taking a few more pictures. Richard scribbled something. It was nothing special: a bed and breakfast room above a pub, neat and clean if not a little out of date like its landlord. The plugin air freshener was a sweet approximation of flowers, and while bearable, it was strong enough to make Rob wonder whether it was preferable to whatever it was trying to mask.

"Think that's us finished, mate."

Rob didn't even flinch like he usually did when his dad called him that. It might well have been the first time Rob could remember actually enjoying being with Richard, apart from now distant memories of when he was a small child. The memories involved a pier that seemed to him to go on forever into the sea. He'd apparently asked them if it was a bridge to the moon, as it disappeared into the horizon. Rob couldn't remember that detail, but it always made Jane laugh. It was the one happy tale involving all of them that she retold, and there was a sadness in that fact.

What Rob remembered was a giant ice cream with marshmallows on top that was as big as his head. Squawking seagulls floated on the wind, diving for chips, their white feathers dazzling in the sunshine, and there had been a feeling of warm happiness that swelled up from his stomach, and which he could feel again whenever the memory was conjured. In his child's mind, the recollection was a slideshow of disproportions, like a Salvador Dali painting where everything was out of kilter to normality, and wonder teetered on the edge of grotesqueness and, as a consequence, fear. Now as a young man living in a world that appeared perfectly proportioned, a kindred feeling fluttered in his stomach for the memory they were making now.

They shut the door behind them. The timing was perfect, coinciding with an almighty clatter that rang through the whole building, vibrating through the floorboards beneath their feet. They jumped again, looking back down the corridor to the crooked window, holding their breath. Nothing. Of course there was nothing, except for the expletives of Amos Blessing down in the bar shouting at himself or whatever had fallen.

Behind them, floorboards creaked. They turned, expecting to see a guest coming out of one of the other rooms to check on all the fuss.

There was no guest.

The figure was almost around the corner when they saw her, the worn, drab skirt billowing out with petticoats, a pulled-in waist, long sleeved arms with twisted hands clasped in front of her, and hair, jet black, lank and dirty covering her pale face, revealing only one eye, which fixed them in a sideways stare for the tick of a long second hand. It was no normal eye. It had no white. Instead, it was a solid orb of dark green, the colour of moss, that for that long second seemed to suck all the phosphorescent light out of the corridor and mark their souls with shadows. And then she was gone.

A cold spike ran from the seat of Rob's trousers to the crown of his head, and a sense of dread more than equal to what he had felt the previous night when his social life had imploded.

"Did you see that?" Rob whispered to his dad, fingernails biting into the faux leather of the camera. Richard nodded.

"Hello, who's there?" Richard called. His voice had lost its trade-mark confidence. There was no answer. Richard gave a hollow "Ha!" to himself. "Quite a performance."

"What, Dad?"

"Seems the landlord is putting on a show for us. Shall we go meet our Mary Hooper around the corner?"

Thank God! Rob thought to himself as the floorboards creaked underfoot on their way to expose the ruse.

"The game's u..." Richard shut up, turning the corner.

A dead end. A short corridor with a bricked up window and one closed door.

Richard walked up to the door. It read 'Store,' on a brass name-plate. He gripped the knob. It was locked, rattling in the frame as he tried it.

"You wait here," Richard said to Rob, turning to stride around the corner.

"But Dad."

Richard stopped and pointed at the locked door. "She'll be hiding in that cupboard. Make sure she doesn't get away. I'll get the key from the landlord." And with that he left.

Rob was alone. He looked back down the short corridor and then at the locked door and the bricked up window, which had taken on a sinister connotation. He felt trapped. Every sinew of his body wanted to run, but he had to be brave. That unnerving moss green eye stared back at him from the dark of his imagination. His artist's eye recalled every detail of her wretched face, and his mind embellished the picture, twisting her purple and split lips into a sneer of hatred that exposed shards of broken teeth, lacerated gums that dripped with clots of claret-red blood. Suddenly, a smell hit Rob, a dank woody odour of decay. In Rob's mind, that was what the sweet plug-in air freshener had been hiding: death. Sound followed the smell. He put his hands to his ears as a rustling noise grew louder; he scrunched his eyes shut, instinctively backing into the corner by the bricked up window, but it only intensified the image of the Witchopper, whose ruined hand with its broken and dislocated fingers reached for Rob, closer and closer.

He blinked his eyes wide to banish the vision. Did that count as seeing her? It was only a glimpse. Did that count? It couldn't be real. *Where is dad? Where is he?* Rob was panting in shallow breaths. Nowhere felt safe; he was exposed, hunted. The rhyme from the playground game his dad had educated him on rang in his ears as his reality warped into one of Dali's paintings:

> *If you see the Witchopper*
> *Then you'll come a cropper*
> *Never mind how hard you try*
> *If you look in her cold black eyes*
> *When it's time to go to bed*
> *You'll be sure to wake up...*

"It's not bloody funny, I tell you. Scared the bloody life out of Rob," Richard's voice interrupted the fear.

"I told you, there are no guests up here at the moment and the cleaners don't come until tomorrow," Amos Blessing protested. "I'm not playing any tricks on you." The landlord was fumbling with a bunch of keys while simultaneously trying to hoist up his trousers.

"Rob, did you see anyone come out?"

Rob shook his head.

"Looks like you've seen a ghost," Amos joked to Rob, noting his white complexion.

"Not funny," said Richard.

"I was only trying to reassure the boy."

"Just open the door and end this farce," snapped Richard.

The landlord slid the key into the deadlock and opened the door.

Rob's heart pounded, and he wanted to leave even more. He had to go. *Please Dad, please, let's go*, he thought, but he could not speak. His mouth was dry, and fear kept his mouth shut tight. For some reason, he thought of children dying of thirst, withering away in the basement with no one to help them. With an act of will he pulled away from his imagination. Superpower? More like a curse.

Richard pulled on the light in the cupboard, urgently looking around. It didn't take long. Packed full of toilet rolls, stacks of soap, and folded bed linen, it was barely wider than the door and only six feet deep. There was no place to hide.

Richard knocked the walls and inspected the floor. He looked up, checking for a hatch to the attic above. There was nothing.

"Satisfied?" Amos asked. "Maybe you've got a bit of a mystery to write about after all? You wouldn't be the first to see things up here," he added, more lightly.

"Yeah, maybe," Richard said.

"I think you'd better take the boy home," Amos said. There was kindness in his voice.

"Don't presume..." Richard turned back and saw Rob shaking in the corner, a dark, wet patch spreading across the crotch of his jeans and down one leg.

14

JANE HAD FINISHED PACKING AWAY the remaining cardboard boxes in the spare room when Richard's keys rattled in the front door. The noise was quickly followed by Rob thundering up the stairs.

"How did it go?" she called, coming onto the upstairs landing. Jane saw only a flash of Rob disappearing into his room.

"Rob?" No answer came. She tried a gentle knock at the door. "Rob honey, is everything okay?"

"Leave me alone," was the muffled reply.

Jane thought about going in, but she took her hand from the doorknob. He wasn't five anymore. That physical distance that grows between teenagers and parents had arrived gradually. She was hardly aware of it until there was no longer a child climbing up on her lap for comfort or seeking a larger hand to cross the road. Despite this, Jane still felt the same pang in her stomach, because he needed her.

Richard was in the kitchen pouring a large glass of water. Jane watched him drink it down in one go, gulping loudly. Some water spilt on his jacket, and Jane noticed he was trembling.

"My God, Richard, what happened?" She went to him, but he stepped back, holding up a hand.

"Bloody landlord played a practical joke on us." All the colour had drained from Richard's face. "Scared Rob half to death."

"What joke?" Jane said, finding it a little hard to believe it would scare Rob as much as it seemed to also have scared Richard.

"The landlord had one of his staff dress up as Mary Hooper."

"The Witchopper? It's a little early for Halloween."

"Don't know how he did it though," Richard said, more to himself. He poured another glass of water. "How did she disappear? It's an old building. Must be a hidden door or secret panel." He downed the glass of water again.

"It must have been something else to scare you both like this," Jane said.

"I'm not scared," Richard almost snapped. "I'm raging."

"Okay, don't take it out on me."

"I'm not. God, Jane, don't make it about you."

ROB COULD HEAR the argument start, but it was the least of his worries. The image of the Witchopper, with her lank and dirty hair and her bone white and broken face stared back at him when he rubbed his eyes trying to clear his head. He almost screamed and opened his eyes. He was thirsty too, like he'd played football in the park on a hot day. Rustling in his school bag, he found a sports bottle with yesterday's water. Only a quarter of the bottle was left, and its lukewarm contents did nothing to shake his thirst.

He stood up from his bed and paced and then noticed the cold wetness of his jeans. Disgusted and ashamed with himself, Rob stripped and hurried to the bathroom. The argument downstairs was growing louder.

The shower was warm, and Rob hurriedly soaped up hoping that the water would wash it all away. He bent down to wash the lather from his legs when he saw it, black and crawling, and he fell back with a cry. From the drain, a long black leg appeared. A jointed needle threading the air. It was slowly followed by a second and a third limb, until finally the spider pulled itself from the drain. It must have been the size of a small child's hand, but thin and sinewy, crouching in the falling water. Rob saw the only thing at hand, a bottle of shower gel, and snatching it up, he brought it down hard on the spider, feeling it crunch beneath the plastic bottle. When he pulled it away, however, there was nothing there.

A knock came at the door, making Rob jump and catch his breath.

"Rob, is everything alright?" It was his mother.

"I slipped in the shower. I'm fine."

"Rob?"

The water fell, and Rob stared at the plughole. "Leave me alone, Mum." It came out harsher than he'd wanted, but... but what? Rob couldn't get his head around this.

He hurried from the shower and dried himself quickly, all the while monitoring the plughole. Back in his room, he felt no safer. He climbed onto the bed and hugged his knees, the familiar sound of his parents arguing floating up from downstairs. He had forgotten, at least for the last hour, about his phone. It buzzed on the bedside table, its case rattling like the shell of an agitated beetle.

Julie, he thought, and with dread he picked up his phone. He shouldn't have. The notifications had piled up across his apps. He searched for her, but none of them were from Julie. They were more of the same.

"You bastard."

"What a dick."

"I've reported this vid you sicko."

And worse. "Nice one Robbo. Legend."

The messages went on and on. Despite Rob deleting the videos, they had reappeared on his timeline, sparking a fresh onslaught.

He scrolled, the hatred becoming a blur. Then as his thumb was about to turn off the phone, one comment caught his eye as the scroll slowed. It was Sally's profile in the chat line.

"How could you?" it read.

It was Sally's profile, but he felt those were Julie's words. "I didn't," he said to the empty room. Immediately, under Sally's words a link appeared from Rob with a link to the video, but Rob had done nothing. He threw the phone against the wall and the screen when blank as if fell.

Slowly, the shadows grew long, and Rob turned on the light - now afraid of the dark. Mary Hooper, the Witchopper lived there, in the black. The light and this world, the one in which Julie and everyone else now hated him, was the lesser of two evils. Both were a torture of impotence. He felt powerless to do anything.

The shouting had stopped long ago. Jane knocked to see if Rob wanted any dinner. He'd said no. She left some anyway and later retrieved the untouched plate of food and knocked again gently.

"Please talk to me."

"Just leave me alone."

"I can't help if you don't tell me what's wrong." There was no answer. "It was only a practical joke."

Rob knew she was talking about the *Witch's Brew*. How could he explain any of this? She might humour him, but she wouldn't really believe what they had seen. He couldn't say anything about Julie, not without looking like a pervert. And so he said nothing.

Night fell. He heard his mother going to bed alone. Every small noise made him tense. Even the space under his bed had become the Witchopper's domain. The bed was the only safe space.

Eventually, exhausted, Rob drifted off to sleep.

He was warm on a soft bed of moss. When he turned over, Julie was there, naked, just like him. She kissed him, coming closer. She climbed on top. She smelt of spring flowers and the earthy freshness following a storm. She wriggled her hips on him. The small thatch of her pubic hair brushed his belly, and everything became cold. Her tongue was a dead piece of grey flesh squirming in his mouth. Her body was as cold as a corpse, and the smell of decay and woodland rot sickened Rob.

When he opened his eyes, Julie had gone and Mary Hooper's distorted face stared back at him. She leered with a mouth of broken teeth, overflowing with clots of congealing blood. Rob tried to get away, but he sank. His bed of moss was now a roiling mass of skittering beetles and worms. The more he struggled, the deeper he sank, smothered, limbs struggling ineffectually through crawling and squirming things of the underworld. Deeper and deeper he sank, gasping for one last breath before the living quicksand covered his face.

Flailing in his sleep, Rob hit his head against the wall of his room. He looked around confused and then recognised the racing cars and superheroes of his bedroom. It was still night. He felt cold and alone, and something else: thirsty. His mouth was dry, and the sickness of dehydration burnt the back of his throat.

He moved quickly across the bedroom to escape the dark under his bed. Quietly he opened his door and crept downstairs. He found his father there, sat at the kitchen table, a jug of water sat in front of him nearly finished. Hearing Rob, he raised his head.

"Thirsty too?" Richard asked.

Rob nodded and got himself a drink, drinking deeply. It wasn't enough, and he poured another glass.

"I don't know what happened." Richard said. "It was just a practical joke. It had to be, right? We were carried away with the story, that's all."

Rob finished the second glass and filled a third.

"I mean, why would this happen to us?" Richard said.

Rob didn't know. Parents were supposed to be the ones with all the answers.

15

Rob wasn't sure if things could get any worse after the weekend he'd had but school was the last place he wanted to go. Between school and home, there was no escape from his troubles. At least at school maybe he'd be safe from his visions.

He left for school as late as he could, avoiding as many people as possible as he walked through Southwell. He would stop and sink into a doorway and then move on so that a group of children walking together wouldn't spot him. He was halfway down Nottingham Road when the bell rang for the start of school.

Reluctantly, Rob broke into a jog. Dehydration at the back of his throat cut sharply like a knife. Initially, he hadn't made the connection between his perpetual thirst and he and his dad seeing the Witchopper. But over the last forty-eight hours they'd both drank copious amounts, never slaking their thirst, and Rob knew this was part of the curse. It was just as much a part of it as his inability to sleep. Every time he closed his eyes *she* was there waiting to distort his dreams. The sinking bed of beetles and worms had only been the beginning. Sunday was worse than the initial shock of Saturday. Between the terrifying visions and the abuse he was getting online, Rob hardly slept. Even through this, he worried about Julie, longing to speak to her and explain, but not knowing how. He looked for her online, but she seemed to have deleted all her profiles, which Rob wished he could, but they kept springing back to life to torture him with the video and the torrent of abuse that went with it.

"Come on, come on."

Rob didn't know the teacher scolding him at the entrance. The corridors were already emptying as students filtered into their rooms. Rob's feet squeaked on the floors as he hurried to his form.

He paused just shy of the doorway, unsure whether he felt sick from dehydration or the dread of what was going to happen today, but especially when he saw Julie. He took a breath, literally and figuratively, and with his head down walked into the form room. His heart ached, noticing that Julie was sitting next to the window crying, with Sally's arm wrapped around her shoulders comforting her. A cheer went up as he entered. Followed by wolf whistles. Rob felt Effie and Sally's eyes, along with everyone else's in the class, on him as he took a seat next to Ally.

He'd dreaded this moment, spun it a thousand times in his head. He should just tell Julie it wasn't him, that he would never do anything like that to her, that it was Ally and the guys. Rob knew that he couldn't prove that with the video coming from his phone and posted on his accounts. He could say that Ally had his phone, and they played a practical joke that was far from funny. Maybe he should just confront Ally. But it was Rob's word against Ally's, and Rob knew he would deny it. But if he could talk to him at break. Try and understand why he did it. God, that would be hard, just thinking about it made Rob angry.

There were whispers and sniggers, and worse Rob could hear Julie sobbing. If only he could find the words. He didn't want to hurt her. Looking at his desk, he clenched his fists beneath it.

"Good weekend, Robbo?" Rob could hear the smirk in Ally's tone. Henry laughed.

The boy sitting behind him cried out when Rob's chair crashed into his desk. The scraping of the chair across the floor immediately silenced the onlookers. Rob grabbed Ally by the collar of his school blazer, pushing down into Henry's lap.

Cries of excitement and shock went up. More chairs scraped across the floor.

"Chill out, Rob. What's up with you?" Ally tried to sound confident, but he was wilting beneath the rage of Rob's glare. Rob was possessed by his anger, and he pulled back a fist ready to smack Ally in the mouth and maybe more, much more.

"Rob Peters, what the bloody hell do you think you're doing?" Mr Bryce's booming voice stayed Rob's hand, and he looked up, rage still contorting his face.

"Put him down now." Rob let go and looked up almost surprised to find himself at registration.

Mr Bryce's gaze swept across the classroom, noticing Julie crying as he did.

"I don't know what's going on here, but we will get to the bottom of it."

"Rob's gone mental, sir."

"Shut your mouth, Strachan. Now is not the time. Rob, cool yourself off on the way to Mr Khan's office. I will see you there once I've registered this lot."

Rob now knew that things could get a lot worse.

16

THE COFFEE WASN'T HELPING Richard feel any better. Neither was the litre bottle of water he picked up from the garage. The first didn't wake him up. The second didn't quench his thirst. He drove the winding road from Southwell to Newark. Sliding between the trees, past the Gothic building of Kelham Hall. Cars slunk past in both directions on their reluctant Monday morning commutes.

Richard rubbed his eyes hard and gave his cheek a little slap to wake himself up. His life had taken on an unreal quality. But he also had a familiarity with that. It was guilt. It must be. He'd done it again, and he felt terrible for having cheated on Jane. He loved her and Rob, he really did, and they were the whole reason for being here at this backwater newspaper instead of in the big leagues down at *The Telegraph* in London. Then that prat of a landlord at the *Witch's Brew* had shocked him. It was effective, Richard would give Amos Blessing that. How he'd pulled it off, Richard still couldn't figure out. Those old buildings often had secret doors hidden in the walls and trapdoors under the carpet. Well, Richard wasn't a man to be made a fool of. The landlord was playing a dangerous game, and he'd lose. Richard had retired senior ministers with his articles. He could crush a small town landlord and his business, with or without its local legend attached.

Richard finished the water and threw the empty bottle into the footwell of the passenger side. A noise in the car caught his attention. Glancing around quickly, he was unable to pinpoint the source of the noise. It was a faint rustling, like wind passing through crispy leaves of birch hedge in autumn. But it was spring, and he was in a car. Then again, maybe it wasn't a rustling. Maybe it was the whisper of wind through the vents in his car, not quite audible. He shrugged it off as nothing, trying to pay attention to the road. It could just as well be the blood in his ears.

He drank the last of the coffee and wished he'd brought another bottle of water.

The prospect of seeing Izzy weighed heavily on him, but Richard told himself he'd clear it up with her. It was a one-time thing. A bit of a fling, that was all. She had seemed pretty blasé about it all. It would be fine.

Suddenly, his heart lurched just as it had on that landing in the *Witch's Brew*, and Richard slammed on the brakes. The car screeched to a stop. Richard was jolted forward and then flung back into his seat pinned by his seatbelt. He'd seen the flash of a woman, straight backed and seeming to glide in front of his car, with billowing skirts filthy with mud, lank black hair covering a bone-white face, and that eye, staring hatefully through the strands of hair, a dark glaucous green. But that's not what it was at all.

An old lady stood frozen to the spot, her face petrified, Richard's car inches from knocking her over in the middle of a pedestrian crossing.

A younger man, dressed in a security guard's uniform and bomber jacket, crossed quickly to the middle of the road and took the old lady by the elbow. Casting a hard look back at Richard, he shouted, "Wanker!" and moved the old lady to safety.

Richard put his hand up apologetically, mouthing, "Sorry." The man in the bomber jacket rolled his eyes.

Putting the car back into gear, Richard got himself to work and parked up in his editor in chief's allotted space. His hand had a slight tremor on the key fob, and there was that noise again, the low rustling. He looked around. The sun was shining and there was barely a breath in the air. Less quick to dismiss it now, he stuffed his keys into his pocket and hurried to the safety of the office.

Inside, people said hello. Richard waved back and headed straight for the water fountain trying his best to appear normal. The thirst was clawing at the back of his throat. He poured himself a drink, followed by another and then another, in the tiny plastic cups. Finishing the third one, water dripping from his chin, Richard jumped at the sound of a voice.

"Hello, Richard," Izzy said behind him. "Sorry, I didn't mean to make you jump."

"It's not you. I didn't sleep very well." He couldn't meet her eye.

She looked at him sympathetically and took a step forward as if she would touch him. Richard took a step back, and she stopped, a small frown on her face.

"Look Richard, about Friday night..." Izzy began.

"Hi, Tim," Richard said to his deputy editor, cutting her off.

Richard and Izzy remained quiet as Tim helped himself to a glass of water. He drank it looking between the two of them and left with, "I'll see you later," to Richard.

"What I was saying," Izzy began, coming closer to Richard who was now backed against the wall with nowhere to go, trying not to look like an animal hemmed in.

She was speaking to him, but the rustling or slithering noise had started again, but louder now. He looked around the water cooler, left and right, not listening to what she was saying. Where was that noise coming from? Richard thought he saw something with many legs and a long body undulating across the floor and hid behind the bin next to the snack machine. He lurched from between the wall and Izzy and over to the bin, pulling it up expecting to see a large millipede type creature there and stamp on it. When he lifted the bin, there was nothing except an empty, scrunched up packet of crisps.

"Richard," Izzy said. "What's the matter?"

Richard looked back to Izzy and nearly dropped the bin in shock. The millipede was pushing its way from under Izzy's eyeball. Its many legs struggled to find purchase. The wriggling of its body distended Izzy's lower eyelid. Izzy seemed completely oblivious and looked at Richard with utter bewilderment.

"What is it, Richard? What *is* the matter?"

The millipede writhed more and more. Inching out from under her eyelid, drooping down with its tiny pin like legs grabbing onto Izzy's cheek. It popped free, as if a boil had been lanced and the pressure released, but instead of puss, four inches of millipede crawled down Izzy's pretty face.

Richard stumbled, dropping the bin in a clatter to the floor. He barely got his feet, steadying himself against the food machine, and when he looked back up, Izzy's face was entirely normal. Furtively, he looked for the millipede, but it was nowhere to be seen and the rustling had stopped.

"Why are you acting like this?" Izzy said.

Richard's mind reeled. This couldn't be happening. What was wrong with him? He suddenly seemed to notice Izzy was there.

"I don't have time for this. Get back to work," he snapped and hurried off to the safety of his office, Izzy looking after him - not hurt but confused.

He shut the door and pulled the blinds on the full-length glass windows in his office and then leant his forehead against them, crumpling it. He needed to think and pull himself together. This was all in his head. The thought occurred to him that he might be having a mental breakdown. How could he have screwed everything up so badly? This was just stress from the guilt. But if it was a one time thing and Jane never found out, there would be no harm. With time, he'd feel less guilty and everything would be okay again. All Richard needed to do was get some focus, some perspective. Just get back into work and do something boring like look at a spreadsheet of finances, or go over some junior journalist's copy and rip it to pieces. That would centre him and bring the world back to normality. Everything was okay. He breathed in and out slowly, telling himself that over and over like a mantra.

His phone started to ring in his pocket and almost, but not quite, made him jump. Yes, everything was calming down. It was Jane. Relief. God, how he wanted to hear her voice right now.

"What's up?" There was cheer in his voice, but then Richard heard his wife crying. And with the thinking of a guilty man he thought he'd been discovered.

"It's Rob," Jane said, trying not to sound too upset. "There's a problem at school."

17

MARY HAD COME to the May Day fair with her Aunt Jenny, passing out remedies in tinctures and posies of dried herbs to the poor folk of the town.

To some, she gave a blessing. Others, a small poppet made of grass - straw men with little arms and legs, tied with delicate knots. Both Mary and her aunt had them laid out over the table in front of the hearth before the fair, uttering blessings in the old tongue. Some, they gave enchantments. The poppets were handed out discreetly to wives in order to put under their angry husbands' pillows. Or they were given to young ladies who'd asked for help attracting the eye of their favoured beau. But with love, there were no guarantees, because love, old Jenny would always tell them, was the oldest of all the magics. It could not be wielded. The most that could be hoped for was to attract love's attention, feed a fire where it might already be kindled. The poppets could help with that.

Neither Jenny or Mary would take payment. "Money does not sit well with Jack in the Green," Aunt Jenny would say. Sometimes Mary and her aunt accrued favours along with an occasional homemade loaf, a knitted garment, or nettle cloth. But mostly, they were given the secret hearts of the townsfolk, which they kept with love and care.

Mary had her own trials in love. Giles Brennan, the tall apprentice blacksmith, was the beau that'd caught her eye. He sauntered nonchalantly around the fair's stalls, chatting to people, crunching on sour apples, seemingly oblivious.

They'd been engaged in this dance for some weeks now. Despite Mary being very poor, with Giles a station or two above her and with significant prospects, including a profession nearly his, Mary had something that none of the other girls had. It was something every man in the town seemed unable to take their eyes from when they thought their wives or girlfriends weren't looking. It had always been the same ever since Mary had begun to bloom, as Aunt Jenny had put it.

Mary stood next to her aunt at a stall, selling preserves. The proprietor, Dorothy Wilkins, was attempting to give aunt Jenny three pottery jars of strawberry jam from last summer's harvest when Giles came up beside Mary. He said nothing, but his hand touched hers. In the secret space between them, her fingers curled momentarily around his. She, soft and delicate. He, strong and rough.

Tall and handsome, he looked down at her and took a bite of his sour apple. He smiled, and she smiled back, and then with a slight cock of his head, indicating for her to follow, he was gone, walking away in the sunshine as if the world was his.

Mary slipped away after him, following over the park at a discrete distance, to where the small bridge crossed Potwell Dyke into the little graveyard, nestled amid flowering hawthorns and evergreen holly trees.

Mary opened the wooden gate under the archway and walked up the path through the middle of the graves just as Giles disappeared into the small copse of trees that lay in the top corner. The graves sprouted like tree stumps from beds of purple forget-me-nots. With the May Day fair in full swing, no one would be coming to visit the dead today. It was a celebration for the living.

Giles was leaning against the trunk of a tree. He threw away his apple when Mary entered the concealing shade of the copse. She came to him. The rest was an ecstatic joining of lips on soft skin, of sighs that quickened to a peak. As a breathless wind rustled in the leaves, and the forget-me-nots grew, their blooms burst with pollen.

When they had finished, they slumped together. The scent of their sweat mixing with the sweet hawthorn blossom. They dressed, and Giles kissed Mary once more, pinching her bottom a little roughly. She gave a playful cry and swatted his hand away. She reached for a final kiss.

"Naughty boy."

"I'll go first," he said with a wink, swaggering off into the sunshine.

Mary waited, like a good girl. When she returned to the fair, her grandmother busied around her.

"Mary Hooper, where have you been? I needed your help. Go and give Ethel Bagshaw this tincture of primrose. Tell her to mix it with warm water twice a day."

"I know, Aunt."

"By Jack, if you knew so much, Mary Hooper, then you wouldn't have disappeared for the last half an hour."

Mary found Ethel Bagshaw, along with her husband and her three children, standing at the bowling pins. He was enjoying a bottle of cider, ignoring Ethel, and talking with the menfolk as they tossed balls at the pins. Mary gave her the tincture, and Ethel wanted to pay, but Mary refused. Ethel's youngest, Tom, a boy of seven, asked if he could play the pins too. Ethel didn't have any money for that. Her husband had spent it all on the cider. Tom looked forlorn. His siblings had run off to seeing their friends, leaving the youngest by himself. Mary crouched down in front of Tom.

"Do you want to see something?" Mary said. Tom shrugged. Mary held out her hand.

"Can you see anything?" she said. Tom shook his head.

"Watch." Mary closed her hand into a fist and blew theatrically. When she unfurled her fingers, a purple forget-me-not bloomed from her palm.

The little boy's eyes grew followed by a smile that rose on his face like a sunrise. Mary smiled too and picked the flowers from her palm and, wrapping one of their stalks around them to make a little posy, handed it to Tom.

"It's our secret," she'd said pressing a finger to her lips. "It will bring you luck."

Over the little boy's shoulder, Mary saw Giles and tried not to let her smile falter as the betrayal turned her stomach.

The apprentice blacksmith was standing with a girl named Helen Banks. He held her two hands in his, not only in public, but with Helen's mother and father by her side.

And Mary's heart broke.

18

THE HEADMASTER, Mr Khan, sat on the other side of his desk, bony fingers interlaced in front of him, index fingers at a peak, touching the tip of his nose. Mr Bryce sat in a chair to the side of the desk, arms folded across a developing paunch, listening, face impassive. The room felt too bright, even as Rob hung his head, sitting flanked by his parents. The magnolia walls reflected the strip-light overhead, leaving nowhere to hide. Rob felt their full glare as Miss Chandra, one of the ICT teachers fresh out of university, went through Rob's phone on Richard's insistence. Rob was mortified as the young teacher inspected the apps on his phone, comparing the activity with the timeline in his story. Her hands moved swiftly over the device's screen, as if unweaving some elaborate spell with precise gestures. Jane sat with her arm around Rob, and he could feel the tension in her body as the full story, with every embarrassing detail including video footage, was replayed to his mother.

Miss Chandra looked up: "Given the speed of the activity across multiple applications, and that Rob has clearly deleted his accounts only for new ones in his name to reopen immediately. *And* given the fact that these accounts are using multiple IP addresses, I have to conclude Rob is telling the truth. He's been hacked and is as much a victim in this as Julie."

"So I think you'll agree suspension is out of the question. Rob is the victim here." There was a hint of derision in Richard's voice.

"It's not as simple as that, Mr Peters," Mr Bryce chipped in.

Rob tightened his fists and his mother squeezed his shoulder, but he couldn't be sure if there was doubt there.

Mr Khan spoke over the peaks of his fingers. "A day, while we investigate and interview all the interested parties and let things calm down. It's as much to give Rob space as anything else."

"Then why isn't anyone else suspended? If you think I'm going to let you make Rob a scapegoat for some sick schoolboy prank, you are much mistaken." Richard sat on the edge of his chair, one hand pointing in emphasis.

The sides of Mr Khan's mouth twitched. "In my experience, Mr Peters, it is best to give everyone time to cool off while we work to see what really happened."

"How much more abuse are you prepared to let Rob take?" Richard said. It was a classic journalistic question, in the same vein as: 'How long have you been sleeping with underaged boys, Minister?' or 'When did you first become aware of the gross misconduct?' The latter was more Richard's style. It had two built in suppositions - there was misconduct and they were aware of it. In defending one, the second might be validated.

"Richard," Jane said, barely above a whisper.

Mr Khan smiled opaquely, his demeanour more inscrutable than a mandarin in the British civil service, who might just benignly say, 'Yes, Minister,' as, "It is for Rob's benefit too. There will be no stain on his record."

Richard glanced at his wife and then back to the teacher's, taking a deep breath and letting out in a slow sigh. "Fine. But we're taking legal advice..."

"Richard," Jane said, but the tender *sotto* in her voice was ignored.

"... while you perform your... investigation." Richard gave a little dramatic twirl of his hand at the final word and stood up. "I think we're done here."

Mr Khan and the larger Mr Bryce stood politely as the Peters family made to leave. Miss Chandra handed the phone back to Rob, who couldn't meet her eye.

They emerged into the anteroom that buffered the Headmaster's office from the rest of the school, guarded by Mrs Birch, his secretary, who sat to the side, glasses perched on the end of her nose, typing. Seats lined two sides of the secretary's office forming a waiting area. With his head still bowed low, Rob didn't see the other three people sitting against one of the walls. Richard and Jane tried to shepherd him out, but not before he heard Julie's father.

"Is that him?"

"Dad, no," Julie said, her voice both tired and fretful.

In the moments before it happened, moments in which time seemingly slowed, Rob couldn't help but look up, drawn to her voice. There sat Julie, eyes red. Her mother looked just as tired, and her father, standing by her side, a dishevelled wreck of a man with a face contorted with rage.

Mr Brennan had a limp, but it didn't stop him. He was younger than Rob's parents, not yet touching middle age, and despite his injury moved like he was once used to a physical life.

"You little bastard," Julie's father said, closing the short distance across the waiting room.

Everything became a rush of chaotic shouts and scuffling.

Rob felt his mother pull him back by the shoulders to shield him with her body. Mr Bryce's commanding boom of a voice came too late, not having the same effect as it did on a room full of teenagers. Richard rushed forward to meet Mr Brennan, tackling him with a hug around his arms, but the punch had swung low. It hit Rob in the stomach, sucking all the air out of his lungs. He fell winded, toppling onto his mother, who cried out in panic. Richard and Mr Brennan tussled in the middle of the room, Julie's father spitting expletives at Rob. Mrs Birch, the secretary, stood up from her chair and backed away, her hands half raised, her mouth frozen agape. Mr Bryce barrelled out of the Headmaster's office, the authority of his teacherly tone coming with him.

"Mr Brennan, *stop*." Mr Bryce was bigger than both of the fathers and inserted himself between them. A fist flailed over the top of Mr

Bryce's shoulder and caught Richard on the cheek bone. A backward stumble from Brennan took most of the force out of the punch, but the hard knuckles still rapped into Richard's face, turning his head.

"Enough! That is enough!" Mr Khan's voice was more shrill than Mr Bryce's boom, but its shrillness cut sharply through the din.

From his position on the floor, in his mother's arms, trying to find his breath, Rob saw Julie crying in her mother's embrace, unable to look at him.

THE POLICE CONSTABLE, Melvin Playfair, took notes from his position next to the door to the Headmaster's office. No one was entering or leaving without getting past him and his pepper spray and side-baton. They were holstered, but his posture said it all. Words, Mel knew, weren't always enough in this regard. In the moments after a violent altercation, language had a tendency to ignite the situation once again. It was one of the things that made taking notes on said altercations particularly troublesome. As such, much could be achieved through body language.

"We want to press charges," the gentleman identified as Mr Richard Peters said yet again. Mel noted the gentleman had made a point of stating his role as editor in chief of *The Newark Advertiser*. With an internal sigh, he scribbled a note on his pad.

"Mr Brennan is a man under a lot of stress and is a veteran," the Headmaster, Mr Khan, added. He'd taught Mel many years ago at this same school, and the Headmaster remembered him when he and his partner arrived. Mel's partner was in another room, dealing with the other side of this altercation. As a school boy, Mel had thought Carney was a self important prick, along with every other teacher. Now, the officer could see the small man carried authority and diplomacy with ease, which is probably why the officer remembered him being much bigger than he now appeared.

Mel could now relate to his former teacher's position of authority and the unique effect it had on people, particularly those who didn't like authority, like the snot-nosed teenager he used to be, and, it appeared, this journalist fella. Mr Peters, editor in chief of *The Newark Advertiser* - one mustn't forget that - reminded Mel of every coked-up, drunk driver he'd pulled over in an overpriced, over-muscled German car. Most of them were like sniggering school boys at first, until things didn't go their way. As soon as they were asked to step out of the car, their confidence would go south. Half of them would become mouthy and then resort to pleading when reality dawned. The other half escalated things. The officer had been called a Nazi about as many times as he'd been told that said German car drivers earn significantly more money than he did as a public servant. Which way this Mr Peters, editor in chief of *The Newark Advertiser*, would go, was still in the balance.

"That doesn't mean he can go around assaulting my son." The newspaper man just wouldn't shut up.

"Richard, please!" The wife, a Mrs Jane Peters, said. She was the calm one in the marriage. Pretty in middle age. 'Elegant' would be the descriptor Mel would use to himself, but not in court. Rather, if asked by a barrister, he would say the witness was smartly dressed, and while visibly shaken she, Mrs Peters, appeared calm and more concerned with her son's welfare. God, Mel hoped this wouldn't escalate to something that needed to go to court.

"No, Jane this is unacceptable." Mr Peters was becoming more agitated, working himself up.

"Sit down, Mr Peters," Mel said, feeding his pen to the hand holding the notebook so that it lay unoccupied and available.

Mr Peters took a step forward. "If you think I'm going to stand by while..."

"Richard, please stop," Mrs Peters tried.

The officer stood, one foot slightly in front of the other. "Mr Peters, please take a seat..."

Alas, Mr Peters had decided to go the *other* way and was talking over the officer. "If you won't do anything, by God my lawyers will..."

"I want to go home," the boy said; a Robert Peters, who sat with his mother's arm around him. He was barely heard over his ranting father.

"What's your name?" Mr Peters asked. *Here we go*, Mel thought, having already told Mr Peters his name. "Come on, your badge number too."

"I want to go home," the son Robert said again. He looked exhausted, as though he'd not slept in a few days.

"We will, Rob, soon," the mother said.

"If you don't..." Mr Richard Peters had raised his voice to nearly a shout.

Ah, the ultimatum. Mel shifted his weight to his back foot just in case.

"I want to go home," the young man repeated, but only his mother appeared to be listening.

"Rob, for Christ's sake, I'm sorting this out. We'll go home in a minute."

"I want to go back to London. I want to go *home* to London," the boy nearly shouted. Tears boiled up in his eyes and overflowed, streaming down his cheeks, and finally the father, Mr Richard Peters, editor in chief of *The Newark Advertiser*, stopped ranting.

"But..." The newspaper man looked at his family, his son in his wife's arms and, finally, he was lost for words.

19

THE THREE FRIENDS sat cross-legged among textbooks, folders, and notebooks spread all over Julie's bedroom floor. Even with everything going on, they still had exams to prepare for. There was only a matter of days before they would break up for GCSE study leave. Effie and Sally were at Julie's on the pretence of homework and revision, but that was only half the reason. As they spoke, Julie's laptop lay open on her desk. The black circle of the webcam stared at the room, and beyond, through networks of fibre-optic cables and signals passing unseen through the ether, someone watched and recorded, and slowly drew his plan together.

"It's kind of lucky they're not pressing charges," Sally said.

"Lucky? " Effie said. "How is that lucky? Rob had it coming."

"I know, but it wasn't him that shared the video, and his mum didn't deserve to get hurt," Sally responded.

Effie rolled her eyes. "She didn't get hurt. She just fell over. Didn't she, Jules?"

Julie shrugged. "I don't know. " Her eyes started to sparkle with tears.

Sally gave Julie another squeeze, but only a small one in case that would set her off even more. Effie gave Sally a look as if to say she wasn't helping. Sally didn't seem to notice, or she was ignoring Effie.

"But, well, how could Rob have shared the video? He seemed nice," Sally said.

Effie tutted. "Well, clearly, he was in on it with whoever took the video. We know it was Ally, Chris, and Henry."

"Then why aren't they getting in trouble along with Rob?"

"I don't know, Sal." Effie sounded exasperated. "The teachers can't prove it or something, but it's all on Rob's timeline, isn't it? The video keeps popping up."

"Maybe he got hacked or something," Sally said.

"Yeah, right. That would be a bit convenient, wouldn't it?" Effie said turning her trigonometry textbook upside down to see if that would help her understand it. "Bottom line," she concluded, "Jules got taken advantage of. I mean, I know the sight of her makes all the boys want to play five-fingered knuckle shuffle - the poor darlings; I'm surprised any of them can still see - but that's no excuse."

Jules frowned. "What do you mean?"

"Come on," Effie scoffed. "There isn't a boy in school that doesn't stare at you if you're within a half a mile."

Julie shifted uncomfortably and looked to Sally for support.

"It's true. You're the fittest girl in school, fitter than any of the sixth formers. You're probably the fittest girl in the whole town. Even my dad looks at your bum when you come around."

"Eew!" Effie and Julie chorused.

"That's gross," Julie said.

Effie pretended to retch, putting a hand over her mouth. "I think I'm going to be sick." And all three girls fell against each other in peals of laughter.

In the middle of their circle sat three phones, screens blank. Julie's phone buzzed, interrupting their fun. Julie picked it up and put it back down again, having checked a message.

Effie narrowed her eyes in suspicion. "Who was it then?"

Julie pretended to be interested in her own trigonometry revision and shrugged nonchalantly. "Danny."

Effie squawked excitedly. "See what I mean? You're right, Sals. It's like a curse for Jules. The poor boys can't handle themselves."

"Shush," Sally said. "What does he want?"

"We all know they want the same thing..." Effie said, not waiting for Julie to answer. She made a circle with her fingers and opened her mouth a little, moving her hand from side to side toward her lips, while her tongue poked out the side of her cheek in time with her hand.

Julie blushed and Sally gave Effie a push, making her lose her balance.

"But apart from that?" Sally said.

"Yeah, what *does* lover boy want?" Lover boy came out as lurver boy, Effie's eyes full of mischief.

Julie tried to act as though she hadn't seen or heard any of this. "He was asking if I'm okay."

"Aw," Sally cooed. "That's so sweet."

Effie tutted. "Sweet? He dumped her because he couldn't get in her knickers."

"But he's *so* fit," Sally said, dragging out the so. "Big muscles. Nice car too. I'd let him do anything he wanted."

"God, yeah," Effie agreed, biting her lip suggestively. "Those muscles. That chiselled face. He's like the male equivalent of you, Jules." She leaned in, tickling Julie under the ribs and puckering her lips, "Oh, Julie, you're so fit. I'm so fit. Let's make fit babies together."

Julie wriggled away from Effie, laughing and batting her hands away.

"Are you going to text him back or not?" Effie released Julie from her clutches.

Julie tried to play it cool, pencil between her teeth and trigonometry of vital importance once more.

"Come on," Sally said. "You know you're curious. It wouldn't hurt to text him back."

"What would I say?"

Effie rolled her eyes again and snatched up Julie's phone.

"Hey, give it back!" Effie stood up in order to get away, already typing out a text with lightning fast thumbs. Before Julie could get to her, the message was sent. Effie sat down and handed Julie the phone.

"Don't worry," Effie said, "I made it sound all sweet and innocent, like you."

The text read: 'Doing OK. Thanx. Just revising n stuff. How r u?' And then she'd put a big X. Julie looked pained: "You put a kiss."

"He put a kiss. You've got to put one back. It's just a bit of flirting," Effie said.

"But I don't..." The phone buzzed and lit up in Julie's hand.

"What is it? What did he say?" Sally shuffled closer in excitement.

Julie chewed her lip as she read.

"Well?" the girls said, leaning in.

"He's asking if I want to meet up for coffee."

And both friends chorused: "Ow! Coffee!" with Effie adding a dirty wink.

Julie put the phone back on the carpet in between them and continued with the farce that had become trigonometry revision, staring at the notes in her lap.

"Playing hard to get?" Effie said.

"Good move. Make him come to you," Sally added.

Julie wanted to pick up the phone. She wanted to say that coffee would be nice, but she'd also been burnt, not just by Rob. Danny had hurt her first. She had thought he was sweet, just like she thought Rob was sweet. The burn was even more pronounced because she knew she had been using Rob, playing with him because of Danny saying she needed to grow up. She'd been looking to get experience with Rob. And well, after that picture Rob had drawn of her, Julie had been embarrassed, yes, but flattered too. Rob was so talented, and did he really see her like that? Like a... goddess? He wasn't bad to look at himself, for a boy in her year, of course. And so after Danny, the picture, and enough wine, Rob seemed like a good candidate. Sensitive, that's what she'd hoped. How wrong she was. So, Julie was hesitant. She wasn't playing hard to get. She didn't know whether she should go for coffee, what that would mean, or where it would lead or what Danny wanted. Effie and Sally made it sound like they had men all figured out, like it was obvious.

She remembered the car, his hands, Effie's lewd gesture. No, maybe Julie *did* know what he wanted. It was what *she* wanted that eluded her.

The phone came to life again, buzzing on the floor. Effie made to pick it up but Julie's hand shot out before her friend could cause any more mischief. Effie and Sally sniggered together, eager eyed, looking at Julie.

Sally could barely contain herself. "Well? What does it say?"

"He says he feels really bad and wants to make it up to me. That he misses me and he realises he was going too fast and no pressure. He just wants to see me again and buy me a coffee."

"Well, Jules, are you going to let Danny put a little sugar in your coffee?" Effie wiggled her tongue between her lips.

Julie shoved her, and Effie rolled backwards squawking.

"Don't pay any attention to her," Sally said. "What do you think? It's only coffee. What's the worst that could happen? You deserve a bit of fun and people deserve second chances."

Lying curled up on the floor, still grinning at her own lewdness, Effie said: "Don't listen to me. I'm only pulling your leg. It's just coffee."

That seemed to make up Julie's mind. 'Coffee sounds nice,' she typed, signing it with an X.

20

EVEN THOUGH SHE'D only been in her new job a matter of days, Jane was enjoying it and welcomed the busyness. It helped take her mind off her troubles. Usually, there wasn't time to think, except now, through some curious anomaly in life's frenetic ebb and flow, the GP's surgery had fallen quiet. Jane sat behind the reception, pensive in the lull.

The events at the school, on top of everything else, played on her mind. She really had nothing more than a fright when Julie Brennan's father had knocked her over in the Headmaster's office. Richard had been furious, wanting to press charges and throw his weight around, but that didn't feel right to Jane. Mr Brennan looked like a man with problems, caught up in the emotion of trying to protect his daughter. And no real harm was done. Taking it further would only make things worse. The policeman had calmed the situation down and separated the interested parties, and he clearly didn't want to escalate things, but the constable said it was up to the Peters. Despite Richard's feelings, Jane had got her way, which in turn concerned her as to why he'd capitulated so easily. That wasn't like him, bullish and headstrong, especially when he thought other big boys were in the room. The whole event had left her more worried than ever about Rob.

Even the fact that Rob had let Jane keep an arm around him during the meeting with Mr Khan and Mr Bryce troubled her. She realised later on that the gesture had been as much to comfort her as him, to find some balance and stability. Rob had always been the one thing that had been constant in their marriage. At first she couldn't believe what Rob was accused of, was relieved when the ICT teacher Miss Chandra supported Rob's account, which gave way to more worry with the realisation that Rob was a victim in this as much as Julie. And then there was Richard. The old warning signs nagged at her. This whole move from London was starting to feel like a nightmare.

A cough reminded Jane that there were two other souls sitting in the room with her, waiting for the automated system to flash their names up on the digital board. It was so quiet even Dr Ken Bishop had come out to reception, but Jane was so engrossed in her troubles, she hadn't noticed him and gave a start when he spoke.

"Fancy a coffee? Thought I'd grab one before the inevitable storm."

"Coffee would be lovely."

Moments later, Ken reappeared with two mugs of coffee and sat on the other swivel chair next to Jane's.

"This is a bit weird. I don't think I've had a break like this since, well, never," Ken said.

He was an easy man to be with. Funny, kind, interested in people. He drank his coffee while flipping through papers lying on the desk, and rocking his chair from left to right in a carefree manner. Eventually, he looked around conspiratorially.

"Where's the dragon?

Jane stifled a laugh. "She took a half-day to see a daughter in Lincoln."

"Phew!" Ken said. He had a boyish grin sometimes. Jane could imagine he'd been an errant schoolboy.

"Aren't you supposed to be the boss?"

Ken now had a look of the class clown playing it stupid despite knowing the answer. "Don't tell Miss Wainwright. She'll have us all fired."

"You're terrible. Don't," Jane said, barely managing to keep herself from snorting her mouthful of coffee.

"I hope you don't mind me asking," Ken said in a low voice so that the two other patients didn't hear. "...but is everything okay with you after that business at the school?"

"You heard about that?"

"It's a small town. News travels. Also, dragons like to gossip."

"The truth is, I don't know. Trouble seems to have followed us here from London." Jane knew Ken was asking about Rob, and she was happy to let that answer mean whatever Ken would take from it.

"Boys get in trouble," Ken said. "If you ever need some time off to sort things out, you only have to ask."

"Thanks," Jane said. "It can be hard fitting into a new place. Rob will be alright." She was telling herself as much as Ken.

A small beep sounded and one of the patients got up and followed the instruction to see Dr Sadiq. The last patient coughed just as the electronic sign called her to go to Dr Thompson's room. Jane and Ken were the last ones left in the reception.

"This is weird. Where is everybody?" Ken said, looking around. "Do you think the dragon has eaten them all? If we go outside, will the town have been laid waste, reduced to a smouldering pile of charcoal and crispy humans?"

"Maybe. She did look a bit peckish yesterday."

"Not to worry then. That must be it. I was getting bored of all those patients anyway. Always whining about being ill."

"How dare they, and in a doctor's surgery," Jane said.

"I know. Selfish buggers."

The automatic doors to the surgery hummed open and an elderly couple came in. The man was struggling to help the old lady along. She had a cut on her forehead and was in some distress, wrestling against his shepherding.

"Help!" she cried out. "Get off me. Who are you? I don't know you. Help!" and then the old lady escalated the situation. "Rape!" she shouted, trying to pull her arm from his grip.

"Not now, love. Please don't, Millicent," the old man said, trying to hide the anguish in his face.

"How do you know my name? Get off me. I don't know you. Help! This man is attacking me."

Ken was already around the other side of the reception desk, and the couple seemed in so much distress, Jane had found herself following the doctor.

"Hello, Millicent," he said kindly. "It's okay. Do you remember me? I'm Dr Bishop."

The old woman focused on Ken. "No, I don't know you," she said, still trying to pull away from the old man.

"I'm a doctor. See?" Ken pointed to the badge pinned to his shirt. "I'm Dr Bishop. I've seen you before, but I've a forgettable face. That looks like a really nasty cut on your forehead."

Millicent tentatively put her hand to the cut and then looked at the blood on the tips of her fingers, surprised to see it there.

"I..." she paused, confused. "I don't know what's wrong."

"That's all right," Ken said, offering his arm as if to take her on an old-fashioned stroll. She threaded her hand through, and he patted it with his other hand. "Will you come with me and let me clean up that cut and put a nice bandage on it?"

Millicent calmed and began to let go of her husband. She reached, like a frightened animal, for Ken's arm, then stopped dead when she saw Jane.

Jane saw that Millicent had the palest blue eyes, like summer skies, but suddenly they clouded as if panicked by the swooping shadow of a winged beast.

"The witch," Millicent said, clutching at Jane and taking her hands. "We've got to save the witch. We've got to save the witch." The urgency of her words were underlined by the deep creases on her face, her blue eyes shimmering expectantly at Jane, who didn't know what to say.

Millicent was apparently not satisfied with Jane's response. "You must understand. We have to save her. Jack's not happy. He says it has to stop. If we don't save her it's going to keep going."

Jane felt worried for the old lady who seemed so distressed. Perhaps the town had been razed by a dragon, and Millicent and her husband had struggled here through a netherworld landscape, losing pieces of themselves along the way. Ken and Millicent's husband were at her side now, caring hands reaching for her, but Millicent was oblivious to their presence, all her attention was fixed on Jane, as if delivering her senile message was the most important thing in the world.

"If we don't, they will both die. We have to save the witch. They will die." Millicent had reached a peak of intensity that bordered on anger. Shocked, Jane reeled back, freeing herself from Millicent's clutches.

"Now, now, love. Don't speak like that," the old man said, gently but firmly pushing down Millicent's hands.

"Get off me. Who are you? Leave me alone."

"Millicent. Millicent!" Ken's voice magically drew her attention as if he was casting a spell on her. "It's okay. I'm Dr Bishop. Remember? I'm going to help you with that nasty cut on your head."

Millicent touched her forehead, the quick stab of pain bringing her back into the moment.

"That's right. I help people. You're okay," Ken soothed. "You come with me. We'll just go through here into this room, and I can make you all better."

"Yes. Okay," Millicent agreed, pulling her other arm from her husband. Jane saw the hurt in the husband's eyes as he tried to smile reassuringly to Millicent.

"I'll take care of her for you, Brian. We'll see you in a minute. Jane, would you get Brian a coffee? Thanks." Ken led Millicent off to one of the consultation rooms.

Brian slumped in one of the padded chairs, put his head in his hands.

"I'll make us those coffees," Jane said and a minute later took the seat opposite Brian. "I guessed you might take milk. Do you want some sugar?"

Brian looked up. He was tired. No, more than tired. *Defeated.* "Thank you. No, Millicent always said I was sweet enough." His voice cracked and his face screwed up into a ball of deep weathered creases. "I'm sorry," he said, regaining his composure. "It's the silly little things that set you off."

"Is there anyone I can call to come and help?"

Brian shook his head. "We didn't have any children. We were never that lucky. It's just me and Milly. Have you any children?"

Jane nodded. "One. A boy. Fifteen."

"It must be a blessing," Brian said, the gruff traces of grief still not quite smoothed from his voice.

Rob *was* a blessing, Jane had always thought so, even with all the trouble at school.

Looking for something to say, Jane said: "I'm sorry about your wife."

He looked towards the door through which Ken had led Millicent.

"She always used to joke that she actually was a witch. Milly was a fantastic gardener, so green fingered. She'd grow all kinds of strange plants and herbs. When we found out we couldn't have children, she always said that the plants were her babies. She still goes out in the garden. It's her favourite thing, even when she doesn't remember who I am. But she stands there talking to them, to the plants, like they are really her friends." Brian stopped before emotion would overwhelm him.

"Is it dementia?" Jane asked.

Brian nodded. "About five years of it now, but this last year it's gotten bad. I wake up in the middle of the night and she's gone. I'll find her in the garden talking to her babies. If I interrupt her, she can get quite hysterical, as if I'm some strange old man who's come to hurt her."

"That must be very hard," Jane said.

"Love is hard sometimes, isn't it? You have to take the bad as well as the good. It's a package deal. You can't expect to have one without the other." Brain smiled and looked at the ring on Jane's finger. "You're married and have a boy, you know that."

It hit Jane then. Yes, marriage and family was hard and this was just a rough patch they were going through. They'd get through it together, somehow. "It has its moments, doesn't it?" she said.

Brian had begun to brighten. "This is just a bit of a rough patch," he said, echoing Jane's thoughts. "She's still my Milly, and she's a little lost is all. It's my job to help her find herself and keep her safe. We all get a little lost sometimes, don't we?"

"Yes, we do," Jane agreed.

21

IT WAS a rainy summer's day and Mary had taken shelter in the archway to Tucks Yard. The sky was fat with dirty clouds. It had been grumbling sullenly all morning until it belched forth a feculent curtain of rain over Brackenhurst Hill, which had swept across the fields of ripening wheat and barley to drench the town. Aunt Jenny sent Mary on errands into the town, picking up supplies and dropping off their herbal remedies and blessings. Mary was already wet, the dampness chilling her skin with its clammy caress. She was finished and could go home and warm herself by the fire, but she had other business to attend to in town. It couldn't wait any longer.

Mary had to tell Giles of the miracle that slept in her belly, growing bigger every day. She had never thought it possible. Not for the likes of her, not for people like she and her aunt. They could never have children. And yet there it was, undeniably. She had not bled for three cycles. Now her breasts were tender and had begun to swell. Mary's normally flat belly had the first showings of a bump. It was still easy enough to conceal under her clothes and shawls, but it was there. She could feel it. By all the blessings of Jack in the Green.

Like the plants of the earth, she could feel the life growing inside her womb. For whatever reason, Jack was letting it happen. The child must be special, that was her hope.

Mary had been waiting as much to pluck up the courage to see Giles as to avoid the downpour. The sky cried its tears without reprieve. Dirty water flowed down the streets in rivulets that zigzagged their way between the cobbles. Mary watched Tom Keating leave for his lunch at *The Wheatsheaf*. He hurried from the blacksmith's which lay down another alley between two buildings, the redbrick of one and pale render of the other were tarnished almost black from the soot of the forge in the yard beyond.

Tom didn't see Mary hiding in the shadows. She crossed the street, to a roll of thunder, and hesitated before cutting down the alley.

Giles stood with his back to her, hammering on an anvil, bending a rod of iron to his will, beating it until it became what he wanted it to be. Over and over, with clean, precise strikes, he struck it with his hammer before turning the metal with the tongs gripped in his other hand. Hitting and turning, hitting and turning, until the metal was too cold to work. He pushed it back into the coals, shaking the tongs in which he held the metal. The rustling produced a blaze of yellow, orange, and green that spat sparks up the chimney.

Mary coughed.

"With you in a minute," Giles said, and pulled his work from the fire. He adjusted his grip on the red hot metal, careful but firm, as if he was a man used to playing with hellfire. He turned from the forge to place the metal on the anvil, and resumed punishing it into shape. As he did, the light from iron held before him reflected orange cinders in his eyes. When he saw Mary, no emotion was written in his features. He positioned the metal on the anvil and began to hammer it again.

"What can I do you for, Mary Hooper?" His tone was formal and distant, as if there had been no familiarity between them.

"I was passing," Mary began, "and thought I'd drop in to see how you were."

Giles paused for a moment and then turned the metal and struck a tuneless toll.

"It's not much of a day to be out for a stroll." Giles ceased hammering and thrust the now curved piece of metal back into the forge. It glowed white hot. The sullen sky growled overhead.

"How have you been? I've not seen you since the fair," Mary said.

Concentrating on the fire, Giles said nothing. In the pile of coals, he turned the iron he was forming into a horseshoe. When the metal was ready, not too cool to work, nor too hot so that it became brittle and would fracture, he drew it from the flames and continued to smith the horseshoe into shape, rotating it around the pointed brick of the anvil.

Finally, over the hard blows of his hammer, Giles said, "I don't have time for idle chit chat, Miss Hooper. I'm not an apprentice anymore. I'm busy."

"That's wonderful. Congratulations."

Giles made no reply and turned his back on her, thrusting the metal into the forge.

Mary took a small step forward. The heat of the smithy's felt stifling and yet soporific, giving Mary a sensation of fevered slumber. There was a silence and Giles clearly had no intention of filling it. She might as well have not been there.

Mary yearned for Giles, despite his betrayal, and yet now he was cold and callous. Gone was his charming swagger. She hoped that he merely needed a good reason to see her, to love her, to acknowledge her. Like he had done that May Day fair, and they had snuck off together and he had lain with her. There was poor Helen to whom Giles was betrothed, Mary knew that. But if he knew her secret, perhaps that charming swagger would transmute into the wondrous shape of gallantry, like the iron in his forge. Putting a hand to her belly, feeling the life, the impossible life that was growing there, gave Mary confidence to say the things that she must.

"I'm pregnant."

Giles stopped hammering. After a moment, he said: "Congratulations. Is that any concern of mine?"

He hit the horseshoe, the broad muscles of his back clenching.

"Of course. We laid together." Mary blushed at having to say something so uncouth out loud.

The horseshoe, turned upside down as if all the luck would run out of it and dirty Giles's boots, tolled coldly as Giles beat it.

"How do you know it's mine?"

"What do you mean?" she said.

Giles stopped hammering and turned finally to look at Mary. The forge's light cast angry furrows into his face.

"How could I know that you've not lain with other men? There could be many men as far as I know. You and your aunt, well, you're not exactly respectable women of the town, are you?

"No! Giles, there isn't anyone else. I've never been with anybody but you."

Giles laughed. It was a heartless laugh, as hard as iron.

"So you say, but why would anyone believe a cunning woman such as you. Everyone knows what you and your aunt do. How do I know it's not a trick, some witchery?"

"Why do you say these things? I love you."

His laugh struck again like cold iron. "Love?" He smirked, and that swaggering confidence was there again, the young man who bit into sour apples, but he did not look the same to Mary any longer. "What do you know about love? I think this is a trick; an act of jealousy."

Mary took another step forward. "No. It's no trick. I'm pregnant." She touched her belly, touching the truth of it.

"How would you know?" he said.

"My aunt and I deliver the babies for the ones who can't afford the doctor. I've not bled for three cycles. I'm embarrassed to tell you this, but a woman knows these things. I can feel it growing inside me. My body is changing."

"Then you and your aunt should get rid of it. You do that too, don't you?"

"No," Mary said and couldn't help but touch her stomach protectively. "I would never. How can you not care?"

"Care?" He hit the metal he'd left cooling on the anvil. It fractured. All his work had been for naught. The piece was ruined. He threw the tongs to the floor and sat down on a stool. He pointed his hammer at Mary, brandishing it as a judge waves his gavel.

"Just what is it that you want, Mary? Did you come here thinking you could trick me, make me love you? Have you got a spell you want to cast on me lurking under those skirts? I've tried the magic that's under those petticoats," he spat. "Nice, but a bit of a common stink about it. Probably from all the other men who'd been there before."

Mary took a step back. "No, that's not it. I love you. I wanted you to know I'm having your baby. I thought you would want to be..." she trailed off in the glare of her foolishness.

"You speak so easily of love. I could never love you or whatever that thing is in your belly. This is a spiteful trick. You know I'm engaged to be married to Emily. She is a fine woman, a much finer woman than you, from a good family, not like you and your cunning aunt. You should know your station, Mary Hooper. I'm a blacksmith now. I have a trade, a future. What do you have, witch?"

Tears ran down Mary's face as she backed away from this man, his eyes ablaze before the forge. She opened her mouth to say something, there was only a bitter sob there. Turning, Mary fled, sprinting through the filthy alley until the rain soaked her black hair. She ran and kept running until she reached their cottage. On the edge of town, away from everyone else, a foolish girl back where she belonged.

22

THE BOYS PLAYED football under a temperamental spring shower. It spat occasionally, then lashed them with tepid rain. It even stopped once to let the sun peek through the clouds: a cruel trick before unleashing another downpour. Rob tried his best to loiter at the edge of the football game, feigning action with short runs up and down, and wishing he could get a drink of water, his thirst only growing worse with exercise. Rob's efforts were a poor show, but Mr Philips, the games teacher, didn't direct his usual berating comments towards Rob. Instead, he let the boys play it out, only intervening when necessary.

It had been impossible for Rob to avoid the PE lesson. He wasn't sick and he'd decided that the open air would allow him some distance between him and his fellow students, not least Ally, Henry, and Chris. But while that was true, it also gave them licence for physical contact. Whenever the ball came Rob's way, Ally, Henry, Chris, and some of the other boys took the opportunity to have a dig, under the pretence of playing the game. Rob had taken elbows in the ribs, a knee in the back of the thigh, studs on the top of his foot, and several hard body checks, sending him sprawling into the mud. Many of these had drawn fouls; Mr Philips' whistle blew again and again. But the more Rob tried to withdraw from the game, the more it drew the fouls to him, until it seemed members of his own team were feeding him the ball to *get him* fouled.

Just as the online abuse hadn't stopped, school was equally relentless, and while Rob could turn his phone off (as it was permanently now), he still had to go to school.

He'd run the scenarios over and over in his head, the same way he did when he was composing a picture in his mind before setting it on the page, and however he drew it out, there seemed to be only one course of action. The least imperfect choice. Solitude.

He existed in a bubble of loneliness, surrounded by whispers, accusing stares, and mirthful looks as he passed through the day. Many students were not discreet about what they were saying. He'd become his year's, and to an extent the whole school's, whipping boy, so that even those groups of outcasts and undesirable individuals who typically drew the ire of the more popular children turned on Rob, happy that someone else was taking the flak which they usually had to endure.

The lesson was nearly at an end, and Rob was already thinking about hanging back to help Mr Philips pack the equipment away. That way, most of the other boys would be done with the showers before he got there. As Rob was thinking this, John Rivers, a small boy for his age, slightly portly too, heard the call of "man on", panicked and kicked the ball as hard as he could, as if the thing were dangerous and might explode if he tried to do anything with it. To John's apparent surprise, and for perhaps the first time in his awkward life, his foot struck the ball on the sweet spot. It flew from his boot in a lofty diagonal arc, half the length of the pitch, and directly to where Rob was standing. An excited cry went up. The sun peeked through the clouds once more so that Rob had to squint, half blinded.

He saw two things too late.

Both came hurtling towards him. One from above, the other from the side. As the ball came into focus and Rob readied himself to try and trap it, Ally came sliding in on the slick grass.

Luckily, Rob's feet weren't planted or else he might've broken an ankle. Instead, the studs of Ally's two feet connected with one of

Rob's, sweeping his legs out from under him, lifting him from the ground. Ally slid underneath, taking the ball with him and off the field of play as Rob landed on his side with a wet slap, banging his head on the grass.

There was another cheer from some of the boys. The whistle blew. Mr Philips, a man in his mid forties, once in shape, but now carrying a little bit too much of a belly, had already anticipated the conflict and was running to intercept. Ally was standing up with a smirk on his face. Rob held his ankle, teeth gritted against the pain as he stood. He took one look at Ally and turned the other way. Mr Phillips came to a stop, a look of slight bemusement on his face at the fact the event hadn't escalated. He helped Rob.

"Can you stand on that, Rob?"

He could, but it was painful. "I'll walk it off, sir,"

"What do you think you're doing, Strachan?"

"Tackling, sir? I got the ball."

Mr Philips was exasperated. "With two feet?"

"Sorry, sir. I thought it was fifty-fifty. Apologies, Robbo." Ally offered his hand. Rob shook it without looking him in the eye as he hopped, the pain in his ankle still bright.

Phillips furrowed his brow and checked his watch, and then seemed to decide there was an easier course of action. He raised the silver whistle to his lips once more and blew it hard three times to signal the end of the game.

"Right, you lot," he shouted, "piss off and get showered."

Ally and the rest of the boys jogged from the field.

Rob was already hobbling to the kit bags dropped at the sidelines and started to put things away.

"You don't need to do that," Mr Phillips said, not unkindly, holding the muddy ball.

"It's okay, sir. I want to help."

Mr Phillips looked towards the boys walking off the pitch.

Ally Strachan, Chris Ward, and Henry Willits were laughing and looking back over their shoulders.

"All right then," the teacher said, squatting down to stuff stray balls into their holdalls, rain beading on the monk-like bald patch on the crown of his head. "You might want to go to the nurse and get that ankle checked out after you've showered."

Rob hammed up the limp to slow down collecting the plastic cones used for shuttle runs and ball skills. Once the kit-bags were full, they hauled the awkward load to the store room. Mr Philips opened the double doors. A waft of dried mud and mouldering grass blew over them, as if they had opened an ancient tomb, but instead of treasure and weapons, there were faggots of hockey sticks, piles of grubby netball bibs, and shelves full of everything from multi-coloured bean bags, to silk parachutes, and dented rounders bats.

Mr Phillips grunted and sighed as he stowed the bags away. When he turned, he looked surprised to see Rob still stood there. Awkwardly, he said, "Thanks, Rob. Go and grab a shower. You don't need to help with any of this."

"I don't mind, sir. Really."

Rob saw the look of genuine puzzlement that one of his students was being so helpful. Puzzlement changed to something else. "You'll be late for your next lesson. Now bugger off." It was firm but not unkind.

"Yes, sir."

Rob sloped off, dragging his feet along the concrete. He waited outside to see if the changing rooms were quiet. They weren't. He waited a few more minutes, doing a calculation of how long it would take him to get cleaned up and limp to his next lesson, Art. Julie would be there. Ignoring him, but there.

The chatter in the changing rooms quietened when he forged into the heavy miasma of body spray and steam. Stares punctuating the silence before the boys started up their conversations again.

Rob expected them to have done something to his clothes, put them in the shower or hidden them, but to his surprise nothing seemed to have been touched.

Ally, Chris, and Henry were toweling off, dripping as they sauntered to their bench. Ally clocked Rob undressing. "What do you think would be the best job in the world?"

"Let me think, Ally," Chris put a finger to his chin, his wet hair a mob. "Maybe porn star?"

A few of the boys left the room, sensing where this joke was going.

"Ah yes," Ally agreed. "Although, I think they prefer erotica artist."

Chris nodded sagely. "How do you get into that business?"

"Rob, any ideas? You like having sex on camera."

With a towel around his waist, Rob put his head down and hurried to the shower, hearing Henry cackle, "I think he's going to cry." Rob hung up his towel and disappeared into the tiled tunnel of showers.

Twelve shower heads continued to blast hot water. Steam churned, rolling over on itself. Rob walked into the cloud, a sharp pain stabbing up through his ankle each time he put weight on it. Rob put his head under the water and the warmth soothed his ankle and muffled the snickering boys. He lathered up to remove the mud caked to his face and limbs. Soap slithered down his body, and Rob closed his eyes to avoid the foam and imagined he was a snake turning his head in the water. His body became the muscular tube of a white viper, its red eyes a glaucous pink. He visualised the foam as scales sloughing away, shedding his old skin. In his mind's eye, he could imagine each scale like an armoured plate no one could penetrate. He wanted to etch them on a page and escape into the detail. Rob the Snake was thirsty and opened his mouth, bearing his fangs, letting warm copper-tasting water overflow like venom.

A young child giggled.

Rob paused to listen - the blind albino snake aware of its surroundings, checking to see if the teenage boys had come into his lair. If they had, he would shed his serpentine form and they would see only a boy like them, but not like them, not beneath the skin. It was a happy fantasy, an act of self preservation, where his imagination was a private fortress against all external onslaughts. But at the second peal of childish laughter, Rob's fantasy crumbled and his skin prickled. He spat out the water, opening his eyes, checking to see if it was the boys outside, but he already knew it wasn't. In fact, he could no longer hear them at all. Feeling exposed in his nakedness, Rob covered his privates with both hands.

Another giggle, this time from the opposite side of the showers.

Rob wheeled in that direction, following a new sound of bare feet slapping wetly on the tiles. The noise seemed within arm's reach through the swirling steam, but he saw nothing.

There were more children now. A squeaking titter from the left; a suppressed snigger to the right. With each he spun to face them, only to see phantoms of churning vapor and hear the sound of small feet running through the water as if to try and catch Rob in a playground game he did not know how to play.

At last, he thought he saw an old-fashioned cloth cap just visible above a thick clot of steam, and then it was gone, barely seen, perhaps only imagined.

Something, solid and yet too light to be water, dropped into Rob's hair. He brushed it off like a leaf and it landed out of sight on the back of his shoulder. It was followed by another and then another. They moved. Their legs pressed lightly on his wet skin and became tangled in his hair. Rob let out a grunt of disgust, frantically rubbing his hair and shaking his body. Three large black beetles, antennae fingering the air, jaws clacking together soundlessly, scurried through the sluicing water at his feet, causing him to hop back and look up to see where the bugs had come from. A deluge of insect bodies tumbled out of the shower. They overflowed up the shower head towards the white tiled wall, only to slip and fall to the tiled floor, bouncing on their armoured shells, then finding their feet and running in all directions, including over Rob's bare feet.

Rob slipped and stumbled, supporting himself with the wet wall, trying to find an exit from the shower. It should have been a few steps away, however when he looked, the wall spread out unendingly in the steam. He snatched short, fast breaths. More unseen children laughed and ran unseen through the mist. Rob's injured ankle almost buckled when his foot found the camber of a drain. He righted himself, only to feel slick and moist worms. Fat and covered in mucus, the worms boiled up from the grate, writhing, and from their midts slithered a slow worm, its tan coloured body winding off into the steam.

The chemical soup of detergent, the sweat of teenage boys, and cloying amounts of spray-on deodorant was overtaken by a pungent earthiness of woodland decay mixed with the scent of abundant spring flowers. Rob could taste the ozone that portends a storm.

The showers shook as the earth tremored.

Rob groped for a wall to steady himself as each of the other eleven shower heads burst forth a slew of living bugs. He flinched away from the unnatural rain, trying, and failing, to find a space between the torrent of insects. The tunnel of showers continued to vibrate in regular intervals, as if one of those unseen giggling children in a nightmare had grown to be a giant and now stomped around the playground. *Fee... fi... fo... fum...* Rob wanted to run, hobbling on his injured ankle, unable to gain any speed through the growing carpet of insects and worms. *I smell the blood of an English man.* The ground rocked. *Be he alive or be he dead, I'll grind his bones to make my bread.*

Run, goddamn it, Rob tried to jump start his body.

Rob waded through the swell of insect life down the endless corridor, feeling them crunch and squelch beneath his feet, oozing between his toes. Perhaps *he* was a giant, being pursued by an even greater giant, in the grimmest of all fairytales. He couldn't move fast enough. The insects had filled the corridor up to Rob's calves, and it was like trying to run through quagmire. The more he tried, the slower he ran, until the steam grew dark under a terrible shadow, lurching forward over the infinite corridor.

Fee...

Fi...

Fo...

Rob threw a glance behind but saw only swirling eddies of mist darkening in the encroaching gloom. He could not see whatever pursued him, but he could feel the giant drawing closer, each of its footsteps made the earth shudder, and Rob couldn't keep his feet any longer and fell into the mass of beetles and worms. The children's playful giggles retreated into the mist. The ground shook, once, twice, and then the unseen behemoth came to a halt.

Rob hauled himself up, bugs crawling all over him, lurched and tripped once more, turning as he fell into the churning mass. White tiles connected with the back of Rob's head. He scrambled back through the insects and, miraculously, out of the shower, whimpering and naked.

Panting, Rob stared wild-eyed back into the steam, expecting whatever shook the earth to emerge at any moment.

The fog had gone. A light steam hazed in the showers, and a trickle of blood ran down the white tiles from where Rob had hit his head. Seeing it scarlet and bright against the white, Rob became aware of the new pain in the back of his head. He touched it and winced, feeling the oily substance.

"Hey, Robbo, having your period in the shower?" Ally smirked, tying his shoelace.

"I don't get it," Henry said.

Chris rolled his eyes. "The blood on the tiles, like period blood from a girl."

Realisation dawning, Henry said: "Oh right. Good one." He gave a belated bark of laughter.

The three boys shouldered their bags and left the changing rooms. For some reason they didn't want to stay and gloat.

"Are any of you boys left in here?" Mr Philips' voice ventured from the door as Rob picked himself up, trying to get a bearing on reality, which came back with a cold slap of realisation when his eyes came to rest on the whiteboard. Usually covered with instructions and timings for sports lessons, instead there was a special message for, or rather about, Rob.

'Julie Brennan gave Rob Peters a blow job, but all he could do was shoot blanks.'

Rob found it neither funny nor accurate. He limped over with gritted teeth to erase it with his wet skin.

The changing room door banged against the wall as Mr Phillips came around the corner, having heard no answer to his question.

"What the bloody hell do you think you're..." Mr Phillips didn't finish his question. He saw enough of the message on the wall and Rob's pained expression to get the gist of things, and he'd undoubtedly heard about the trouble with Rob and Julie. Rob saw the pity in the teacher's face.

"All right, son. You leave that. I'll take care of it. What happened to your head?"

"I fell in the shower, sir."

"Did you really?"

"Yes, sir. That's when they put this up."

Mr Phillips paused, considering the options. "Get yourself to the nurse after you're dressed. No ifs, buts, or maybes. There's a chance you've got a concussion. I'll speak to Mr Bryce and Mr Khan about this."

"Please don't, sir."

"Some things you can't solve by yourself, Rob. Who did this?"

"I don't know, sir."

Mr Phillips sniffed, as if he didn't believe that. "Alright. I'll bring it up delicately with Mr Bryce. Now, get yourself sorted."

"Yes, sir."

"And Rob," Mr Philips added, wiping clean the board.

"Sir?"

"Keep your chin up."

23

RICHARD OFFERED TIM, his deputy editor, a glass of water from the jug which was now placed on his desk every day. Tim declined and Richard filled the glass to the brim. He picked it up and gulped it down in one go and refilled.

"Thirsty?" Tim said.

Richard wiped his face on his sleeve. "I think I need to get a diabetes check."

Tim nodded and patted his belly. "Good idea. I had one four years back, pre-diabetic. I even go to the gym twice a week. The weight never seems to come off though. I think I'll be on the pills by next year."

The deputy editor was affable and dependable. Richard had worked out that much already. In fact, he was probably too nice for his own good. By rights, editor in chief should have been Tim's job. He was a more than capable journalist from what Richard had observed. He'd put his time in. He was a local man. He knew the ins and outs of the business side of print journalism, from the finance and advertising, to the people monitoring, to just being a darn good desk editor for his junior journalists. Tim was the model of what a local newspaper editor should be, and yet, Richard was sitting in Tim's chair. But still for Richard, just like Goldilocks, the seat never felt just right. Tim seemed neither jealous nor angry. He'd been nothing but helpful, like a tubby Clark Kent.

"So," Richard began, taking a gulp from his second glass. "What have we got on the books for this week?"

"There is a meeting at the new town hall with the Lord Mayor. You should probably make an appearance at that. He hasn't met you yet. The Mayweather garden centre business, they've a store in your neck of the woods, another in Mansfield."

"Apache country," Richard joked.

Tim smiled politely and went on: "And another here in Newark. They want to take out more ad space in the build up for summer. We should probably do a few interest pieces on gardening and outdoors. Ten things to grow in a veg patch. Health benefits of gardening or some such. The Saville butchers in Mansfield..." Tim looked to Richard to give him the space for the joke, but he was looking through his window out across the office. Tim followed his gaze to see Izzy bent over a colleague's desk and went on. "They want a bit more ad space too, and were sniffing around for an editorial piece, local artisan butcher, something like that."

"Sounds fascinating," Richard said.

Tim nodded and smiled affably. "It's not the hustle and bustle of London, but these kinds of pieces are the lifeblood of *The Advertiser*. I scratch your back. You scratch mine. It's not so different to Westminster village, or what's going on in the City of London, is it? It's just on a smaller scale. A bit more personal, more local."

"I know, you're right. I'm sorry. Still adjusting."

"You're doing a good job," Tim said. Richard didn't believe him.

"It's true. Maybe not in how you think. We already do all the usual stuff well. But print journalism is dying. Local papers are closing everywhere. We need a bit of zing, a little pep in our step. We needed something to set us apart from the rest, and that's you. It's like having a Premiership football star come and play for the local pub team, well maybe not a pub team, but a Conference side. The younger ones look up to you. Most of us cut our teeth on the local scene, but only a few make it to the big leagues. They all dream of that, of playing on the big stage. You've shown them it's possible. You've raised the bar for them. I can tell. There is more of an edge to them. They want to impress, and they do that through their writing. Even this ghost story thing that Izzy's been leading on. She's showing initiative, imagination, and she's organising her colleagues, chasing their copy. She's a woman of many talents, isn't she?"

Like a good journalist, Tim let that last sentence hang in the air, let the reader draw their own conclusions as to its meaning. Richard drew his gaze from Izzy, still leaning over her male colleague's desk, and looked at Tim. He couldn't read his face. There didn't seem to be malice there. Which way did that comment cut?

"Yes, she seems very gifted," Richard agreed.

"She is, but that's not my point. She writes good copy. She never misses a deadline, and to be honest, she is ambitious. But before you came here, she was probably treading water. You seem to have woken something in her, let's say."

What did that last phrase mean? Was there something else he was hinting at with Izzy? And as if to prove you should never speak the devil's name, two quick knocks came at Richard's door. Izzy popped her head in.

"Sorry. Busy?"

Richard looked at Tim, who nodded. "It's okay. We're having a meeting, but if it's a quick one..." Richard nearly winced at his choice of words as she slipped into the office. With Tim opposite, Richard tried not to linger on the tight white blouse Izzy was wearing, with the top two buttons popped open, showing the cleft between her breasts. His eyes fell on her narrow waist and the curve of her hips, emphasised by the tight pencil skirt she wore. Richard reached for the water to have something to occupy his hands and drank deeply, draining the glass.

Izzy had a folder in her hands. "I was following up on the research for the ghost stories," Izzy said to them both, standing next to Richard's desk so that he was forced to look up at her.

"Go on," Richard said, filling his glass.

"Gerald, Zeynab, and William's are coming on quite well. They've all got nice local pieces. I'm doing one on the ghost of Welbeck Manor. And I also took the liberty of chasing up a couple of those contacts for you." Izzy fished inside the folder and handed Richard a sheet of paper. "The Reverend Lovegrove. I got his number and phoned him. He'd be happy to talk to you about his thesis. And about the Witchopper. And another one for Dr Josephs. Uh, or maybe it's Professor. I'll double check that for you. She's an anthropologist who specialises in curses and folklore down in University College London. I've sent her a preliminary email and she responded favourably. How did you get on at *The Witch's Brew*? I never got a chance to ask you."

Richard stopped drinking. Fear and guilt spiked up his back and he hoped they didn't show on his face. He put down his glass and coughed. "Okay. Yes. Good. I took Rob, my son. Um... he's quite the artist. I got him on the camera. He took photos for the piece, to get him to know the local area. The landlord was interesting..." Richard rambled but emphasised that last word.

Richard thought he could feel Tim's eyes on him again.

"Oh?" Tim said, unreadable.

"He's a... how should I put it?"

"Bit of a misogynistic bigot," Izzy finished the sentence for Richard.

"He's possibly to the right of Genghis Khan," Richard said and Izzy laughed, touching him on the shoulder. Tim smiled and watched.

"I haven't got round to the fluff piece for the pub yet," Richard told Izzy, opening the document on his desktop to show her. She placed the file in front of Richard and then lightly rested her hand on his forearm as she read, the smell of her perfume wafting over him. Richard's mind flashed to that night when she'd sat next to him in his office, showing him the original paperwork before they, well, before they did what they did. He tried to bury images that both excited and terrified him.

"I'll finish it off for you, if you'd like? Is it on the common drive?" Izzy offered.

Richard said it was; she took her hand away. "Okay, well I'll leave you chaps to it."

She left, closing the door behind her and this time Richard noticed Tim looking at the pretty girl's behind as she left. There was only a flash in Tim's eyes that told Richard he knew he had been seen, but then his face was impassive again. Richard didn't judge.

"You see?" Tim said. "She's ambitious and clearly wants to please. Just a word of advice."

Richard tightened but kept on his journalistic mask. "Any advice is welcome, Tim."

"Don't coddle them too much. Don't get too close. Do you know what I mean? We're journalists. We're like sharks with copy to write. They might not be the big sharks you are used to, but they are still sharks. Izzy will do her best work if she feels you're dangerous." Tim took a big breath and held up his hands. "I know you know this."

Richard nodded. "Thanks Tim; I appreciate it."

He smiled and picked up his glass of water, the thirst pestering him like insatiable questions. Richard was wondering whether what Tim had said was a veiled threat. No man could be *that* nice. Heck, he wasn't a man, like he said, he was a journalist, a shark. Was that what Tim was trying to say? Maybe he knew something, or had worked it out, smelled the blood in the water perhaps. Was it that obvious? God, if it was, had Jane noticed? Could she smell it on him, the guilt dripping like blood from his mouth?

The questions dangled like bait in Richard's mind, but it was hard to worry about them, because somewhere in the dark a monster was waiting, not for the questions but for the man who dangled them there.

24

"YOU'RE lucky you don't need stitches," the nurse told Rob. She had cleaned the wound and put a steri-strip on it in order to pull the skin together. She followed it up with a large bandage that wrapped around his head in a ridiculous headband. "Keep it dry for as long as you can. It looks worse than it is. Heads bleed like water from a tap. It's all the pressure up there from those brains."

The nurse pretended to tap him on the skull, clicking her tongue in time. She was old to Rob, grey roots down the parting of her bobbed hair, nests of wrinkles around her eyes, and a roundness probably from hours of sitting dunking biscuits in tea while she immunised, applied plasters, caught sick in a pan, and checked the temperature of the endless stream of children who came to her office. While she spoke to Rob like he was eleven, and not sixteen, he knew she was being kind. The caricature he'd drawn in his head was not too unkind: a rotund mother hen with an old-fashioned nurse's cap and upside-down watch pinned to her plump breast, fussing at the front of an endless queue of tiny chicks wearing school blazers and little neckties.

Having checked his eyes, getting Rob to focus on her finger in various ways, and asking him a series of questions to deduce if he was concussed, she wanted to send Rob to the GP's surgery or at least call his mother, which would have amounted to the same thing. But Rob said he was fine, neglecting to tell her about the stinking headache that pounded in the back of his skull. He didn't want to ask her for any paracetamol. He knew she would be reluctant to give them out in school. She'd definitely want him to go to the doctors then, and Rob knew his mother would have to be involved and everything would escalate. Besides, the last time she and his father had been at the school, things didn't exactly end well. Rob instead followed his father's suit, and deflected her attention with his ankle.

The nurse sucked through her teeth at the swollen ankle, the bruise already maturing into a deep maroon. "You've been in the wars."

"I'm fine, really." Rob could have laughed out loud at how ridiculous that was. *Go on, tell her about what happened in the shower*, he thought. *It won't be paracetamol and the GP's surgery they'll prescribe to you.* Rob wiped away the sketch of dishevelled caricature of himself in a padded cell with his arms wrapped around himself in a straitjacket; his eyes the swirling disks of a cartoon hypnotist.

"You look tired too. Is everything alright?"

"It was a rough tackle, that's all. An accident. And then I slipped in the shower because of my ankle. I'm having one of those days. Honestly."

"I've had a few of those," the nurse agreed, finishing off the accident form as Rob slipped back into his school shoe, now a little tight due to the bandage under his sock.

When Rob finally got away, the bell for lessons had long gone. The halls were quiet. Stretching out long and empty, they evoked a memory of the shower and that thing looming over in the fog. Rob could imagine the fog beginning to seep into the hallways as he limped as quickly as he could to Art, his feet instinctively starting to carry him that way, drawing him towards what he most desired. All the while, he looked around and behind, but no mist appeared. When he reached the classroom and peered in, everyone already had their heads down.

Miss Longman had her back to the window. They were supposed to be working on the last of their portfolio submissions before the break for exam leave in around three weeks. Through the glass, Rob could see Julie engrossed in her work. For once in what seemed like an age, she looked normal, biting her lip in concentration. She frowned, and that only made her look more beautiful. Rob didn't want to spoil that. He stood reflecting, Julie unaware of him watching her, but as he gazed, the memories of the changing room crowded in on him. The Witchopper reaching for him. The streaming mass of insects crawling over him. The giant thing which shook the ground and loomed enormous and concealed in the mist. Rob turned away from Julie and the memories, a powerful urge to escape school rising within him. At least for the rest of the day. He didn't care if he got detention. He'd just say he misunderstood the nurse, and after leaving her office, feeling sick, he thought he'd best take himself home.

Rob took his time, making sure that he wouldn't be seen. When he got to the main road, he had one quick scout around to check he wasn't being watched and crossed quickly up Lees Field, the short road that led to an alleyway, taking him off the beaten track. From there, Rob made his way along the back streets until he reached the top of the hill. A large playing field stretched out below with two large horse chestnut trees sitting in the middle of the hill, which belonged to the town's primary school, the oddly named Lowes Wong, taking its name from the Old English for field. A high wire fence surrounded the school, hemming in the grass. Rob walked around the edge of it, following the path, flanked on the other side by a copse of trees overgrown with brambles and nettles. In spots like this, the town and nature knitted together. It was as if the town had grown up like a patch of weeds where once there had only been a thick and wild forest, and over the ages the trees were cleared until only remnants of the dark wood remained, its deep and ancient roots covered up.

There was a rustling from the copse as Rob passed.

The children were out for break time. Excited shouts filling the air, drowning out the whispering leaves. Rob's ankle throbbed as he limped. With the effort of walking and the after-effects of the football game, his thirst had become a powerful urge. He fished the large water bottle from his backpack and drank as he walked down to the edge of the school, but as he approached the children's playground, he heard them singing, and the words brought him up short.

There was a group of girls, maybe seven or eight years of age. They were playing a game that looked to Rob like Blind Man's Buff or What's the Time Mr Wolf. One girl stood with her eyes closed and her back to all her friends while she sang and her friends slowly crept closer. He had never heard the nursery rhyme sung before, only remembering his father saying it as they were about to step into the grotty pub. It should have seemed harmless, but Rob's hand holding the water bottle began to shake.

"If you see the Witchopper
Then you'll come a cropper
Never mind how hard you try
If you look in her cold black eyes
When it's time to go to bed
You'll be sure to wake up dead."

As the little girl playing the Witchopper came to the final line, two of her friends were tiptoeing within a few feet. On the final word, *dead*, the Witchopper swung around, her eyes wide. All the other girls screamed and tried to close their eyes, but the Witchopper had caught one.

"Sophie Ashton, I see you. You're dead," the little girl Witchopper pointed. Sophie Ashton opened her mouth and then her eyes, which she had squeezed tightly shut, as if she was going to complain, but she accepted her fate. Quickly brightening, Sophie skipping over to take her place as the vengeful undead spirit of Mary Hooper.

"Hey you, boy," came the teacherly voice, its tone rather than its volume penetrating the wall of sound from the playground.

"Boy! You at the fence. Yes, you. Shouldn't you be at school?"

Rob snapped back to reality. Two teachers, coffee mugs in hand, stood looking at him from the dated single-storey school building.

As Sophie Ashton took her place as the new Witchopper, Rob put his head down and walked off briskly, gritting his teeth at the pain in his leg. The rustling of leaves followed him to the top of the Rope-walk, crossing as quickly as he could with furtive looks. He was nervous, both because the Witchopper game had brought back the terrifying experience in the showers from only an hour before, and because he was close to the centre of town here and on a busy thoroughfare, with the risk of being seen, either by teachers or his mother, working at the GP's surgery on this road.

Rob needn't have worried. The town throbbed with only a gentle hum of activity. He crossed unseen and cut off the main road as soon as he could to rejoin the network of alleyways that threaded through the town, like capillaries on a leaf, where he would be safe from being spotted. Always in a hurry, adults move around by car and only know the places they live in terms of the broad strokes of those main thoroughfares, and not the small spaces in between, which the children discover on foot while in transit to the servitude of school, or in gangs of push bikes on parole for the weekend. Rob wasn't completely familiar with the town yet, but had begun to explore these lesser trodden paths getting to school and in avoiding contact with other people. He wished he had more water, but home was less than a five-minute walk away.

As Rob hobbled towards the entrance to an alleyway edged with high wooden fences, the rustling noise returned. There was a light breeze and yet the rustling sound was loud and there were few trees and bushes nearby. He checked behind, feeling pursued. As he entered the alley, he heard the tittering laugh of a child from behind. Propelled by fear, Rob hurried as fast as he could down the narrow passage. Some twenty yards ahead a kink in the alley prevented him from seeing beyond, but Rob was more concerned with the rustling from behind, which had not only grown in volume, but turned into a hiss. Running footsteps behind the fence, accompanied by another childish giggle, spun Rob in a circle of panic. At the bend in the alley, to go back was as bad a choice as to plunge on. Rob looked back from where he'd come. The passage seemed to elongate, now an impossible distance to cover. While empty of any form, living or dead, it was filled with a barrage of noise, rasping and angry. Rob had run in the showers and escaped - and so he would run again now.

Rounding the corner and still looking behind, Rob nearly stumbled into a thicket of brambles that blocked the way. He stopped, wild thunder in his chest and a cold sweat on his back. It had been merely a day since he'd used this alley, but now it was completely overgrown. The bramble's branches, leathery in texture and as thick as broom handles, were riveted with thorns. They had twisted and coiled into an impenetrable briar, spread over from the two gardens either side of the alley, spilling over the fences. There was no way through and yet the rustling was coming ever closer. Rob was transfixed by the briar, the rational part of his mind wondering how it got there, another more primitive part, the part with a lust for survival, screaming at him to go. But go where? Rob was caught in a loop.

The briar lashed out with one of its barbed tendrils, cutting Rob over the eye. He reeled back. The hissing became the rattle of an angry snake. The briar was now moving, coiling and uncoiling, squirming and thrashing over itself. Serpentine, another tendril reared up ready to strike. It whipped through the air and Rob leaped out of its way, the pain in his ankle now a familiar friend telling him he was alive, and that this was real and he needed to escape. More tendrils rose up to strike while another snaked along the ground, forcing Rob back the way he came and around the corner, towards the very thing he was trying to escape.

The way was clear no longer. Rob half expected to see the Witchopper. At least then there was a chance, however small, that this really was all in his head. Instead, Danny Broad was strutting up the alley, apparently bunking off school as well. He took one last bite of the apple he was eating, its juice spraying his chin. He'd seen Rob, and knew *exactly* who he was. He sneered and tossed away his half eaten piece of fruit.

Rob didn't know what to do. Forward or back. His life had been reduced to a binary of terrible choices.

"Rob Peters, isn't it?" Danny said, and without waiting for an answer added, "you sick pervert."

Rob bubbled, "What? Me? No." He put his hands up, and looked behind to see if the briars were still there. "I didn't..."

"Yeah, you did," Danny said, coming up to Rob. "Don't be such a pussy. At least own up to it. See, the problem is Rob, Julie's my girl, and you, well you're a scumbag, a pervert. Nobody likes perverts, Rob.

In jail, they have to be kept apart because they'd get killed by the other inmates. Funny that, isn't it? The only place real justice gets done is in jail." Danny was in Rob's face now.

"I didn't do anything. I swear it. We were only kissing and..."

"Yeah, well you see Rob..." Danny had taken him by the lapels of his school blazer. "...like I said, Julie is my girl. You don't *get* to kiss her." Danny punched Rob in the stomach. Rob bent over, wheezing, the wind knocked out of him. Looking at his own feet, Rob reached up a plaintive hand.

"Please. Stop." The words came out as a breathless croak.

Danny batted away Rob's hand and punched Rob with a swinging left hook. The blow caught him where the bramble had cut his eyebrow. Rob's head whipped to the side, and he fell to a knee, the cut opening up further. The world pitched and swayed as Rob tried desperately to breathe and protect himself. Danny stepped over him grabbing Rob by the hair and pulling his face to the sky. The sun had just begun to break through the clouds, casting an ironic halo around Danny, who pulled his fist back like an asteroid hurtling from the sun's orbit and slammed it into Rob's mouth. Pain bloomed exquisitely from Rob's burst lips. The metallic taste of blood on his tongue. The dark angel above him raised his fist for another strike and hammered it into Rob's other cheek, knocking Rob's head back into the fence. Finally, his legs gave out and his first lungful of air caused him to cough blood down his chin. In the delirium of pain, the thought crossed Rob's mind that Danny could bludgeon him to death here and no one would ever know. Maybe they wouldn't even care. *Mum would care*, he thought wanly.

"Hey, you! Stop that this instant."

Rob felt the grip loosen on his collar and release.

"What do you think you're doing? Danny Broad, is that you? Let go of that boy."

Rob slumped back against the fence. Danny's legs disappeared from his shaky view.

"Come back. I'll be telling your father about this," the voice said, but Danny didn't listen.

"Piss off, you God-bothering wanker," Danny threw back, and then he was gone.

Rob looked up. The sun haloed a new figure, not the dark angel that had just beaten him. Someone else, someone that was familiar, that in the pain and confusion Rob couldn't immediately place.

"Crikey, Rob Peters isn't it?" It was the Reverend Lovegrove. "Lie still. Let me help you. I'll call the doctors. They'll be here in a moment."

The Reverend thought it was a moan of pain when Rob gave a short laugh. *That's what you get for bunking off*, he thought.

25

RICHARD LEFT TIM IN CHARGE, deciding to cut out early to change for the event with the Lord Mayor. He was planning to drop in and surprise Jane at the GPs, and then swing back via Mansfield to follow up on the Saville butchers. He'd already got a few quotes from them over the phone, but as their ad spend was big, Tim thought it was a good idea for Richard to press the flesh.

"Last time I got two-kilos of pork and leek sausages out of it," Tim said, patting his stomach. Jane used to make a great toad-in-the-hole when they were first married. They hadn't had that for years, and suddenly Richard felt like being editor in chief of a backwater rag might just have a few plus sides after all. Although, maybe Tim's paunch was a portent of his future.

The morning had gone smoothly too, considering Richard still couldn't sleep. That damn practical joke had put his imagination into overdrive, setting off some stupid childhood memories of the Witchopper he'd long suppressed. He was still damnably thirsty, but as he'd joked with Tim, maybe it was diabetes. On the topic of Tim, Richard had reflected on their conversation about Izzy earlier that day and decided he was reading too much into it. Tim was that rare thing: a genuinely nice guy. Rare in life and even rarer in a journalist. In short, it had been a pretty good day. Even the temperamental showers had stopped and the sun was coming out, cascading across the road in sheets of iridescent gold as he drove. Yes, he thought, this Witchopper business was all in his head, conjured from the stress of moving and his inability to keep his dick in his pants (again).

As the car slunk towards Kelham, for some reason Richard thought of Lesley Tibbits, the former Minister for Justice, and how he had helped to end Tibbits' career. The Minister was partial to - now what was the word Richard had gone with? Ah yes - 'fruity' parties with transgendered escorts, cocaine, and amyl nitrate. Great word that - fruity. Older connotations of homosexuality, a hint of end-of-the-pier lighthearted smut, and above all, mocking. It jarred perfectly with the illegality of the act - or rather acts. Tibbits was a habitual user of transgendered prostitutes. So much so that he had a nick-name among their Westminster cohort: Hookey, on account of the character of his penis. Richard didn't put that in the articles. He'd been willing to, but the first one caused the resignation, and Lesley turned up dead after the second. His wife found him strung up on the back of their bedroom door in their constituency house, his old school tie wrapped around his neck.

Richard was no prude. As far as he was concerned, Tibbits could shag all the consenting adults he liked, snort bags of coke off whatever body parts he wished. Trouble was, Tibbits voted against the gay marriage legislation in 2013 and 2014. He even went on those dreadful Sunday morning discussion shows to call gay marriage a sin against God. He claimed to be representing the view of the vast majority of his rural Surrey constituents, and he might well have been.

However, hypocrisy and a slow news summer made Richard pull the trigger on the story. He'd been sitting on it for weeks. There were rumours Tibbits might be in line for the Home Office top job in an autumn reshuffle. In a way, Richard was doing him and the Tory Party a favour by cutting Lesley Tibbits down before he reached the top. But the thing Richard really remembered was the twenty pound note Tibbits had paid the cabbie with for Richard's taxi ride to the London Press Club Ball.

Richard was pissed and had lost his wallet between the pub and the hotel venue. Lesley was walking into the hotel with his wife,

Charlotte, and came over and settled the bill with such grace Richard didn't feel embarrassed and the cabbie's anger immediately abated. When Lesley rejoined Charlotte, she'd given him such a look of adoration as they walked arm in arm into the hotel reception. Charlotte, only a little bird of a woman, had cut down Lesley, whose autopsy report put him at 241lbs, and cradled him for nearly three hours until their son came home on leave from the Royal Navy and found the home smelling of his father's bowels, a detail Richard gleaned from one of the Surrey police officers for, ironically, a twenty pound note. As he rounded the sharp corner through Kelham, and heard the low rustling noise again, Lesley Tibbits was stuck on replay in Richards head, shaking his hand and passing the cabbie a twenty as if this had been preordained.

It was as much like a snake hissing in the grass as wind blowing through the trees. From somewhere deep and instinctual an icy wave flushed across Richard's skin, snapping him back to the present. But when he tried to listen, the hissing had gone. He laughed at himself.

"Silly bugger," he said out loud. He'd merely touched on a dark spot in his memory, not that he had anything to feel guilty about. He didn't need to be a psychologist to work out what was going on. Jane, London, guilt about the past - and the present.

"Get a grip man." *Guilt is a powerful emotion*, he asserted to himself. Lesley Tibbits was testament to that. The move from London was too.

Something light dropped onto Richard's shoulder and he brushed it away, thinking nothing of it. It could have been the movement of his suit jacket, or the prickle of his skin settling after the cold flush.

Then came a tickle at his collar. He scratched and the itch stopped.

The car was nearly through the village of Kelham, transforming into a wood surrounding a country house set back from the road. The trees lined the road ahead, their canopy stretching up to the mottled sky, creating a tunnel filled with speckled sunlight.

The itch again. Reaching behind, Richard scratched harder and this time felt something under his fingers. He caught it and pulled it in front of him and opened his hand. A large black beetle, the size of a fifty pence piece, struggled on its back. With a cry of revulsion, the memory of its legs still on his neck, Richard threw the beetle into the footwell of the passenger seat.

A car blared its horn, skimming by Richard's wing mirror. Richard saw it as a flash of grey as he looked up and corrected course, pulling his own vehicle back into the middle of his lane.

"Jesus!" he breathed, calming his nerves. When he checked his rearview mirror to see the passing car, he froze.

Instead of a car retreating into the distance, Richard saw the reflection of the Witchopper in the backseat, staring at him through orbs of dark green moss, hair dangling in front of her ruined face like vines wet with rot.

Instinctively, his body tensed and his foot pressed hard on the accelerator. He turned and looked behind, less to face his fear and more to check his sanity. She would be a trick of the light. She had to be.

"Oh Christ!" Richard said in a strangled cry.

She really *was* there, sitting in the middle of the back seat, the smell of woodland decay filling the car. But no sooner had he laid eyes on her than the nightmare deepened, as Mary Hooper dissolved into a mound of bugs. A mass of earthen coloured things, squirming bodies and writhing legs, the slime of their forms glinting dully in the dappled light through the corridor of trees. The bugs fell in a wave, filling the base of the car. Spilling over Richard's ankles, they began to crawl up the legs of his trousers. He brushed frantically, trying to clear them, but their sheer numbers scuttled over his hands, and they were quickly running up his chest, over the skin of his neck, into his hair and on his face. A millipede wrapped around Richard's wrist as he flailed maniacally.

A second horn blared like a foghorn through the cloud of Richard's fear, causing him to look up, startled. Lights flashed directly in front of him. With his foot jammed down on the accelerator, the car's engine revved, careening him towards the front of the articu-lated truck at eighty miles an hour. Richard hit the brakes and pulled hard on the steering wheel. Tyres screeched, the smell of burning rubber pervaded. The car turned, and for a fraction of a second,

Richard was certain he wouldn't make it. The truck was going to smash into the side of him. But he was wrong. The deep horn of the truck sounded again. Richard's turn became a spin. Through the whump of air left in the wake of the passing truck, the world was a whirl of images. Trees, road, sky. Jane weeping. Trees. Jane on their wedding day. Rob learning to ride his bike seen on Jane's mobile phone. Road, sky. Rob wetting himself with fear in *The Witch's Brew*. Trees. Mary Hooper's death stare. Road, trees, sky. Deborah lying on his desk in *The Daily Telegraph*. Road, trees. Izzy and her pencil skirt. Road. Trees. Sky. Lesley Tibbits' bulging tongue in an autopsy report. Sky. Trees. Rob and Jane eating ice-cream on Southend Pier. Road. Trees. Sky. Two twenty pound notes, one handed to a cabbie, another to a police officer.

It all came to a sudden stop. The seatbelt constricted Richard's chest painfully. The airbags deployed. The sound of metal and plastic crunched at the front of the car. A ditch, filled with water, had stopped the car being impaled on a tree trunk.

For a few moments, while his car alarm wailed, Richard was in a state of dumbfounded shock, staring into the white airbag. Gradually, he became aware of himself, the annoying cycle of the car alarm, the pounding of his heart, the shaking of his limbs. Suddenly, he took a huge gasp of air. His eyes widened and he looked around, but there was nothing there. No beetles, no worms, no spiders or millipedes. Just Richard Peters, Editor in Chief of *The Newark Advertiser*, husband, father, adulterer, going slowly out of his mind.

26

6TH NOVEMBER 1810

Bitter and wet, it was a harsh autumn. Rain drummed heavily against the shutters of Mary's cottage as she screamed in pain and memories of recent events haunted her.

THE LANGUID DAYS of late summer, full of sweating bodies toiling in the fields and orchards to bring in the harvest, in a great reaping of life, had withered into autumn. And with it Aunt Jenny had fallen ill.

The fever came on quickly and would not shift. Jenny hacked in the pews next to Mary, at the back of the Minster during Sunday service, drawing reproachful stares. But they were not here for their god. The perception of propriety was merely a convenience, like a powdered wig on the bald head of a syphilitic aristocrat. In truth, the Minster sat upon an older place, its foundations piled upon deep running roots. They did not listen as the Reverend Moseley preached fire and brimstone against those that shunned the one true faith. Aunt Jenny wheezed, her breath a rattling snake at the tree of knowledge.

None of their knowledge of herbs and plants could help. No poultice could extract the poisonous humours and no enchantment could bring energy to the old woman's limbs. Jenny had seen enough death to know it was upon her. And with the bleeding of October into November, on a deathbed pulled next to the hearth, the old witch joined Jack in the Green, blown away like a leaf on her final breath.

The town's poor folk mourned her passing, squeezing Mary's hand on the street when they met. Many more said nothing, relieved that at least one of the witches had taken their secrets to the grave with her. Less pleased that her apprentice might know of their moments of shame and weakness.

It would not have been her wish, but Jenny was buried in the consecrated ground of the Minster, at the Reverend Moseley's insistence. He even paid for a coffin made from used planks of pine. In an unmarked pauper's grave next to the gravedigger's shack, tucked away at the edge of the graveyard, Jenny was lowered into the earth, facing east to west, "So that she may see the resurrection of our Lord and Saviour Jesus Christ," Moseley had intoned.

Dagund, Mary thought in the old tongue. *Midsumor, herung!*

The bitter weather gave cause for Mary to hide her growing belly beneath layers of shawls and a heavy cloak. The rain soaked her hair, falling like wet vines around her face, as the Reverend canted judgement from his book. Under her cloak, Mary's hands cupped her belly, and Aunt Jenny's warnings tolled in her mind as the church bells struck the hour. "The likes of us cannot have children of our own. What grows there can never be." Mary had thought Jenny's words had been proved false, and by the blessings of Jack in the Green, Mary's belly had continued to swell.

Once the Reverend Moseley had given the liturgy, the few mourners took Mary's hand or embraced her. Feeling the bump of her belly against them, the women said nothing, but gave Mary knowing looks full of sadness and told her to take care. And then Mary stood with only the Reverend Moseley by her side.

"Your aunt was a well regarded woman, Miss Hooper." The way the Reverend said it reminded Mary of an adder's hissing in the long grass. She stiffened but said nothing, politely nodding her head in recognition, and waited for the adder's next move.

"There are many troubling rumours about your Aunt and your-self. You live on the edge of town. You come and go. People visit you. God," the Reverend said with a sharp laugh like a hiccup, "sees everything."

The adder was poised.

"I don't know what you mean, Reverend."

The Reverend's tongue darts over his lips. "It's very difficult for women of your position, such a lowly station," his voice whined. "Now you're all by yourself, without even the protection of your aunt. It would be very easy for someone such as yourself to become desti-tute. I've seen it many times. Not just here, but in the bigger towns like Newark and Nottingham and beyond. I have seen the work-houses that are being built to shelter the penurious. I would hate to see that happen to you, Mary. Have you considered your prospects?"

Unseen, Mary touched her belly, that place of hope, that one thing deep inside her that was hers. The thing she would live for. She wasn't naive. She could do what her aunt had done. Her kind were needed. They always had been, more than the workhouses and alms.

"I should get out of the rain, sir," Mary said.

The Reverend stepped closer and reached to take her hand. To keep her belly a secret she met him halfway, and encouraged, Moseley smiled. His hand was clammy. Mary wished to flinch away, but she did not. The adder had not yet struck. To flinch would give away her intention.

"I am without a wife, as you might have noticed. This is not for want of looking. I have many prospects, being a respected man in the town. A man of some importance and yet still in the blush of youth. The future lies ahead of us both. Just as this great institution lies behind me. I shall rise up the ranks. The Bishop's Mansion lies there. He was once a man like me, you know? A humble vicar. But as it is written in the good book, a man needs a wife. It seems to me you are in need also, and I am in a position to graciously help. I would do that for you, Mary. I would become your husband."

Moseley caressed the back of her hand and Mary was repulsed. But not by his pallid complexion and serpentine features. Nor by the hook of his thin nose, nor the small black eyes. It was the feeling of predation, to which Giles Brennan had awoken her. She did not much believe in beauty on the outside. A dandelion was one of the most beautiful of all Jack's plants. It would struggle through the hardest of earth, even break out between the cobbles to daub the roads with bright sunspots. They were good eating too. Abundant and nutritious, though eat too many and they were an even better cure for constipation. No, her revulsion was because something of the adder's venom had permeated to corrupt the entirety of the snake.

"That's very kind of you Reverend. I should certainly consider it, but after the death of my dear aunt, I need time. In my moment of grief, I could not in good conscience take you up on your offer."

It was the Reverend who stiffened now and removed his hands from Mary's, and with a haughty sniff, he said, "As you will. As a Christian: it was my duty to offer, even though it could hurt me a great deal, marrying so beneath my station." He looked away from her, straightening his coat.

"It is very kind of you, sir," Mary said. "It warms me to know that someone such as you is looking out for me."

A smile twitched at the corners of the Reverend's mouth.

"How gracious of you," he said flatly and fished inside his coat pocket for his fob watch. His small eyes barely looked at it before he clicked it shut. "I must be going, I bid you good day."

The rain drummed on Aunt Jenny's coffin. It was not a good day, but Mary hoped that one would be delivered soon.

MARY SCREAMED out in her cottage, wracked by a cramp in her belly as the November rain pelted and the wind snatched at her door.

"No," she pleaded, her pacing faltered in front of the hearth.

It was too early. He couldn't arrive now. But the pains were coming closer together. The fire was dying and Mary bent down to poke it to life. As she threw the damp log on the meagre flames, another contraction ripped through her body. It was so painful she nearly swooned and fell, but steadied herself against the blackened stones of the chimney.

Once the spasm abated, Mary hobbled over to the table and assumed the position they often helped women deliver their babies from. She squatted, holding the top with both hands to steady herself. The vase on the table top, filled with winter's blooms of holly, ivy and mistletoe, wobbled. Sweat beaded on Mary's brow, and she blew out slowly from flushed cheeks.

"Not now, little one. Don't come yet. You're not ready. Mummy's not ready. You just go back to sleep my little duckling."

She knew it was a pointless request, born of desperate hope. For if a baby came this early, there was little chance it would survive. And for the mother there were risks as well. Childbirth was dangerous at the best of times.

Mary screamed at the top of her lungs with the next contraction, and the fire roared, sending flames up the chimney and causing the damp log to spit in a choleric fit. The sweat ran down her face and drenched her back. With the next scream of pain, Mary felt as if the earth would rumble beneath her feet, and the small dirty mirror they had above the mantle cracked into a spider's web.

Panting against the pain, Mary reached between her legs to see if she could feel the top of the baby's head. It was there, her baby's crown. Then another contraction hit her body. Mary grabbed the table top. Her legs almost buckled. Her scream rattled the table, making the vase dance. At the table, a chair toppled to its back. The fire spat and roared, burning white hot, with Aunt Jenny's rocking chair seesawing back and forth as if the old woman sat there worry- ing. Mary's knuckles turned white. The nail of her index finger ripped from its root, as her world was rent apart with a primal cry. And then there was a release.

Mary's son fell into her waiting hands. She caught him between her legs with her last vestiges of strength, until she lifted him to her breast and collapsed to her knees. The fire in the hearth calmed to a gentle crackle and pop. The room stilled. A whisper on the wind, the little boy's chest rose and fell as weakly as Aunt Jenny's on her deathbed. Mary petted his back. On the table, the unripe green and orange holly berries swelled and turned scarlet.

Mary fell to her backside exhausted, rocking him back and forth.

She would need to cut the cord, but she had time, and the after birth would come soon. She wept with joy, rubbing his back to try and bring forth his first cry of laughter. But the little boy was silent as the storm outside pulled at the door and shutters. Mary rubbed more vigorously.

"Come on my duck. Give a shout."

His little chest stopped its laboured rise and fall. The evergreen plants in the vase withered, and their vibrant greens turned sullen. In the hearth, the fire dulled to an ailing glow.

Hoisting him to her shoulder, Mary spanked his bottom as they would for lethargic babies to remind them life was born in a scream. He did not cry. His tiny weight lay heavy on Mary's chest. She tried again, the little slap like the cracking of a small twig in the forest, but he did not cry. Clearing the mucus from his mouth, Mary cradled him and rubbed her knuckle into his fragile breast plate. In response, his head shook from side to side, as if to tell his mother none of this would work and he had already gone to Jack in the Green.

As her tears fell, she rocked, alone on the flagstones, smothering him with kisses. Cold ashes lay in the hearth, and on the table the black desiccated husks of once vibrant plants crumbled to nothing.

27

THEY SAT MAKING polite chit-chat in the front room, drinking tea, skirting around the edge of what had happened, since it had already been covered in Dr Bishop's consulting room as he checked Rob over and patched him up. On the sofa, Jane kept her arm around Rob, who stared into his empty mug. The cut above his eye stung. His head throbbed a little. His lip was fat with a bruise, which managed to be the location of both numbness and a nebulous ache. But none of that compared to his thirst. He wanted to fetch another drink, but he feared he might drag his mother with him, or draw a million questions about where he was going, or why he was so thirsty. Then she'd worry more and look anxiously at Ken to see if this was a sign of a concussion or worse. And if these were the questions, how could Rob answer them? Well, Mum, I've been cursed by the ghost of a long dead witch who haunts the local pub, and not only does the curse make me unquenchably thirsty, I see visions of her rancid body in my dreams as well as in the showers at school, where, by the way, everyone hates me and thinks I'm a pervert. Oh, and while we're on the topic, the witch sent a plant to kill me on the way home, only the beating that psycho Danny gave me is hiding the cut and he might actually have saved me from being torn to shreds by some shrubbery.

Ironically lucky, eh? Instead, Rob kept his mouth shut and his head down.

The Reverend had called the surgery when he found Rob, and as it was only over the road, Dr Bishop had run across along with Rob's mother. She'd kept him close ever since, reluctantly moving away only when Dr Bishop tended Rob's wounds and checked for concussion, which by some miracle Rob didn't have. Taking his mind from the stinging iodine, Rob drew a mental caricature of Danny squeezing his neck, with bulging muscles as large as the quiff in his hair. Rob's face was a comedy of swollen black eyes and a maniacal gap-toothed grin, as Danny gasped: a mix of exasperation and exhaustion. A sinister briar of thorns lurked in the corner of the page, and above the fence, like a nosey neighbour, dark eyes stared through lank, black hair at the violence.

From the surgery, they'd driven the short distance home. Jane sat in the back with Rob, holding his hand, while they phoned the police. Once inside, Dr Bishop sat with Rob and Jane while the Reverend disappeared into the kitchen, refusing all offers of help. He navigated the kitchen with an almost preternatural sense of where to find things in a stranger's kitchen, garnered from a career of pastoral tea making and biscuit dunking in parishioners' homes.

The Reverend appeared with a tray, rattling with crockery and laden with biscuits, when the police constable turned up. It was one of the same policemen from that day in Mr Khan's office. He was a man as tall as he was broad with a full beard, which, in Rob's head, made him a dancing bear dressed as a policeman. It was a crap image, neither cutting nor insightful. Rob discarded it, feeling mentally drained.

Dr Bishop was watching Rob carefully as the policeman asked questions and Jane stroked his hair, even though he was much too old for this kind of attention. When asked, the Reverend Lovegrove had to admit that he hadn't seen a punch thrown, only Danny standing over Rob with his fist cocked.

"But you didn't actually see Danny hit Rob?" the Constable asked the Reverend.

"Well, no but..."

"And Rob, you say you had a bit of trouble at school today?"

Rob shrugged in agreement.

"Isn't Rob's word enough?" Jane asked with a tremulous edge to her voice.

"I'm making no judgments, Mrs Peters. My notes need to reflect all the facts."

"Will it record the fact that Danny's father is the Chief Constable?" Dr Bishop asked, his voice level.

The policeman looked up from his notes and without missing a beat, he said, "The occupation of someone's father will have no bearing on my notes. I'll be visiting Danny and his father next."

His questions asked, the policeman left. The Reverend made another pot of tea, and Rob tried not to chug it down and burn his throat. Jane checked her phone, reluctantly letting go of Rob.

"Where's Richard?" she said to herself, sending another text.

Rob didn't know which was worse, the thirst or the slow purgatory of sitting around with these three, when thankfully, in silent affirmation, Rob saw the Dr and vicar exchange a look.

Reverend Lovegrove stood and said, "I think we better leave you two."

Dr Bishop took his cue. "Yes, we'll get out of your hair. Call me if you need anything, Jane. Anything at all."

"Indeed, do," the Reverend agreed. "I took the liberty of leaving my card on the kitchen counter, in case you need to chat. Day or night. It doesn't matter."

Jane showed the men to the front door. Rob stood too, but they told him to sit. As they stepped out into the dimming light of early evening, a roadside assistance truck pulled up in front of the house, with its lights twirling. The yellow flashes drew Rob to the window. His dad got out of the truck, which drove off towing his car behind it. One of the front wheels was buckled and the fender hung loose. Richard looked tired and stressed and something else that Rob had seen that day in the Witch's Brew: afraid. However, Richard's face changed to one of puzzlement when he noticed the two men at his door.

"Take tomorrow off work if you need it," Ken told Jane.

"Thanks, Ken, but I'll try to be there."

"Call if you need anything," the Reverend reiterated as Richard came to the door.

"What's wrong? A doctor and a priest at this hour. Has someone died?" Richard said it without humour, but as soon as the joke had left his mouth, his bubbling annoyance changed. "Rob? Where's Rob? Is he..." Richard looked to the front window and saw his son there looking worse than Richard felt. "Bloody hell! What happened?" Without further greeting or farewell Richard pushed past Jane and hurried to Rob.

Jane said goodnight and shut the front door. "I've been trying to reach you for ages. Why didn't you answer?"

Richard was holding Rob at arm's length checking him over. "Car accident. Skidded off the road. Nothing serious. I was on the phone to the roadside pick-up guys and then the insurance company this whole time. The car will be out of action for a day or two."

"Was anyone else hurt?" Jane asked.

"No. I lost concentration. Swerved to avoid a truck. Ended up in a ditch. The front suspension, an axle or some such, is buggered apparently. Hell of a day, but what happened to you?" he said to Rob.

"Nothing. Just a fight after school," Rob said, but his eyes were fixed on his father's and in them they could see the reflection of what the other had been through that day.

"Right," Richard nodded, trying to process things. "Okay," which was not what he meant.

"It's not okay," Jane said. "This is getting out of hand. Do you know who hit him?"

"Of course, I don't. I've been in my own trouble all afternoon."

"It was Danny Broad, Julie Brennan's boyfriend."

"Right."

Jane shifted uneasily at Richard's uncharacteristic lack of bullishness. "He's the son of the Chief Constable." That should have got him going, but Rob could see the concern for the other thing he knew they had shared.

"Right," he said like another man, a weak and indecisive person, but one who now saw his son and held him with concern.

"First those boys roughed him up in games and nearly broke his ankle. Then he slipped in the shower. And having had enough, he decided to play truant from school and bumped into the wrong guy at the wrong time. Ken says it's a miracle he's not concussed but to keep an eye on him."

"Ken?"

"Dr Bishop. My boss. The guy who wasn't the vicar you pushed past."

"And this Danny, did all this to you?" Richard said.

"Mostly," Rob replied in a whisper.

"Aren't you listening? The boys in his class played hard at football too. I bet that was why you slipped in the shower. It's all connected, and it's getting out of hand." Jane looked frustrated at the impotence of her words. "If the Reverend Lovegrove hadn't come along when he did, who knows what would have happened?" Jane paced back and forth in quick turns.

Richard put a hand on his son's shoulder. "It'll be alright, mate. I promise, we'll sort it out together." Rob knew there were two meanings here; one for him, another for his mother. He nodded and played along.

Jane sat down heavily in an armchair. "The boy's father is a senior police officer. This will be brushed under the carpet."

"I don't want to press charges. It'll only make everything worse," Rob suddenly said.

Jane looked shocked.

"Alright, mate. Whatever you want," Richard patted him on the back.

"It's not alright." The muscles in Jane's jaw rippled. "For Christ's sake, Richard!" Normally, she was the calm one, but somehow in this damn town their roles had inexplicably reversed. Nothing made sense, and to Rob that seemed like the normality of this place.

Richard ran his hand through his hair, which only added to his harassed look. Jane stood to remonstrate with him, when Richard's phone rang in his pocket. His face fell when he saw the number.

Without answering it, he hung up the call and put the phone away. Rob saw his mother's face change too. Tears welled in her eyes, drowning the words that had been forming in her mouth. Bitter and salty, she swallowed them, hurrying from the room before the pull of conflicting emotions swept her away.

28

THE REVEREND LOVEGROVE stared at the blank screen of his laptop, sitting on the messy desk in the vestry. Late afternoon had turned to early evening, and the light was beginning to fail. It seemed barely able to break through the old million windows. Lovegrove turned on his desk lamp and rubbed his eyes.

He considered the chaos around him: there was a jumble of loose papers, stacks of old dusty books, academic articles which he'd downloaded, printed out, and then scrawled over with a fluorescent yellow highlighter and a cipher of marginalia understandable only to him. Around his desk, the room was a clutter of vestments and coats hung on hooks between overstuffed bookcases, a chipped khaki green filing cabinet standing against a sandstone wall, and the threadbare carpet of once rich Ottoman reds now faded and rumpled on the flagstones. The room bore no resemblance to the spartan order of a medieval monk's cell.

Lovegrove picked up his tea and winced as he sipped it: it had gone cold. He put it down with a sigh.

"The book won't write itself," he said, and sighed again. "The words won't appear as if by magic." He laughed, given the topic of the book.

The tome of his PhD monograph lay on the desk beside his

laptop, open at one of the middle chapters. He'd been working on it for the last two hours, since his pastoral duties had finished for the day. However, procrastination, Lovegrove knew, was the real word for what he'd been up to. In all that time, not a single new word had survived long enough to remain on the screen now. Some had made a valiant attempt, but their directionless rambling made them easy prey for Lovegrove's inner judge, who consigned them to their fate with the stroke of his 'delete' key. Sometimes, the vicar thought that he'd only get this book written once the delete button had worn out, which could be any day now, with God's help. *God helps those who help themselves*, he thought with another sigh. *If only you believed that.*

Somewhere, on the computer, there was also a contract from a small academic publisher for Lovegrove to turn his PhD into a book. He'd signed it eighteen months ago and things had not progressed well. He didn't know what it was. A bit of writer's block or resistance to the idea of putting the book out into the world. It was one thing to write a PhD that would remain unread on the dusty shelves in a university library, its spine facing out into the world as year after year of undergraduates passed it by not knowing of its existence. There was a safety in that hidden knowledge. *Hidden knowledge.* The phrase made him laugh again. Ah! That was it. The chapter he was pondering over was the relationship between various epochs and the land, how things were laid on top of each other. Essentially it was the concept of geomancy. He'd so loved to read about it, that and fantasy novels, as a boy. Some authors had coined the term 'Sacred Geometry'. That term really applied to buildings and man-made structures, which went as far back as the Neolithic era with stone and wooden circles. It also applied to the medieval masons, who built the great cathedrals of Europe, as well as the lesser ones such as the Minster he sat in now. Still, it was magnificent in its own right, but in a more genteel way.

Lovegrove's thesis was, in part, about Nottinghamshire and the Minster in which he worked. But it posed him a particular problem. Why here in Southwell? It's such a small town, with a population hovering around 10,000. Why build a cathedral here, rather than, say, Newark, with its formidable castle on the river and history as a centre of power? Why not in Nottingham itself, even larger and more important since medieval times? Yet the Normans, who understood how to dominate the landscape, built the county's cathedral here in a town of no strategic military importance, nor on a main trade route. It was nothing more than an idyllic backwater, then and now.

The vicar got up from his desk and wandered out into the nave to look up at the huge golden figure of Christ looking down on the hall below. The coloured glass in the windows had darkened to deep reds, greens, and blues, depicting tableaus from the bible. The smell of stone, polished wood, and the faint residue of incense perfumed the air. He let his mind wander, drifting through the vaulted space to the Roman mosaic laying under a pew near the south entrance. Visitors hit a large white button to illuminate it. Nothing too impressive, faded white squares that only hinted at something more. At the turn of the millennium, when developers bought the old sixth form site of the school and promptly levelled it to make way for more houses, they made a quite miraculous discovery. An enormous Roman villa complex, one of the largest ever found in Britain, which put an end to the development and tied the town up in a legal dispute for years.

Again, Lovegrove wondered, *why here?*

Those who seek power often build over the significant religious sites of those they conquered. The Romans did it to the Celts. The Normans did it to the Anglo Saxons. The British Freemasons in Hong Kong deliberately built in violation of indigenous Feng Shui practices. There are countless other examples throughout history from all over the world. All led him to the conclusion that Southwell, at least in some distant epoch, must have had a religious significance that had long since passed out of memory from a pre-Christian, perhaps even pre-Celtic, culture.

Alas, it was hard to write a book when there was no hard evidence. *Isn't that the nature of belief?* he thought wanly and looked up at the effigy of Christ.

"It used to be that belief was enough for you," Lovegrove said to himself. Christ offered no advice, and so the vicar wandered slowly from the nave to do his final checks before leaving for the day.

Just before the vestry, he turned down the short passage towards the Chapter House. His mind wandered to the local fairytales. His particular interest in this, as a local boy, had been the story of the Witchopper. His PhD had led him to explore folklore in relation to religious belief from an anthropological perspective in a post-Christian landscape. (It was a good way to lose friends at a party.) In the new book he wanted to go beyond that, to the root of it all.

The case of Mary Hooper sounded like an old folktale, except at two-hundred years, it really wasn't that old. The rhyme and game had all the marks of an oral culture, encoding essential information, but not always on the surface. But without direct connection with the practices of the past, so much information was lost. Lovegrove felt that Mary Hooper somehow had become the physical embodiment of a lost cultural memory that recorded the pagan traditions of this place. It was an image remembered from the depths of childhood, but without context it meant nothing. There were other clues, too, in Southwell, and in strange serendipity as he entered the Chapter House, he saw one of those things.

Lovegrove wandered over to one of the many wooden seats lining the room. Sat like a tiny man in reverie was a straw poppet no bigger than his palm. He'd been finding these every few weeks, from his very earliest time serving his parishioners over the last eighteen years. Although, he never remembered seeing them as a boy growing up in the town. When he'd asked around, making small talk in the pub or at the Women's Institute coffee morning, no one seemed to know anything about them.

The straw man, a vivid green from freshly picked grass, weighed nothing, as if it was hardly there. He turned it over in his fingers. It reminded him of the deep past in this place, and of how one culture had built on top of the previous one, blending with it. From the church walls, the Greenman stared back at him, branches and leaves sprouting hideously from his mouth, a thatch of foliage for hair, almost like the mane of a wild animal. The Greenmen murals were all around this room, omnispective. Some of the finest examples in the whole of Britain.

Sighing yet again, Lovegrove put the poppet in his pocket and closed up for the night.

There was very little light left. The shadows of the gravestones had long since moved past, stretching out like fingers clawing to hold onto the day and blending into a soft grey blanket, putting the town to bed.

A contemplative pint in the *Witch's Brew* tonight seemed the order of the day. Perhaps he'd find inspiration there. But as he was leaving the graveyard, a strange thing caught Lovegrove's eye. He stopped and peered into the gloom. Sure enough, Trevor Hempstead, the grounds-man, was operating a small earthmover, digging a grave. The Reverend walked over.

"Good evening, Trevor."

The groundsman looked up startled. He'd been engrossed in his work, a trance-like state of focus the Reverend wished he could obtain when writing his book. Trevor seemed almost surprised to find himself sitting in the digger, wearing muddy jeans and a flannel shirt rolled up to the elbow, as the dew condensed on the grass.

"Could I ask what you're doing?"

Trevor paused, looked around himself, and then down at the hole that he was digging, and replied, "Digging a grave," almost like it was a question.

Quite genially Lovegrove said: "I don't remember there being a funeral in the books. But, it's entirely possible I missed something."

Trevor put his hand on the lever to start digging again. "Must be."

"But I don't think I did - miss anything - I mean," the Reverend said. He was usually very good about such things. The pastoral side of his job was the bit he still believed in.

Trevor shrugged. "People are always dying."

"That is true."

Trevor yanked the levers back and forth, and the digger's arm twitched like a drunk robot and then lurched down into the hole.

"Do you have any idea who the poor soul might be?" Lovegrove raised his voice to be heard over the machine.

"Not a clue," Trevor said. "It won't go to waste. Someone is bound to die soon."

"Well, that's true," the Reverend shouted pleasantly, "but I wouldn't want anyone falling in it, if it isn't needed soon."

"Good point," Travis said, rotating the digger to drop the bucket of earth on a growing pile at the grave's edge. "I'll be sure to put some cones around it. Be good if you could rustle someone up to go in this hole for me, though."

They both laughed at this.

"I'll see what I can do. Good night."

"Night, Reverend," Trevor said, already slipping back into the trance of his work.

With even more unanswered questions, the Reverend Lovegrove took himself off for a pint at the *Witch's Brew*. As he walked, he let his mind wander away from his thesis, away from the unknowable mysteries of the past. Instead, he thought of Rob Peters and how he found the boy yesterday. Strangely, and completely unconnected, he had a message from a junior journalist on behalf of Rob's father. Lizzy was her name, or maybe it was Izzy. She was sounding out the vicar about a possible meeting with Richard Peters to discuss, of all things, the Witchopper folktale. The Reverend had come up in a library search, apparently. *The knowledge was not so well hidden*, he thought with a smile.

Life certainly was full of coincidences. There was a time he'd have seen God's hand in it all.

"Alas," he sighed once more.

29

JULIE WAS in front of the bathroom mirror again, wiping an arc that wanted to steam up as soon as she'd cleared it. The ritual sting of deodorant on shaved armpits followed. *Why do we even bloody shave them? No one but me and the other girls in the changing room has ever seen them. Except tonight, maybe.* The spritz of her mother's Dior perfume to hide what she really smelled like. The pulling on of stolen underwear, as concealed as the non-existent hairs in her armpits. *Except tonight maybe.* And the padded bra, filling it all out and pushing it up. If everyone took part in the lies, did that make them true? Julie looked at the results in the mirror. Her heart beat faster, but not as fast as it had done before. She tingled, but the excitement felt more controlled and familiar. There was no need to turn at the hips to inspect herself. This time, she knew what she was doing, slipping her phone into her back pocket and returning to her room.

It was cold. Julie pulled on a sweatshirt and began to dry her curly hair. The house was freezing from trying to save money on the heating bill. The warm air made her shiver as she brushed out the tangles, looking at her cacti lined up on her window sill. She turned the hairdryer on them.

"Hey, guys. You must be cold. I know, summer is nearly here."

They were a small prickly family, each with their own personality.

One short and dumpy, one round and fuzzy, another hairless and waxy. *Like my armpits*, Julie thought, *only without the thorns. Though they could come in handy sometime.* Julie loved the Aloe Vera, it had a medicinal sap she'd dab on pimples. There was a Bird's Nest, or Nipple Cactus, but she wasn't about to tell Effie its name. Another of her cacti was tall and coated in fine hairs that looked soft but stung like hell if it touched anyone's skin.

"It looks like a cock," Effie had snorted when Julie bought it from the florists with Christmas money.

"Cocks aren't furry on the..." Sally made a gesture.

"Shaft?" Effie guffawed. "You can say cock, but you can't say shaft. What's that about? Anyway, how would you know? That porn addiction getting out of hand again, Sals? Get it? Out of hand. Like wan..."

"... Just ignore her, Sal. Anyway, it's a Armatocereus Godingianus."

"Ow! Fancy. Still looks like a hairy cock," Effie had smirked.

Julie liked to talk to the cacti. They never said anything back, not in words anyway. But plants had ways of communicating, if anyone took the time to notice, and Julie did. They wore their condition on their skin. She liked the way people made all the wrong assumptions about them because of the way they looked. The truth was, they were nature's survivors and that was real beauty.

Julie's phone buzzed in her pocket, interrupting her cactus conversation.

'Looking forward to tonight XX,' the message from Danny read.

'Me too. See you soon XX,' Julie replied and slipped the phone back into her pocket to finish drying her hair. The cacti stared at her without judgement.

Earlier in the week, coffee with Danny had gone well, really well. He was sweet and asked questions about how she was doing. She didn't even like coffee but pretended to. The one hiccup had been when Julie asked if Danny had beaten up Rob. Danny said they got into an argument after school one evening, but that's all it was.

"It's not as if Rob doesn't have a track record in lying about stuff," Danny had said, taking Julie's hand across the table, sending a thrill through her.

"I guess."

"What? Do you still like him after what he's done?" Danny removed his hand.

"No. Not at all. You're right," she said, and the hand came back.

The date, because that's what it was, had gone so well Danny got them a second cappuccino. Later that afternoon, Julie thought she was having palpitations, while Effie made lewd comments (and gestures) and Sally tried to read between the lines of every word and action Julie could remember Danny making. She and Danny then exchanged messages. Sweet selfies competing in who could look the most bored or most confused about their revision. Then Danny asked if she'd like to come around on Friday night for a takeout and a movie. Effie and Sally said they'd cover for Julie. As far as everyone's mothers were concerned, they were all at Effie's.

After coffee, Danny walked her home, and they'd held hands. At the corner, before anyone in Julie's house could see, they'd kissed, their tongues touching briefly. Julie's head swirled like helicopter seeds falling from a sycamore. That spin had carried her through the rest of the week to tonight as she walked to Danny's house from the council estate on the edge of Southwell. It was only a fifteen minute walk to the nicer part of town. On the way, hugging her arms in a jacket too thin for a spring night, Julie didn't see Rob looking out of his bedroom window as she passed his house.

IT WAS like Danny punching Rob in the gut again. He wanted to run outside and explain everything to Julie, but he didn't. He couldn't. Besides there were other more troubling things in his life, exams being the least of them.

Rob's laptop lay open on his desk as he went through his geography revision. In a matter of days they would break up for exams, and Rob was still playing catch up from the move from London and everything that followed. He punctuated cramming facts about glacial deposits with constant sips of water. A sharp pain had started in his lower back in the morning and refused to go. It could have been from the beating Danny gave him, but he knew it wasn't. He pushed the pain aside and wrote a description of a drumlin for the fourth time, hoping it would finally stick.

One of Rob's message apps pinged on his laptop, which was unusual as he'd not only cancelled all of his accounts but also deleted the apps from his phone and laptop.

'Pervert,' it read in all caps. There was no recognisable sender, only a generic image. Worse, Rob's account was fully active again. Its most recent post was the video of him and Julie, the image paused with her head near the crotch of his jeans.

Another message popped up. 'Why don't you fuck off and die?'

'Good idea,' the next read.

'Everyone hates you, pervert.'

'Even your mum thinks you're sick.'

'Things would be better without you.'

'Do everyone a favour and kill yourself.'

Each was from a different sender, none of whom Rob knew, all with pseudonyms as lurid as 'Shag69'. He deleted the video, and then all the messages, but before he could finish, the video was reposted on his page, and he was locked out. Rob slammed the laptop shut and snatched up the water bottle. He took long gulps until the water sloshed in his stomach, but it made no difference, so he slammed the bottle back down. *What was the point?* He was thirsty whether he drank or not.

Taking himself off to the bathroom, Rob turned on the light and tried to pee. Finally, it came in a weak stream of dark yellow. He washed his hands, and a wraith stared back from the mirror. His lips looked dry, and dark rings were forming under his eyes from lack of sleep. Life had become the part of a nightmare where the world falls away, and Rob should have woken up. But he didn't, because the nightmare was real.

"I don't think you'll need to kill yourself," the wraith in the mirror told him through gritted teeth.

———

RICHARD STOOD over the kitchen sink, filling and then drinking his third glass of water. His mouth remained dry and his thirst burnt acidly at the back of his throat. There was a tremor in his hand as he placed the glass on the draining board, and for a second it rattled like Marley's chains. The image of Mary Hooper dissolving into a squirming mass flashed across his mind. He tried to shake it off, the memory of the bugs all over him making his skin itch.

Jane's voice came from behind him. "Please tell me what's wrong."

The weight of the world was in those words.

Richard wrung the shakiness from his hands, still facing the sink. "It's just proven harder than I thought. Managing a team. The chaos of the move. The stresses of the business side of things. I've never had to do any of that stuff before. I thought it would be a step down. Much easier. And then this business with Rob."

"You're sure that's it?"

Richard turned around, but he didn't meet her gaze. "What else would it be?"

"I don't know. But we can talk. You know that, right?"

He felt and looked deflated. "I know. I just need a good night's sleep. That's all, love. If I can't, maybe your boss could sort me out with some sleeping pills. I'll head up now."

"Alright, love."

As Richard walked out of the kitchen, Jane made a step to come to him, but something more than a kitchen table seemed to lie between them. He left, too distracted by his troubles to notice.

WHEN JULIE PUSHED THE DOORBELL, it felt like electricity was running through her entire body, as if she could feel everything around her, the trees, the sky, the dirt beneath the gravel. The bell produced a slow bing-bong, like a gameshow contestant just got an answer wrong, and the crowd laughed with mirth, while a man with white teeth and a deep tan looked smugly into a camera and slowly shook his hair implants from side to side.

The house was so large, new and with at least six bedrooms, in a mock-Georgian style. The walls, rendered a light blue, were broken up by white sash windows. Doric pillars stood either side of an anthracite coloured front door, which loomed imposingly on top of three stone steps. There was a pause after the gameshow bing-bong, and Julie, despite knowing for sure this was the right house, doubted herself. Self-conscious, she looked back down the drive, which, while in reality only a few feet longer than her own front yard, seemed to suddenly stretch out forever, past the two-seater Jaguar sports car parked there. The wind rustled agitatedly in the trees, and shadows cast by the street lights could have been gateways leading from twilight to a forbidding nether of darkness.

There was a noise inside. Julie shifted from foot to foot in the chill, her hands stuffed into her armpits. *No spiky hairs there.* A voice, not Danny's. A woman's. And footsteps rushing down stairs. A snib clicked, and the anthracite door slung in.

Julie tried not to wince at the light which cut into the dark, sending the gateways to the nether rushing for cover.

"Oh my," the lady squealed. "You're so pretty. I can see what all the trouble was over now. Judy isn't it? Come in, come in."

The lady, maybe in her late twenties, and dressed in a tight, but long, chocolate brown dress, stepped aside. She wore diamond earrings and a matching necklace that glittered with starlight under the chandelier. In her high heels, which chiselled sinuous lines into her calves, the lady made a sweeping gesture with her arm, like a game show hostess - *come on in and see what you've won.*

Danny had made it to the bottom of the sweeping staircase, his freshly pressed polo-shirt pulled up, exposing his biceps.

"Do you mind? I said I'd get it. And it's Julie not Judy. You know that."

The woman made a face, pursing together her scarlet painted lips in a manner that was either mocking or condescending, Julie couldn't decide.

"Danny boy," she mewed, reaching to pinch his cheek. "There's no need to be so embarrassed. Oh look at the two of you. Get closer together and we'll take a picture."

The lady, who had an accent, Eastern European maybe, put a

manicured hand on Julie's shoulder and cajoled her towards her prize. *Congratulations, Judy you've won your very own life size Ken doll. Terms and conditions apply. No purchase necessary.*

"Aaron," the lady squawked down the hall, putting her aquiline nose and unnaturally large and gravity defying breasts in profile to Julie. "Bring your phone. These two are adorable."The four syllables of the final word were each separated and stressed.

"Seriously, Karolina. You're so embarrassing. Please, piss off," Danny said, lacing his fingers into Julie's and starting to move away.

"Stay right there!" The voice boomed down the corridor, both commanding and edged with delight. "And don't talk to your mother like that, boy." A man, tall and balding but wide at the shoulder like Danny, came marching down the black and white chequered tiles in full police dress uniform, hat tucked under his arm.

"She is *not* my mother," Danny muttered.

Danny's father joined the game show model, his phone already fished out of his pocket, and the two of them smiled maniacally into the little screen.

"Put your arm around her, son. Come on, smile."

"How can you not smile, Danny boy. She's so gorgeous," not-mother Karolina said tapping the palms of her hands together. Red lipstick had smeared her front teeth, as if she liked to eat babies during the ad breaks. "Isn't she beautiful, Aaron?"

Mr Aaron Broad checked the picture and, happy with the results, pocketed the phone. "She most certainly is. Chip off the old block." He pulled Karolina into a kiss that left dead baby smears on his lips.

"Dad!" Danny moaned, already flushed red.

"What? Me and your mum are just happy."

"Thrilled," Karolina agreed, her hand draped on the Chief Constable's shoulder.

"Julie's a girlfriend, Dad. Not a knighthood."

Girlfriend? I'm a girlfriend, Julie thought.

"Well, you know, son, we thought..."

"You thought what?" Danny said.

"We thought you were gay, silly," Karolina reached forward and gave Danny a patronising pat on his muscular forearm.

"Jesus, Dad! Seriously!" Danny looked mortified. "You're going to let her say that?"

Danny's dad gave an over-the-top shrug, and now Julie felt just as mortified for Danny. Her dad, with all his problems after the army, could be embarrassing, a liability even, but this was something else.

"You know," not-mother Karolina tried to explain, "with all your lifting weights..." She made the actions, like pumping alternate invisible dumbbells and puffing out her cheeks. "...and perfect hair," she preened her own perfect hair, "all the nice clothes," she straightened an invisible collar, "and no girls. Not one. Never." The last word came out as 'nyever' in her accent.

Danny was speechless and covered his face with a palm. Julie squeezed his other hand.

"Alright, that's enough teasing." A seriousness came over the Chief Constable, and he put on his hat, Karolina still draped over his shoulder, grinning at them. "There's cash on the counter, and you've got your own card. Call Charlotte, my PA, if there are any emergencies. There better not be. And we'll be back late on Sunday. Make sure you do your revision. Second and last chance on these exams, son. I'm not paying for another year at that overpriced school just so you can fail, so get it right this time."

Even Julie felt the power in the man's voice. *Do not pass go. Do not collect two-hundred pounds, and go straight to jail, without your life-size Ken doll.*

"Yes, Dad," Danny said, head bowed.

Without a hug or even a pinch on the cheek, Chief Constable Broad and not-mother Karolina left arm in arm. Karolina smiled wryly over her shoulder at them and batted a fake eyelash in a slow wink. The anthracite door slammed shut behind them and moments later the Jaguar's engine roared and wheels then crackled over gravel.

Julie and Danny stood in silence. Danny's chest rose and fell in stiff breaths.

Squeezing Danny's hand again, Julie said, "I'm sorry," mostly because she didn't know what else to say.

"What have you got to be sorry about?" The words were dark.

"I just meant... I don't know. Parents are embarrassing. My mum still spits on a hanky and tries to wash my face with it sometimes." Bing-bong, and the game show audience laugh at another stupid answer from Judy, not Julie, Brennan.

But Danny's face softened, and a smile slowly bloomed there. His head came up and he turned to her, muscles bulging, hair perfect, clothes immaculate, like her very own life-size Ken doll.

30

MARY HELD her little boy weeping silently. She kissed him and cuddled him until he grew as cold as the November wind outside. Then she remembered to cut the cord, as she had done so many times with her aunt Jenny, with so many women. But never to herself.

She placed him lovingly on a blanket and cleaned herself as best she could. The physical pain she had, torn and bruised, was nothing to the pain in the heart. Mary relit the fire, igniting kindling with a tallow candle that still burnt, and warmed a pan of water.

Mary bathed her son, washing away the blood and mucus of birth, until he was a perfect little blue man. Such a good boy, he never cried, not once. Such perfect little hands and feet, and a tiny round face. Black hair like his mummy. So peaceful with his eyes closed and those perfect baby lips pursed into an eternal kiss. There he was ready but for one thing. His name. Edward she would call him, because it was a name that meant guardian in the old tongue.

When he was clean, Mary swaddled Edward in a clean blanket, wrapping him into a perfect little bundle, singing to him as she did.

"Lavender's green dilly dilly, lavender's blue; If I love you dilly

dilly, you'll love me too. Call up your men dilly dilly, set them to work; Some to the plough dilly dilly; some to the cart; Some to make hay; some to cut corn; Whilst you and I dilly dilly, keep safe and warm"

But Mary wasn't warm. She felt cold to her very soul.

Mary strapped her son to her chest, holding him close to her heart, and threw a shawl over her shoulders and pulled on her winter cloak. Beneath that she hid a shovel and stole away into the night.

Moving through the biting wind and driving rain she skirted the town. When two rowdy men barrelled out of *The White Lion* inn, both as drunk as bishops, Mary stole behind a sycamore, calling the ivy to spread around her and keep her hidden. The drunkards started up Church Street towards the Minster and went out of sight. Mary set out into the wind and rain once more.

Stopping. Staring. She moved off the main tracks, until she found the stream that traced along one edge of the town, connecting places most people had forgotten. In the dark, moving by memory and the sense of the plants and life around her, Mary found the stepping stones. The grass on the bank reached mournfully for her as she struggled onto the first step. Each step was made with a muffled cry. On the final leap to the far bank, she slipped and would have fallen into the swollen waters but for the ivy and a small rowan bush who bent to her rescue, catching and righting their mistress.

Panting on the bank, Edward, yet so small, felt like the weight of the world. The rain seeping to her skin, Mary caught her breath and hoisted herself up using the shovel for support and pressed on.

She found the old willow as easily as if it was daylight. It was a place she had come to many times with her aunt ever since she was a child to nourish her *cunning* ways with Jack's help. This night, Mary worked with Edward wrapped to her chest, savouring every moment she could with her son. She dug a shallow hole near the roots of the tree and unwrapped Edward, finally taking him from her breast. Kissing his perfect little face one last time, Mary laid the bundle in the shallow grave. Kneeling at Jack's feet, she made her offering in the old tongue.

"Geopane min leofes, Jack grenemon. Him brycyst ond þu gehal gehalode!

The wind picked up, shaking the drooping branches of the willow. Rustling whispers grew to answer the wind and the roots of the old willow began to move. They snaked from the ground, coiling and twisting, slowly entwining around the little boy, wrapping him carefully until he was encased within a cocoon of caressing tendrils. Mary's tears salted the dirt as her son was gradually pulled into the earth. When the little boy had gone to be with Jack in the Green, Mary placed her hand where he had once been. A mother's final, longing touch for what she could never have.

31

THROUGH A WEB OF UNSEEN CONNECTIONS, beneath the earth and cast invisibly through the sky, he hunted his prey, gathering information, setting traps. Some doors were closed to him but were easily opened with lines of code or with the aid of wireless devices no one thought to protect with passwords. The not-so-smart lightbulbs and plugs, speakers that listened, and baby monitors - by far the easiest to corrupt: in their multitude he turned them to his dark purposes, mindless familiars he would send through the web to break down their defences. And so his control grew, machine by machine, device by device. Gathering information. Bank codes were useful, but not as valuable as guilty secrets or private moments, naked before their screens, which stared back at their unknowing watchers. Recording all.

Of the many devices and homes he invaded there was one he looked for above all the others. On the way to find her, he played with another of his victims, taunting him through untraceable proxy accounts, revelling in giving instead of receiving the torment for once. At first, she wasn't where he expected, but with a little effort - and Julie was worth it - he found her through message apps and the GPS in her phone. He smiled watching them. Tonight he would have a front row seat. It would be easy to imagine himself in

Danny's place, and someday it would be him for real, one way or another.

JANE SLID into the bed next to Richard, trying not to shiver at the initial coldness of the bedcovers. She pulled them up around her chin and curled into Richard's back. By the way he was breathing, she could tell he was still awake. Jane kissed his neck and let her arm reach around to his chest. Words having failed, she had followed Richard upstairs after looking for courage at the bottom of her wine glass. But instead, words from Brian, whom she'd met at the surgery with his confused wife Millicent, had surfaced from the dregs.

"Love is hard sometimes, isn't it? You have to take the bad as well as the good. It's a package deal."

Jane kissed Richard's neck again, leaving her lips to linger, her hand moving slowly down Richard's chest. The seconds moved as slowly as her hand. At last, he rolled towards her and looked into her eyes. His eyes shone faintly in the dark, as if reflecting a timid moon that pulled at Jane's heart. He seemed hesitant, like a school boy, and then he took her by the waist and gently pulled her to him. Their mouths opened. Their bodies relaxed as they dived into each other, the timid moon dissolving in ripples.

Shouts came from Rob's bedroom. They heard the thuds of things being thrown. The moment was gone. Jane pulled away from Richard.

"Rob?" she called, and went to her son.

IT HAD ONLY BEEN a week since Julie and Rob had run from the police. There had been a thrill that night as they ran hand in hand away from one trouble only to find another. That same thrill fluttered in Julie's chest now as she sat next to Danny on his bed while they drank cider, ate pizza, and streamed the remake of *Carrie* on Danny's laptop.

Danny held her hand and kept his own cider just as topped up as

Julie's. A pink blush had risen on his cheeks and across the top of his chest, and Julie imagined she was just as flushed. Danny hadn't mentioned anything more about his dad and not-mother Karolina. He'd given Julie a quick tour of the house. The open plan kitchen at the back, with its chrome finishes and granite worktops that sparkled almost as much as Karolina not-mother's jewellery, was the size of the entire downstairs of Julie's home. There were paintings and prints on the walls, some lit by their own small lamps. There were also photographs, a lot of them of Karolina and Mr Broad. Some had Danny in them, looking sullen or forcing a smile, but not many. But in Danny's room, on his bedside table, there was a small photo frame containing an old picture of a woman with sandy hair hugging a boy of maybe five. The boy was laughing with abandon, his head thrown back against his mother's chest.

"Who's that?" Julie had asked, as they opened the pizza box and searched for a movie.

"My mum, my real mum," Danny'd said.

"She's pretty."

"Yeah, she was," Danny had replied flatly, topping up their cider, which was already going to Julie's head. He wasn't forthcoming with any more information and Julie didn't want to press, not right now.

The pizza was nice, the cider was sour, and the movie was good. Horror wasn't usually Julie's thing, but she felt for Carrie. How could she not? Carrie wasn't the monster in the movie, and as Julie thought about the bullying Carrie endured, the constant taunting, the girls filming her in the shower while she had her first period, Rob appeared in her mind with the mix of emotions from that night a week ago. Julie had really liked Rob. He was cute and gentle and talented. That picture from art class, how could someone their age produce something like that? It was embarrassing and flattering in equal measure and twice as confusing as a result. Why did people have to look at her? Rob made art, but art wasn't what the other boys saw. They all thought she didn't notice them watching, the way their eyes followed her out of a room, like the gaze of a painting, always on her. At least, here with Danny tonight, no one was watching.

Julie put her head on Danny's shoulder and he wrapped his arm around her. Carrie was about to be made Prom Queen and the cruel joke would have its punchline, as Carrie tried too hard to fit in.

Danny kissed Julie on the top of her head and she looked up at him. He was so handsome. Danny hesitated for a moment, as if unsure about something, and Julie thought it was her, and then they kissed. It was hard and not tender like Rob's. Danny's stubble scratched, and he tasted of tart apples. A high-pitched keening erupted from Danny's laptop, and he broke their kiss. Everything became blood and fire and death as Carrie dispensed her justice. Julie was drawn into the carnage. Carrie was pure in her vengeance, intoxicated with rage and yet the effects were both sweet and sore. Those that deserved it died, but so too did the ones whose crime was laughter, as did the ones who just stood by and let it happen. That's what made it ring true, even though it was a fantasy.

As the credits started to roll, they drank the last of their cider. Julie felt light-headed. Danny turned off the movie and the frozen screen stood blank and open.

"Stupid bitch," Danny said.

Julie thought at first he meant her. "What?"

Danny nodded towards the laptop. "Carrie. Why did she let everyone treat her like that? Why did she let her mum walk all over her? Why did she have to die like that at the end when she's a super-human? I mean if I had a power like that..." Danny didn't finish his thought. Julie could feel his whole body tense, and then when she looked into his face, his eyes were on the verge of tears. Whether it was the cider, or the way his parents treated him, or the picture on his bedside table, there was a swell of emotion that looked ready to explode out of him at any moment. Julie put her hand on Danny's thigh and arched up to kiss him.

THE TWO TENTATIVE knocks came at Rob's door, followed by his mother's voice.

"Rob, darling, are you okay?"

Rob wiped away his tears and sniffed. "I'm fine."

He did a poor job at disguising his state of mind. His door handle turned, and his mother did not wait for permission to enter.

"Robert!" She looked around the room. Rob sat on his bed amid the mess of notebooks, folders, sketch pads and sheets of paper tossed around the room like oversized confetti. His desk was swept clean, which included his laptop, which lay ajar on the racing car carpet. The desk chair was upended.

Jane came to him. Sitting next to him on the bed, she pulled him close, and Rob allowed himself to cry.

"Darling, what's the matter? Tell me, please."

The same unbelievable secret stopped him from saying anything. What good would telling her do, if the father who knew exactly what was happening and had experienced it himself didn't seem to have a clue?

"It'll pass. I promise. It's just a bit of bullying. I'll speak to Mr Khan and Mr Bryce. We'll get it sorted."

His mother had accepted her own truth, an entirely plausible and rational one. Rob let her believe that's what was wrong.

Rob let her stroke his hair and rock him like when he was a small child. He closed his eyes, and at least for a few moments he could smell the sea and hear the seagulls call as they ate ice cream on Southend Pier. They were precious moments of reprieve, until the rhythm of the waves became a menacing rustle of a wild wood and the seagulls collapsed into a fermenting mass of maggots, forcing Rob to open his eyes.

FOR THOSE THAT could hear it, there was always the faint effervescence of life. The infinitesimal movements of deep and ancient roots beneath the soil. The scuttling and squirming lifeforms, churning the earth through their guts. Eukaryotic kingdoms devouring and creating in their mycelic web. Teeth and claws red with blood and lust. The micro-biotic viscera and their infinite digestion of life. All in perpetual motion. Life begetting life.

It stirred Millicent from a dark and terrible dream in which she'd lost her mind. A strange man lay asleep next to her, and it seemed the dream would never end. She swung her feet over the side of the bed, and, trembling, she stood, dressed only in her nightgown. The rustling was louder now, calling to her. She had forgotten many things, but not this. She followed it.

A blade of light from the hallway cut across her bed, hitting the strange man's face. He mumbled and turned over. She shut the bedroom behind her. The man did not wake.

Moving quietly to the back of the house, Millicent pulled open the French windows which hissed as they slid. In her bare feet, she stepped onto the grass, padding over to the flowerbed, where the rustling was loudest.

As she approached, the plants moved expectantly. The old witch, Millicent, dropped to her knees, finding her mind once more.

"I'm here, my darlings."

"Yes, I'm fine. Thank you for asking."

She petted them one at a time.

"Is it really?" Millicent was shocked. "Have I been away that long?"

The plants rustled as they gently wound around her hands.

"No! She can't. That's too quick. What does Jack think?"

The plants shook vigorously.

"Tonight? But I already passed on his message. At least, I think I did. Didn't I?"

The plants quivered timidly.

"Angry? Well, you tell that silly old fool to do it himself, then."

"Okay. Okay, I'll do it. Subtlety is usually his strong point, except when it comes to *her*."

An owl hooted.

"I know she had more than good reason. But *had* is the operative word, so yes, I agree with him that enough is enough. He's cutting it a bit fine."

The roots of fronds sought the touch of her hands once more. They caressed her tenderly.

"Yes, yes, I know my time is running out too. No matter. We can all be together soon."

She pulled her hands away but one stem was reluctant to let her finger go. She peeled it away like the hand of a small child.

"Now, that's enough. I might not be back to see you. Don't you worry about me."

The plants gave one last urgent rustle.

"Okay, I'll do it now."

Millicent plunged her hands into the dirt, letting the mud ooze between her fingers. Once her hands were sufficiently covered and her eyes had glazed to a rough green, she was ready to begin.

THEY LAY TOGETHER in the light projected by Danny's laptop.

The stolen yellow knickers were crumpled amid the rest of their clothes.

This was what he wanted, wasn't it?

It was what Julie wanted, surely?

Danny's jaw clenched and unclenched in the dull electrical glow. His eyes had been closed all through their urgent fumbling, but now, standing on the precipice, he opened his and looked down at Julie. She touched his face, and together, hearts pounding, they didn't so much as leap, as stumble into each other.

THINGS CALMED DOWN, the bullying put into perspective, Jane helped Rob tidy his room. She didn't react when she found the picture of the nymph in the wild wood, though her chest fluttered at her son's talent, so precocious it was almost frightening. But the picture which disturbed her and made her pause was of the face of a woman, with one eye glaring blackly through strands of lank, wet hair, her twisted hand reaching out of the page. The dark imagination behind the composition unnerved her. Questions began to form about what it was and why he had drawn it, but then he could conjure so much from his mind's eye, why not this? The possibility of an over-talented son with a troubled mind also troubled Jane. But now was not the time. More than likely it was a natural, perhaps even healthy response to bullying and being pulled away from everything he knew in London, and that made Jane feel guilty and selfish. Finished, she made Rob cocoa like he was eight-years-old again, kissed him on the top of the head, and reluctantly left him be.

Closing the door to her bedroom, Jane found Richard in bed reading over a dossier of notes with an intensity that reminded her of him popping Adderall and pulling all nighters to meet a deadline.

What mood there was had gone, but Jane didn't want to reject him. Not now. She needed to rekindle it, with the hope that it would ignite their marriage, otherwise the move north, the new jobs and school, the years of their lives would have been for nothing.

"Is Rob okay?" Richard asked, looking over the rim of his glasses.

Jane undid her dressing gown and let it fall to the floor. She stepped towards Richard's side of the bed and pushed the straps of her nightie from her shoulders, standing before him naked.

Richard gawped.

Jane bent down and placed a kiss on his lips. She wasn't sure. Did he tighten? Did he find her repulsive? But then Richard relaxed. Jane pulled back the covers and climbed astride him, and even through his pyjama bottoms she could tell he did still find her attractive.

IT WASN'T hard to catch a rat, not for Millicent. She squatted on her haunches by the greenhouse and let the old words slip from her lips, repeating the whispered incantation.

One of Jack's priestesses, she could feel all his creations vibrating in a giant web of life. She only had to reach out and find the right harmony with the thing she sought. There, a little squeak in the night, drawn to the whispered chant. Its small body came over the grass and stopped in front of Millicent, her hands dangling between her knees. The rat stood up on its hind legs, forepaws beneath its chin, and sniffed. Between beats of its heart, Millicent snatched up the rat in her muddy hands, and with the noise of a snapping twig, broke its neck.

DANNY HADN'T LOOKED at Julie at all. His eyes closed, he'd turned in on his own world and surrounded it with layers of rigid muscle.

It wasn't the experience Julie had imagined it to be, even though that imagining remained vague and more of a desire than a clear thought. Whatever it might have been, in reality it was short and painful.

Finally, Danny grunted, somehow tensing even more, and slumped forward onto Julie. The weight of his body was suffocatingly heavy. He breathed heavily, his skin tacky with sweat, and rolled away. Julie took a deep, juddering breath, the wetness in her eyes glinting in the glow of the laptop's screensaver.

RICHARD TRIED TO FOCUS, concentrating on the shape of her breasts. Jane had retained her figure and still looked fantastic. A few more wrinkles, a few more stretch marks, a tiny bit more padding, but still a gorgeous woman who wore the marks of time like gold leaf. Richard held her hips. She arched back on top of him.

Richard was glad it was dark to disguise his frown of concentration from holding on to his arousal. He opened his eyes, looking up at her. She was moving faster. Richard tried to block out the images that threatened to flood his mind: beetles and worms writhing under the dirt; a spider's insidious creeping towards the struggling butterfly trapped in its web; the rotting carcass of a fox on the woodland floor. But the louder Jane moaned, and the more she moved, the more vivid the images of death and decay became. The rotting carcass dissolved in seconds before his mind's eye, white maggots turning into black flies, scratching and buzzing, devouring flesh. The animal's fur peeled away as the macrobiotic process of putrefaction stripped the bones to leave a husk of skin and bones, which sunk into the dirt of the forest.

The putrid smell caught in the back of Richard's throat. He tried not to gag. Jane gasped, her movements more urgent. Richard felt his gorge rise, and his mouth filled with salty saliva. He needed a drink of water. In desperation, he fixed his wife in her moment of ecstasy with a hard stare, trying to hold onto that image. When an icy chill enveloped Richard's privates and then swept over his body. He gasped, his breath billowing in a white cloud, and Jane was no longer astride him.

Mary Hooper leered down at Richard through the tangle of black hair, which dripped ice cold droplets. A congealed clot of blood leaked from her mouth, landing with the droplets on his belly. A grey worm of a tongue licked her black lips and the smell of rotting death made Richard heave. In blind panic, he reached up and pushed the cold corpse off him, and tumbled out of bed.

Richard scrambled away across the bedroom floor, but when he looked back, Jane was on the bed looking shocked and hurt.

"What's the matter?" She was already covering herself with bed clothes.

Richard's chest heaved, his heart a machine gun in his chest. A cold sweat of revulsion beaded on his skin.

"I'm sorry," Richard swallowed back the bile. "It's not you. I don't feel... I don't feel right." He began to dress quickly.

"What's wrong, Richard? Please tell me. Talk to me."

He picked up his glasses and the dossier from the side of his bed.

"It's the stress of work," he lied. "Maybe I can get pills for that and sleep." It was a thin joke, and Jane didn't laugh.

"I don't know. I'm sorry," he said, and hurried from the bedroom.

THE COCOA FINISHED, Rob sat hugging his knees. He heard his father going downstairs. Unable to sleep, he stood and picked up the picture of the wood nymph from the pile his mother had tidied.

He touched the figure resembling Julie with the tips of his fingers. Standing in the middle of his bedroom, his curtains were ajar, and movement on the street outside caught his attention. An old woman dressed in a white nightgown stood across the street. Long grey hair hung around her shoulders, and she clutched something in one hand that Rob couldn't quite make out. Her feet were bare. Her hands were darker than the rest of her pale, liver-spotted skin, and the front of her nightgown bore a long dirty stain right down its front. But worse, the thing that caught his attention was that now too familiar sound that bristled his skin and quickened his heart. Instinctively, he backed away and, not looking where he was going, bumped into his chair. Eyes shifting to the obstruction, hand catching his balance, Rob's attention wavered for only a moment, and yet when he looked back to the street, the old woman was gone.

The rustling grew louder. Rob wanted to run and hide, but already knew there was nowhere she, the Witchopper, couldn't reach him. He felt the paper crumple in his hand and stared down at the picture. Suddenly it seemed to come alive. The great tree behind the nymph was moving. It was a man not a tree. No. More than a man: part-tree, part giant, the Greenman breaking free from the forest floor. The wood nymph knelt penitently, as roots snapped and dirt, in the greys of Rob's pencil strokes, sprayed up in explosive jets.

Rob dropped the picture and watched it seesaw through the air in slow descent.

DANNY SNORED on his side next to Julie. She got up and picked up the discarded yellow knickers from the floor, and her phone from the desk.

Danny had an en suite, and as noiselessly as she could, Julie crossed his bedroom to it. She shut the door without a sound, and groped blindly for the light switch. When she found it and the light overhead blinked on, her eyes were puffy from crying. And when she went to clean herself up, blood spotted the tissue paper.

There was a message from Sally's phone, but Julie knew it was from both of her friends.

'How was it???'

RICHARD FLICKED through the dossier at the kitchen table, a glass of water almost finished in his hand, failing to do the job of quenching his thirst. He'd calmed his nerves but still felt on edge and guilty he'd left Jane upstairs like that.

He needed answers, and the dossier Izzy had put together was his only hope of that at the moment. Most of the articles *The Advertiser* had published over the years were of no help. The deaths were largely associated with the former foundling house, now a pub. The demise of heavy drinking and smoking publicans was hardly mysterious. The story always referenced the Witchopper in a tongue-in-cheek fashion, regurgitating the same distillation of the myth, until it was as benign as a playground chant. The Halloween piece filled in more of the back story, embellished with either modern twists or journalistic license, and nothing Richard hadn't heard before. The baby killer makes broth from the bones. A ghost who haunts the halls of the pub-come-bed-and-breakfast. Sightings of the Witchopper's corpse swinging from the Hanging Tree under full moons. Of course the moons were always full. There must be something. There had to be or... *or else you and Rob are just as dead as a twelve pints a night landlord*, Richard thought in despair.

Each page might as well have been another paper cut of slow torture, until Richard turned to the section at the back. Izzy had put in a red divider, and a yellow sticky note on the first page read 'Academic Research and Leads.' Richard moved the sticky note to the top of the page so he could read. The first page listed three books on curses written by a Professor Sandra Josephs, at University College London. Izzy had annotated the page to say the books were on order to the Newark library, and in the printout of an email exchange on the following three pages the professor had agreed to the interview request. Richard wrote in the top corner, 'FU ASAP'. FU his shorthand for 'follow up.' Maybe the professor had answers. After this was another printout with another sticky note which read 'Local Vicar.'

Richard skimmed the abstract from the front of the thesis. Most was background he knew but then something different caught his eye:

As time has gone on, the myth has been regularly associated with deaths particularly, but not exclusively, associated with the pub known as The Witch's Brew, which was of course, formerly the foundling house where the dastardly crimes of Mary Hooper were proportionately carried out.

However, it is this thesis' assertion that all is not as it seems, particularly when we cast in light the town's relationship with pre-Christian pagan folklore and its strong connections with the traditions of the Greenman, also known as Jack in the Green. Of particular importance is...

Richard froze in his reading. The noise was back. Like the metronome for one of Pavlov's dogs, Richard reacted to it, memories skittering on his skin and leering in his mind. He looked cautiously around the kitchen to see what could be distorted. Would the table dissolve into a shower of squirming things? Could Mary Hooper peel from the shadows by the back door, or her face loom from the dark at the kitchen window? Richard braced himself. The rustling grew to an all pervasive white noise, pounding like waves in the shore of his mind. Richard's hands ached, gripping the tabletop.

The rustling stopped with such suddenness it left a whine of silence in its place.

In short, sharp gasps, Richard breathed in and out, in and out, straining to hear. At first, there was nothing, but then he heard scratching coming from the front of the house, which lay in darkness. Where exactly was it coming from? The dark was the answer. Richard stood, caught between curiosity and fear. There it was again. Faint. Scratch, scratch. A pause. Scratch. A pause, and in the silence Richard stepped closer, seeking the source of the sound despite his racing heart and legs heavy with adrenaline. Scratch, scratch, pause, scratch. *Oh god!* Now the dark enveloped Richard, and he slapped on the light. Scratch - slow and soft. It, whatever it was, was at the front door. Scratch... scratch... scratch.

He was at the front door now, and turned on the hall light at the bottom of the stairs. Whomever, whatever, was making that noise was standing on the other side of the front door. Richard was braver in the light and stood for long seconds listening, craning to hear. It had stopped again. The door seemed charged with danger. An invisible field that attracted and repelled him in equal measure. The desire to flee the worst fantasies of his imagination; the need to face those phantoms and see them evaporate in the cleansing light of reality. The sound had definitely stopped. Richard could hear nothing more.

"You're jumping at wind, man." Richard shook his head at himself. "Dad?"

Richard jumped. "Jesus! Rob, you scared me."

Rob was standing halfway down the stairs behind Richard.

"Is someone at the door?"

"I thought there was. But I think..." Richard looked back at the door unsure, "but I think it was nothing. Probably just the wind."

"There's not even a breeze outside," Rob said.

"Houses move and make noises."

"Like rustling?" Rob said.

"You heard it too?"

"I hear it all the time. Don't you?"

Richard hesitated. "Yes, yes I do."

"It's part of it, the curse, I mean."

Richard cast a look behind Rob. "Shh, your mother will hear," he whispered.

Richard saw his son's face crease with worry. A sense of protectiveness ached in his chest. He'd been sitting on his bloody hands, spending most of his time in denial. He'd seen enough now. It was up to him. He was going to solve this and make it right between him and Rob and Jane.

Scratch, scratch.

"Did you hear that?" Rob said, one foot already retreating up the stairs.

Richard nodded, and with conviction running through him, he slowly turned, lending his weight to the desire to see and throw this phantom into the light.

Scratch.

Richard reached for the handle.

Scratch, scratch, and muttering now.

His hand closed around the handle. It felt cold and alien.

Scratch. Muttering. Scratch, scratch.

"Dad, I don't think this is a good..."

Yanking down on the handle, Richard flung open the door, ready to scream in the face of Mary Hooper and drive her from his home and his family, even if that meant she dragged him to hell.

The scream died in a glottal stop. Richard was perplexed. Their door was covered with symbols daubed in red, dark brown against the grain of the wood. Circles, crescents, the tiny figure of a stick man and many others he didn't recognise. Outside, standing in bare feet, was an old woman in only her nightgown, covered in mud. Her hands were stained with what Richard now understood was blood, which dripped down her forearms. In one hand, the old lady held her inkwell: a dead and disemboweled rat.

Richard had frozen again.

"Mum," Rob called.

Richard blinked.

"You must save the witch," the old woman said.

"What?" Richard said.

"You must save the witch," the old woman repeated.

"Save the witch? You mean Mary Hooper?" Richard said. That was the logical deduction to make in the illogical mess.

The old woman seemed dissatisfied with Richard's questions and lurched forward, grabbing hold of his pyjamas with her bloodied hands.

"There isn't much time. Save the witch. That's the key. You must save the witch. She's coming for you. You can only stop it by saving the witch." The old woman was desperate now, searching Richard's face for comprehension.

"What do you mean? How can I save Mary Hooper?" Richard's own desperation nearly matched the old lady's, but then she became hysterical.

"Save the witch. Save the witch. Save the witch," she pleaded. Her eyes then glazed over as if a light switch had been turned off. The old woman looked up at Richard in surprise. She released him and stared at the blood and mud on her hands, before cowering away.

"Who are you? Where am I?"

She began to weep.

Jane appeared at the top of the stairs behind Rob, tying her dressing gown behind. "What's going on?"

"Jane, this woman is..." but Richard didn't know how to finish the sentence.

"Millicent," Jane seemed to answer with clairvoyance. She hurried down the stairs.

"You know her?" Richard said, standing aside.

Jane stepped outside. "It's alright, Millicent. We met the other day at the doctor's." She was carefully approaching Millicent as she might have startled a fawn until the old woman was safely in her arms. "Go and get my phone from the kitchen. I need to call Ken. That's it, Millicent, come on in and get warm."

JULIE CREPT BACK to the bed and sat on the edge in just her knickers, the pale light of the laptop still watching over them. Danny was sleeping. He looked so peaceful now, more like the little boy in the photograph with his mother. All the hardness of earlier had gone. Why couldn't he have been like that? She touched his face, and he murmured. The carefree little boy was in there, somewhere. Julie reached forward to the laptop screen, her bare chest lit blue. She didn't know the small camera, like an all seeing eye, watched her covetously, having filmed everything between her and Danny, and filmed her still as she shut the laptop with a quiet *snap.*

32

IT TURNED into a long Friday night for Jane and her family. They'd phoned Ken, who was still up, and said he'd be straight round. Jane tried cleaning Millicent up but the old lady clung to the dead rat like a child with a comfort blanket, its grey-blue innards hanging out of the hole in its belly. She only relinquished the rodent once Ken arrived with Brian, her husband. There was a vague flutter of recognition in Millicent's face, which then fell into confusion.

"I know your name, don't I?" Millicent said to Brian, as Ken took Jane's place with the old lady at the kitchen table.

"Yes, Milly. I'm Brian."

"Where did we meet?"

"At a dance, in the old cinema."

"What were you doing at a dance? You're too old. Do you run it?"

Brain smiled and tried not to make it look strained. "No, but I did help put the bottles in the floor."

Millicent's face lit up. "Oh, I love those. It's like dancing on gemstones."

Both Ken and Jane gave Brian a quizzical look.

"The floor used to be made of thousands of empty glass bottles turned upside down and sunk into polished concrete."

"What do you mean used to?" Millicent said.

"It closed down," Brian explained.

"Oh that's terrible, where will we dance?"

"I'll take you to one in Newark, if you like?"

"That's so sweet, but I think you're a little old for me," Millicent said, raising her eyebrows at Jane as if to say, *bless him, the silly old fool.*

They'd cleaned Millicent up with warm water and towels, which Brian insisted on taking to wash, but Jane wouldn't hear of it.

Once they'd left, Jane couldn't get to sleep. By Richard's breathing, she guessed he was awake too but pretending to be otherwise. At some point, her whirling mind finally succumbed to exhaustion. She woke with the sun shining brightly through the curtains. She stretched languorously, enjoying the warmth of the bed, before the events of the previous night came back. With a pang of guilt, Jane realised she hadn't dreamt about them, not even with bizarre dream interpretations of her emotional state, like her dream of having their beloved dog, Suzie, put down, when she was fourteen. That dream replayed whenever Jane faced a decision she didn't want to make. But last night her sleep had been deep and dreamless.

The bedside clock read 11:02 a.m. The time was a silent alarm propelling her from the bed, rushing her downstairs to see where Rob and Richard were, hastily tying her dressing gown around her as she went. She found her two men sitting at the kitchen table with glasses of water in front of them. These days, neither of them ever seem to be without one. Perhaps both of them needed a diabetes test. They stopped talking when they heard her coming, as if keeping a secret between them.

"Have you seen the time? You should have woken me. Have you eaten?" Jane said, rattling off the words as she touched Rob on the head. She patted the teapot's cozy to see if it was still warm.

"No, I'm fine," Rob said.

"Me too," Richard agreed.

"It's brunch. When was the last time we had a lazy Saturday brunch together? Come on, I think we've got some bacon. I'll do French toast and we'll pour golden syrup all over it."

Rob and Richard shrugged their consent.

"Okay, great," Jane said, feeling like a warm-up act trying to get the crowd in the right mood. The sun was shining. It was a new day. *Come on campers, rise and shine. The knobbly knees competition starts at 11:30 next to the shuffle boards.* "You put on a pot of coffee, Richard. Rob, you're in charge of orange juice."

Jane was a dervish of activity, lighting the stove, cracking eggs, dipping bread, flipping bacon until it was crispy. All the while she thought of Brian and Millicent, and how positive he was, how he lived for his wife even though his love wasn't always returned. By the time she laid the plates in front of Rob and Richard, and pressed the plunger down in the cafetière, Jane knew what they were going to do, at least in the short term.

They ate in silence. Although the boys mostly pushed the food around the plate, Jane smiled through mouthfuls of food, feeling energised. When she felt the time was right, shortly after her second cup of coffee, she fished in her handbag, which hung from the back of her chair.

"I've been thinking, we haven't really been spending much time together since we moved, and that was the whole point of it. What with starting new jobs, a new school and unpacking the house, we haven't made time to be a family." She was rifling through the contents of her bag as Richard and Rob exchanged looks. "So, I've had an idea."

Jane held something beneath the tabletop. The drummer could have started a roll on his snare drum, as the magician shoved her hand into a bottomless hat.

"They dropped a pile of them in the surgery this week. I picked it up to be polite, but then I was thinking it might be fun." Jane produced a brightly coloured flyer, flattening out the folds as she spread it across the middle of the table.

Richard didn't have his reading glasses and squinted to see what it was.

"It's a fun fair. They're setting up on the Burgage common right now," Jane explained, trying not to be put off by the tough crowd. "They come a few times a year apparently. There are rides and games and candy floss. I know it's silly, but it could be a bit of fun."

"I remember that," Richard said, picking up the flyer for a closer look. "They'd been doing that ever since I was a boy. Gypsies, I mean travellers. Then they move about going from town to town. I'd forgotten all about that." He smiled.

"Do you remember we took Rob to that one when he was seven? We were staying in that cottage on the Norfolk Broads your old editor let us borrow," Jane said.

Rob looked none the wiser, but neither was he complaining. The crowd was finally warming up.

"God, yeah, I'd forgotten about that," Richard said, clearly enjoying the memory.

Jane took another swig of coffee only to find it was empty, but persevered anyway. "Well, I've decided we're going to go this week. We're going to talk to Mr Khan and Mr Bryce this week and sort things out at school for Rob. Richard, you'll go into work and clear the decks a little bit so make sure you're free. You said Tim's a great deputy editor. Delegate. Give him more responsibility. We're going on Wednesday night, because we haven't been having the best luck with Friday nights recently, so let's mix it up a bit. So what do you think?"

The answer came as a wordless shuffling of shoulders from Rob.

The flyer still in his hand, Richard looked as though he was about to complain, but then said, "Whatever you think. Yeah, it sounds great. Good idea."

And although there was a flatness to his voice that didn't match his words, the sun was shining. It was a new day, and Jane was going to take it as a positive sign.

33

MARY SAT ALONE on the wooden pew outside the meeting hall. Times had been lean, and her many shawls for the cold weather hid how thin she had become. There had been several years of poor harvests, not terrible but enough for there to be little for folks to spare. Mary's body reflected the fortunes of the town. When people were poorer, they asked for her help more but could pay even less. Mary got by. There were always nettles or dandelion roots to be gathered. Mushrooms to be picked. A favour for a farmer's wife might produce a rabbit or a few hen's eggs, and people still brought her favours when they could, usually dropping them in secret at night. But the harder things were, the more people took and the less they would give, so Mary sat on the pew waiting, hoping. She needed and wanted this.

A frost still clung to the inside of the windows, muting the light as the sun limped towards midday. Mary blew on her hands, clothed in fingerless woollen gloves, with more holes than she had fingers to fill them with, and closed her eyes.

Her lips moved in a murmur. '*Worda swæ honig to þe bee sindon, ond cuman.*'

The words from the men beyond the door grew in her mind like echoes from a dark cave.

"We are in agreement then?" It was the Reverend Moseley.

"I am still unsure. Is it really wise to choose such a woman?" That was Zachary Hawthorn, the Provost, a man with only a ridge of grey hair just above his ears, as if his halo had faded and fallen from lack of use. "The rumours about her and her aunt before her, well, they are hardly..."

"Christian?" finished Thomas Hempstock, the gentleman farmer. A titter of laughter rang in Mary's mind. She was getting cold and wouldn't be able to keep listening in for much longer. Perhaps if she'd eaten more and wasn't so weak. 'Perhaps, perhaps. Don't worry about perhapses and look to what has and will happen,' Aunt Jenny would have said.

"Gentlemen, that is precisely why we should keep Miss Hooper under the Church's purview, among other reasons," Moseley told them.

"She is a fine woman indeed to keep an eye on," Mathew Ridgely, the merchant who owned one of the large houses set back from the road on Church Street, overlooking the Minster.

A mirthful chuckle rippled around the table.

"My..." Moseley's voice was sharp and shrill, rising above the laugher to cut it down, "intentions are pure. As I'm sure are the motivations of this council."

"Aye right," Thomas Hempstock muttered under his breath.

"So, we are in agreement. Mary Hooper shall be appointed governess of the new foundling house," Moseley said.

Mary's hands were turning blue and shook with the cold and effort. She could not listen anymore, even if she had wanted to. Opening her eyes, she squinted against the light, as if she had emerged from the darkest part of the wood into a glade bathed in the brightest summer sun. Only it wasn't summer. Mary blew on her hands once more, the warmth of her breath causing her hands to ache terribly. The room was duller, since the frost had expanded during her eavesdropping. It had spread out in crystalline branches, covering the window with a layer of ice that crept over the stone cills and mullions and onto the walls.

The door to the council room opened and the Reverend Moseley looked down on Mary. He then noticed the window, perhaps because of how cold it was. His mouth was ajar for a moment, as if the thought was a spider which had become trapped in its own icy threads. Without a word, his eyes moved back to Mary and his mouth shut, shaking off whatever he was thinking.

"Miss Hooper, if you would please join us."

Mary stood and followed the Reverend into the council chamber. There was a scraping of chairs as the men around the square oak table rose. Mathew Ridgely even gave a short bow to Mary, to which Mary lowered her head and smiled.

Moseley then said, "Mary, we would like to inform you that after careful consideration the Church Council, along with Mr Ridgely and his generous endowment for the new foundling house, have agreed to instate you as governess of the house and guardian to the children."

"Oh thank you, gentlemen. Thank you a thousand times. You won't regret it. I will care for them as if they were my own."

"Miss Hooper, you will care for them as if they are children of the lord God on high," the Provost interjected.

Mary settled herself. "Of course, sir." She lowered her head.

"Of that there is no doubt." Moseley stepped closer to Mary. His presence made her flesh crawl, but she smiled sweetly. Sometimes the only warm place with food was in the adder's nest. "Now, let us get to why we are really here." Moseley strode off to the far end of the hall to another wooden door next to the open fire, which crackled and spat with a green log. The other gentlemen rounded the large oak table and took up position next to the fire. Mary followed them, unsure of where to stand and how to carry herself.

Moseley opened the wooden door. "Come, come this way, children," he said.

Mary's heart quickened. The cold in her bones began to melt and an excited glamour prickled in her fingers and toes, so much so that she had to be careful to calm it.

From the room came a girl, Mary guessed to be about nine years old. Taller than the rest, she held a baby in her arms and led another by the hand. After them came four more, aged perhaps from seven to three. They looked thin, and as if a great deal of dirt had been washed away, but no matter how presentable they had been made, their sadness could not be scrubbed from their faces. They looked at the floor as Moseley ushered them in front of the fire. Mary knew many of them. She had been to one or other of their desperate mothers to deliver an unwanted bastard, an incestuous child, or one they simply could not afford. Mary herself had found the baby the eldest girl now held. It had been abandoned in a ditch, left to die. Mary didn't know the mother. She could have been someone passing through the town looking for work on a farm, desperate and destitute. But she could just as easily have been pushed from the loins of a merchant's daughter or a scullery maid and discarded because of fear and shame. Mary had heard it screaming one night as she travelled between her errands. Its cord had not been cut properly. Mary had to put a knot in it. She carried it to the vicarage, where Moseley had welcomed her in, his eyes glinting in the candle light. Something had to be done, he had said, and the Church was not the place to raise these foundlings. And that night an idea had been born along with the little lost soul she gave to the Church.

"Well, children, say hello to Mary," Moseley told them. They said nothing, keeping their eyes on the ground. "Children," he scolded, and the little one, holding the eldest girl's hand, recoiled.

"It's alright, my ducks," Mary said softly. She crouched down and peered around at the little girl. "I'm Mary. I'm going to look after you." Mary heard the eldest sniff at that. It wasn't loud, just loud enough for Mary to hear.

"You must be Lily," Mary said standing up. "You're the mummy of the group, I can see. What a fine job you are doing. Who is this one?"

"This is Ethel," Lily said. Mary could tell her measure was being taken. "Say hello." Ethel clung to Lily.

"Ethel," Moseley butt into their meeting, "say hello to your new governess. Manners are next to godliness." He made to grab the little girl, and she shrank away behind Lily, who shielded her protectively.

Mary saw a wild edge in Lily's eyes, like a once smooth pebble which had been thrown against the rocks until she became as sharp as flint.

Moseley's eyes narrowed, black in the flickering light from the fire. "Come here child, this instant." Mary's hand touched his. He looked at her, startled, and then melted at her touch, his eyes fixing upon hers.

"Please don't be harsh on them, Reverend. They don't know me yet. A little time to warm up to me is what they need. That's all." Mary left her hand upon his, as she turned to say those words to Lily.

"As you wish. But they will need a firm hand, and good Christian teachings," Moseley said, trying to remain stern.

"Of course, they will," and Mary gave a wink to Ethel, but it was as much for Lily. Mary let go of Moseley's hand and bent down to Ethel. "You take your time, my duck."

The fire popped, letting out a long hiss, as if a snake sizzled in the flames, and from behind, unseen by the rest of the council and children, Mary felt the Reverend's hand rest on the rump of her buttock.

34

"Ah, great, give me a swig!" Henry snatched the bottle from Ally's hand. He was already raising the bottle to his lips, with Ally smirking silently, when Chris put a hand on Henry's arm.

"Don't drink it, you muppet."

"What? Why?" Henry sounded disappointed. "I'm thirsty. Didn't have time for breakfast."

Ally started to laugh and took the bottle back, screwing the cap back on. "You're no fun, Wardy. That could have been epic."

"What?" Chris said earnestly.

"It's a special little concoction," Ally said.

"What's that mean?" Henry looked between them.

"It means, our little Northern Irish hacker friend here has been busy online. If you catch my drift." Chis explained, but Henry, like most days, wasn't catching any drifts.

"It means I managed to purloin us a few special ingredients, which I've added to this here bottle of water to test out."

"Test what out?" Chris said, frowning like he was in chemistry.

"To see whether it has the desired effect, of course," Ally said, as the three boys walked down the alley towards the Burgage on their way to school.

The funfair was setting up on the expanse of grass. The Burgage sat in front of the old jail, now little more than a barely noticed tourist attraction. The common sat slightly elevated from three roads that edged it. Sycamore and oak trees standing around its margins would flourish in late spring, their once vivid new buds now deepened to earthy greens. Except for the Hanging Tree, whose branches lay bare. A small community of fairground workers were a bustle of activity. Men and women shimmied up makeshift scaffolds, or lifted dodgem cars into place. Trucks and vans were transformed into stalls selling candy floss, popcorn, burgers, hotdogs, chips, and drinks. Tents were secured and the rides bolted back together. At least two diesel generators coughed continuously, powering the travelling amusement park.

The three boys crossed the road and walked the pavement edging one side of the Burgage, heading towards the town centre.

"I still don't get it. What are we doing exactly?" Henry asked.

"Looking for a test subject, after Chris vetoed your generous volunteering," Ally said.

Something dawned on Henry's face. "I don't mind. I could be the guinea pig."

"No mate, you really don't want to." Chris said.

"Ah!" Henry whined.

"Gentlemen, I think I've found what we need," Ally said, his eye fixing on the potential test subject.

"Great!" Henry grinned trotting alongside Ally. "But what exactly are we doing?"

"You'll see," Ally said, unscrewing the top of the bottle. "Here, boy!" He made a series of friendly clicking noises with his tongue. "Here boy; there's a good fella. Thirsty, boy?"

The dog was tied up to the back of one of the trailers by a line of rope. It sat with its head resting stoically on its forepaws as the three boys approached, its tail mutedly thumping on the grass. As Ally got within arm's reach, the dog shuffled back suspiciously. It sniffed the air, eyeing them.

"It's okay, boy," Ally said.

"I think it's a girl," Henry said. "Yep, it's definitely a bitch."

"With your mum, you'd know all about bitches," Chris said.

"Wanker!" Henry punched Chris in the arm. The dog gave a little bark and shuffled back, its line of rope preventing it from retreating too far from the boys.

"Will you two stop pissing about?" Ally whispered calmly. "You're scaring him."

"Sorry, Ally. But it is a bitch," Henry said, happy to be the one who knew something the others didn't for once.

Ally shook his head. "That's it *girl*, sorry if I offended your gender." Ally coaxed the dog. "I'd like to apologise for all the crimes you have endured at the hands of the patriarchy." The dog gave a whimper.

"Maybe she identifies as a boy?" Chris said in a low voice, matching Ally's tone and volume.

"Well then you'd have a lot in common," Ally said calmly, and shot them both a look. "But if you'd be so kind as to shut your pie holes, we can get this done."

The dog had a bowl sitting on the grass, half filled with water. Ally picked it up, emptied it out, refilled it with the contents of his bottle, and placed the bowl back down, nudging it towards the dog.

"That's it, girl. Come and have a nice drink."

The dog took one pad forward sniffing the air a few inches from the bowl.

"This is going to be epic," Chris said. "What do you think will happen?"

Ally answered as though he was still encouraging the dog. "She should become very friendly, won't you, girl? Even more than you are now. Maybe even a little sleepy. Suggestible. And you should get quite the psychedelic experience as a little added bonus."

"I still don't get it," Henry whispered.

The dog's nose was just above the water. It looked up to Ally for reassurance.

"Rohypnol and LSD," Chris said, by way of explanation.

"Like the date rape drug? Are you kidding me?" Henry snapped his fingers in the air. "Who are we gonna use it on?"

The dog looked up, surprised by Henry's outburst. Suddenly, she didn't like the look of these boys. Her muzzle wrinkled, exposing her canines. The fur bristled along her spine and the bitch lurched forward, snapping. Ally tumbled back, scrambling away from the dog. Chris and Henry stumbled, teetering on the edge of the pavement into the road. Barking, the dog jumped forward, only to be held back by its leash. Its hind legs overturned the bowl as it scrambled to break free from its tether, spilling the contents onto the grass. The dog kept lunging forward, barking and snapping. Chris helped Ally to his feet, face pale with shock, when the shout of adult voices issued from behind the trailer.

"What's going on?"

"Leg it," Henry shouted, and the three boys sprinted up the road towards the town centre.

Ally looked behind to see an old woman, with a head of wild, silver hair, bend down to take the dog into her arms, stroking its scruff, her grey beady eyes fixed on his.

They didn't slow down until they reached the market square, coming to a halt to catch their breath. Ally bent over and then straightened up, both hands on his head.

Hand on his knees, Chris spat between his legs. "How can we test it now?"

"I guess there's always Henry," Ally said.

"If you want," Henry agreed.

"No way. Piss off, Ally," Chris said, putting a hand to a stitch in his side.

"I guess we'll be flying blind then."

"I still don't get it at all. Who are we going to use it on and what for?"

The three boys started to move off again, dragging their heels to school. Ally put his arm around Henry's shoulders.

"All will be revealed, mate."

35

EVEN THOUGH MEL WAS A POLICEMAN, he never thought of it as littering. He always left the last sip of tea and a crumb of his iced bun at the Fairy Well. A blackbird trilled from a bough overhead as Mel took one last bite, tossed the nugget of dough next to the well, and tipped out the dregs of his tea on the ground. The blackbird flew off as Mel sucked the stickiness from his thumb and forefinger and headed for the centre of town. The well was a lovely spot just off the old train track. Nothing more than a boulder with a hole either chiseled or weathered in the top (it was hard to tell which). It was more of a bird bath than a well. The boulder sat at the edge of a clearing under the hawthorn trees, between the track and town on one side, and seemingly endless fields on the other. Mel had no clue how long the well had been there. His father was the one who introduced him to it, and Mel's grandfather had introduced his father to it before him. As a child, they'd go there on walks. His father would tell him stories of Robin Hood, Jack in the Green, Dick Turpin, and the Witchopper. Mel navigated his way around his beat making various small offerings. He thought little of it. It was something he'd always done.

As Mel walked, he thought of his father.

"You always leave something for the good folk," Mel's father told them, although 'something' came out as 'summit'. The 'good folk' was the name he gave to all the magical spirits in his stories. Trees had elves, as did houses. Gnomes, of course, lived at the bottom of the garden. Trolls under bridges. Nymphs and more elves in the woods, and the ghost of one witch in particular resided at the Hanging Tree. While Jack in the Green was king of the Wild Wood. When Mel asked where the Wild Wood was, his father would smile. "Everywhere. And nowhere. It used to be here. The whole world was a thick forest. It was hacked back like weeds generation after generation, until there was nothing left. But it's still here beneath our feet. They cut down the trees, but the roots stretch to the heart of the world, connecting everything."

Mel's childhood had been full of such wondrous spirits in fanciful tales. Not that his father had been a particularly superstitious man. He was a car mechanic all his life, but also took periodicals on advanced engineering, delivered every quarter in the mail. Mel remembered he was also the first in his class to have a computer, one with a green screen. His father found wonder and magic in machines as well.

Some people went to church, at least on Sundays. Mel kept a different routine, honouring various sites around the town. He wasn't particularly pious about it. They were places rooted in his childhood that he regularly visited to be close to his father, who died some two years past, and his grandfather fifteen years ago. Visiting the sites also provided structure to his beat. Mel started at the Devil's Heel - a rock set in the ground with a cloven hoof-shaped indentation - located at one corner of the town. From there he'd walk up to the town centre and pick up an iced bun from the bakery and amble back out to the Fairy Well, following the spokes of a cartwheel. From the well, he'd head back up to the centre of town where he found himself now.

"How do, Mel?"

The memories were put on hold. "How do, Amos?" Mel touched his index finger to his cap, returning the landlord's greeting and stopping on Main Street. "What you got there?"

Amos Blessing blushed a little, standing outside the florist's with a large bouquet of flowers. "It's the wife's birthday."

"You old romantic."

"Aye. Cost a bloody fortune, they did."

"Can't put a price on that woman's patience."

One of Amos's bushy eyebrows rose. "Aye, you can. Forty quid for things that'll be dead in a week."

"We could all be dead in a week. How's business?"

Amos puffed out his stubbly cheeks theatrically. "Could always be better. Been waiting on a piece in *The Advertiser*. Bloody editor came around a few weeks ago. Haven't heard from that dicky-bird since. Thinks I set him up on a practical joke."

"It wouldn't be like you."

"Aye, I know. But I didn't, not this time. Even though he was a right prat. Felt sorry for his boy though."

"Wait. That wouldn't be Richard Peters and his boy... Rob, would it?"

"Aye, that's them."

"What happened?"

"Peters reckons I dressed up one of the cleaners to be the Witchopper, and then somehow magically made her disappear through a secret trap door. As if I'm bloody Houdini."

"And you didn't do it?"

"Wish I had. Bloody brilliant idea for scaring the guests - they love that kind of thing. Probably pay extra. But no, I didn't."

"You said you felt sorry for the boy?"

"Aye, pissed his pants, poor bugger."

"Really?"

"Aye. Why? You know them?"

"Aye, I do. It explains a few things, is all."

"Nowt queer as folk," Amos said, checking his watch.

"And we're all folks." Mel touched his cap again, and both men said together "Aye," as they parted ways.

Mel nipped into the chip shop, said a greeting, and put in a lunch order. He purloined a sachet of salt to spread on the roots of the Hanging Tree, where he was headed next. After that, he would carry on down the hill, past the old Mill, track along the riverbank, and then cut under the boughs of the big willow tree. And if needs be, he'd clear away any cans of cider and bottles of cheap wine, which again, didn't feel like littering.

His radio crackled on his chest. It was a report of schoolboys antagonising one of the fairground owner's dogs.

"Heading there now."

Mel always liked to touch base with the travellers when they blew through town. They were an easy target for people to blame, but they were also a little prickly about the police turning up. But then so were coked up men in BMWs, teenage boys and, Mel remembered with dread, the Chief of bloody Police, when he spoke to him about his son beating up the Peters boy. It turned his stomach that nothing came of that assault, just as Mrs Peters and Dr Bishop had implied it wouldn't. Mel didn't need to be a psychologist to see that Danny Broad had some issues. Something in his gut made Mel uneasy about the number of times he'd come across the Peters family in recent weeks. Anyway, the fairground needed his attention now. The last thing he needed was a bunch of teenagers setting the fairground workers on edge hours before money and alcohol got added to the mix this evening. Thankfully, he'd be off duty by then.

At the top of the Burgage common, Mel surveyed the encampment. They were finishing their set-up of the various rides and stalls, busying over them like industrious ants. He looked between the various temporary buildings, caravans, fun rides and stalls searching for the likely candidate. A woman by the name of Siobhan O'Leary had made the call. Control had said she might be elderly. Mel could see a few women, but none of them looked old, but voices can be deceiving, and so he set off ready to make his enquiry.

Stepping onto the grass was like moving between worlds. As if to mark him as an outsider, the last of the dew gave Mel's boots a high reflective shine and they squeaked as he walked through the fairground, like a leper's bell. He saw a man with auburn hair, approximately six-foot tall, in jeans and a Metallica *Master of Puppets* T-shirt fastening down guy ropes. Might as well start there.

Mel assumed his squeaking footfalls would have been heard, but the man continued to work on the ropes like an old sailor securing the rigging as if he wasn't there. Mel let out a polite cough, but still the man continued testing and adjusting the tension of his ropes. Mel was beginning to think he was being ignored, and knew he was when the man with auburn hair turned from the ropes and walked straight past him to work on another rope, refusing to meet the policeman's gaze.

"Excuse me, I wonder if you could help?"

Without looking up from his work the man said, "Doubt it."

"We received a call from Siobhan O'Leary?"

The man fished a hammer with a rubber head from his belt and began banging the peg into the ground.

"Can you tell me where I can find her?"

"Never heard of her." The man continued to hammer, making the strings issuing from the fingers of the Master of Puppets dance on his chest.

"Don't you know someone who might?" Mel had a bad feeling about where this conversation was going.

The man tested the guy rope was taut, stood, and without looking at Mel, strode off and disappeared between two trucks.

"Good talking to you." Mel touched his index finger to his hat.

A young woman with red hair, barely out of her teens, stacked cans of soda into the back of a fast food truck across the way. Maybe she knew where to find Siobhan O'Leary. Mel put on his best smile.

"I'm looking for Siobhan O'Leary. She called for the police." The young woman disappeared from view, ducking down behind the counter.

"Paddy might know." The redhead popped back up like a jack-in-the-box, hands full of cans, and jerked her head in the direction of a portly gentleman with forearms like ham hocks setting up the coconut shy. Paddy was preposterously burly and wore a flannel shirt rolled up to the elbow. His belly hung over his jeans like a gigantic cannonball, pulling up his shirt to produce a giant hairy smile of flesh.

"Afternoon. The young lady in the burger van says that you might know where I can get hold of Siobhan O'Leary."

Paddy was reaching up to hang stuffed pink bunnies and giant yellow fluffy ducks on hooks for prizes at the shy. Mel prepared himself for being ignored again, when Paddy turned around and gave him a conspicuous look up and down. Paddy sniffed.

"Can't say I do." Well, it was an improvement on being ignored. The big man scratched his balls as he hawked in the back of his throat, leant forward over the counter, and spat past Mel. Okay, maybe not an improvement. The wad of mucus disappeared into the green grass. It was well wide of Mel, but the intent was clear: a challenge had been laid down.

"Nasty cold you have there. There's a chemist up in the town who could give you something for that. Not your normal drugs and cough syrups either. Local girl, Wendy. If you say Mel Playfair sent you, she'll make you a camphor rub for your chest and honey with elder and primrose to put in a hot toddy. Works every time."

Paddy sniffed and scratched his chin, taking in the policeman for a second, when with a jerk of his head that more than reminded Mel of the young lady in the burger van, he said, "You might find her over there helping out in the house of mirrors."

"Much obliged."

Paddy grunted and hung up some more fuzzy ducks.

The house of mirrors was the largest construction on the site in terms of floorspace, although it wasn't as high as the ferris wheel or the skyrocket, which hurtled people fifty feet in the air on a pole and then dropped them even faster. It was a wonder the fair hadn't closed years ago under the weight of spinal injury lawsuits. The house of mirrors was a safer bet for funfair goers. The size of a four-bedroom house, with at least three levels overlapping each other, linked by gangways that threaded in and out of the building, like an optical illusion.

However, Siobhan wasn't to be found at the house of mirrors either. Frustrated, Mel found himself standing under the Hanging Tree. The naked boughs creaky like a hangman's rope in the breeze. A friendly dog was tied up to a trailer next to the tree with a length of rope. Mel ruffled the dog's ears. The dog licked his hand. Mel then fished in his pocket for the sachet of salt and tore off its top. He sprinkled the salt onto the roots as his father had told him to. He remembered eating fish and chips on the Burgage bench with his dad before sprinkling the salt from their wrappers around the base of the tree. "Tree elves like salt; ghosts and witches not so much." They weren't the only ones who did it, and Mel wondered if the tree had finally given up due to high blood pressure.

Smoke drifted across Mel's vision, as he gazed up into the bare canopy, transfixed by the rocking branches. The woody tobacco smoke could have been a mist rolling in, or the fog of a dream. It sometimes happened in these places. Mel would find himself gazing into nothing, thoughts meandering to places he'd never been but felt so familiar. A dark wood, with a whispering stream, trees wearing coats of ivy, branches shaggy with moss. A chorus of chirps and ribbits. The rustle of leaves. Snap of twig and slurp of mud. Desiccated life crumbling away into death. Death fertilising life. The original womb of life and the glade of death. From whence we came and would return. And still the branches of the Hanging Tree creaked.

"A fine place is this," the voice of an old woman broke Mel's reverie. He drew a long breath through his nose, as if rousing from a dream, finding himself beneath the Hanging Tree.

The old woman watched him through her pipe smoke, content to wait.

Mel played with the meaning of her words in his mind. What did she mean by this "place"? *What was this place? Here? Now? Under this dead tree? Or that other place, at once a fantasy and yet more vivid than this life?* Mel wanted to laugh like one of the many kids he'd dragged home to their parents for smoking weed. With this he remembered himself, and the wild wood evaporated like smoke drifting into an afternoon sky.

"It is at that." There wasn't a wrong way to agree with her statement. The old woman had a tangle of thick, grey hair, with streaks of white and copper so light, it was like the sun's last rays in an autumn sunset. He imagined her hair had once blazed with all the fire of the earth's mantle. Her nose had a gentle hook, but he could tell it had once been a handsome face, now wrinkled with time.

"You wouldn't by any chance be Siobhan O'Leary would you?"

The old woman gave a laugh: half bark, half phlegmy cough. "You have the sight."

"No, it was a guess. I'm Constable Melvin Playfair." Mel offered his hand, and the old woman shook it warmly. Her fingers were gnarled into misshapen knots, but it was strong and warm.

She looked at him, puffing on her pipe, and Mel got the feeling she was seeing something more. Every so often she would look up into the branches and then back to him.

"You called the police. I'm here following up."

Siobhan took the pipe from her mouth and pointed at her dog, smoke escaping from her mouth as she spoke. "Three boys were messing with my Molly. Made her bark."

"Does she bark a lot?"

Siobhan drew on her pipe. "She's a dog."

"Maybe she was being protective of the camp."

Siobhan gave a short, dismissive shake of her grey mane. "Those boys were up to something."

"Any idea what that might be? Boys will be boys."

"Nope. Nothing good, whatever it was. Had that look about them."

Mel was starting to feel that frustration he'd felt in the rest of the camp. He knew the futility of his next question but asked it anyway. "What sort of look would that be?"

Siobhan considered this for a moment, enveloped in a cloud of smoke. "Trouble."

"Trouble?"

"Trouble," the old woman said with a nod.

"Could you give me a description? I could see if they were seen anywhere else causing... trouble."

"Just boys, maybe fourteen or fifteen. They all look the same, don't they?"

Mel cringed inside, fearing where this was going. "Do they? Who's they?"

"School kids. All wearing the same uniform. My eyes aren't what they were. Maybe fourteen or fifteen. Brown hair."

"Okay!" Mel said by way of bringing this to an end. "I'll see what I can do." And he would. He'd ask at the school and check with the local shops. But as Siobhan had described about three-hundred suspects with no distinguishing features. He didn't hold out much hope.

"Much obliged."

Mel moved off, pausing to pet Molly.

"Are you coming to the fair tomorrow night?" Siobhan suddenly said.

Mel turned around and saw her looking up into the tree again.

"I..." Mel hadn't planned to. The last time he'd been to the fair he was a young man in his early twenties on a date. "I wasn't planning to."

The Hanging Tree creaked and wild wood whispered.

"Think you should," Siobhan said, her eyes still fixed on the branches overhead. And Mel did think that he should. He wasn't on night duty for another week, so a trip to the fair could be fun.

"I'll tell you your fortune," she said, almost disappearing in a billow of smoke.

"That would be fun, thank you." Mel touched his index finger to his cap and strode off up the street and wouldn't remember for some time that his next stop should have been the old willow tree.

Picking a piece of tobacco from her lip, Siobhan watched the policeman go and ruffled Molly's head. Before she left, she looked one final time into the branches of the Hanging Tree. Mary Hooper hung there with dozens of bodies. Their tongues stuck from their open mouths like swollen blue grubs. Their eyes glared bloodshot and bulging, as the branches of the dead Hanging Tree creaked.

36

RICHARD HAD TAKEN to keeping a refillable gym bottle with him wherever he went, but even with that, it wasn't enough to shake his thirst. The waste bin next to his desk was filled with an assortment of empty plastic bottles bought from vending machines and service stations.

But aside from his thirst, Richard had relaxed a little and things were coming back into perspective. The more he thought about it, the more stress and, he sneered at himself, guilt, were the likely culprits. But what about Rob? part of his journalist's mind, always probing, asked.

In a move that had become a habit, Richard reached for his water bottle. He needed more. *The thirst? What was that? Diabetes, probably, but you know it's not.* Richard laughed hard. It had been a few days since the incident with Millicent and nothing else unusual had happened. Apart from his kidneys being sore in the morning, like he'd taken a punch to his lower back, things were feeling normal again. His stomach gurgled, and he belched. *Too much water*, Richard thought. He sat looking at the article he needed to finish on *The Witch's Brew*. It was little more than a puff piece. In a parallel document he had opened there was nothing but a blank screen and the title 'Witchopper'. He had nothing, literally or figuratively.

Richard felt his gut move. He put a hand to his lower belly and burped again. The taste was foul.

He had a block and more than with any deadline he'd ever faced, Richard knew he needed to act. But what? The strong skeptic inside still pulled him towards a rational, scientific explanation. What is more likely, that they had both been cursed by a local legend for god knows what reason? Or, he and Rob had both experienced the same stress - moving home, leaving friends, school, work, the city they knew as home? Then that ridiculous landlord at *The Witch's Brew* played a prank on them both. Wasn't it more likely that they were having a shared psychological experience? He'd had no problem finding a rabbit hole of scientific papers to prove this point with a quick internet search. But he knew he was lying to himself and this wasn't what they needed. Seeing was believing, and he'd seen enough. The answer lay somewhere else. Maybe buried in the old stories, in the folklore. He needed to look there. If it was in the dossier, he couldn't see it, but maybe someone else could.

A sharp pain, not from his kidneys but from Richard's bowels, accompanied another loud gurgle. He suddenly felt uncomfortably hot as though he was about to lose control in the most embarrassing way possible. He belched and the foul taste filled his mouth again as he stood and hurried to the bathroom.

Tim stopped him in the open plan office, halfway to safety. "Richard, I hope you don't mind, but I've taken some of the sausage puns out of the piece on the Saville butchers." Tim was grinning, like he'd enjoyed the joke.

"Too much?" Richard's guts squirmed. A hot flush ran through him, and he clenched his buttocks together.

"I love the title: Saville Ahoy! - Mansfield hails award winning sausage maker. I love a good pun. But we don't want to seem like we're taking the piss."

"Great, great, whatever you think." Richard was hopping now. "I've got to rush."

Richard sped off in a tottering wobble, trying to hold back his bowels. He banged through the toilet door and rushed into the cubicle, simultaneously locking the door with one hand and pulling the toilet seat down with the other, praying that he could hold it together.

"Argh!" It was both a sigh and a grunt, as Richard's bowels loosed in an explosion of semi-liquid slime that slapped wetly into the bowl. Relieved in more ways than one, Richard pulled a length of toilet paper from the dispenser. Doubling it up, he wiped and paused. Something wasn't right. He felt it through the paper, long and squishy and dangling down towards the water below. Richard grasped whatever it was between his thumb and forefinger and pulled. He felt it inside him, being drawn out, like a swollen length of spaghetti. Had they eaten pasta recently? What else could it be?

Pulling it free, Richard held it up to inspect it, dread already forming as he nearly fell off the toilet seat with a cry of revulsion. He dropped the squirming earthworm. It landed on the titles where it slowly writhed, twisting and coiling. Looking between his legs at the bowl below, Richard jumped from the toilet seat. With his trousers around his ankles, he buffeted around the cubicle, shaking its flimsy construction. Calming himself enough to edge back to the toilet, Richard investigated its contents. A mass of pinkish brown worms, squirming over each other, piled up above the waterline. Richard felt sick and heaved but managed to hold it back. Feeling violated and unclean, and wanting to get away, he pulled up his underpants and trousers, staying as far from the toilet as he could, which in the confines of the cubicle wasn't far enough. The worm on the floor slithered towards him, nearly at his shoe. He flung open the cubicle door, tumbling out, as the door to the communal staff bathroom opened.

Izzy walked in and put her handbag by the sink. She fished inside and produced a lip gloss and began to reapply it in the mirror.

"What's up, boss?"

"I..."

Richard looked back at the cubicle. There was nothing on the floor. He walked back into the toilet and warily checked the bowl. There was nothing there apart from the clear water of an unused toilet.

"I forgot to flush." He pulled the handle and started to wash his hands in the sink next to Izzy. Another social embarrassment formed and occurred to Richard. "Isn't this the gents?"

Izzy drew the lipgloss on as she spoke. "Ladies are full. I thought the gents were empty. Are you sure you're okay?"

"Why? What would be the matter?"

"You know." Izzy stopped applying her gloss and looked around to check they were alone and lowered her voice. "Because of the other night." She rolled her lips together and inspected the results.

"No. Like you said, it was just a bit of fun. Nothing serious, right?"

"Right," Izzy agreed, straightening the hem of her tight fitted blouse. She pushed her chest forward, turning from side to side inspecting how she looked. Richard looked at her breasts through the mirror, and then looked away when Izzy caught him. She undid a button from the top and opened her collar a little more. The crease between her breasts was just visible. "I've done a bit more work on the ghost story project. I could show you what I've got again after work. It could be another bit of fun."

Richard dried his hands on a paper towel. "Last time was nice, but it was a one-time thing. Like you said, I'm the boss. It wouldn't be right."

"Sure, no worries," Izzy said quickly. "I didn't mean, well... I value your input."

Was that a pun, a euphemism, and *double entendre* all rolled into one?

"That's great. You've got real talent." *Jesus! Stop with the euphemisms at least.*

"You really think so?"

"Absolutely. You've got all the right attributes..." *Oh bugger, stop it,* "to be a great journalist. You just need a little tightening up in a few places." *Jesus wept, man.*

"So you'll stay tonight? Help tighten me up? Just work, nothing... too fun."

Richard swallowed. "I'm sorry, I can't. We're having a family night out at the local funfair. It's silly, really. Rob's probably too old, but

Jane wants us to spend some quality time together. I do too," he added quickly.

Izzy smacked her lips together and ran her tongue across her teeth. "Sounds... fun." She picked up her handbag, and her heels clipped across the tiles to the door. "Guess I'll just work on those attributes myself tonight."

37

When the bell rang for a break between lessons, school became a no-man's-land of loneliness for Rob. No one wanted to talk to him, not during lessons or at break time. There was no one to walk with to or from school. The snickering looks, the whispered comments, the things written on cubicle doors and penned on classroom white-boards had not stopped, but phones were banned at school, which was a small mercy. Rob had regressed to a new phone that merely made and sent calls. All this only reaffirmed Rob's resolve to with-draw from the social life of school. It was by far the safest strategy that he could come up with, and moved that problem to the side so that he could work on the far bigger problem that his father seemed unable or unwilling to recognise.

Rob packed up his chemistry notes before the teacher, Miss Gould, dismissed them. She noted him hovering at the edge of the class, but said nothing. At her words, "You can go," he was out of his seat and first to the door, followed swiftly by Ally, who was grinning ear to ear.

"Ally Strachan, I haven't got your final homework."

Ally halted, his prey disappearing out the door. "You have, Miss."

"Wait while I check." Miss Gould rifled through the stack of workbooks.

"Silly bint," Ally muttered to Chris.

"Ah, yes. You are right. Off you go."

Ally and Chris slunk off. Rob was long gone.

There were only a few days left of school before the break for study leave exam preparation for the GCSE, but the break only heightened tensions rather than relieving them, and that wasn't helping Rob's own situation as the default whipping boy.

Rob navigated his way from the school building through the playground, ignoring the younger children, who took the opportunity to laugh at him, passing on comments from the older students they probably barely understood. He reached the expansive playing field at the back of the school onto which children of all ages had flooded. Numerous games had already sprung up; cricket and rounders in addition to football. Small groups sat on the dry ground in circles. Younger pupils chatted in a carefree way, while the older ones fretted over text books.

When Rob reached the far corner, he joined the path that ran along next to the small stream called Potwell Dyke, which acted as a natural boundary between the school playing fields and the town's park. He followed the path, flanked by mature trees on the opposite bank of the stream, and looking over his shoulder to see that he was not being watched, Rob slipped from the school grounds. Less than twenty yards on was the entrance to a graveyard, an overflow from the Minster, hidden away in a corner. A wooden archway with a quaint tiled roof and a wooded gate in need of a touch of paint marked the entrance. Rob needed a quiet place, and he'd discovered one amongst the graves trying to avoid other pupils on his way home. Closing the gate, Rob already had a sketchpad and pencil in hand. Forget-me-nots were in bloom, covering the tombstones in a gossamer blanket of pale purple. His artist eye looked for an appropriate frame, an interesting arrangement of shapes, a contrast of colour, light or shade. Rob was so engrossed that he was already halfway up the path running through the middle of the graveyard before noticing someone else sitting on the bench at the top of the path.

Heart sinking, Rob was about to stop and turn heel without a word, following his plan that avoiding the abuse was better than taking it head on, when the boy met his gaze. Without hostility, the boy raised a hand, waved and said, "Hi."

It was Jason Potts, one that everyone else in his year called Potty. Hardly an original twist on a surname for a piss take, but linguistic finesse was hardly the point of such things. Rob automatically raised his hand in response.

"You're Rob, right? Rob Peters?" Potty went on.

They were in the same year but had never met. Having not been at the school long, and then making friends with Ally, Chris, and Henry (what a mistake that had been), Jason had been, well, what had he been? He had been Rob: an object of derision, a whipping boy, the one everyone likes to make fun of, just as long as it wasn't them. Jason had jet black hair but fair skin with freckles that didn't quite ring true with the hair colour. Rob suspected he was naturally auburn. The strange boy - *look who's talking* - also painted his finger-nails. One black nail on each hand, and there was eyeliner beneath his eyes in thin black lines. To finish the picture, Jason had a notepad open on his lap with a fountain pen in his hand. Rob's mind had already drawn it as a flamboyant quill.

Too far in to go back, Rob approached slowly kicking at some gravel on the path. "Yeah, that's me." He half expected a comment now, something to twist the knife. Maybe Jason was happy that he was no longer the butt of everyone's jokes.

Jason stuck out a hand. "I'm Jason."

"I know." Rob shook it.

"Do you want to sit down?" Jason shuffled across even though there was plenty of room.

"Thanks."

They sat in silence for a few moments, then Jason closed his note-book. "What have you got there?" Jason pointed at the sketchpad with his fountain pen.

Rob put his hands protectively across the cover. "It's my sketchpad."

"Cool! I come here to write." Jason tapped his notebook with his pen.

"Cool!"

"Can I see?" Jason turned on the bench to face Rob.

Rob bit his lip, hesitating. Was this when the knife would be twisted? But it didn't seem so.

"I heard you're a pretty amazing artist."

Rob was unsure. Opening the pad was opening up himself. It was risky. He really shouldn't do it, and yet his hands were already moving. He was tired of being lonely, and he'd heard it all before, so Rob took a risk and prepared himself. "Sure," he said and opened the sketchpad. Jason leaned over.

"Fucking hell! These are amazing."

Rob was a little taken aback by the ferocity of the boy's enthusiasm. He seemed absolutely genuine in his astonishment.

"Can I see?"

Tentatively, Rob passed over his sketchpad. Part of him, still emotionally tender, waited to be hurt. Jason flipped through the pages slowly, stopping at each picture to consider it in detail. Every so often he would let out a small gasp of astonishment or a whistle through his lips or simply say "Amazing!" or "Brilliant!" Finally, Jason looked up.

"People weren't wrong. You are a freak." He was almost laughing and then noticed the hurt look on Rob's face. "No, I didn't mean it like that. You're really talented, like incredibly so. That's what I mean when I say freak. It's a compliment. Honest." Jason handed back the sketchpad. "Tread softly, lest you tread on my dreams."

Rob was glad to have it back in his hands. "People talk about my art?" He wished he hadn't said it. He'd just opened himself up for it, something he told himself he should never do again.

"Of course, even to me, not that many people admit to doing that. Or rather, they did say stuff about your art, you know before...". Jason shifted uncomfortably and looked away from Rob, flushed with embarrassment.

"Right." Rob understood, but still expected the put down to come any minute, only it didn't. Then Jason cracked the silence.

"People are dicks."

Rob couldn't help but grin in agreement. It was the first genuine smile he'd had in weeks, since everything went so catastrophically wrong with Julie.

"Yeah, total dicks."

Jason was smiling as well. The two boys sat in happy contemplation of just how dickish people, by which they meant their peers, were.

"What's that?" Rob indicated the notebook Jason held.

"This particular notebook is hopefully going to be a novel."

"Wow, you're writing a book? What about?"

"It's my second novel, actually. I wrote another one last year, and I'm always doodling short stories and stuff, you know? This one is like most of my stuff, an epic fantasy mixed with sci-fi and horror. Kinda like space opera meets irradiated brain eating space cannibals."

"How long have you been writing stories?"

Jason took a moment to consider this. "I think probably about six years. Ever since I could really write properly I've been making up stories. Little things first but they got longer and longer until..." He gave a kind of Gallic shrug, "I had to write a novel."

"I've never met an author before," Rob said.

Jason laughed. "I'm not an author, not yet. But I will be." He was sure of this, so absolutely confident, that Rob believed it, but also realised this was something special he was being shown. Like his drawings, Jason had just bared his soul, or at least a bit of it, to Rob.

"Cool!" Rob said.

Rob asked about the novel and Jason became animated, detailing the story set in a future where humans spread out into space. They formed different factions around various solar systems, developing separate religious and political systems. One of the factions, thought lost, turn up like space pirates, raiding warring factions. The twist is that they have cultivated something Jason called the prion gene, which meant they were almost exclusively cannibals, who loved nothing better than chowing down on their fellow humans. Then Jason asked Rob about some more of his pictures and one in particular. He got Rob to flick back through the notepad until it fell open at the picture of the wood nymph standing in front of the ancient oak. Rob told him where the idea came from about that day in the Chapter House at the Minster and thinking about the Greenman and how sometimes he's not even aware of what he's drawing, it feels like he's channelling something else, something beyond himself.

Jason was still animated. "Sometimes, I'll be working on a bit of a story and get lost in it, and then read it back and think: *Shit! Did I just write that? It's actually not total crap.*"

Their conversation was taking on that same feel. There were only the two of them, and whether it was that or Rob's loneliness and growing desperation he suddenly changed the subject, taking another chance.

"Do you know anything about the Witchopper?"

"Sure, everyone knows the ghost story. It's the same as the playground game. If someone sees her then a whole series of horrible accidents will befall them until they die gruesomely. Though the details on that bit are always a bit vague." Jason said it matter-of-factly, and then noticed the worried look on Rob's face and was puzzled. "Why'd you ask?"

Rob shrugged. "My dad was doing a story on it for the local paper. He is the editor at *The Newark Advertiser*. He dragged me along to take photographs at *The Witches Brew* for an article he was writing. It was supposed to be dumb father and son bonding time, but..." Rob left it hanging.

"What? Don't tell me you saw the Witchopper?" Jason was smiling at this, apparently thinking that would be the punchline to a joke. But Rob's face fell further and his colour drained.

"No... friggin... way... You saw the Witchopper? Holy shit!"

Rob still had a mix of emotions: terror at touching the memory, nerves that he had just said out loud what he had been afraid to, and a small bright thrill. Jason apparently didn't think that he was completely ridiculous. On the contrary, he seemed to have taken it at face value.

"Well, yeah. Both me and my dad saw her. My dad thinks it was a hoax put on by the landlord. But we checked. She went round a corner on the upstairs landing, and when we turned down that passageway, it was a dead end. No one there. Just a locked door. My dad stormed off to get the landlord to open it. But when he did it was full of laundry sheets and stuff for the bedrooms. Nothing else."

"So the nursery rhyme is true?" Jason said, in all seriousness. "Has anything happened to you? I mean, I know you're not dead. Are you?"

Rob shook his head and even managed to smile. "No, I'm not dead. Well, not yet anyway. But things have definitely been weird since it happened." Rob couldn't believe that he was telling someone this. The feeling of elation was growing. He hadn't realised just how much he needed to talk to someone about it, and the more he spoke the better he felt. He felt lighter. But there was still a part of him that was tender and wary.

"Like what kind of things?" Jason asked eagerly.

"Maybe it's nothing. You know stress from moving and stuff at school." Rob didn't need to say what stuff.

Jason eyed Rob. His eyes assessed Rob above the eyeliner. "Bull-shit!" Jason said it like he'd known Rob for years and was cutting to the chase. "Something happened and it's freaking you out. I can see it. Something other than the legion of walking phalluses we go to school with. What is the collective noun for penis?"

They both seriously considered this for a second. "A crotch?" Rob suggested.

Jason laughed. "Nice. I'm going to write that down."

"You don't think I'm nuts though?"

"What's nuts? People do crazy stuff every day. Think about the crotch of dicks over there." Jason cocked his head towards the playing fields. "Think any of them are actually happy? School is like torture, playing some ridiculous game to fit in. All those guys are going to wake up one day and realise they've been living up to other people's expectations about what's normal. Some of them won't even wake up. They just transfer to a crotch of other dicks at work, trying to fill their vapid little lives with new cars and phones and holidays and bigger houses, all to fit in. Now that's crazy, but to them it's totally normal. And that's not even the really crazy stuff like nukes and biological weapons and burning fossil fuels even though we know its melting ice caps." Jason was building to an almost frenzied intensity. "Christ! Life existing on this little green and blue rock, hurtling through space at twelve-thousand miles an hour, narrowly missing asteroids and cosmic radiation, now that's crazy. So no, I don't think you seeing a ghost and any of the weird crap that followed is at all crazy."

The school bell rang in the distance. "Perfect!" Jason rolled his eyes and put his notebook back in his backpack.

Rob stood up. "We better get back."

"You don't get out of it that easily, Rob. You gotta tell me every-thing that happened."

They walked back down the graveyard through the forget-me-nots. When they reached the gate, Rob had decided something. Being alone sucked. "It's a long story, but are you going to the fair tonight?"

"I wasn't planning to," Jason said. "I haven't been since I was about ten. Why?"

They had rejoined the field. Rob couldn't help but picture all the pupils filtering back to class as a herd of disembodied penises, replete with legs, arms and school ties, waddling back towards a building that looked remarkably like their school but for the sign which read, 'Meat Grinder.'

"My mum wants us to do some family bonding. The last time dad made me do some bonding things didn't go too well. I'm not exactly looking forward to it, but..."

"But what?"

"But I was wondering, maybe, you know if you're not doing anything..."

"Are you asking if I want to come to the fair tonight so you can tell me all about the curse?"

"Well, yeah."

Jason splayed his fingers and inspected them. "Normally I'd be doing my nails, but for you, why not? What's the worst that could happen?"

38

8TH FEBRUARY 1820

The kitchen was a bustle of activity. It sat in the basement of the foundling house, its high windows peeking out onto the pavement above and letting in meek shafts of light. Mary sat around the table with four of her charges: Annabel aged four, Simon aged five, little Ethel who remained small for her age and was actually aged six, and Dorothy was nine. The baker's wife Mrs Hegarty had brought them a loaf of bread in thanks for the cold remedy Mary had prepared for her husband three weeks previously. The four children round the table now gorged happily on thick slabs of bread covered with a thin layer of butter and a dollop of honey. It was a rare treat besides the meagre rations that Mary was able to provide from the monies the church bestowed upon them each month. Mary was made to go to the vicarage each time to receive the money from the clammy hand of the Reverend Moseley.

They might not have had much, but Mary could not have been happier. She had the family she had always wanted. Her life was filled with children. Her eldest, Lily, stood in front of the hearth with the newest of her charges, a little boy of two named Amos. He sat on Lily's hip, his little legs curling around her waist and his arms draped over her neck. The little boy's head lolled on Lily's shoulder, and she rocked him back and forth singing quietly to him while poking the fire into life. Mary touched Lily lightly on the shoulder. Lily smiled and nestled her head into Mary's hand. Mary kissed Lily's hair and said, "Here my duck, you give Amos to me and help yourself to some bread and honey."

The little boy murmured a quiet protest as Lily handed him over. He then settled back to sleep, clung to Mary's front.

There was a knock at the door above, and several of the children playing upstairs shouted with excitement. Mary climbed the narrow staircase and walked through from the back of the foundling house to the front door. It was broad daylight, and so she wasn't sure what to expect. A knock at the door at night could well mean receiving a new small child left on her door, perhaps with a note, more often than not without. Or it would be someone requiring her help, a sick loved one, a new baby's arrival taking too long. Mary did not know what to expect but neither would she be able to guess at what she found.

Down the step onto the pavement stood Emily Brennan with her four children in tow. Marriage had not treated her as kindly. Child-bearing had taken its toll on her once slender figure. The many sleep-less nights and harsh realities of marriage had been worn into her face and not just with wrinkles. Emily wore a hat that poorly disguised her black eye, several days old by the looks of it. The bruise had turned dark purple with brownish-reds spread over her cheek.

"Good day, Miss Hooper. Giles, leave your sister alone."

"Good day, Miss Brennan, but you don't need to be calling me Miss Hooper. Mary's just fine, me duck."

Emily gave a laboured smile. "Then you should call me Emily."

"Then that I will. And how can we help you today, Emily?" Amos was still clung sleeping in Mary's arms, and several other children who'd been playing upstairs hung from her skirts.

Emily looked skittishly up and down the road. They were towards the edge of town, but still this was a main thoroughfare and many people strode about as it was nearing lunchtime.

"Might I come in?"

"Of course, you can, me duck." Mary stood aside to let Emily and her brood file into the foundling house. Mary closed the door behind them, and for a moment the two women stood opposite each other in silence. Mary waited; Emily frowned and looked at her hands. The two opposing sets of children also stood curiously looking at each other.

"James, why don't you go and show Miss Brennan's children your toys, or play a game of hide and seek?"

James didn't need telling twice. He thundered down the hall, and skidded to a halt halfway remembering. He turned and shouted, "Come on, follow me." They ran like rabbits fleeing the gamekeeper's buckshot. Their small feet hammered on the wooden floorboards, soon disappearing into whatever magical worlds their imaginations would create together.

Her eyes still cast down, Emily remained silent.

"Do you know what? I fancy a cuppa tea. We've some fresh bread and honey downstairs. Would you like some?"

"That would be very kind," Emily almost whispered.

When they reached the kitchen, Mary passed the sleeping Amos back to Lily, and in a wordless conversation of exchanged looks, Lily took Amos and the other children off to play. Mary made the tea, leaving the pot to brew in the middle of the table as she cut and buttered slices of bread.

Mary blew on her tea. "What brings you to see me, Emily?"

Emily stared into her tea, struggling with the weight of her burden. "People say that you could help."

"Do they?

"Yes, they do."

"And what kind of help would that be?"

Suddenly, Emily broke down. She sobbed, covering her face, crumpling in on herself. Mary rose and rounded the table to the weeping woman and then knelt beside her, taking Emily's hands in both of hers, gently pulling them from her weeping face.

"There, there, don't cry, Emily. It'll be alright. What help do you need? I can make you a poultice for that eye. It'll bring out that bruise in no time."

Emily drew a hand away to fetch a handkerchief from inside her coat to blow her nose and wipe away the tears.

"Thank you, but that wasn't why I came to see you."

"Then what has you in such a state?" Mary said softly.

"I'm pregnant," and with those words Emily began to cry again.

"And it's not congratulations I should be saying?" Mary squeezed Emily's hand, having had this conversation with many other women before.

More tears flowed down Emily's face. "It should be, shouldn't it? But I..." Whatever she wanted to say was impossible, and the weight of it broke her down once more into a series of choking sobs. Lily appeared at the kitchen door, and with a wordless shake of Mary's head, Lily disappeared again, shutting the door behind her.

"You take your time, my duck. It's just good to let it out. There's no one here but us. No one here to listen or judge or anything else." Mary lifted Emily's chin with the edge of her finger to look at her black eye. Emily demurred, trying to hide her bruise.

Finally Emily said in little more than a whisper, "I cannot have it." A hollow deadness had come over her voice. "I cannot have another one. I'm so tired, and he promised that three was enough, and then we had our fourth. I thought it was all over with. Little Billy's four and just getting to that manageable age. But Giles comes home drunk like he always does and wants it. Sometimes I can put him off. Sometimes I can't. If I'm lucky he's so drunk he passes out in the middle of it. If I'm unlucky, he can't do it, you know, get it up, and then that's my fault. But sometimes there's no stopping it. Oh Mary! I just can't go through it again. I know it makes me sound like a terrible wife and an evil mother to want to get rid of the little thing growing inside me. But it'll kill me, I know it will. God forgive me!"

Emily broke down into uncontrollable tears. Mary pulled her close. She stroked the top of Emily's head, feeling pity for the woman, pity at the hand fate dealt her. Mary felt mad at herself too for the twinge of relief she was feeling at not being married to Giles Brennan. And to think once she had not only envied but felt a streak of hatred for this poor woman. But Mary was younger then, filled with the foolishness of youth, just as Emily must have been. Whereas the women had grown and matured from their childish ways, Giles remained a petulant and swaggering colt.

When Emily finally stopped crying, her words came as a plea. "Can you help me, Mary? I've heard that you can. There are stories about you. You're the one they come to, to deliver their babies when they can't afford the doctor, and the one to come to when..." Emily didn't want to finish that sentence. Mary could tell it would make it too real.

Mary stood and patted Emily's hand. "Drink up your tea, me duck, before it gets too cold. I can make you a powder. Take it with warm milk. It'll help the taste. But it will hurt, and you will bleed a lot for most of the day, and then it will be like a heavy time of the month for at least five days. You'll need to make sure he's out of the way, and if you can, the children too. The cramps will be bad, and it can be dangerous if you're too far along."

Emily realised this was a question. "It's maybe two months. Not much more."

"Can your mother help?"

Emily shook her head. "She would never approve."

"Is there anyone?"

Emily was sure that there wasn't.

"Then can you come here? Perhaps make an excuse that you're out of town seeing a family member or a friend over in Newark or Mansfield, Nottingham even?"

"He would never allow it," Emily said. "He asks where I've been every day, and after here I must go and see him at the Forge. If I don't, he's furious from not knowing what I've been up to all day when he comes home. He gets jealous, and if he gets jealous, he gets suspicious, and when he gets suspicious he gets angry and..."

Mary reached out again across the table and took a hand. "Okay, there there. Then you have to do it yourself. You'll have to be brave."

"But I'm not, Mary."

"Yes you are. You're brave coming to see me. No one ever considers doing such a thing lightly. And so you are brave, and you must believe it. Now, enjoy your bread and tea, and I will get everything ready for you. It'll be alright, Emily. I promise."

39

ROB SAW his father take his mother's hand as they walked in front of him on the way to the funfair. The thirst was still with him, as it always was, but at least tonight, since meeting Jason, he felt hopeful. And even though outwardly he put up a pretence of resistance to his parents, Rob was looking forward to this. His mother was right: it had been far too long since they'd done something like this together, something just for fun.

Other people were heading in the same direction. The noise of the funfair played in the air. Cries of excitement. The quick crescendos of a cheer. A dinging bell and sirens whirred on various rides, from dodgems sliding and thumping into each other, the skyrocket launching small groups into the air, to the squeal of children as they slid down the spiral of the helter-skelter. The cacophony grew louder, drawing them in, and as they reached the bottom of the Burgage, a lone figure stood waiting for Rob. Jason was wearing a feminine-looking raincoat pinched in around his waist and tied with a belt at the hip. His collar was adorned with various pins: a dragon, a typewriter, a rainbow, a space rocket, a CND badge. He waved sheepishly when he saw Rob, who returned the gesture. Richard and Jane looked behind.

"Who's that?" Jane asked.

"It's Jason." Rob pushed between his parents, not wanting to answer any more questions. He started to speed ahead but stopped.

"Is it okay?"

"Go on, mate. Me and your mum will be alright." Richard pulled Jane in for a kiss, and Rob made a disgusted face, before running off with a pang of hope flaring just a little brighter inside him.

"I wasn't sure you'd come." Jason had his hands stuffed in his pockets and was wearing thicker eyeliner than in the graveyard. Mascara fattened up his eyelashes. Dark purple eyeshadow matched his lipstick, which looked almost black in the failing light.

"Me neither," Rob said.

The two boys crossed the road to the Burgage common, passing between two of the parked trailers, and entered a fantasy world made of plastic and metal, lit with bright lights and filled with tumbling layers of noise that fell over each other in peaks and troughs of excitement.

"What do you want to do first?" Jason asked.

"Oh, crap!" Rob was looking over Jason's shoulder. Jason spun around and saw the source of Rob's worry.

Ally, Henry, and Chris sauntered past the dodgems.

"Screw them. Let's give them a wide berth." Jason grabbed Rob and pulled him in the opposite direction. But it wasn't only Ally and the guys Rob had seen. There was a glimpse of a dark lifeless eye filled with earthy green peering through lank, black hair accompanied by the billowing of long dirty skirts.

And then, when Rob looked again, there was nothing apart from the swarm of people at a spring funfair.

Rob and Jason stopped by a burger van. Jason bought them drinks. He got a Diet Coke and bought Rob a bottle of water. Jason watched him drink it in one go and then wipe his mouth.

"Thirsty, then?"

"It's to do with, you know..."

"Really?"

"I'm thirsty all the time. Doesn't matter how much I drink. Dad is the same."

"So, what happened exactly?"

A family with four kids in tow came up to the burger van. Two of the children close in age screamed at each other. Both parents seem oblivious as the sibling conflict escalated to shin kicking and arm punching.

"Not here," Rob said. "Let's find somewhere easier to talk."

ALLY SAW Rob out of the corner of his eye, but he didn't say anything to the guys, not yet. The night was young, and there was a great potential for fun to be had. Ally hadn't counted on Rob being part of the fun, but now that he was here there was every chance he could be worked into the plan. He had filled in Chris and Henry, explaining which of the two bottles was safe to drink, even though at a cursory glance they looked like bottles of water. The ruse was twofold however. They appeared to be bottles of water but both contained spirits, one of vodka the other of white rum, both purloined from the drinks cabinet in Ally's house. He was careful to take the measure of the bottles and add back in a little water. Outwardly the bottle looked innocuous, so they could get drunk in plain sight. But the second layer of the ruse was that one of the bottles contained the additional ingredients Ally had sourced from the darker part of the web, via careful use of an onion browser and a VPN to disguise his identity online. It was simple really if you knew what you were doing and knew which sites to go to. The sellers even posted it to you, so the Royal Mail could deliver it directly to the buyer's door. Paid for with cryptocurrency, and bought with the credit card details Ally had acquired during his online poaching, everything was untraceable back to him. A touch of Rohypnol, a pinch of LSD, and whomever drank from the wrong bottle would be in for one helluva ride. Ally leered at the word 'ride'.

Ally knew Julie and her friends would be there tonight. It was too easy to watch them online, hacking their emails, social media, and messaging accounts. Even installing tracking apps wasn't that hard for Ally. Some apps were harder to hack than others, beyond even Ally's coding skills. The thing was, it wasn't the code there that was the weak spot. It was the dumb-ass people that used the apps, never changing the security code from the default, being so tiresomely predictable that it was easy to work out from enough snooping. There was always the old school method too. People wrote things down, like passwords in the back of notebooks. Julie Brennan did this. Ally didn't even need to get her notebook while she wasn't looking. He simply hovered a moment, pretending to talk to somebody else in the form room, and a glance down gave him all the information he'd need to unlock the puzzle of her passwords. So, Ally knew that Julie would be here tonight along with Sally and Effie, and unfortunately, Danny. Now, that couldn't be helped, no plan should expect to run perfectly. And in fact, Danny might come in quite helpful. It could work to their advantage if both he and Julie were incapacitated. It wasn't as if Julie didn't already have a history with this kind of thing. There was video evidence showing as much. And Danny being the police constable's son, older and messing around with someone who was technically a minor. It wouldn't be the first time two teenagers got a little too drunk and things got out of hand, but neither of them could quite remember what happened. Even that rumour about Danny beating on Rob would be helpful. Seems Danny was a bit rough, tut, tut.

And as if on cue, Ally spotted Julie and her friends looking around, presumably for Danny. What kinda guy would Ally be if he didn't go and help out the ladies in distress?

"I don't know what you two fruits want to do, but I'm going to see if those girls would like a drink." Ally stalked off.

The plan was in motion.

———————

JANE SQUEEZED Richard's hand as they watched Rob go off with his new friend. "You see? Things are going to get better. We just got off to a rocky start."

Richard looked at her. He really had been a fool, mocking the majesty of this woman he loved. She stood by him, and saw something he couldn't see in himself. She was wonderful and beautiful. No longer the girl he'd fallen for at university. She was much more than that now. Every small line on her face and grey hair like a fine patina. She had matured into something far more interesting and deeper. Richard was not sure he could say the same about himself. And in that gap between them, his heart yearned for her.

"Come on, I'll win you a flammable cuddly toy," Richard said as they ran across the road hand in hand.

Every single ball missed the coconuts on the first try. Richard paid another two pounds for three more balls and only hit a pole on which a coconut stood, but the hairy nut stayed in place.

"Bugger!"

Jane laughed, and he was happy to be her fool. "You can't even say it's fixed. Let me have a go."

Richard handed over another five pound note to the enormous man with auburn hair and a giant pot belly. He plunged a ham-sized hand into a pouch hung like a flap of skin from his distended belly and handed Richard his change. Jane closed one eye, her tongue protruding slightly from her lips, cocked her arm back to her ear, and let rip with all she had. By the time she finished the throw her eyes were tight shut, but the ball hit a coconut dead in the middle, knocked it from its perch, and then ricocheted to the side to take out a second. Richard cheered and Jane squealed.

"Did I win?"

"Need three," the enormous man gruffed.

"You've two more balls. Maybe don't close your eyes this time," Richard said.

"Is that your expert advice?" Jane teased.

"Good point." Richard bowed low. "Carry on, m'lady."

Jane narrowed her eyes again, tongue sticking out even further this time. She shifted her weight onto her back leg, cocked her arm and let it rip, shutting her eyes again. The ball didn't go straight, but its path was true, clipping the farthest edge of the remaining coconut. It teetered on its small plinth, tipped and seemed to pause as if it were afraid of heights, and then finally gravity made up its mind. The coconut pitched over. Richard and Jane cheered. Richard hugged her, holding her up as though they'd just won the league. Jane threw her arms around his neck and kissed him on the lips.

"Which one do you want?" The fat, grumpy man pointed to the top row of enormous stuffed animals.

"I'll have that one." Jane pointed to a three-foot tall yellow duck with an orange bill and matching feet.

The fat man reached up with a hook on the end of a pole and fetched down the duck and handed it to Jane.

"Oh, it's not for me. I won it for him."

The fat man gave a short snort, which Richard thought might have been a laugh, and handed the giant yellow duck to Richard.

"Wow, thanks. It's beautiful."

"Cheeky bugger. Well, I am quackers about you," and Jane kissed him on the cheek.

Richard blushed, and the guilt stabbed, making him aware of his thirst again.

They wandered around until he found a burger van selling drinks. Richard tried not to guzzle his water; almost too hot to hold, Jane sipped from a paper cup.

"Oh no," Richard said.

"What is it?" Jane followed his gaze.

"Over there. It's that Julie Brennan girl. Where's Rob?"

Jane turned his face back to her with a gentle touch of her fingers.

"It'll be alright. He's with a friend. If he needs us, we're close by. It's a fair; everyone is having fun. We're having fun. Everything is fine. Look at that. Do you want to know your fortune?"

"Piss off, Ally," Effie said. "We know it was you that filmed Julie."

"Me? No way. I would never do something like that. I can be a bit of a cheeky prick, but come on, that's just sick, isn't it guys?" Ally even impressed himself with how sincere he sounded. He had been practising in the mirror at home, playing out each scenario. He knew they'd suspect him of being involved, but as long as no one could prove anything, there was always doubt.

"Look, no hard feelings. Fancy a drink?" Ally offered Effie the tainted bottle. Effie, of course, was not the main target, but there were many possible permutations to the plan. If they got lucky, maybe they could get a clean sweep of all three girls, one for each of them. Ally was also ready for the contingency that only one of them drank it and started to feel funny and their friends would ferry them home before they could separate them from the safety of the pack. No plan was perfect. But there was always more than one route to the prize. *If at first you don't succeed*. Like computers, if one entry was blocked there were always others. Nothing was impenetrable. Not a firewall. Not Julie Brennan.

"I'm not thirsty." Effie made a sour face at the offer.

"Oh, it's not water," Ally said.

Effie looked at the bottle suspiciously. "What is it then?"

"Just white rum with a bit of lemonade. Try it if you want."

Chris supported Ally's act by swigging from the safe bottle and wincing at the alcoholic burn.

"He's here." Julie waved to Danny who was sauntering towards them.

"Who are these guys?" Danny put a proprietary arm around Julie's waist and kissed her.

Effie answered deadpan. "No one."

"Ah Effie, you protest too much. My name is Ally, Ally Strachan." He held out a hand.

"What the fuck are you, Irish or some shit?" Danny just looked at the hand.

If he had been as big as Danny, if he'd had the same muscles, then Ally would've loved to have punched him right in his smug face. But Ally knew muscles weren't where his strengths lay. He had other weapons. "Isn't that Rob Peters over there with that weirdo Potty?"

It had the desired effect. Danny stiffened immediately and spun around. "Where?"

"Over there," Ally pointed. "Going into the house of mirrors."

"Danny, don't," but Julie could not hold on to Danny.

"Oh shit, sorry Julie," Ally said. "I thought you'd want to know in case he was stalking you or something."

242

"That is fucking it." Danny spat each of the words, storming off towards the house of mirrors.

ROB HAD SEEN HER AGAIN, in a sweep of old-fashioned petticoats; glimpsed and then evaporating like a phantom when the crowd moved. He was glad to keep on moving.

As Jason had bought the drinks, Rob paid for the house of mirrors, and they slipped inside the maze. Nothing was as it should be. The first few steps nearly tripped them up as the gangway suddenly projected down at an angle, and then they were walking up an undulating path of warped floorboards. Not a wall or ceiling was straight, each had an angle leaning in or out, warping around. Mirrors lined everything, reflecting distortions into an infinite kaleidoscope of refraction.

"Don't keep me waiting then," Jason said. "Tell me about it. Tell me everything."

And so Rob did, telling Jason every detail as it happened to him. From their tour round *The Witch's Brew* and their first sighting of the Witchopper, to the dreams and hallucinations leading to a lack of sleep, the ever growing thirst, and how he seemed to be fading away whenever he looked in the mirror but that no one else seemed to notice. And finally, Rob told of how he kept seeing the Witchopper, even tonight. Jason listened to it all, only to occasionally interrupt with a clarifying question.

When Rob was done, Jason puffed out his cheeks, running one hand through his hair. "That's a lot to be dealing with, especially on top of the other crap you've been putting up with at school."

Rob shrugged as they snaked through an S-shaped corridor and came to a doorway that opened into a room some ten feet across. Its walls were inlaid with mirrors warping reality in a multitude of ways: elongating, compressing, twisting. There were freestanding mirrors too, presenting the boys with multiple distortions of themselves. But the oddest of the mirrors, given present company, was the one fixed in the dead centre of the room. Rob found himself in front of it, with

Jason next to him. He saw himself reflected into infinity. Rob after Rob in the never-ending corridor. It was as if he was looking into an infinite abyss, where all the reflections were drawn to one focal point.The mirror drew everything to the centre and brought three things colliding together. Rob had fallen silent, and Jason grew anxious at the look on his face.

"Can you see the Witchopper now?" Jason whispered.

Rob was about to tell him no and reassure his friend, and then she appeared.

"Yes," Rob said, a quiver in his voice. The colour drained from Jason's face.

She did not show herself on his shoulder, to be reflected with all the other infinite Robs. Instead, she passed across the corridor of a Rob some ten times removed from himself, looking down demurely, only to turn ahead at the last minute and to spy the real Rob with one moss green eye.

The earthy sweet smell of woodland decay permeated the mirror room. The noises of the fairground outside were joined by one now familiar portent of the Witchopper's presence.

Mary Hooper now stood next to the Rob four removed from himself. He stood transfixed. His nails bit into the skin of his palms, but in a blink Mary was no longer in front of him. A swirl from a reflection in his peripheral vision made Rob turn to follow it, and he clumsily bumped into Jason.

"What is it?" There was panic in Jason's voice. "Where is she?"

Mary moved from mirror to mirror, always one step ahead of Rob, never quite where he expected her to be, her movements matching the unfathomable distorted logic of the mirrored room. With Jason close at his side, Rob backed up until he bumped into something solid, letting out a cry. Yet another mirror they'd missed in the kaleidoscope of glass all around them. Attached to the ceiling on the floor in its middle, the mirrored panel began to turn on its axis; a mirthful laugh mocked the boys.

"Couple of gaylords screaming together."

Danny stepped into the room. Rob saw Mary linger momentarily in a mirror behind Danny and then disappear as soon as Rob tried to fix his gaze on her.

"You'll try to screw anything with a hole, won't you, Rob?" Danny laced his knuckles together and cracked them against his ribs.

Rob was looking from mirror to mirror, trying to find the Witchopper as the panelled mirror spun like a roulette wheel.

"Who's this?" Jason whispered in Rob's ear.

"Danny Broad. Julie's boyfriend."

"He's, erm, a big boy isn't he?"

There was nowhere to turn, or at least, no obvious way in the shifting labyrinth of reflections. Their backs were pressed against a mirrored wall whose distortion stretched the two boys like strands of chewing gum.

"Sorry for interrupting you two queers." Danny continued to close the space between them. "Me and Rob have got some unfinished business. Are you even paying attention, Rob? I'm talking to you."

Mary appeared and disappeared in the swivelling panelled mirror next to them - there and then not there, there and then not there, while the funfair droned in a maniacal whirligig.

"You're such a fucking weirdo." Danny grabbed Rob by the collar. Hoisted onto his tiptoes, Rob still looked around trying to spot the ghost in the mirrors. Danny raised his fist casually, as if he was about to throw a ball at the coconut shy.

Another fist flew through the air, one with black nail polish. Danny's head whipped around. He took a step back, shock on his face, having been caught off balance and off guard.

Rob snapped out of the paralytic spell the Withopper's presence cast on him only to see Jason wincing, holding his hand in pain.

Now the fight really began.

Danny sniffed and wiped the trickle of blood on the back of his hand. His face was sanguine as all six foot two inches of him ran at Jason, knocking Rob to the side. He took Jason in a rugby tackle under the ribs, lifting him a few inches from the ground with a grunt, and drove him into the nearest wall. There was a bone shattering crash, and a tremendous shower of glass as one of the walled mirrors broke into hundreds of shards. Rob shielded his face. When he looked up, Danny was climbing on top of Jason, who was gasping for breath.

Danny grabbed Jason around the throat and began to squeeze. Jason's hands pulled ineffectually at Danny's arms. Mary Hooper now forgotten, Rob hauled himself off the floor and, without thinking, launched himself at Danny, catching him around the neck in a headlock and knocking him off the top of Jason. The two of them rolled, glass grinding into their backs, and with the momentum Danny tumbled free, coming up to his knees. They faced each other. Blood dripped down Danny's face from a cut at his hairline and another on his cheek; his face looked like a macabre carnival mask through which his eyes blazed white hot.

Rob's limbs trembled with adrenaline. He was unfrozen. He would not run, not anymore. Not from Danny or anything else. The mirrors had shown him the corner he was in. But as trapped as he might be, he wasn't prepared to accept his fate, not without a fight.

"Fuck you." Rob clenched his fists ready to meet Danny head on.

Something caught Danny's eye on the floor in front of him, and a moment later in a terrible realisation, Rob saw it too.

The shard of glass was maybe ten inches long, tapering like an ice pick to a point. Danny smiled maniacally and picked up the weapon. Rob, already standing and backing up, looked for something, anything he could use. Another piece of glass perhaps, but everything else was too small or crumbled into tiny fragments.

Danny lunged with everything that he had, plunging the huge shard towards Rob's belly. Rob put out his arms to protect himself, but they were knocked aside.

"No!" Jason shouted, jumping in front of his friend. The glass dagger stabbed hard into Jason's stomach, and all three of them tumbled to the ground.

Danny, still in his fit of rage, quickly got to his knees, rising above the two boys, preparing to strike another deathblow, this time on his intended target. Rob didn't have time to think. He saw his friend holding his stomach. His own rage burned as hot as Danny's, and in the peak of adrenaline, he hauled Jason out of the way with one arm just as Danny came in to strike for a second time.

Rob lunged for the nearest thing to him, and with both hands slammed the rotating panel of glass into Danny's face. Like the wall before it, the panel shattered, covering Danny in another deluge of glass. Rob felt the solid connection with Danny's skull. Head whipping back, stunned, Danny stumbled. His legs wobbled beneath him like a boxer clipped in the tenth round, and then he fell heavily.

For a split second, Rob thought he'd killed him. But then Danny's legs began to move, and he groaned. Fists clenched, ready for more, Rob looked down at his friend on the floor and couldn't believe his eyes. The shard of glass had broken in half, and stuck out of Jason's stomach. But there was no blood. Jason was propped up on his elbows and opened his long coat to inspect the damage, revealing that his notebook had taken the damage on his behalf.

Danny groaned again, and his arm flung spasmodically across his body in a pantomime of a B-movie monster coming back to life.

"Let's get out of here, now," Rob said, picking Jason up under the arms. The two boys fled the hall of mirrors as Danny came back to life.

40

"OH GO ON, it'll be fun." Jane's arm, laced through Richard's, pulled him along.

This funfair outing was turning out to be a good idea after all. It was a frippery, detached from their normality, in which ironically they could be themselves, or at least the version of themselves they wished for, amid the bright lights and the sizzling of cheap beef burgers and the smell of sweating onions and gleefully shouting children.

"Okay, okay, let me grab another drink before we go in." Richard tugged them over to the confectionery van and ordered himself an extra-large soda.

"You know, if it is diabetes, that won't help." She wasn't nagging, not tonight. In the topsy turvy world of the funfair, it was a joke.

"Sugar, man's greatest foe," Richard said as if narrating a wildlife documentary, happy to still be her fool.

They paused in front of the tent's entrance and faced each other. The huge yellow duck, bent double over the crook of Richard's arm, stared blankly at the grass as they kissed. Jane still tasted faintly of toothpaste, clean and fresh. It made Richard think of how pure she was. And from there it was only a small jump to feelings of inadequacy. Behind those lay resentment that Jane was almost too perfect, and behind that were Richard's own insecurities. A Babushka doll of little demons, malevolent and brooding, stacked one inside the other to maketh the man. By the time their kiss had broken, Richard's mind had tumbled into a collage of his affairs, only some of which Jane knew of, and the last of which he prayed she never would. They were cold thoughts, as her warm fingers wrapped around his, and the Hanging Tree creaked behind Madam O'Leary's fortune telling tent.

Jane went in first, pulling back the flap, leading Richard by the hand. The setup was everything that Richard would have expected from a sideshow charlatan. The space was hung with heavy velvet material and embroidered throws replete with a hodgepodge of mystic symbols borrowed from various cultures, everything from third eyes to yin-yang symbols, pyramids to mandalas. Madam O'Leary sat replete with gypsy shawl, an over-the-top mop of grey hair with wisps of white and streaks of gold, and what Richard thought was the perfect amount of staged unkemptness. And there, in the middle of the table before Madam O'Leary's bejewelled hands, the cherry on the proverbial cliched cake: a crystal ball.

"Welcome. I am Madam O'Leary, teller of fortunes, psychic and seer. For the price of admission, I will look into your futures, but beware, I am but a messenger." Madame O'Leary held out her hands, inviting them to take the seats across the table from her.

"Oow, I'm a Pisces in alignment with Aquarius," Richard whispered not inconspicuously to Jane. She gave him a chiding look as they took their seats and handed over a ten pound note to cover each of their fortunes. Madame O'Leary slipped the note into a pouch she wore around her waist, jangling the change within.

"Thank you, Deary." Madam O'Leary's voice crackled like waves pulling away from a shingle beach. "What will it be? I can read your tarot, or look into my crystal ball. I could read your palm." She took Jane's hand between her gnarled digits. "I can tell you if this strapping lad will be up peeing all night." She laughed, looking at the enormous soda Richard held. "Maybe it's safer to stay away from the tea leaves tonight."

"I think you're right," Jane laughed lightly. "I've never had my palm read."

The old woman turned over Jane's hands, shuffling forward on her seat to get a better look. Richard was amazed she wasn't in agony. Every joint of her fingers was swollen and misshapen like the roots of an old tree. She cooed and purred, looking over Jane's palm, considering it in great detail. Finally she looked up, the many creases of her face bunching together around her eyes and mouth. "You have a very interesting hand. It tells me you are kind and trusting, too trusting at times."

Richard rolled his eyes, disguising the pang of guilt. But Jane, she listened intently. Did she stiffen a little at that last comment?

The old woman went on. "This line here," the woman slowly traced the tip of one of her gnarled fingers across Jane's palm. "It means that you work hard, but it also means that you work hard for other people. This one here is your fortune line."

"We are going to be rich?' Richard mocked.

The old woman ignored him. "Fortune is not always about money. Some of the poorest people live the richest of lives. Either way, your fortune line shows that you will lead a rich and fulfilled life."

"Is there a lifeline as well, or am I wrong about that?" Jane said, still listening intently.

"Ah yes, of course, Deary." Madam O'Leary enclosed Jane's hand in both of hers and patted her palm. "You have a very long and strong lifeline, like an oak tree." She chuckled. "You have a good root, so you will endure."

That's a funny way of putting it, Richard thought. He looked around and wished he had another soda to drink, slurping at the bottom of the one he had. The noise of the funfair outside was barely dampened by the tent. Sirens whirred, bells rang, unseen people shouted and screamed in delight. Richard felt odd, as though this night was just a dream, a temporary fantasy.

"And now for you, Deary," the old woman said, not sounding nearly as warm as she had with Jane.

"Tell me who wins the three fifteen at Ascot, Madam O'Leary," Richard said a little too sarcastically as he presented his hand, crushing the poor yellow duck between himself and the table. The duck stared with its dead eyes at Richard.

Richard was surprised at how hot Madam O'Leary's hands were. He nearly pulled away believing he would be burnt. But he let her take his hands in hers, and while they were distorted and ugly, they were also soft and cosy. She inspected his palm, opening it out. Richard grinned at Jane. She wiggled her eyebrows up and down in the excited way that she did sometimes. When Richard looked back at Madam O'Leary, her brows were knitted together. Was that a look of concern? Did he present a puzzle? Richard caught himself being drawn into the charade.

"Oh God, I'm going to die?"

Madam O'Leary said nothing at first. She continued to study his palm and then wet her lips, pursing them slightly, nostrils flaring. It was the nostrils, why were they flaring? And Richard caught a whiff of it, and his thirst now became a sickening burn in the back of his throat. He could feel his hand trembling in the old woman's, and he could also feel her steady him. The sweet woodland decay, it's earthy yet sweet musk, so sweet it was nauseating. The susurration grew in those few seconds, which stretched into an eternity. The roil of thousands of tiny creatures writhing in the soil, churning and eating the earth, dying and rotting and growing again in an endless cycle of life and decay. He could hear worm-eggs hatching, the stretching of their guts, the desiccation of their exoskeleton husks, the putrefaction of their soft cells becoming the rushing torrent of the Earth's bloodstream, crashing and pounding, until...

Madam O'Leary clasped Richard's hand in hers, as she had done with Jane's, and patted them. "Such a complex palm."

"Will we grow old together?" Jane said, looking every bit the college girl whom Richard fell in love with, innocent and sweet and impossibly perfect and utterly unaware.

The old woman made a noncommittal articulation, which sounded something like "hmm," and could have meant "yes, of course" or something else entirely. Richard tried to pull his hand away. Madam O'Leary held it firmly. The warm knots of her fingers biting into his. "You two have something special, don't you?"

Richard knew she was talking about Rob.

"Thank you. We met at college," Jane said.

"That's nice, Deary." Madam O'Leary remained fixed on Richard, glassy grey orbs looking beyond the veil. "You should spend more time together. In fact, you should go home right now, but remember, turn right when you leave, and if you do there's a chance you'll get what you desire."

The old woman let go of Richard, and now he wished she hadn't. She was talking about Rob. He could fix it for Rob. Did that mean he couldn't fix it for himself?

"Thank you, Dearies. Enjoy the rest of your evening." Madam O'Leary was turning away and bending down beneath the table. She was done with them. Jane was already beginning to stand. Richard found himself sitting in his chair as if he'd been entranced by a movie and the house lights had suddenly turned on and everybody had left. He caught himself, almost laughing at how he'd been sucked into the theatre of the cold reading, even though she hadn't told him anything really, and told Jane what she wanted to hear.

"Thank you," Richard said, finding that his voice was dry and cracked. He coughed to clear his throat.

Madam O'Leary was still rummaging for something under the table, and waved a hand goodbye. "Remember, turn right not left."

All of a sudden the instruction seemed ridiculous, part of the charade. Or perhaps he should view it differently: the old woman was well on the way to senility, and it was good that she could still find work among the people at the fairground.

Jane opened the tent flap and they ducked out. The noise washed over them like a wave. The light seemed brighter now. The night was darker, seeping from the sky like a clogging oil. People bustled by, bumped into them. A child, alone, cried, its cheeks bright red, tears streaming down its face, its eyes crushed into plump wrinkles, until a young mother and father found it and scooped it up, and still it cried, sobbing into the mother's shoulder, and the father patted its back to no effect.

"At least I'm going to live for a long time," Jane said. "Not sure about you, old boy. Hey, what's the matter?"

"Nothing. Just surprised people can still get away with that kind of nonsense in this day and age."

"It's a bit of fun. We're having fun, aren't we?" There was a twinge of doubt in Jane's voice.

He forced himself to brighten. "Yeah, of course we are darling. What should we do now?"

"I haven't been on dodgems since that time we took Rob to Southend Pier when he was five. He sat in your lap, do you remember? You and he chased me around that dodgems bumping in the back of me. I had a bruise on my hip for about a week after that. Let me get my own back now. You haven't got Rob to protect you this time."

"Sounds great."

"I think it's over here."

Jane pulled them to the left.

They skirted a queue for the Skyrocket, which just shot a group into the sky screaming, when they bumped into another couple. Richard dropped the yellow duck and bent down to pick it up.

"Richard, my God, funny seeing you here," Izzy said.

"Richard?" The large muscular man standing next to her said. He was at least three inches taller than Richard, and at least fifteen years younger. "Richard, your boss?"

"Yes, Will."

Richard already felt the cold tingle that something wasn't quite right. Izzy had not said she was coming to the fair tonight when he had mentioned it. But he was still trying to put his finger on what it was, while simultaneously wanting to get away, which made him too slow. The realisation was forming when Izzy's boyfriend grabbed for Richard. He placed his two large hands in the middle of Richard's chest and gave him one almighty shove. Richard went sprawling back landing on his backside. Jane was shouting. Izzy watched with a hint of a smirk.

"You slimy bastard," Will shouted, his face reddening, as he stepped over Richard. Jane was already reacting, trying to get in between them. She stopped when she heard the rest of what Will had to say. "You think its okay to pressure your employees into having sex with you?"

"What? No. I..." Richard said dumbly.

Horror dawned on Jane's face.

"I ought to knock your teeth out." Will looked as though he was about to do just that, when another large man with a beard intervened. He placed a hand lightly on Will's chest, but didn't shove.

"That's enough now, son."

Will batted the hand away, but the big man, seemingly familiar with physical confrontations, merely ensnared Will in a bouncer's lock. Will tried to pull it away.

"Piss off. This has nothing to do with you."

Calmly, the bearded man said, "Less of the bad language, son. I might be off duty, but will still arrest you and get you put in the cells to cool off for the night."

A look of confusion spread across Will's face.

"My name is Constable Melvin Playfair. And this is my beat. We'll not be having any trouble tonight, will we now, gentlemen?" It clearly wasn't a question, and the situation was diffused.

People had stopped to stare. Abashed, Richard scrambled to his feet, the rest of the parties in this confrontation seemingly held in suspended animation, when a piercing scream let out.

Richard's first instinct was to look towards Jane. But it wasn't her. She was the only one glaring at Richard, looking at the fool she'd married. Everybody else looked to the exit of the house of mirrors. There came another animalistic cry, disturbing enough to tear Richard and Jane from their own confrontation.

A young man had staggered onto the grass in front of the house of mirrors. He lurched, swinging one way and then the other. Blood covered his face, dripping all over his shirt and jacket. His hands were cut and blood dripped from the tips of his fingers. He looked for all intents and purposes like a zombie risen from the grave, disorientated and raging with anger. People nearest to him backed off. Staggering, the bloodied young man swung his head back and forth as if drunkenly looking for something.

"You two wait here," Constable Playfair instructed Will and Richard, as he headed straight for the boy covered in blood. He muttered as he went. "This was supposed to be my night off."

41

AT FIRST THERE was nothing but the pounding of their feet and the heaving in their chests. Then Rob and Jason slowed. They'd run from the funfair up towards the middle of the town but quickly turned off into a carpark, which presented options for fleeing down various alleyways. Safely ensconced in the shadows between buildings, they caught their breath. Jason had his hands on his knees, and Rob leaned against a high fence. Jason looked down and opened his coat to pull out his notebook.

"I guess he didn't like my writing," he said, pulling a shard of glass from the pages. It wasn't even funny, but both boys burst out laughing. The thrill of their ordeal still pounded in their chests.

They heard voices.

"Come on," Rob said, not because he thought it was Danny, but because their ordeal had drawn them closer together, bonded in brotherhood of adversity, and Rob at least did not want to share that with anyone else. They ran off, still laughing, until they got back to Rob's house, where they took refuge in his bedroom.

"I like your taste in wallpaper. It just screams seven-year-old, darling."

"Piss off," Rob said, jumping onto his bed, smiling.

"No seriously," Jason went on, now looking at the carpet, "you're clearly in touch with your inner child. Do you want to play soldiers or tag, maybe?" Jason took the seat at Rob's desk.

"I think we just played that with Danny."

The brightness of Jason's face flickered off and then came back on brighter than ever. "Kicked his ass, is what we did," Jason said, giving the air a one-two combination.

"Thanks, though," Rob said.

"What for?"

"Like, taking a giant spear of glass for me." Rod held out his hands indicating the size of the shard.

"What are friends for?" Jason said spinning around to Rob's desk.

Friends? Yeah, Rob guessed that's what they were and the fight with Danny had accelerated their friendship through months of getting to know each other. As if to prove it, Jason was flipping through Rob's drawings, which covered his desk, like he was an old friend, and Rob didn't mind at all. He felt no protectiveness, no trepidation at being judged.

"Thanks for pulling him off me too," Jason added casually. "I thought he was going to kill me."

"I think he was."

"Yeah, my life flashed before my eyes. It was disappointing. I need to masturbate less."

Rob nearly choked on his laugh. "You're hilarious."

"It's a curse," Jason said, settling on a sketch that had been hidden under several others. "And you're a fucking savant," he said, holding the picture up to examine it.

"A what?"

"A savant. A kind of genius. A total freak," Jason said, turning the picture to Rob.

Rob flushed.

"This is the one, isn't it?"

"The one what?"

"The one everyone in the year was talking about? The one that seemingly impressed the fittest girl in the year, if not the school, so much that she let you snog her, and, well, fucked up everything else for you in like a cataclysmic fuckstorm of shit."

"When you put it like that... Yes?" Rob ventured. He'd never really thought about it like that, not the bit about impressing Julie, and the idea hurt.

Jason had turned the picture back around to look at it more carefully. Then he eyed Rob equally as carefully, before putting the picture down."Mate, a talent like that on top of you being a good looking guy - don't blush; it's true, and while the rumours are true and I like boys, it's not a come on. You're not my type, all moody and artistic, wrapped up with your blonde locks. The problem with you Rob is you're a Hollywood cliche. Talented, handsome - it's a curse. It's why they picked on you, you know that right?"

Rob shrugged at the barrage of revelations and straight talking, but again he didn't mind. It felt natural between them, that this was Jason's role in their friendship.

"Julie too. Too pretty for her own good that one. Half the school has a permanent stiffy when she's around, and the other half are either gay or don't have a penis. Or they don't have a penis and are gay and therefore offer a bit of bushy texture to the otherwise permanent sea of tents pitched in the campsite of school trousers. She must be tortured."

"I guess," Rob said.

"God you'd have beautiful children. No wonder the covetous forces of avarice couldn't allow that to happen."

"What?"

"Ally Strachan and the rest. Spiteful little fuck is he. How the hell did you end up friends with him?"

"It just kind of happened. We moved here and I sat next to him in registration."

Jason put his hand to his chin, considering Rob once more with deliberate theatricality, but under it, Rob could tell his keen mind was working.

"We need to take control of all this." Jason waved his hand over Rob. "Too much of the sad, put-upon pretty-boy thing going on. *Oh Julie doesn't love me! Oh I've been cursed by a witch and might die!*" Jason said, clasping his hands to his cheek.

"Don't pull any punches."

"Robert, that I will never do."

"But what can we do?" Rob sat up straighter in his bed. Jason's tone, while lighthearted, Rob knew was also serious.

"We need to try and figure this out. Work out what caused the curse, if we can."

"But why? How will that help?" Rob said.

"So pretty," Jason said, "not much of a thinker."

"Hey!" Rob said.

"I'm only kidding, mate. But if we can work out what caused the curse, maybe we can figure out how to break it. We need to gather all the possible information about the Witchopper."

"My dad has a dossier of stuff from the newspaper for the story he is writing on her," Rob realised.

"Brilliant! What does it say?" Jason said.

Rob looked ashen faced.

"You've not read it, have you?"

Rob shook his head.

"Poor love, so pretty, yet so..."

"Mate, enough already."

"I'm sorry, but that would be the smartest thing for us to do. Is it here, in the house?" Jason asked.

Rob was about to say he wasn't sure but that they could go and look for it when a wail from the road outside interrupted his thoughts.

With the window directly in front of the desk, Jason had the clearest line of sight to the road. "That's your parents, isn't it?"

Rob was off the bed and looking out of the window now as the wail ceased and Rob's mother pushed his father away from her, breaking the embrace he was trying to hold her in, along with a preposterously large, yellow, cuddly duck.

"You fucking bastard" she screamed, and Rob could see that neighbours were popping up at windows to see what all the commotion was. Richard staggered back.

"Jane, wait," he called after her. She was running up their short driveway, wiping tears away with the back of her hand. Richard

258

started to follow her, but when she reached their front door, Rob's mother turned and screamed at him.

"Wait? Wait for what? Wait around like a good wife while you fuck the office junior? You arrogant wanker, Richard." Then she slammed the door behind her.

Rob slumped down onto his bed, deflated. Jason didn't say anything. When the front door slammed again a few moments later, both boys winced. The argument started ringing through the house, and the past, which they had tried to leave behind in London, had finally caught up with them. Suddenly, the racing cars and space rockets on his carpet and walls seemed to fit Rob. He regressed into them. If only he and his new friend could get lost in a make believe world where they played hide and seek in lands filled with dragons and trolls, where every wardrobe was a dark cave, a bed was a safe magical island protecting its occupant from all the evils of the world. Rob drew his legs up to him and hugged his knees, wishing that could be true. But it wasn't. The carpet wasn't his and neither was the wallpaper.

The argument reached a peak when something smashed, but only after all his father's infidelities had been laid bare.

"You crazy bitch," Richard shouted, followed by his footfalls pounding up the stairs.

Jane must have been standing at the foot of the stairs when she shouted, "I must be a crazy bitch staying with you, while you slip your prick into anything that moves. Crazy for thinking you had changed!"

Richard wasn't responding, and so Jane climbed the stairs to take the fight to him. "Where are you going?" she said. Rob could tell they were both down the landing in their bedroom.

"I'm going to sort this out."

"By running away? You fucking coward."

"I can't talk to you when you're like this."

Rob heard his mother scream. It was an animalistic screech, a sound filled with equal parts pain and anger. A sound that made Rob hug his knees even harder. Jason came to sit next to him. He put an arm around Rob's shoulder. There was a struggle as the scream became a guttural grunt of effort.

"Jane, calm down," Richard said through the gritted teeth of physical effort. Their bedroom door flung open and Richard fled down the stairs. The front door opened and immediately slammed behind him, vibrating through the house. Jane followed, flinging the door open.

"That's right, run off to London. Run back to your other whore."

"Tell Rob I'm sorry and I'm going to sort this out." Rob heard this and stood to look out of the window. Richard was looking up at him, his car door half open. He looked like a haunted man.

Jane had lost all control. Her words were coming like cars crashing into each other, skidding into a pile up on an ice covered motorway. "Tell him yourself, you fucking prick. I fucking hate you, you bastard."

"Jane, please."

"Fuck off and die."

Rob watched his dad wave to him weakly and then disappear into his car, its front end still battered. The headlights switched on. The engine revved. Jane lurched for the car, clawing at it, slapping the window. Richard reversed and Jane pitched into the space, nearly losing her feet. The car paused for a moment as it found its line on the road, and then Rob's father was gone.

42

LILY HELPED Mary take the last of the little ones to bed, tucking them up with kisses, hugs, and lullabies. The soft breaths from the deep sleep of ten little souls blew like bellows in the furnace of Mary's heart. She cast one final look over her sleeping brood and closed the bedroom.

They slipped down three flights of stairs to the basement kitchen where they could carry on with Lily's training. Very few had the gift, but Lily did. Mary had seen it in her, an aura imperceptible to most people. It was in the way animals of all kinds were not only drawn to Lily but were also calm in her presence. When Mary took the children foraging for whatever plants were in season, Lily had an intuitive sense of which were edible or medicinal or poisonous or perhaps all three depending on how much would be used or how they were prepared.

Most people trampled blindly through their landscape. Even many farmers who were more sensitive to the changes in the seasons, what they saw as weeds very often could be used in a poultice. A dandelion had many usages. The whole plant was edible and its sap could make a basic glue. Its roots could be seeded anywhere and provide a bountiful crop to be harvested later. Not only did Lily seem adept, she was also eager to learn.

The fire had quelled to a smouldering rubble of red and orange. Lily picked up another log and tossed it onto the embers. Yellow and green flames began to slip and slide over the underbelly of the log, giving off thin ribbons of bluish smoke that were pulled up the chimney, like the wheeze of an old man's pipe.

Lily took a seat opposite Mary and laid her palms out face up just as she did.

"Concentrate," Mary said. "It's a feeling. Think of the plant. It could be anyone, but the smaller ones are best: bluebells, snowdrops, primroses. Mine are forget-me-not. Here, let me show you."

As she looked on her charge kindly, Mary's eyes began to change, from hazelnut with their deeper flecks of walnut, to a green as forest's moss and lichen. The whites then transmuted to match that green of her irises. The crackle of the fire was joined by the whisper of the world churning. Once the change was done, a forget-me-not began to grow. First one green shoot pushed through the skin. The nubile green stem unfurled, and the tiny knot of a bud raised its head, opening to a delicate purple flower. Quickly more followed, spreading out, coiling around Mary's hand and fingers. Despite that this was not the first time Mary had tried to teach her this, Lily watched in awe.

The demonstration was done. Mary picked the flowers from her hand and wrapped them into a simple wreath. "What flower did you pick?"

"I thought I'd try nettle," Lily said.

"Why nettle?"

"They're as good as any other plant, better even. We can eat them, use them to make cloth, and treat swollen joints."

Mary was pleased with her. She was showing wisdom beyond her years, not beguiled by pretty little things, she had the appreciation of the function of the plant, its many benefits, and in that was held extreme beauty.

"That's good, Lily. Now feel the plant."

Lily furrowed her brow and concentrated. Nothing happened. Her shoulders sagged.

"Don't imagine the plant," Mary said softly. "*Feel* the plant, my duck. It might sound strange, but we are all connected through Jack, every piece of brick, every plant, even the metal of the pots and pans comes from the ores of the earth. They all have a different feeling, but at their root, they are all of the same place, the same essence, like your hair or your toes and the heart that beats in your chest are all part of you, but they are different. Try and feel the difference in the nettle. It's already in you."

Lily readied herself, closing her eyes, and took a large breath. She exhaled and looked at the palms of her hands. She was trying too hard and as such would be *thinking* not *feeling* the nettle that she wanted to call forth. Mary knew that she would get it in the end. It was just a matter of time.

Hard and fast banging rattled the front door, breaking Lily's concentration.

"Mary Hooper, you bitch. I want to talk to you."

Lily flinched, tensing with fear of the noise and the memories from her past that it evoked.

"Don't you worry, my duck. It's just a drunken fool. I'll deal with him." Mary patted Lily on the hand and rose from the table, ascending the stairs to the ground floor of the foundling house. She took a candle with her. The little orb of light floated in the darkness before her. When she reached the front door, Giles Brennan was still shouting, banging on the door again as he slurred his words.

"Come on, you bitch. You witch. You bitch witch." A drunken titter at the accidental wordplay. "Open the door."

Mary carefully unlocked the front door, keeping her foot firmly behind it, and opened it a few inches.

"Giles Brennan, you're drunk and my children are sleeping."

"They're not your children, witch. I want to talk to you." Giles pointed at her through the gap in the door.

"Come back when you're not so drunk and the sun is up. You've a wife and children at home," Mary told him.

"Some bitch isn't going to tell me what to do." Giles took a lurching step forward and found his balance with the help of the brick wall of the foundling house. "I know what you did to my Emily."

"I don't know what you're talking about. Now go home."

"Yes, you do, you spiteful bitch. Think you can take one of my children away from me just because you're an evil and barren witch. God would never give you children, even though you would lie about it."

Mary bit her tongue lest it would become forked. "Goodnight, Giles."

She shut the door.

But before she could lock it, Giles rammed his shoulder into the oak. Mary tumbled back. The candle flew from her grasp, skittering across the floorboards and snuffing out, its wisp of grey smoke invisible in the dark. Mary struck her head in the fall. The room tilted and Giles' silhouette swayed for a moment in the doorway, the lamps fluttering on the street outside, and then he stumbled forward.

Before Mary could do anything, he was on her. One rough hand closed around her throat, while the other forced her legs apart and yanked up her skirt. Words died unspoken as Giles' hand closed more tightly around her throat.

"Shut up, bitch." His breath reeked of the tavern. The smell of sweat and iron dust oozed over her as he spat the insult and unfastened his belt and breeches.

Mary struggled, trying to squirm away, but as she did, Giles squeezed his strong blacksmith's hand harder around her throat. There was the ripping sound of tearing cotton as he pulled away her undergarments. The world throbbed in and out of focus.

"Stay still, you dirty witch," Giles growled through gritted teeth and reached behind himself. Mary heard the blade being drawn from its leather pouch sheath. Its edge glinted in the light of the street lamp bleeding through the open door. He turned the blade to her throat.

"Stop struggling, or I'll open your throat, witch. Get what's coming to you. Remember when you were my May Day whore? Didn't even need to pay. That's how cheap a whore you were."

The pressure on Mary's throat released as the cold blade pressed into her skin. She could breathe again but dared not draw a large breath for fear that the blade would cut her. Between her legs, Giles was struggling with his manhood. Flaccid, it poked ineffectually against the flesh of her thighs and the rounded flesh of her buttocks, unable to find its mark. He grunted with effort and frustration.

Mary's senses came back to her, crystallising with the focus of the room. Air filled her lungs. With a knife against her throat and the violation about to be done to her, Mary's anger surged.

"Jack grenemon! Min sweostorum oder deorcholt sendan!"

Giles fumbled and grunted again. His phallus bumped against her coarse hair.

"Deop, digol wudufeorh, to cuman!"

The door slammed shut. An unseen force stirred in the room, a sound like paper crumpled and tossed on a fire, or deep hillocks of dried autumn leaves kicked up in twirling dervishes, as a gale rushed through a wild wood. The whites of Mary's eyes glazed moss-green. With the urgent grunts of a ravenous hog, Giles thrust. Mary searched and found them, feeling the plants, calling them to her in a time of need. Angry, rushing, tunnelling, from between the floorboards coiled vines of ivy, brambles, and a host of weeds in a twisting briar. They coiled around the hog's ankles, which at first he was unaware of, so fixed on hauling Mary back.

"No you don't, witch!" Giles pressed the knife harder to her throat. Mary's skin wept a tear of blood beneath its sharpened edge.

"Swine bewiscan, swa þes deofollufu ic acwellan."

A vine of ivy slithered along the floor towards Giles's wrist. It coiled around it, ripping the knife away from Mary's throat. A second vine of knotweed, weaker but persistent, ensnared his other wrist, and together they pulled Giles to his knees.

Mary still spoke in the old tongue, but now freed from the knife, the words thundered from her throat. The plants grew beneath her, lifting her preternaturally to her feet in one swift motion, so that she towered over Giles, queen among gathered shadows. The blacksmith knelt penitently before her, arms outstretched.

Mary's skin shone like the pale moon. Her black hair tousled in an unfelt gale.

"Ecg mid bealu slean!"

The ivy restricting Giles's knife-hand began to pull his limb down towards his genitals. He grunted, resisting, and a tendril of a thorny bramble struck, lashing his wrist. Giles was unable to resist now. He glared at Mary, not fully comprehending what was happening to him. He began to grunt and struggle, but the plants held him firm.

"You cunting witch," he spat, but another bramble whipped through the air, gagging the swine's petulant mouth. He bucked and pulled against his bounds, which held fast and turned his blade slowly, inexorably beneath the sack of his scrotum. Mary meant to geld him and free him of his offending appendage.

The realisation dawned on Giles with the cold touch of the blade. His bucking became a small tremulous experiment at movement. The weeds tightened. The sharpened edge drew a red tear, whetting the steel. One jerk would see it sliced through his scrotum. Giles whimpered. Salt water glistened at the corner of his eye and tumbled through his stubble.

A stifled cry came from behind Mary. She whirled, still Jack's priestess, borne above the ground by the plants of the wild wood, her eyes green and black hair billowing like a Valkyrie's wings.

"Mary!" Lily was pulling little Henry's head into her nightclothes. The little boy must've heard the commotion and got out of bed to see what was wrong. More children stood on the stairs behind Lily and Amos.

The vines withdrew, lowering Mary. The knife clattered to the floor. Mary's eyes returned to normal; her hair lay flat around her shoulders. The room was suddenly still. Except for the sobbing of Giles Brennan.

Mary hurried to her charges and gathered them into an embrace. She kissed the top of Henry's head.

"It's okay, my ducks. Lily, take them back to bed."

"But, Mary?" Lily said, worried eyes alighting on Giles.

Mary regarded him coolly. "Mr Brennan was just leaving. I will see him out. Meet you upstairs shortly. Now go, my ducklings."

As the children hurried upstairs, casting curious looks behind them as they went, Mary turned to see Giles was already on his feet,

266

pulling up his britches and staggering to the door. She followed him and paused at the entrance to the foundling house, looking out onto the street. Giles lurched in frantic drunken steps. He stumbled, grazing his knees and hands on the cobblestones. He righted himself, panic still in his eyes, but feeling that he was at a safe distance from Mary now, he turned and gesticulated at her with the V of an English longbowman. "You are a fucking witch. I'll not forget this Mary Hooper. I'll see you get what's coming to you."

Mary descended one step at the door of the foundling house, and Giles paled. He turned and blundered into the night.

43

RICHARD DROVE through the night down to London. He pulled in at a roadside services to fill up. It was a bleak, empty place, harshly lit and grubby, despite the reek of detergent, as if covering something up. Like lilies at a wake. The plump checkout girl, her yellow polo shirt too small, disinterestedly read out the price for the three large bottles of water he bought. Her distant eyes flickered inquisitively to Richard stuffing the bottles into a plastic bag, but the flame of curiosity died with a tut when she was compelled to say, "That'll be five pee."

Richard went to the toilet out of habit, but nothing came out. When was the last time he'd been? He walked to the coffee shop, a lone traveller in a doldrum of empty chairs, and sat looking into a cup. Muzak played on an endless loop, almost quiet enough to be ignored - almost. Richard deflated and pulled out his phone. Maybe this was hell. Or possibly its waiting room.

Richard's phone buzzed, causing agitated ripples across the coffee's muddy surface. The message was from Rob.

'Fuck off.'

It was fair enough, and that's what he was doing. But he'd make it up to Rob, he would. He'd get to London and find the solution. They still had some time. How much he didn't know, but there must be some left. There *had* to be some left. He had to save Rob. And Jane?

The weight of it being over felt unreal. Richard gave a short huff of a laugh. *What was real? Jesus, how did his life get so metaphysical? Because you can't keep your dick in you pants, stupid.*

Richard's problems were a tempest, and he was the captain of a sinking ship. But disaster had left him only one choice. Up to now, Richard had been playing the good husband, trying to be father, playing at being a leader, when in all three of those jobs he was woefully unqualified. Maybe the truth of it was that he was a shit. He was good at that. The distraught face of Charlotte Tibbits at Lesley's funeral, snot glistening on her reddened nostrils, morphed into Jane screaming, tears streaming, and then Lesley handing over a twenty pound note to a cabbie, who became a policeman with a guilty look who took the twenty from Richard. *See? World class shit. Could be useful that. A self-serving prick will do anything. Imagine the motivation if his life depended on it?* But the shit seemed to have buggered off for a fag as the ship went down. Richard couldn't find him and it only made the feeling of isolation more profound. *There's only you now, start bailing, rig a mainsail, or do whatever the fuck a salty dog does, because you are a dog remember.*

Richard called his friend and former colleague John in London.

"Rich?"

"Not too late is it?"

"Nah, not sleeping tonight. Banged two Adderall, met the print deadline, now just finishing off the packing." John sounded almost manic, speaking a little too fast. Richard recognised it and missed it; ADHD medication was the mainstay of elite journalism. Booze and weed to level out, tempered with a little coke in the ladies - never the gents - toilets. Might as well snort it off a sewer pipe otherwise. Good times.

"Packing?"

"Didn't you hear? I got the Washington gig. Land of the brave, home of the fat fucks and all that. Flying out first thing from the Babylonian whore's anus that is Terminal 5."

"No, I didn't hear. Congratulations."

"Cheers, mate. Was a time it would have been yours. How is it in the Styx? You got chickens and a dog named Archie yet? Or are you phoning me from the grave because you died of fucking boredom?"

"Not yet. Working on it."

"Which one? The chickens or the slow agonising death?"

"Both."

John laughed.

"Listen, John, I need to ask a favour for old time's sake."

"Fuck! You're starting out with shit clichés, it must be serious." The copious use of the f-word and a thousand-and-one-word games was also a side effect of the Adderall. "Shoot, brother. It's a game of two-halves, give it everything you've got, don't count your chickens, leave it all on the table..."

"John!"

"Sorry, proceed, my good man."

"Can I crash at yours? I need a place for a few days. Maybe a week."

"Praise the fucking Lord. I'm off to the States and Jesus already loves me." John's voice suddenly changed to a mix of Elvis and a Southern Baptist preacher. "Hear me now, brother Peters, you are my rock upon which I will build my church. You've come to me in my time of greatest need. And though you do walk in the shadow of death, I shall fear no Airbnb scammers, because the Lord hath delivered you upon me, in Jesus' na... "

"So, that's a yes?"

John back to normal, "Well sure, Rich. Anything for you. I'll never forget that time you bailed me out over the thing with the donkey and Prince..."

"Is tonight okay?"

"Tonight? Shit, yeah. Like I said, I'll be up. We can have a single malt while I finish packing. Think I need to level out."

Previously, Richard would have felt a pang of envy for his friend getting the Washington beat covering the White House. But that all seemed another lifetime away now. He thanked him, told John he'd be down in a couple of hours.

Izzy's dossier sat in the passenger seat. He hadn't found anything in the pages so far. He hoped London, and the specialists she'd outlined, were the key. They *had* to be the key. Someone must know something.

A vague plan had formed in his mind. Get to London. Check *The Telegraph's* database for other curse stories. Follow up on the UCL professor. See if he could chase down any other experts, and then armed with that information, circle back to Southwell. See this Rev. Lovegrove. Put the pieces together, solve the puzzle, save the boy and the shit, and then pray there was a way back to Jane. It sounded tenuous. *Keep bailing*, he thought, remembering the lost boy look on Rob's face as he got into the car and drove away.

Glancing at the folder, the oval script of Izzy's handwriting caught his eye. God! The trouble he had caused himself. What did she think she was doing, turning up like that to the fair with her boyfriend? But Richard knew exactly what she was doing, and he had been a fool. *In the land of the sighted, the man with the one-eyed penis is blind, or whatever.* If only he'd kept his prick in his pants. None of this would have happened, but of course it... A thought glowed in his mind as chevrons slid under the car in a monotonous metronome. Richard's realisation, or maybe not a realisation, his leap, was that his infidelity was the key. Was that what started it, and not just the obvious trouble with Jane? He rubbed his eyes. Focused on the road. He was tired and thirsty, and everything was a knotted briar of cause and effect that he couldn't unpick, not yet, but maybe -- just maybe -- he could see the end of the knot.

When he arrived, car-shaped and bedraggled, at a Victorian townhouse chopped up into flats in the Brockley district of London, John opened the door and greeted Richard with a brotherly hug in the flat's narrow hallway. They threaded their way past the suitcases which were already packed and ready to be thrown in the back of a cab come the morning. The flat was nothing more than a bachelor pad. One bedroom, a kitchen, and a dining area that opened out onto a small living room. It was enough for John, a man with no family, married to his job. Richard thought it might suit him forever more. John offered Richard a whiskey. Richard took it, but the fiery liquid burnt his throat, making his dehydration all the more excruciating.

"You look terrible, mate," John said.

They sat the rest of the night reminiscing. Richard caught up on what he'd been missing. The inside gossip on celebrities, politicians, and royals. The sexploits of his colleagues.

"Remember Margot Williams-Smyth? Yeah, big tits and chicken legs. Had that blog about women's sexual liberation under that pseudonym we all knew was her because we'd shagged her?"

"What about her?" Richard played along.

"Seems she had a come to Jesus moment, so to speak. Got sprogged up with three of the little shits and moved over to being a programme controller for children's TV at the Beeb. She was on Woman's Hour last week spouting off about having never been so fulfilled. Christ, she must have forgotten about that threesome she had with Zeb Jaffar - remember he's the chief sports correspondent - and Littleworth, the England goalkeeper."

"Maybe she changed?"

"Oh, she changed alright. Took up pie eating along with thunking out demon spawn." John puffed out his cheeks and indicated the width of Margot's hips with his hands.

There was a time Richard would have loved this. Tonight, he was just glad this meaningless tattle kept him from sleep, where unsettling thoughts lurked in the spaces of his imagination. John only stopped talking when the sun finally came up and his phone alerted him to the taxi outside. Richard helped John throw the cases in the boot of the cab. Handing Richard the keys to the flat, John looked back at Richard with commiserations and seemed to be about to say something reassuring. But the moment for male intimacy passed the next instant, disappearing with John to another continent. Thankfully the cabbie was in a hurry.

"You two ladies need time for a snog, or can we go?"

John jumped in the cab which quickly performed tight U-turn and sped off.

The flat was quiet. Richard sat at a small table and opened the dossier, spreading the papers out. He drank deeply from a glass of water and looked at the riddle in front of him.

Richard quickly got absorbed, scouring but finding nothing.

When at 7:45 the doorbell rang, an hour and a half had passed. Thinking it must just be the postman, he opened the door.

"Hello, Richard."

It was Deborah Keeley, the other half of the affair Jane had found out about, the one that nearly destroyed their marriage, causing them to leave London and start again, stranding on the doorstep.

Richard stood stunned.

"Going to invite me in?" Deborah was smartly dressed in a pinstripe trouser suit, a three-quarter length camel coloured raincoat over the top, tied at her slim waist. Her blonde hair sat in a short bob around an oval face with high cheekbones. She was, Richard had always known, a younger version of Jane.

"Yes, of course. Sorry!" Richard stood aside. Deborah mounted the steps and turned sideways to edge by in the narrow hall. When they came face to face, she went on her tiptoes and kissed him on the cheek. Her lips lingered for only a moment, long enough to give him time to react, but he didn't. The message delivered and understood, without a word of reproach, Deborah walked through to the other room.

Richard made them tea and they sat awkwardly across from each other at the table, the notes messily arranged between them. Finally, Richard said, "You look well."

"You don't. In fact, you look bloody awful. I thought the plan was supposed to be a clean break. Starting afresh somewhere new. No stress, no distractions."

Richard knew what distractions she referred to.

Richard sighed. "It was. How did you know I was here?"

"That's changing the subject," Deborah said, blowing on her tea. She put the mug down, tilted her head, taking in the exhausted and dishevelled man sat across from her. "John told me. I'm glad he did."

"Good old John. Thought he was a mate."

"Don't be a prick, Richard." Deborah still had that journalist edge, Richard noticed. It was one of the things he liked about her. She was a shark, like him. There was no bullshit with her, no pretence, and in that way she was utterly different to Jane.

She wasn't finished. "I still care about you even though you don't deserve it. But I get it. I was the other woman. Things didn't break my way. We had fun. I thought it could have been more, but you decided otherwise. All the upheaval and stress, for what? I actually cried over you. Don't look surprised. I do have emotions. You clearly do too. Maybe we don't know each other as well as we thought. I don't just cry for anyone. I haven't cried since I was fourteen."

"Sorry," Richard said, mainly because he didn't really know what else to say.

"Don't give me that. I don't need your fucking sympathy, Richard. You'll piss me right off, and don't give me puppy dog eyes. It doesn't suit you. Makes me feel stupid for wasting tears on you. Christ, you've hardly been gone, now you're crawling back here and you look like you're on the edge of a nervous breakdown. What happened? Did the running away not solve it?"

"No." Richard visibly deflated. "Wasn't anything like that. Truth is I had another affair and Jane found out."

"For Christ's sake, Richard. I'd fucking throw you out. Now you *have* pissed me off." Gritting her teeth, Deborah couldn't look at him for a moment.

"I know. I've said it all to myself as well. I know it was stupid, but actually that's not what's wrong. Or rather, it is... it's part of it. Only, it's more complicated than that." Richard sank his head in his hands.

"I don't see what's so complicated about it. You were fucking me and then Jane found out. That was the end of that. I get that. But you're barely a few weeks up the road, living in the back arse of nowhere, and what? You can't keep your dick in your pants and end up nailing the office secretary?" She still had anger in her eyes, looking for an answer. "Jesus! You *did* fuck the secretary."

"She wasn't the secretary," Richard said. "She was a journalist on my team."

"Oh, brilliant. Now I feel like another cliché. You can shake hands, Richard. You don't have to stick your penis in every woman."

"That's not fair."

"I'm sorry," Deborah said. "Actually, I'm not. What was it then that made you need to bump nasties with the yokels? Was it not enough for Jane to throw you out? Christ, that woman's a saint."

"Don't talk about her like that," Richard said.

Deborah visibly prickled, but then softened a little. Maybe it was journalistic curiosity or maybe she still had deep feelings for this man. Whatever it was, her tone changed once again, "What was it then?"

Richard raised his head from his hands. "You won't believe me."

"Try me." Deborah reached across the table and squeezed his hand. "I've never seen anyone looking more like they're in a crisis than you. So, I guess you've got nothing to lose? Stop keeping it all inside and tell someone. I'm here. It might as well be me." She let go of his hand and sat back, taking hold of the tea once more. She waited.

Richard's eyes danced across the papers in front of him. Then he took a deep breath and told Deborah Keeley everything that had happened to him. She did not speak. This was his moment to get it out, however unbelievable it was. He told her about the Witchopper, that he suspected he and Rob were cursed. He explained that he thought time was running out, that he felt as though he was wasting away from the thirst, and that he was haunted and couldn't sleep, that he had visions and visitations, things that seemed so real. Deborah noticed the papers on the table and how they related to what Richard was saying. When he finished, he said, "That's it, the truth and the whole truth."

Deborah said nothing at first, she was thinking, and then swept a hand over the papers on the table. "So, all this is... research?"

Richard nodded.

"You think I'm insane."

"Do I believe you've seen a ghost and now you're mortally cursed? No, I probably don't believe that," Deborah said, not unkindly. "But I do believe that you *believe* you're cursed. And I believe that you need help. Whatever was between us before, whatever that added up to, still means that I want to help you. I know a psychiatrist..."

"No psychiatrist." Richard held up his hands. "Not yet. I've not ruled out the fact that I might be crazy, but Rob, he's experiencing the same things." His voice started to sound more desperate, and his eyes became wet with tears. "What I need... What I need, Debs." Richard could barely keep it together and he was grinding his index finger into one of the pages on the table like stubbing out a cigarette. "What I need, Debs, is to find a specialist in this kind of thing. Someone who knows about curses and folklore. I've got someone here." Richard rifled through the papers urgently until he found what he needed. "Here, this woman." He handed over the piece.

Deborah read.

"She's a professor at University College London, in anthropology?"

"That's her. I need to get in to see her this week, Debs. She's willing to talk to me. I just need to get in to see her as soon as possible." Tears brimmed his eyes.

"Okay, okay," Deborah soothed. She reached across the table to him again, taking his hand. "Tell you what, I'll phone her now. Bring the influence of *The Telegraph*." She looked at her watch. "It's still a touch early. We'll give it a minute. But will you do one thing for me?"

Richard looked up at her, tears still in his eyes. "What? Anything."

"Go and take a fucking shower, clean yourself up, and pull yourself together. You need to make yourself look presentable. Now piss off and do that while I phone work and get you a pass, and then I'll phone this Professor Sandra Josephs."

It was the friendliest kick up the arse he had ever had, and apart from a shower, it was just what he needed.

44

"THAT IS TOTALLY WEIRD," Jason said, once Rob had downed not only his but also Jason's glass of juice. Jason's mother had brought them a tray of biscuits, to which Jason had said, "She must think we're still eight years old." But he said it not only without rancour but with a fond look at the door as his mother closed it behind her. It was the weekend and they had arranged for Rob to come around on Saturday morning. He left his mother red-eyed and sitting in front of the television. She didn't want to cry in front of Rob, but he could hear her at night. Once, he found her in tears at the kitchen sink when he walked in. His dad had messaged him, and Rob thought about replying, but he couldn't bring himself to do it after his 'fuck off' text. It felt like betraying his mother, and the negative feelings that Rob had towards his father from his initial affair and then move from London was still a barely healed wound, that his father had ripped open again. They would finish up at school next week for exam leave, and with everything piling up, Rob couldn't wait to get to see Jason.

"You can never drink enough, then?" Jason asked.

"Nah, I've never drunk so much and, well..."

"Well what?"

Rob looked embarrassed. "It's my pee." Jason pulled a face of trepidation. "It's practically brown, like I'm dehydrated all the time."

"Nice!" Jason put down a biscuit, having lost his appetite, and swivelled in his chair to start looking at the computer again.

"So like I was saying, before *ma mère* so rudely interrupted us, I was researching what I could online about Mary Hooper and the curse. Well, it's not described as a curse as such." Jason clicked through various tabs on his laptop's screen.

"Did you find anything?" Rob said. Jason's room was covered in posters. Half of them were for old bands, like Nirvana, and others he'd not heard of, such as The Smiths and The Cure. He recognised one of the posters as David Bowie, a red-flash of lightning painted across his face, cheekbones high and red hair standing on end. It was the other posters that interested Rob more. There was a Frank Frazetta's *Conan the Barbarian* and one of his *Death Dealer* paintings, along with several Josh Kirby posters from the Discworld novels. Rob knew these from books his father had, and he remembered copying them when he was ten. He liked this kind of art very much. It had a level of detail which he now saw had influenced his own style. But the colours in these paintings were more developed, richer than Rob had ever dared to try. He was a technician, he knew. In many ways, he was approaching what those greats could do with form, but he was now having a sudden revelation about his limits and beyond that, the possibilities he'd cut himself off from. He'd tied himself to pencil and charcoal, venturing into colour only when he had to and with an unconscious caution. Suddenly, he wanted to be reckless, to experiment and paint. He tingled with the possibilities of the unknown.

"Earth to Rob. Hey, mate, did you hear any of what I just said? Are you having another... visitation?" Jason said the last word in a whisper, looking around to check for unwanted spectres. They'd never had a good time to debrief about the funfair. Rob's dad leaving had put an end to that night, and school had been a whirl of preparation for the impending exams, filled with instructions and timetables and last minute checks. Their peers had spent the second to last Friday of school signing each other's white shirts with permanent markers. No one wanted to sign Rob's. Jason had no interest in the tradition. Instead, he made the sound of a sheep baaing as he walked through the corridors, drawing dirty looks. Michael Tillitson took exception and told Jason to fuck off. Jason replied that he'd love to but as Michael's dad wasn't present to ride, he was unable to oblige. Michael had turned puce as his friends laughed at him. He was about to take a swipe at Jason when the imposing figure of Mr Philips, the PE teacher, appeared in the corridor. He'd caught a preternatural whiff of danger, the kind of instincts twenty years of teaching bestowed.

"Tillitson, did you break a nail?"

"What, sir?" Michael was bemused.

"A nail, did you break one?"

"No, sir."

"My mistake. Then clear off before you end up in detention for your last week of school."

"But sir, Potty said..."

"Don't tell tales, Michael. You're not a seven-year-old girl. Or am I wrong about that as well?"

"No, sir."

"Good. Then why are you still here?"

Jason glided off, blowing Michael a kiss behind Mr Philips's back.

Whenever he'd had a spare minute, Jason had been looking into his new friend's problem. He'd checked a couple of books on folklore out of the library too, but they contained nothing helpful. However, while trawling through pages of search engine results, he'd happened upon a subreddit chat about the Witchopper.

"No, she's not here," Rob said. "I was looking at your posters."

"The Frazettas?"

"Yeah, I love him."

"You should do some stuff like that."

"That's what I was thinking."

"You could illustrate a story of mine. But we'd better stop you dying of a curse first." Jason tapped his laptop with his middle finger.

Rob shuffled his chair closer to Jason's. "Sorry, I've a few things on my mind."

"Understatement of the year," Jason said, clicking on the track-pad. "Here." He handed the laptop to Rob to read the chat in the subreddit. It was about supernatural deaths. The other posts were from all over the world, but there were a few among them connected with their little town. After the preliminary outline of the Witchopper story for those that didn't know, the hanging of a witch that cooked up the children in her care and fed them to the other children - a little turn Rob hadn't heard before - and then the development of the playground game and accompanying song, the writer *NottsFC69* went on to say:

No one has noticed that every death associated with the Witchopper and the Witch's Brew pub are men. Every one of them. They all seem to die suddenly from some sort of chronic disease like a heart attack or liver failure. Since several of them were landlords, you can bet some booze pickled their livers over the years. But what I find interesting is this. I've looked into every case I can find about her, and there is another pattern on top of it all being men. We only get this information in a few of the reports that actually mention the victim saw the ghost, and they say...

First the screen froze. Rob swiped on the track pad again to no effect. He tried one of the cursor keys, but still the screen was frozen. He was about to say something to Jason, who was reading over his shoulder, when the screen went black but for a small piece of text contained within arrows, like an old piece of MS-DOS programming language.

<POTTY SUCKS COCK>

The text lingered like a death rattle and the computer died.

Jason took back the laptop and started to press his keys ineffectually. "Shit!" he said. "I've revision notes on this; and stories. Shit! Shit! Shit!" He was now hitting the keys.

"What happened?"

"Not what, Rob. Who? And I've a good idea."

"Ally?"

"Who else?" Jason slumped back into his chair. "I'm in Computing with him. He's a fucking wizard. Who do you think has been torturing you and Julie online?"

"He can do that?"

"That and more. What you can do with a pencil and I can do with a pen, Ally can do with code."

Rob thought for a moment. "But what did the rest of it say?"

"Three to four weeks. That's what the guy said. A few of the stories mention seeing the ghost three to four weeks before they die."

Rob paled. "But it's three weeks today."

45

MARY SAT with all her children outside the Reverend Moseley's study. The housekeeper had shown them in and informed the Reverend of their presence before scuttling off. With so many people stuffed into it, the hallway was cramped. Little Amos coughed, and Mary pulled him to her. She felt the rattle of phlegm on his chest. Several of the children had the same terrible cold and wiped their snotty noses on their sleeves before either Mary or Lily could hand them a hand-kerchief.

A grandfather clock ticked slowly in the hallway. It was consider-ably warmer inside than out, but still the cold would not thaw from their bones. The vicarage stood in the great shadow of the Minster, leaving them in a thin shroud of light. Next to the door, a grandfather clock counted off seconds with ticks as slow and viscous as the phlegm on Amos's chest. Growing bored, many of the little ones pushed each other. Small curious hands sought out unfamiliar objects. Mary whispered in their ears and cuddled them into behav-ing. But even Lily had become distracted as the grandfather clock ticked. Blooming into a young woman, her body was changing, hips filling out, chest pluming, and with them her powers grew. In her boredom she unfurled a hand, and from her palm a small and succulent nettle uncurled.

"Not here, my duck." Mary placed her hand lightly on her wrist. It broke Lily's concentration, and the tiny nettle withered in on itself and disappeared into valleys of fortune crisscrossing her skin.

The children jumped when the door of the study swung open, and the slender form of the Reverend Moseley appeared, shoulders rounded, neck too long, black hair swept across his pallid forehead. When he smiled, little Amos and the others shrunk away. Moseley's smile twitched.

"Ah, Miss Hooper, come in." Reverend Moseley stood aside to allow her to enter. Peeling him from her skirts, Mary handed Amos to Lily.

Moseley shut the door behind them. The study was darker than the hallway. Dust motes floated in feeble shafts of light. A fire crackled, scattering muddy shadows beneath the furniture. There was a smell of dust and sweat and a sweet note of port in a crystal decanter. Bookcases filled with many volumes lined the walls, adding to the foreboding gloom. On a large polished mahogany desk before the window were neat piles of parchment and a pen, left at rest on blotting paper next to an engraved silver inkwell. It was another world to Mary, a strange place where the alchemy of wealth turned banknotes into luxuries and a warm crackling fire.

"Do take a seat, Miss Hooper." The Reverend gestured at one of the wingback chairs squatting next to the fire. He poured himself a glass of port into a small crystal goblet and took up the seat opposite Mary on the other side of the fire. Taking a sip of his port, Moseley savoured it for a moment, letting it sit in his mouth with his eyes almost closed, before swallowing it and reclining in the wingback chair.

"And how may I help you this day? I trust that you are well?"

Mary sat straight-backed, perched on the edge of the chair, hands clasped in her lap. "Thank you for seeing me, Reverend. I've come to see you about the matter I tried to raise at the last church council meeting."

Moseley nodded solemnly. "I'm afraid we had no time to consider your request. The church is frightfully busy, as I'm sure you understand."

"Yes, Reverend," Mary wrung her hands together, "but if you will, it is very important. Could I perhaps ask you to consider the request now?"

"I'm terribly sorry, Ms Hooper. I did, of course, read your note. The church, as you know, takes a great interest in the foundling house. What good Christian wouldn't? And we already pay to maintain your house and those children under your care, do we not?" Moseley regarded Mary looking down the end of his pointed nose and took another sip of port.

"Indeed, sir, but if you will, with the weather being so cold this winter and now into spring, we spent much more of our money on fuel for the fire. The children are in need of new clothes and shoes. I've done my best to repair them, but the real problem is food."

"I hear children can be picky eaters. I have a brother based over in Lincoln at the cathedral. His children are nearly adults now, but little Lucien, his youngest son, went through a phase of eating only eggs."

Mary moved uncomfortably, unsure if Moseley was being deliberately obtuse. This meeting had been hard to get. He'd refused to see her three times, so she pressed on. "Eggs would be wonderful, but we can barely afford bread from Gatsby's. We've relied on the charity of several kind souls in the town."

A green log rolled in shifting embers, and sap sizzled in the flames.

"Charity is the most blessed of things. It warms my heart that our fellow man is so generous to these poor foundlings."

"But it's not enough," Mary said, a little more forcefully that she had meant to. The Reverend stiffened, fingers coiling taut around the stem of his glass.

"That is a most ungrateful thing to say, Ms Hooper. A slap in the face to those who have shown you nothing but goodwill."

"Oh, I didn't mean that, my good Reverend."

"Didn't you?" The Reverend raised an eyebrow and took another sip.

"We are also so grateful for all that the church, I mean to say, for all that *you* have done for us."

There was a soft and dangerous quality to Moseley's next words. "Is that so?"

The green log in the fire gave a viper's hiss, and its sap bubbled like flesh roasted on a spit.

"Yes, sir. But, if I may, Reverend, the children have been sick this winter and much of our money went to Doctor Goodyear when you insisted we call him out."

"It would have been foolish not to call a doctor when the children were sick, would it not?"

"Yes, sir, but money is scarce, and I..."

"And you *what*, Miss Hooper?" the Reverend interrupted. "Do you remember our arrangement? In exchange for your position, a roof over your head and what we in the church council believe is a more than generous stipend, you were to desist in your previous activities."

"Yes, sir, I have..."

The fire hissed once more and the Reverend cutting in again. "Have you, indeed?"

"Yes, sir. Of course, sir."

"That is good, Miss Hooper, as the church would be exceedingly disappointed if we were to find otherwise."

Mary cast her eyes down and nodded. Moseley's mouth twisted up, causing his already dark and beady eyes to narrow further. "Well then, I'm glad this has all been sorted out."

"But, sir," Mary blurted out. The Reverend, who had been half out of his seat, sank back into his chair.

"What is it, Miss Hooper?"

A globule of sap fizzled sibilantly in the fire.

"Sir, the children are losing weight. They're nothing but skin and bones. They remain weak after the colds we had through the winter. Couldn't the church just..."

"Just find you more money?" The Reverend finished the sentence for Mary.

"Yes," Mary said, keeping eyes on the silk rug between them. She could not see the smile crawl across the Reverend's face as he sat forward, rearing up like a snake.

"Money? Thirty pieces of silver. Jesus at the temple door steps. The root of all evil. I'm afraid the church has no more money to give, my dear Miss Hooper. But..." The Reverend let the word hang in the air, dangling it before Mary as desperate as she was.

She looked up into his cold eyes, shadows dancing across his sickly complexion. "But what, sir?"

Moseley slunk forward, perching on the farthest edge of his seat. His hand crept across the space between them until it came to rest on Mary's knee.

"But *I* am a man of some means. Not all of my family are godly men. My grandfather was Geoffrey Moseley of Norfolk and much of the land is in the family's hands today. I had a calling and whilst the church pays me a Christian salary, I also have funds of my own."

"Yes?" Hope rose in Mary. It could have been hunger or desperation or the effects of both that dulled her senses, leaving her unprepared.

"As you know, I remain a bachelor. I have often considered myself married to the church. I am first and foremost a good Christian man. As such, I, Mary, could make some of those personal funds available to you..."

"Really, sir? I..."

"If," Moseley raised his voice, preparing to strike, "if you were to become my wife."

Mary looked up with a start. She suddenly felt cold and unclean in front of the fire. Hidden in the shadows, the Reverend's hand had become a dangerous animal. Mary swallowed the lump in her throat and resisted the urge to flinch. This could be the answer to her problems. They so desperately needed money for food, for the fire, for new clothes and shoes. Could she do it? Maybe? Many women had done such things before. She wouldn't be the first. Who has the privilege of marrying for love? Then again, how many of those poor souls came to her, with bruises on their backs, black eyes, and children in their bellies they did not want? These marriages made wounds not visible from the outside, and there were no remedies for their sadness. Many of the children stood outside the door were a result of that. She might be poor, but that didn't make her stupid. She knew Moseley had been manoeuvring her, manipulating her life since Aunt Jenny passed, and now she knew why. Mary forced herself to look at the Reverend. Once more she wanted to recoil from him. He looked at her through the small black eyes, and all Mary could see was a viper who'd been lying in wait, calculating, who had reared up ready to swallow its prey whole now that she was vulnerable in his lair. Could she do it? Could she marry such a duplicitous man?

"Thank you, sir. It is a most gracious offer. But I could not ask you to marry me out of duty. That would make neither of us happy. You do not love me..." And she would come to regret this final sentence, "and I do not love you."

Moseley snatched his hand away from Mary's knee. It was both a reprieve and the judge's sentence. The Reverend's face became hard. The muscles in his jaw rippled.

"Then good day, Miss Hooper. I have much work in urgent need of my attention."

He finished his port with one gulp and turned his back to Mary, staring into the flames that hissed and spat.

Mary rose and left the study. She hurried her brood from the hall-way. The grandfather clock's tick echoed, counting away the hours of their lives.

46

His hands moved swiftly over the keys. Other than the quiet whir of the internal fan cooling the computer's tower, the only sound in his bedroom was the clicking of his finger strikes. He probed, testing the defences where they existed, breaking them down where they were weak, circumventing or fooling them with false protocols where they were stronger. He was untraceable, for all but the most skilled of hackers. He had disguised his IP address, and a programme ran bouncing him randomly between servers in foreign countries. Another program of his own devising laid false trails of breadcrumbs, creating patterns of attacks within which to hide. It wasn't hard, not for Ally. He picked up bounties for 'ethically' hacking company websites and reporting the weaknesses. It wasn't much of a challenge, but it gave him a source of legitimate money, which had its uses. But money was less fun than information, little secrets: the browsing history of teachers and members of the community; caches of pictures they really shouldn't be looking at; even videos of them masturbating in front of webcams, tut, tut. He collected their secrets and kept them stored away, trophies in a virtual box he kept locked with an encryption of his own making. The door to his bedroom burst open.

"Are you ever *not* on that thing?"

Ally left the screen alone. It was lines of code his uncle Callum wouldn't understand, even if Ally explained.

With heavy-lidded eyes, his uncle held a glass of wine, and from the way the edges of his words were slurred, Ally guessed it wasn't his first.

"Spoke to your da." His Belfast accent thickened when he was drunk. The affectations of the Law degree he got from Queen's University Belfast fell away so that he could have been back on the Falls Road, carrying packages for out of work freedom fighters who'd exchanged peddling dreams of freedom for other wages of sin. Both were funded by the same things: drugs, guns, moneylending, and girls.

"When?"

"Just now." Callum took another gulp of wine. A few drops splashed on his pressed shirt.

"Can I speak to him?"

Callum looked like he was about to laugh. "No. He never asked for you. Can't call everyone from prison."

"What did he want?"

Another gulp and a misjudged lean against the wall that sloshed wine over Callum's hand. He didn't seem to notice. "His appeal was turned down. Seems like we're stuck with you." He pulled out a key from his pocket. "Here." He tossed the metal shard. It fell short of Ally, landing on the carpet at his feet. The fan whirred, cooling the computer. Ally didn't bend to pick it up. "Suit yourself. Eat if you want to." Callum peeled himself from the wall and staggered off.

Ally left the key where it was. He'd had a copy made months ago, so he could unlock the cupboards of food and the small fridge which they permitted him to eat from. There was a file in Ally's box of trophies, a box within a box, which contained a chimera of secrets about his uncle Callum and his charade of civility, running shell companies to wash all his father and his associates' dirty laundry. The irony was that Ally could have done it infinitely better, without the old school subterfuge, punishment beatings, and people trafficking. Not that Ally judged. Morality was a construct like a computer programme, built to serve the herd who needed a simplified user interface to navigate the complex web of the world. But Ally wasn't cattle; he was a virus.

Tapping at keys, Ally put away his box of secrets. That was a side issue for now. He slid through the ether and opened a door he'd long had a key for. Food was a need, but it wasn't the only one. He had full control over Julie's computer. It sat on her desk with a view over most of the room. He kept the screen off, but the webcam was on, an unseen eye watching, recording everything.

———

THE GIRLS WERE GETTING CHANGED. They had been studying together, but now it was time to get into pyjamas and watch a rom-com. It had been Sally's idea.

"I don't know about you, but I can't wait to never have to calculate the angle of the hypotenuse ever again. I mean, seriously, when will that ever be useful?" Effie peeled off her T-shirt and held it dangling from one hand, with her other hand on her hip. "It's basically child abuse. They don't even make rapists and murderers do trigonometry in prison. It would be against the Geneva Convention of Human Rights." She folded the T-shirt and reached behind to unfasten her bra.

The camera watched.

"I don't mind it so much," Sally said, down to her underwear, and brushing her hair in the desktop mirror next to Julie's computer. "There's always a right answer, as long as you know how to work it out. Bingo! You get an A." She turned to look over her shoulder at her reflection to see if she'd brushed out the kinks at the back.

Julie stood before a full-length mirror in her bra, the top button of her jeans undone. Her hand drifted over her belly. Her eyes glazed, looking into the mirror but not seeing the young woman standing there.

Sally stripped off her underwear. The camera zoomed in. She hopped quickly into her pyjama bottoms and pulled the baggy T-shirt over her head.

"What do you think, Jules? Jules?" Effie said, still in nothing but her knickers. "Jules," she came behind Julie, "stop looking at your fabulous self and tell us, to trig or not to trig, that is the question?"

"Huh? What?" Julie seemed surprised to see Effie there.

"To trig or not to trig? Not to trig, right? Pointless crap." Effie lay her arm across Julie's shoulder and looked at her through the mirror. "What's up, babe?"

"Wow," Sally said, "Have you seen this?" Sally was leaning over Julie's desk looking at the windowsill.

Effie tutted. "What is it?" She left Julie at the mirror and walked over to Effie, not seeing the camera following her. Julie stripped off her jeans, and had her fingers in the elastic of her knickers about to pull them down, when Effie said, "That is weird. You must have damp or something."

"Damp?" Sally said. "No, it's mould you get with damp, not... What is that?"

Julie had stopped undressing and joined her friends in front of her desk. "It's a forget-me-not," she said, curiously.

"Right, but what's it doing growing out of your windowsill?" Effie cocked her head to the side.

Julie leaned in. "Beats me."

Sally dove onto Julie's bed and Effie moved away, her curiosity satisfied. She finished stripping off and pulling on her pyjamas. Julie reached for the wild flower that had burst up through the white-painted wood next to her family of cacti. As she did, the flower appeared to bend towards her fingers. Julie thought there must be a draft, although she felt none. When she moved her fingers away, the flower straightened again, as though standing to attention. Life bursting forth, so delicate and beautiful. The thought not only frightened Julie; it terrified her. Tears began to smudge the flower in fractals of colour.

"What are we watching then? I've got Dad's card details loaded into my Amazon account, so we can watch whatever movie we want." Effie laughed. "Or we could just go on a spending spree and bankrupt the old boy."

"I fancy that new one with Channing Tatum," Sally suggested.

Julie stood in her bra and jeans in front of her computer. The tears rolled down her face. The camera zoomed in, focusing on her chest.

From the bed, Sally said, "I want to see that new musical."

Effie pretended to puke. "You couldn't pay me to watch a musical."

"What if Channing Tatum was in a musical?" Sally said.

"Then I'd turn the sound down and switch the lights off." Effie made a scene of closing her eyes and running her hand down the front of her pyjamas as she chewed her lip in mock ecstasy. "What about you, Jules?"

The question was like a switch that turned the lights out. The room went black, and there was the sound of true silence, where all the electrical machines died and the background hum became perceptible only because of its absence.

Effie and Sally let out a mock scream of shock.

"What happened?" Sally said.

Julie was sobbing. "Mum and dad must have forgotten to pay the electric bill again."

Effie and Sally hurried to Julie through the dark. The streetlights shone in a pale reflection on Julie's skin.

"Hey, hey, Jules," Effie said. "It's okay."

Julie knew they thought she was crying through embarrassment. It wasn't the first time her parents didn't have enough money to pay their bills.

"We can watch it on my phone?" Sally said.

"It's not that!" Julie wiped her eyes, unable to stop the tears.

"What is it then?" Effie wrapped Julie in a tight hug.

"I'm late." Julie sobbed into Effie's shoulder, who mouthed 'OMG!' silently to Sally.

"Oh, Jules!" Sally joined the hug. "Are you sure?"

Julie sniffed. "I'm always clockwork. It should have started a week ago."

———

HE HAD HER, about to get naked, and the screen had gone blank. Ally checked and double checked. It wasn't something at his end, so it had to be a local problem. Julie's computer was offline. That could mean several things, none of which Ally could fix on his side. Still, he had some nice footage of both Effie and Sally naked, and Julie down to her bra. Not a bad day's fishing. There would be other chances, and he had plenty of other footage of Julie and many other women changing in the privacy of their bedrooms, not to mention the footage of Julie with Danny.

Ally clicked his mouse, running back the footage, cutting out the unnecessary pieces until it was a short movie of the best bits. Effie wasn't half bad, and he'd work on access to her devices tomorrow. For now, he unzipped his fly and before rewinding the movie to the start, Ally stared at Julie's small firm breasts hidden teasingly behind a thin piece of fabric. His eyes darkened as his hand slid inside his boxer shorts. He pulled at himself, knowing that there was nothing in the world he desired more than Julie Brennan, and he would do anything he could to make her his.

47

THE SKY WAS A MOLDERING blanket of greys hanging over Southwell. It leaked a fine rain with no beginning or end, which had blighted the harvest. Hops, wheat, barley and even the hardier hemp crops had drowned. For the poor folk of the town, rations were scant and generosity hard to give. In the meagre dawn before Sunday service, the foundlings grumbled half asleep, putting on cold and threadbare clothes as Mary and Lily readied them for Church. With emaciated arms above their heads, ribs poked through their skin so they looked like a troop of little skeletons raised from the dead. Their bellies had begun to distend with hunger and growled feebly for the thin gruel Mary struggled to put together. Lily had scavenged the last of the nettles in the hedgerows, blotching her hands with welts. They added the weeds to the remaining handful of barley in the jar, flavoured with a pinch of thyme and thinned with water. Mary refused to take her own portion, giving it instead to Lily, whom she looked on with pride as they put on their winter coats and travelling cloaks, assembling in the hall of the foundling house.

"Everybody hold hands." Mary led them like a mother hen to

church. Lily followed up the rear, making sure that none of their ducklings strayed.

"Good day, Mr Hawthorne, Mrs Hawthorne." Mary bowed her head deferentially. With nothing more than a hard stare, the Hawthornes crossed the road in front of them. They hurried their way to Church, heads down and collars up against the rain.

As always, Mary was given the back pew at the Minster. She and Lily settled the fidgeting little ones, encouraging them to be quiet. It was in vain. Their hacking coughs echoed through the austere nave. The reverberating choir of sickness produced ruffled feathers, reproachful glances, and exchanged whispers like fleas hopping between dogs. As the incense burned, and the sermon droned on, many of the little ones dropped off, only to wake when all stood for hymns. They would then hack a parody of the joyful praise being sung. When the singing stopped, they sunk back into their seats and leaned against one another, eyes drooping, their limbs heavy.

The Reverend Moseley was the final priest to give a sermon in the Sunday morning liturgy. He slunk from his pew dressed in all the glory of his vestments and ascended the carved oak pulpit that rose above the congregation. From there he surveyed them with small black eyes. His tongue flicked from his mouth to wet his lips before he spoke. He read from the book of Revelations 3:19.

"Those whom I love, I reprove and discipline, so be zealous and repent."

"God is love," Moseley said. "But I say *what is love*? God is the father. And could we say that a father loves his children if he does not tend to their misdeeds? Would we say he is a good father if he stayed the birch or belt should his child be rude and sinful? We would not. Such a man would be weak and deplorable. Does the Bible not say the Lord giveth, and the Lord taketh away?" The Reverend nodded solemnly and many of the congregation nodded along with him. "And this is the true description of the word. There is no love without justice. Love is the reward for our good behaviour. When we behave as a good Christian made in His image, then we are love. But stray from the path of righteousness," the Reverend's voice rose shrilly, "and then, like any loving father, we should expect His wrath. For it is

God's love to judge the wicked. So in these hard times, look not to the Lord God on High," the Reverend raised his finger into the air, casting it reproachfully across the congregation, "instead, look at what punishments He has given us for our sins. Look at yourself and ask if you are a good Christian. Look around you, open your eyes to the sinful, heathen ways which make you stray from God's path, tempted as if by that serpent in the Garden of Eden. For did not the serpent easily tempt Eve, who then led Adam astray? And what did God do? He showed them, because He is a good father and loved His children. He punished them, banishing them from paradise so they may learn the error of their ways. A long, harsh winter is to come if we fall from His good graces. We must behave as good Christian men and women and punish those who stray from the path of the righteous. Through stern judgment we act as the loving hand of God."

Silence fell across the nave, only to be broken by Amos' rattling cough from the back pew. A collection of bones wrapped in damp clothes, Mary gathered him to her, as many heads in the congregation swivelled to cast their judgement.

The service ended and Mary and her children remained seated, while the rest of the congregation filed out. This was one of the many conditions of Mary's employment. They were to be a reminder of the Church's good works. Seven-year-old Sarah, with a crow's nest of blonde hair, stuck out her tongue at the Hawthornes when they looked down on the foundlings.

"Don't do that, my duck." Mary put a hand on Sarah's shoulder to remind her of her manners.

"They are a blight," Mrs Hawthorne told her husband, who nodded agreeably at the assertion.

Lily shot Mary a look but knew to stay her tongue. Mary was already averting her eyes so no one would see. The Hawthornes approached the towering west door of the Minster. Mary opened out both hands, stretching out her fingers, and whispered.

Min sweostorum, cuman. Fyrenwordun beswican. Heo acwellan swa swa beame.

Mrs Hawthorne did not see the thin brown root squirm from between the flagstone to make a loop, like a rabbit snare. There came a sound like birds fluttering in a hedgerow, in fields far away. The toe of Mrs Hawthorne's boot caught in the root. Just as they were about to shake hands with the Reverend Moseley, she let out a squawk and pitched forward, almost taking her husband with her. He righted her and they both flushed with embarrassment before the vicar. The root slunk back between the flagstones; they looked for the cause and found none. Moseley cast a glance at Mary. Her back was turned to him, but she could feel his eyes.

With the church empty, Mary rose with her children. Seeing her, Moseley moved off before she could reach the door.

"Reverend Moseley! Sir, could I please have a moment of your time?" He did not come back, and Mary hurried her family after him, but they were sick and tired, and moved like millstones with no grain. By the time they rounded the side of the Minster, the Reverend was already through the gate of the vicarage, without a look back.

Mary and her troop of little skeletons stood alone in the grave-yard, as a sky of grey ribs grumbled, as if for a thin gruel that would never sate its hunger.

48

JULIE CARRIED the heat of a dandelion on her back, which smouldered in a near cloudless sky. Nerves turned her stomach on the walk to the Hanging Tree. She was meeting Effie in town later to buy a pregnancy test, making this feel more like a walk from the cells for sentencing. But before meeting Effie, Danny was waiting for her under the guise of escaping the drudgery of exam revision and the anger of his father for what happened at the funfair. Julie's impending exams now felt irrelevant as she walked to the weekend soundtrack of lawnmowers chomping through back gardens, TV chefs demonstrating recipes no one would make (drifting through half-open windows), and cars humming down roads, ferrying children to dance classes and martial arts lessons. A life was growing inside her, and Julie had never felt so powerful and so vulnerable. She should tell Danny, but wasn't sure what to say. 'I'm pregnant, well, maybe. I don't know.' The future hadn't been something Julie thought about much. Now it loomed as a huge and uncertain terror.

Danny leaned against the dead tree in his T-shirt with a picnic blanket rolled up under his arm. Bandages covered his forearms. Six black stitches pulled the flesh back together along his Ken doll hairline. Smaller lacerations peppering his face had granulated into hard scabs. A bruise spread from his right eye to his temple and down to the meat of his cheek, marking the side of his face like oil edging a muddy pool. Seeing Julie, waiting to cross the road with arms hugged around her belly, Danny jogged over.

"Are you cold, babe?"

Butterflies churning, Julie shook her head. "Where are we going?"

"Thought we'd take a walk." He pulled her close.

They kissed, and Danny's tongue forced its way into Julie's mouth. The growth on his face was rough and Julie tried not to pull away. Hands grabbed at her buttocks, and something irked her. Danny was rough, yes, but his body was tense, and Julie had the sense of this being forced, as if he was making himself do it. He was like this that night when they.... when they made love, and now part of him was growing inside her - maybe. A pulse of panic rushed through her like icy saline in her veins. It was the cold thought that after all he'd put her through, he didn't like her, and that he'd grown bored already. But then she could feel his hardness pressed into the soft belly. She wanted to pull away protectively. But didn't. Finally she pulled away from the kiss, needing to breathe, and looked up at the stitches across his forehead.

"How are your cuts?"

Danny let go of Julie so suddenly it was almost as if he was throwing her away. Julie rocked back on her heels. "They're fine. Let's go."

"Did Rob and Jason really do that to you?"

"Don't be stupid. Like I said, I just wanted to talk to Rob, tell him to stay away from you. When they saw me, they ran and I slipped. Fell into a fucking mirror. Cheap shit shattered all over me, didn't it? They should pay me compensation."

Danny told his father something different. It turned out that at least in the circumstance of being involved in an assault in a public place, having a father as Chief Constable went a long way towards removing any legal action. Danny told his father he was jumped in the house of mirrors. In the confusion of reflections, Danny claimed he couldn't tell who it was. Ally, Chris, and Henry had played dumb. And although Sally wanted to tell the truth, she went along with Julie and Effie, who said what Danny wanted. The fairground workers wanted to press charges for criminal damage and demanded compensation. When the renewal of their permit for the rest of the spring and summer season came up, the travellers moved on out-of-pocket and without justice.

"At least it wasn't Rob, then." Julie didn't know why she said it. Maybe just to have something to say as they walked towards the mill.

"Why do you give a toss about him? After this, I've definitely got a date with that pretty-boy." It was a strange choice of words, Julie thought. Rob *was* pretty, and her stomach fluttered again. Suddenly, Julie felt as though her life was a series of conditional ifs with unknown answers. *If* she was pregnant; *if* Danny liked her; *if* she had a baby; *if* she didn't: then what? The fluttering in her stomach was now a tingle of nerves that fizzed to her fingertips.

"I don't care about Rob. I care about you getting in a fight." It came out sounding needy.

Danny came to a stop and threw his head back laughing. "Oh, babe, you don't need to worry about me." He pulled her to him. "But that little prick is going to get what's coming to him." His mouth was on hers again, forcing his way inside, body still taut. They were some way off, but Julie thought she could hear the stream beyond the mill. It hadn't rained for days, and yet it sounded as though the water was a swell of angry whispers.

Danny broke away, and the whispering stopped. "Come on; I've got something planned."

They reached the old mill and crossed the stream at the stepping stones. The water babbled, little more than ankle deep. Birds flitted to and from their nests. Lambs, ready for the spring slaughter and a future lying on polystyrene trays wrapped in clingfilm, bleated in the fields. Then they reached the willow tree, and Danny parted the drooping boughs covered in leaves of yellow and electric green. As Julie passed inside, he placed his hand on her buttock, fingers in its cleft, and pushed her through.

The detritus of the previous night's teenage bacchanal still littered the ground: discarded cans and bottles of cider and cheap wine, cigarette ends and the roaches of joints. Danny cleared a spot near the trunk of the willow and laid out a blanket. Julie stood hugging her arms, trying to hide her hesitation when he patted the rug next to him and reclined on one elbow. Julie sat cross-legged next to him, looking around, remembering the last time she was here, with Effie, Sally, and Rob and the rest. It was different in the daytime. Light sprinkled through the canopy in hazy glimmers of gold.

Danny stroked up Julie's inner thigh, moving closer to the crotch of her jeans. She took his hand in hers, lacing the fingers together, and lay on her side so she was propped up on her elbow in the mirror image of Danny. She wanted to talk about that night they had made love for the first time and say that it was her first time. She wanted to tell him that her period was late, and she thought she was pregnant. The weight of that idea, of the consequences that would follow from the reality of being a teenage mother at sixteen, weighed impossibly heavy on her. So when he pushed himself up onto his hand to look down at Julie, casting a shadow on her thoughts, and then lowered his face to hers, his mouth opening once more, as if to swallow her, she allowed his tongue to silence the words that needed to be said. She lay back, and he leaned against her, the weight of his body pressing her to the earth. The stream was whispering again. The lambs bleated. It was as if she could feel how carefree they were, and it made Julie sad.

Danny explored her mouth deeper and more aggressively. His body was still tense, his eyes closed, as if he was off in another place, his hands roaming over Julie's belly and then under her shirt and up to her chest, cupping and then squeezing her breasts as he pressed his crotch rhythmically into her thigh. Soon he grew frustrated and placed her hand on the fly of his jeans. She rubbed him as much to placate him as anything else. The noises of the town were not far off. The willow was not an uncommon place to come; people roamed the fields or walked their dogs along the nearby nature trail. They could be discovered at any moment. Julie didn't like the idea. Maybe Danny did. Maybe that was why he was so tense and urgent?

Still Danny pressed on, pushing forward eagerly into Julie's hand, grunting into her mouth. His hand roamed lower, slipping beneath the hem of her jeans and then of her panties. Julie stopped rubbing him and pulled his hand gently up back to her chest. He stayed there a moment. Julie's mind raced, wondering what to do next. How to stop this without hurting his feelings? How to get the courage to talk to him, properly talk to him about things that mattered. Then Danny changed position and put his arm behind her head and laced his fingers through Julie's free hand. Her other was trapped between the two bodies. Now she could not prevent his hand from roaming. It headed straight for her crotch. The whispering of the stream grew angry again. The chirp of birds was sharp and clear. The nerves tingling throughout Julie's body were now electric. Every sense was acute and she wasn't sure where *she* ended and the trees and grass and the animals in the hedges began. She could feel them all. The fluttering of their tiny hearts. The furtive twitches at potential dangers. The pulse that connected everything.

Danny undid the button of Julie's jeans and slid down the zip. Julie tried to move her pinned arm to no effect. The whispering stream hissed. Something rumbled, a vibration like blood tunneling through her veins, coursing through her eardrums, but felt through the air and the ground beneath them.

His fingers slid beneath the thin material of Julie's underwear. Danny's knee wedged between hers, forcing apart her legs. She tried to say no, but it came out as a garbled moan in Danny's mouth and only encouraged him. The rumble of a distant train, or maybe it was the babbling stream, suddenly deluged with water. His hand moved between Julie's legs and there was nothing more she could do without making a scene.

"Shit! Something stung me."

Danny sat up and held his wrist. Fresh blood trickled from one of his scabs. Freed of Danny's weight, Julie sat up, scrabbling back and pulling up her knees. She thought she saw a vine of thorny brambles slinking back into the earth next to Danny. With a sudden whip of a door being shut, the stream silenced, the rumbling stopped, but the pulse of life around them still throbbed under Julie's skin.

Danny was sucking at the wound, grimacing. "Must have been a bee or spider." He looked around.

"Are you okay?" Julie scanned to see if anything else had come from the ground as she fastened the buttons of the jeans.

"What the hell was that?" Danny scowled, looking in the air for the culprit.

She could still feel it: everything. Was this part of being pregnant, becoming sensitive? The breeze was like a baby's breath on the leaves. The bending of blades of grass. The hard nubs of blackberries, still green, but with fermenting alchemy of life popping effervescently within their cells. The heartbeat of the world, pounding out the rhythm of life. It was exhilarating. Powerful. Julie's fears blew away like a dandelion clock. She was confident.

"Danny."

"What?" The blood continued to trickle from his wrist.

"I want to tell you something."

"What is it, babe?" Danny sank back on the rug, kissed Julie's lips and her neck. Julie could have tutted in exasperation. The ground seemed to quiver.

There was a sudden flurry of movement in the branches of the willow, then a large labrador broke through. He gave two quick barks of excitement and then ran over to Julie, wagging its tail, muscling between her and Danny and knocking him back.

Julie laughed with joy. She loved dogs, but her parents had always said they couldn't afford one. "Hello, boy." She rubbed behind the dog's ears, who closed his eyes in pleasure and raised his chin so she could scratch him there too. "Good boy?" The dog licked Julie's face, its slobbery tongue wetting her ear.

"Timmy! Timmy!" The man's voice preceded him blundering through the canopy moments later, looking flustered and chagrined. He was middle-aged, with dishevelled sandy brown hair. Panting, he had apparently been running after Timmy for some time. By the joyful look on Timmy's face, eyes bright, tongue lolling in a mouth wide in a beaming smile, he thought it was an excellent game.

"I'm terribly sorry, young lady," the man said. "Timmy, come here at once." Julie laughed. Timmy didn't listen and nuzzled into Julie, licking her hands and face. She made a fuss of him. Eventually, the man gave up waiting to be listened to and hauled Timmy off Julie by the collar. Julie stood up with them.

"It's alright, I love dogs."

"Well, you can have this one," the man said lightheartedly. "Won't listen to a bloody word I say."

Julie squatted in front of Timmy. The dog looked at her, wagging his tail furiously, padding his feet in the mix of leaf litter and cigarette butts.

"You're a good boy, aren't you, Timmy?" Julie scratched him behind the ears again, and as if to prove that she was correct, Timmy dutifully plonked his behind on the floor, his tail sweeping enthusiastically side to side in the dirt. He licked his snout and stared at Julie as if awaiting instructions.

"Blow me! He has never done that in his entire life." The man attached a lead to Timmy's collar and tugged him away. "Sorry again. Come *on*, Timmy." The man pulled Timmy back through the canopy. Timmy looked back at Julie with mournful brown eyes.

Danny brooded on the blanket.

"Let's go. It's not private here. I've got to meet Effie for a coffee in town soon."

Danny gathered up the blanket. Julie held out her hand. He took it with the grace of a sulking child. Pulling back the canopy, Julie gave the ground around the tree's trunk one final scan. There looked to be nothing out of the ordinary, but something powerful still throbbed beneath her skin.

49

"WHAT ARE YOU DOING HERE?" Rob whispered to Jason, tying his shoelaces.

The boys were all changing slower than usual. This was the final PE lesson before they broke for exams. For those who wouldn't go onto the sixth form, it would be their last ever PE lesson at the school. Even those who approached school as if it was a custodial sentence felt the significance of their final lessons. Exams would be a parole board meeting. Soon they'd be out in a world not governed by the institutional regiment that had given them both a structure and a moral code to both live by and resist. Not even shanking a classmate in the showers could prevent the end of their sentence. It felt as inevitable and unjust as death and was equally as undiscussed. For students like Rob and Jason, and Ally and Chris, who fully intended to stay on for A-levels and then go to university, all the *final this* and *final that* only added to their pent-up energy before exams. Although for Rob it was becoming increasingly difficult to focus on anything. The assassin of time slipped away invisibly, bleeding Rob with a thousand cuts. His only hope was in Jason.

"I thought you might need a little moral support." Jason pulled his socks up to below his knees, whereas all the other boys let them rumple around their ankles.

"Why would you voluntarily do cross-country?"

"Some of us don't have a curse to keep fabulously skinny."

"Wanker!" Rob grinned, but his thirst was a flaking rust.

"You don't know the half of it, my dear boy."

"Are you sucking Rob's cock now that Julie Brennan won't?" Ally shouted across the changing rooms, to which most of the boys burst out laughing.

Without missing a beat, Jason fired back. "You seem awfully interested in whose cock I'm sucking at the moment, Ally. Is there something you want to come out about?"

"Oh!" Several boys shouted in unison, approving of the cutting riposte. Ally reddened and punched Henry on the arm for laughing.

"Fuck off, you gay." Ally's Belfast accent thickened, his usual facility with words seemingly stifled.

The boys made a high-pitched and elongated "Ow!" to the sub-par counter.

Jason rested an arm on Rob's shoulder. "Sounding a bit too frustrated there, Alistair. You're protesting just a little too much. If you're not careful, everyone will suspect you think cocks are more delicious than Guinness."

Ally rounded the bench, hung with school uniforms when Mr Phillips walked in.

"All right, ladies, shut up. Potts, what the hell are you doing here?"

"You know I am a fan of physical education, sir, and I had a free period. Rob informed me we'd be taking a leisurely run on the cross-country course today. And I thought what better way to spend one of my final days at school than with a spot of cardiovascular training, what with obesity being such..."

"Okay, that's enough, Jason." Mr Phillips put his hands up in mock surrender. "If only your feet ran as fast as your mouth, we'd win the County Cup every damn year, and I'd be a legend in my own lunchtime. Right snowflakes, outside and line up next to the goalposts."

A chatter of voices ricocheted off the changing room walls, and the boys filed out, with Jason and Rob following up the rear.

Mr Phillips gave instructions, including stern warnings that if any other boys took this as an opportunity to bunk off for the day or take two hours to turn back up at school, then there would be serious consequences. Whether or not it was their final day at this fine educational establishment, they could still get detention. Rob stood holding his side. His kidneys felt like a ham-fisted mechanic had jammed a screwdriver into them and waggled it about whenever Rob had the audacity to breathe. His tongue felt like a carcass desiccating in the desert heat. Sleep deprivation had become normal, and he'd adjusted to its disorientation. It was like a combination of alcohol and coffee, teetering just on the edge of inhibition and mania, but never quite overstepping, leaving him in a limbo where he could feel their presence was never far away.

Mr Phillips finished his speech and Rob hadn't noticed Ally, Chris, and Henry had manoeuvred behind him and Jason. Mr Phillips strode ahead of the class, turning his back to them. Jason moved off, taking him out of the line of fire, as Chris stamped down hard on the back of Rob's Achilles. Ally missed the opportunity with Jason. Rob cried out and fell, holding his ankle. Jason caught up with what was happening and shoved Ally in the chest.

"What's going on here?" Mr Phillips was running over.

Ally was about to open his mouth, but Jason got there first.

"Ally kissed me, sir, and without my permission." He sounded truly mortified.

"He's lying..." Ally was red again, clenching his fists at his side.

"Shut it, Strachan. Why is Rob holding his ankle?"

"I fell over, sir. Trying to stop Ally groping Jason."

"This stops here. All of you, do you understand?"

Ally glowered. Jason pulled Rob up.

"I said, do you understand?" Mr Phillips had raised his voice.

"Yes, sir," all five boys droned.

"Right then, you three come with me. Jason and Rob, line up at the other side of the pack. Let's have a bit of distance between you, shall we." As they moved off, Ally turned to jog backwards and held up his middle finger, his eyes burning black crusted magma.

"They are so predictable. This is exactly why I am here," Jason said.

"If they're so predictable, why didn't you see that coming?" Rob was trying to run off the pain.

"I can't see everything, Rob. But when you told me you are doing cross-country, I knew it would be one of the last times you'd be out in the open and they could have a shot at you." They joined the back of a group. "Besides, I've been doing cross-country at the school for five years. Or rather, I've been avoiding doing cross-country at the school for five years. I know all the shortcuts, my young apprentice, and today I will pass on my knowledge."

Phillips blew his whistle. His cheeks puffed out like a small woodland animal who'd stuffed as much food into its mouth to prepare for the long, lazy winter, which to Mr Phillips, was six weeks of summer holidays without a single student in sight. The boys set off. They were to circle the playing fields and then head off site at the corner of the school grounds. There, they would join a path that led along hedgerows and up to the top of the hill that looked out over the town. From there the route cut through a small wooded copse to undulating scrubland where swarms of gnats waited to attack them. Lungs burning and insects between their teeth and itching their scalps, they would run back down the other side of the hill to double back along the hedgerows and rejoin the school playing fields at the corner from which they left. It was a two mile circuit, and even the poorest runners could do it in around thirty-five minutes, Mr Phillips had told them, although it sounded more like an order.

"They keep looking back at us. They'll wait for us at the copse," Jason told Rob.

"Should we run up into the pack? Get some safety in numbers?"

Jason shook his head. "I've a better idea. The class could still take Ally's side. You're not exactly popular, and neither am I. The pack likes seeing a couple of runts put down. It would add some spice to the tragedy that is their tortuous march towards mediocrity, which they call their lives."

Rob's legs burned on the incline of the hill. He wanted to be sick and felt a little lightheaded already. The first of the boys were disappearing into the copse at the top of the hill, and Rob could see Ally in the middle of the pack looking over his shoulder. Shortly after, Chris and Henry checked too. They disappeared into the trees to wait for their prey.

Jason slowed his pace, and Rob matched him, giving them a little distance before the last man, a grossly overweight boy by the name of Paul Carter. When Paul huffed and puffed through the trees, Jason veered to the left. "This way."

Rob on his heels, Jason found a hole in the hedge and squeezed through. Rob followed, being careful not to receive too many scratches from the hawthorn. They broke through to the other side to a field containing rapeseed already iridescent yellow. They ran along its edge to a holly tree in the corner and crouched behind it in the long grass, getting their breath.

"Have you heard from your dad?" Jason watched for the leaders of the pack.

"Yeah, I thought I'd better answer his texts. Feel bad for my mum though."

"At least you've got a dad."

Rob knew that Jason's dad had died when he was seven, in a car accident. Jason told him in one of his fast track monologues. It was as if Jason wanted to get all the background stuff out the way so they could get on with their friendship, like they were making up for lost time.

"That's what I thought. He was making an effort with me. It's weird: before we came here, he was never home. I hardly knew him. We've only been here a matter of weeks, and I actually started to like him. The curse brought us together. How messed up is that?"

"Makes total sense really." Jason was monitoring the path. The fastest boys would be along soon. "It's like war; a band of brothers. In normal life, people totter along enduring all kinds of chronic unhappiness. Like the crotch of dicks we go to school with. But in times of crisis people get thrown together."

"I suppose." Rob had an image of him and Jason, dressed in army fatigues, WWII rifles in hand, crouched in the long grass, looking out for Ally, Chris, and Henry who were Nazis searching the trees with dogs. Chris was a smart army officer, Ally wore the long leather coat of the Gestapo, and Henry was a dopey looking corporal whose helmet was too big.

Two boys ran along the hedge and Jason ducked down. Rob was away, drawing in his mind.

"Earth to Rob. So, what was your dad saying?"

Rob snapped out of it. "He's going to see some professor about curses. Seems to think she's an expert, and if anyone has the answer, she will."

A steady stream of boys ran along the other side of the hedge, skinny legs trailing a scent of sweat and industrial applications of spray-on deodorant. Rob followed Jason and ducked down. The grass they crouched in was lush and long. The rapeseed behind them rippled like a yellow sea.

"That's great," Jason whispered. "But we'll keep looking too. Did you ask him to send you a copy of what he has so far?"

"He said he'd email it over soon."

"When?"

"Dunno."

"That's okay. It's not as if it's a matter of life and death."

"I'll text him again tonight. Daren't phone him, in case mum hears?"

"Only if you have time. There's no hurry."

"Wanker!"

"Robert, we all touch ourselves. That's like calling me a Homo Sapien." Rob opened his mouth, but Jason raised a finger to interrupt. "The homo joke is too predictable, Rob. You can do better."

"Just a twat then?"

"Now I sound like a feminist icon."

A vajazzle joke was forming in Rob's mind, but Jason put a finger to his lips. Poor Paul Carter huffed and puffed past.

"Let's go." They hurried out from behind the holly tree and broke into a jog. As they came back down the field, they caught up with Carter, who nodded at them, unable to speak, sweat rolling off his ruddy face. Mr Phillips was checking his watch as they reached the playing fields. They had hardly run at all, but Rob still couldn't wait to get to the changing rooms for a drink. Most of the boys collapsed onto the floor, either sitting holding in their knees or laying prone, chests heaving.

Mr Phillips frowned, looking round at the boys. "Where the hell are Ally, Chris, and Henry?"

"Don't know, sir," someone panted.

"Carter, you were near the back. Did you see them?"

"No... sir," Carter gasped, hands on his knees, looking like he was about to be sick.

"Jason, Rob, do you know anything?"

Rob was going to say no, but Jason, faking heavy breathing, said, "Well, sir, I'm not one to tell tales. But they did look to be having a rather good time in the copse?"

"What's that supposed to mean?" Mr Phillips scowled like the summer holidays couldn't come fast enough and looked up to the clump of trees on the hilltop.

"Like I said, sir, I don't like to tell tales. I'm not exactly sure what I saw. Just three boys, having a little pit-stop, huddling up trying to hide something. I couldn't imagine what they would need to hide from a breeze. Probably the trauma of their home lives."

At that point Ally, Henry, and Chris came running back onto the playing fields, with a dash still ahead of them to reach the rest of the class.

"Right," Mr Phillips shouted, "you lot," he pointed to the boys who'd already finished the run, "get your backsides in the changing rooms. I'd like to say it's been a pleasure teaching you all these years. Enjoy your exams."

Ally, Henry, and Chris reached Mr Phillips, gasping for air in their sprint to make it back. They staggered after the rest of the class, holding stitches in their sides. "Not you three." The three boys stopped. "You've some explaining to do about where the bloody hell you've been and what you were doing. Do you not remember our little conversation about detentions?"

Mr Phillips beckoned them to him. Grinning, Rob and Jason

turned to enjoy the reprimand that was about to begin. They caught Ally's eye, who looked past Mr Phillips. Jason blew him a kiss followed by a wanker sign. Ally stared back with nothing in his eyes. The smile flickered on Jason's face, as if he'd just looked into the eyes of a shark who thought of only two things.

50

MARY HAD CLEANED little Amos so gently, bathing him in a barrel of water boiled in the kettle. Little Amos couldn't feel the heat anymore, but Mary knew this was the right thing to do, to clean up the little soul, wash away the dirt and filth of this life, none of which had been the boy's fault. She would carry him in death as she had in life. She would bear his burden and that of all the other little souls whom the sickness had taken. Amos was the fourth of them.

Exhaustion and hunger and anguish drained Mary. The Church would give them no more money. The doctor would not come. Nothing Mary did, none of her remedies, no poultice, tincture, balm or ashes, and no incantation would work. The town had forsaken them. No one came with favours for the things Mary had done for them. She was desperate and angry and grief stricken. She would not, could not, have the children buried in an unmarked pauper's grave, like Aunt Jenny. They were *her* children, and like her beautiful Edward, they deserved the same honour in death. The Church might not recognise them, but she would, and so would Jack. Nothing else seemed to matter. Death came slow and inevitably, like a botched hanging.

It had been her lot to care for the foundlings in life and now in death. The sickness had ravaged them, a pestilence that sucked them dry. The little ducklings couldn't keep any food or water down. Not that there had been much to eat for months. Even the soup had become more water than nettles.

All she had left were the old places, the sacred places, the ones even the churches had forgotten to squat on. Mary knew them and had kept their ways, just as she kept secrets for many people in the town.

Mary would head to one of the old places shortly, under cover of mist and darkness, beyond the town and through the fields and spinneys and along the stream, as she had many times in the last few weeks. To the place, the original place, where she had gone as a girl many years since to have her own duckling, the bastard son of the apprentice blacksmith Giles Brennan. She buried Edward there in the old sacred place, under the weeping willow, where Jack in the Green took him back into the earth with the worms and beetles, to be part of the world again.

Amos had barely turned four when he died in the morning as the sun rose. Mary had given him comfrey and dandelion for diarrhoea, and elderberry and wild garlic for his fever, but it wasn't enough. The skeletal bellows of his little lungs wheezed no more. Rank with excrement and vomit, Mary cleaned him and washed his hair, singing until all trace of the sickness except for his skinny bones was washed away. She rubbed his skin with lavender oil, dried and brushed his hair. He would always complain when the brush tugged at the knots, but not now. He was a good boy. Finally, she dressed him in clean clothes and put a pomander of dried sage in his pocket, tied up like a little toy man, a poppet to take with him.

Once a pall of darkness drew over the town, Mary lifted Amos to her breast and swaddled him there to another song, the one she'd sung to Edward:

"Lavender's green, dilly, dilly

Lavender's blue
If I love you, dilly, dilly
You'll love me too"

As Mary readied to leave, Lily sat in a chair by the fire, nursing Sarah. The fire spluttered, as weak as Sarah's wheezing. Lily stared wildly into the dying embers, her cheeks sunken in, her lips cracked, a wraith succumbing to the sickness just like the smaller ones. Without taking her eyes from the fire, Lily asked, "Why does Jack not help us?" It was a hoarse whisper, dry as smoke.

"It's not Jack's way. His is the way of the plants and animals. Life and death are two sides of the same penny. Death is life and life death, my duck."

Like a corpse floating in the river, Lily bobbed her head weakly. She may have cried but for the fact her eyes were red and looked as though she had no more water left for tears.

"Will you be back soon, mother?" Lily's voice could have floated up the chimney.

Mary came to her, pulling Lily tightly to her belly, and then bent to kiss atop her head. "Soon as I've put little Amos to bed with Jack, I'll be straight back."

Mary swooned and steadied herself on the back of Lily's chair. Although she hadn't succumbed to the sickness, she was exhausted. Bones poked through her skin, and it had been many weeks since any of them had a proper meal.

She grasped at thoughts and feelings, but they had become as murky and intangible as mist. Anger was there. It was the clearest of all the emotions, black and acrid, like burnt hair. She was furious at the Reverend Moseley, at the Church council, at the whole town for abandoning them when they were most in need. Abandoning them, when Mary and her aunt before her had helped them so many times and without judgement, keeping secrets for them so they might live new lives and flourish.

It was because of this betrayal that Mary could not give her children to the Church, to allow them to be covered over in an unmarked grave, so the town could forget them again. She would take them back to the land, give them to Jack in the Green, who was as he had always been: the great circle, connecting life and death. And as one of his priestesses, Mary knew where her loyalties lay. He was their only hope, and perhaps the giving of these children's bodies might turn their fortunes yet.

Mary paused at the bottom step of the kitchen. Her remaining children struggled to hold on to life, and she knew she must hurry.

51

BRIAN PREPARED THEIR BREAKFAST. Rounds of toast with jam and butter. A pot of tea, spout smoking like a fisherman's pipe. A few chocolate digestive biscuits on a saucer. He added a small jug of cold water to the tray to cool down Millicent's tea. Otherwise she might try to drink it piping hot and scald her mouth. Included on the tray was the plastic pill holder, containing today's portion of drugs for Millicent's dementia. Not that they seemed to be working. Millicent's decline had gathered speed. Soon, Brian thought, there would be nothing left of his wife. She would regress into a frightened shell, a husk of an old woman on the outside, an empty childlike mind trapped within, remembering nothing and no one, forced to live in a purgatory of forgetfulness.

Picking up the tray, Brian's hands shook with age and pain, terrible pain. He walked through to the living room, the crockery chattering. Millicent was watching the TV enraptured. Brian poured the tea and added the cold water to Millicent's cup. He prepared himself for the battle of getting her to take her medicine. She might have forgotten him completely, and at best she'd grow agitated, at worst she'd be terrified and scream at him. He would gather her in his arms, quivering until the fight was gone out of her and she calmed.

"Millicent, my love, breakfast's ready."

Millicent turned as if woken from a dream, her eyes glittering with recognition.

"Breakfast, oh how wonderful. Tea and toast, my favourite. Is that the jam I made last summer?"

"Yes, it is, darling." Brian lied with a broad smile on seeing his wife returned to him. She hadn't made jam for more than three years. This came from a jar bought from the Co-op around the corner on the Ropewalk.

Millicent shuffled forward to the edge of the sofa, still dressed in her nightgown. She picked up a knife, spread her toast with butter and jam, and took two huge bites. It crunched. Crumbs sprinkled down her chin. She rolled her eyes in delight and took a sip of tea to wash it down.

"Brian," Millicent said reproachfully, "this tea is freezing."

"Is it, my love? I must have poured yours first. Have mine. It's still hot. I'll make another pot in a second."

"We'll share it," Millicent said, sipping from the hot cup of tea and savouring it as if it was the elixir of life itself.

Brian marvelled at his wife. He loved her so deeply, so completely. She was his entire world. Dementia broke his heart. But she was here now, her old self. But for how long? The thought brought tears to his eyes.

"Oh darling, what's the matter?" Millicent laid a hand on her husband's knee.

"It's nothing, Millie."

"Don't give me that, you silly old goat. I've known you far too long to know exactly when you're lying."

Then the pain gripped him like a primal beast that would devour him from within. His eyes tightened to a knot of wrinkles, and he clamped his jaw down on the agony.

"Oh darling, what is it? What's the matter?" Millicent was now afraid to touch him in case she hurt him. His body had become rigid.

The pain searing, Brian tried to clear his mind. She was here, listening, that could mean he could tell her he'd been living with cancer for three years. It had gone into remission and then it had returned. It all coincided with the worsening of Millicent's dementia.

318

He prayed so many times that she'd die before him. But now he knew he would go first, physically at least, and his Millie would be trapped alone, her body here, her mind somewhere.

"I've cancer, in my bones," Brian managed to say as the pain lessened. Millicent was using a napkin to damp the sweat from his brow.

"Cancer! Since when?"

He could not lie to her, not his Millie. "Three years, my love."

Millicent was shocked, her mouth agape. "Three years? But why didn't you tell me?"

"You wouldn't have remembered, my darling."

"What nonsense. I'm not that old."

"Could I have a sip of tea?"

Millicent handed him the cup. His hands visibly shook. She waited, concern creasing her face.

Finally, Brian was able to go on. "Millie, I couldn't tell you. You don't remember things anymore. You have dementia. I don't expect you to remember, my love, but you know I'd never lie to you."

"Dementia? Silly," Millicent said, but there was doubt. That idea seemed familiar to her. Brian could see her searching memories of the recent past and finding nothing there.

"My dreams, what were they?" she said to herself, and seemed to find nothing there. She raised a hand as if trying to pin down an image. "The silly man on the television, talking about how to poach a perfect egg... and then you came in with breakfast." The words were as quiet as a murmuring stream. Realisation dawned.

"Oh, my darling!" Millicent took his face in both her hands and kissed him long and lovingly. "You silly old fool. Have you been living with this all this time? I bet you have. Struggling on like a martyr."

"Dr Bishop has been very helpful and the Reverend Lovegrove pops in now and again."

"How bad am I?"

"I haven't seen you for a week." Brian's voice cracked. His face creased and wrung out all the tears he'd been soaking up for a year. He wept into his wife's shoulder, letting it go in a flood of relief.

"My darling, how bad is it for you? How far along is the cancer?"

Millicent patted Brian on the back once the worst of his crying calmed.

"Stage four. I'm riddled with it, like bloody blue cheese."

"How long have you got?"

"A few months, maybe six if I'm lucky." He laughed, but it was as humourless as an oncologist's waiting room.

"And how many of those will you be able to look after us?"

"As long as I can." Brian picked himself up and wiped his eyes. "As long as I can."

"That's not an answer."

"I will need male nurses in a matter of weeks. Dr Bishop is already putting services in place for palliative care, but he says you'll need to go into a home at that point. We'll be separated."

"You've had to do this all by yourself?"

Suddenly, they both felt a familiar pang at the absence of children in their lives. It was something they had long learnt to live with, but at times like this, they were reminded of what they never had.

"Well, I'm here now. Why don't I mix one of my old cures to help you with that pain? How does that sound? I'll nip into the garden and see my old dears, and then see to this old dear here, you silly old fool." Still in her nightgown, Millicent slipped on a pair of plastic sandals used for the garden. She slid open the French doors and stepped out onto the patio. The spring air was still cool and fresh. The plastic sandals glistened as they gathered dew in her walk across the lawn. When Millicent reached the bed at the far side of the lawn, she squatted down.

"Hello, my darlings," she said, moving her hands amongst the plants. They rustled and came to life, stems and leaves, fronds and branches reaching out to caress the old woman's hands, like children in the nursery stretching up for their mother at home-time. Then Millicent reached into the pocket of her gown and pulled out a small pair of garden clippers Brian had fetched for her from the kitchen drawer.

"I just need a little bit of this." Millicent clipped some of the purple nightshade. "And... a little bit of that." She reached for the mistletoe growing around the trunk of a tree. "And lastly... could I have a little root and some leaves? Thank you." She harvested the mandrake.

"Yes, I know. Don't you worry about me.... I don't know how many more times I can come. Oh really? Doesn't he now? Well, I have my own mind, so that's enough. I don't care what Jack thinks. All right, I do, but..."

The plants rustled agitatedly.

"Don't get shirty with me. There's always someone else to tend the garden. That's how life works. We all have our time and then it's somebody else's turn."

The plants shook their leaves and then suddenly fell still. From the earth came a purple-hued bramble, covered with sharp thorns. They twisted into the air, stretching.

"Hello Jack... But I want to go... Oh please, not now. He is in so much pain... One last thing, you promise. When?... I suppose that's not long. I can wait until then. And then I will go. But really, do you think that will work? She is still very angry. I can feel her... I agree enough have suffered, but curses are not so easily broken. Particularly, the one she laid down. I'm not sure it's possible at all... You really think this one can do it? We should have found her earlier... Yes, indeed, she can have it all. I will give her all that I can. But then I must go... Yes, I promise... But then I really must go... Yes, I swear it too." To prove her point Millicent offered her hand. A branch of the bramble snaked forward and swept across her palm in a swift movement. Millicent sucked sharply through her teeth and clenched the fingers of her hand into a fist. The blood flowed from the gash. When she opened it again, her darling plants began to move, swarming over her hand, drinking the offering.

"Alright, alright, that's quite enough." Millicent pulled her hand away, making a fist to stem the bleeding.

"It will be done, Jack, and I'll see you soon."

Millicent rose from the flowerbed and began to walk back across the lawn to the house. Only halfway there, the mind of the old woman faded, until, when she reached the patio in front of the French doors, she felt so terribly lost and scared in such an unfamiliar place. The old woman reflected in the glass was a horrible trick. She looked around as a scared animal might when lost in a part of the dark wood it did not know. She shivered and hoped that there might be warmth inside. The patio doors slid open and the house was warm, but she did not recognise it. There were many pictures on the walls of a man and a woman passing through life together, growing from young to old. They had the faces of strangers. She gave a start when a man sat on the sofa, whom she had not seen, spoke.

"Did you get what you need, Millie?"

"Who? Where am I?"

The man turned around. To Millicent he looked sick and angry. He stood up, lurched towards her, grimacing.

"Get away from me." She shrank back towards the glass doors.

"It's all right, Millie. Don't you remember? It's me, Brian. Your husband."

This was a nightmare, and this man was coming for her, old and shrivelled like death itself.

With tremulous terror, Millicent cried, "No, get away." The man had his arms open to grab her.

"Help! Please, someone help," Millicent shrieked. The old man bore down on her, grabbing her in his arms as she struggled for her life.

52

THE SKY DARKENED, mixing its palette first with royal and then navy blue, dashing it with wisps of white, and smearing a falling smudge of burnt orange along the horizon. Rob stared at it through the school art studio's windows with numb awe. Despite everything, he couldn't help but see the beauty of it. They had been working late in the final art class, going over strategies for the exam, whilst Miss Longman went through each student's portfolio. It was a class of quiet conversation, except for Rob, who, without Jason, sat alone. He watched at a distance and always from the corner of his eye as Julie worked pensively over her pages. He thought once that she was looking at him, but when he looked up, she was sharpening a pencil. She slipped away early for an appointment with the French teacher Miss Wheatley.

Rob felt alone without her. Even through everything, he felt an inexplicable pull to Julie. It hurt all the more knowing it would never be; a series of cliches scribbled across the canvas of his mind. Bridges burning. Time personified as a doctor healing wounds. Rob, a caricature of himself, fishing in an empty sea. Greetings card cute puppies, pining as a rain of tiny hearts soaked them. The smolts of the final image snapped Rob out of it. They were all self-indulgent, but the last picture was both weak and commercial.

It was Rob's turn with Miss Longman. Seemingly, she'd left the best till last. She flipped through his portfolio. Rob drifted off. He tried to tell himself there were more important things than Julie Brennan, like not dying from a curse. He felt in limbo, exhausted, weak, and thirsty, so thirsty it seemed to be the only thing keeping him awake, burning sickly every time he swallowed. Yet Julie floated through all of that. Miss Longman turned the page and gasped again. There Julie was, a wood nymph at the feet of the Greenman he'd drawn in the Minster. The picture had an aura since that night the old woman had come to their door and painted symbols in the blood of a rat. It had come alive, the giant tree breaking free from the earth. Rob had stuffed it hastily at the back of his collection with the other associated images: pictures of a dark and wild wood, close-ups of insects, spiders and worms, light glistening wetly from their exoskeletons and slimy skin. The bed of living quicksand, a figure too much-like himself being sucked beneath. Abstract work in charcoal on A1 sheets of paper, weaving briars of thorns that blurred like half-remembered dreams at the edges. A series detailing a woodland animal through stages of decomposition, made vivid with rich colours, inspired by the Frazetta posters on Jason's walls. Colour was a new frontier he thought he'd never get to explore fully.

And finally images of the Witchopper herself, Mary Hooper, hidden behind a rank curtain of black hair, one eye infinite in its darkness, broken and twisted hands reaching out of the page to the viewer. He'd worked in moments of manic possession, the pages his only means of venting everything inside, everything that made no sense. Miss Longman swallowed with difficulty at the end, her eyes shining with tears. She had to cough to clear her throat.

"I hope you will be back for A-levels with me, Robert."

Rob made a motion with his head and shoulders that could have been interpreted as *yes, no, maybe,* or *I haven't thought about it,* the lattermost being the truth. He was thinking now of the old woman that'd turned up at their door again and wanted to slap his forehead, but didn't. How was she connected to the curse? Maybe she knew something? But then again, Rob understood from that night Millicent had bad dementia, so perhaps she would be useless to ask? Her husband could know something, however. He needed to talk to Jason. They'd planned to walk home together. The clock was ticking, and had almost run out. His dad had sent copies from the file he had obtained in London, which seemed to confirm the subreddit story; only men were affected by the curse. But why?

"I have a friend who lectures at the Royal College of Art in London. I'd love to send him examples of your work. He takes a summer school each year and I think he'd be delighted if you would go. Rob, Rob, *Rob*, is everything okay? You seem very distant. You have nothing to worry about in the exam."

"Thanks, Miss. Sorry, I was thinking about history. It never seems to make sense to me."

"Ah, I see. Between you and me, Rob, and Mrs Chatsworth would kill me for saying this, but I don't think you'll have any need for history with your talent. Who cares about what happened eons ago when you create worlds of your own?" She gave him a conspiratorial nudge. "But let's try to get a C grade."

"Yes, Miss."

"Good lad. I can't wait to see what you do in the exam. Blow us away, Rob. Now, off you pop."

Miss Longman done with him, Rob packed his rucksack and the large rectangular portfolio, which contained the remnants of art-pieces which didn't make the cut. He carried it like an obscenely large briefcase batting clumsily against his legs as he threaded through the school to meet Jason at the main entrance. The school was quiet but still with remnants of students and teachers trying to make the cut for exams. Voices and the banging of cupboards echoed like restless ghosts down the hallways. Rob could feel their presence, but maintaining a watchful guard had become a habit, even in his exhaustion.

Jason pushed off the wall he was leaning on, seeing Rob coming through the school entrance. His breath frosted in white jets. With his long raincoat tied at the waist, he became a hard-boiled detective from a dystopian future, where everyone dyed their hair, painted single nails, and defied their Captain by putting eyeliner under just one side.

"It's all over but for the wake?" Jason said.

"Are we talking about exams?"

Jason gave a small nod of defiant confidence. "I hope so. There's got to be something we're missing."

The two boys moved off towards the car park laid out in front of the school. The smudge of burnt orange in the sky had turned to a pinprick red glow, ready to blink out. Rob stopped in his tracks. Jason, a few steps ahead, realised he'd lost his friend, stopped also and looked back puzzled.

"What's up?" Jason paled, anticipating one of Rob's nightmarish visions of death and decay.

Rob nodded ahead of them. Jason followed his gaze and rolled his eyes with a gasp of exasperation before setting off towards Julie, who stood by herself holding her arms.

"What are you doing?" Rob hissed, but Jason wasn't in the mood to listen. He walked right up to Julie and tapped her lightly on the shoulder. Rob hung back, not knowing where to look. Embarrassment, shame, awkwardness, and if he was honest with himself, hope, swirled around in his head. Jason spoke. Julie listened, her eyes occasionally looking over Jason's shoulder. Rob would quickly look away again, the crappy image of pining puppies popping back up. Jason shook his head, and even from behind looked exasperated. Julie then shook her head. Rob's heart fell and wanted to stop his friend, but his feet appeared cemented to the pavement. Jason gesticulated, looking even more exasperated. Rob imagined Julie was at the other end of some of Jason's straight talking.

Finished, Jason leaned forward and gave Julie a hug. She didn't resist and hugged him back, dropped her head briefly to his shoulder. To Rob she looked alone and sad, and his heart ached for her. He knew he could not go to her, and even felt a small pang of jealousy towards Jason, before nearly laughing at how repulsed Jason would be at kissing a girl, let alone doing anything else with one. Jason was beckoning Rob and moving away from Julie. Rob put his head down and strode briskly, lifting his eyes briefly as he passed. He couldn't be sure, but she may also have looked at him. Rob broke into a run to catch up with Jason. Out of earshot at the main road, he said, "What were you doing?"

"What you should have done weeks ago."

Rob was annoyed. "What was that, then?"

"Keep your boxer shorts on. I was merely pointing out that you're a good guy. A really nice guy, actually. Who didn't have a bad bone in his body. Apart from the fact that you were friends with Ally Strachan, but we all make mistakes. Don't worry. I told her you had absolutely nothing to do with that video. That you were just as much a victim of this as she is, and it would be better if you were talking about it to each other like, well, I dunno, *grown-ups*."

Jason was looking up and down the road as he spoke, waiting for an opportunity to cross. An expensive small hatchback sped around the bend of Nottingham Road, its lights on in the early evening dusk.

"What did she say?" Rob said, a little overeager.

Jason grinned. "Ah, young love. Ouch!" Rob punched him in the arm. "She said she'd think about it."

"Think about what?"

"Taking all her clothes off and demanding you give her babies." Jason retched comically at the idea. "Talking to you, of course."

The hot hatchback slowed as it passed them to turn into the school car park.

"Really?"

"Of course she did. Julie is lovely. But it's hardly asking a lot?"

"I know, but..."

"But in the world of young love, what does it mean?" Jason had grown theatrical. "Could she, does she love me? Is it only a matter of time before we move out of our parents' homes because they can't sleep with all our beautiful babies crying?"

"Was only asking."

Jason threw his arm around Rob's shoulders and kissed him on the top of the head. "Rob, you are a romantic and an optimist. You have the Sword of Damocles about to drop, and I think you might spend more time thinking about Julie Brennan than your impending death." They crossed the road. "Now, let's get back to yours and go through what we have."

"I had another idea, about that old woman who came to our door."

Rob did not get to finish his thought. Instead, an angry shout came from behind them.

"Oi!"

The two boys spun on their heels. Danny stood on the pavement, glaring at Rob, his car parked next to Julie. He shouted at Julie to get in the car, but she was protesting. He threw his hands in the air and, without his girlfriend, got back into his car, slamming the door. The engine revved, wheels screeched, and the car accelerated towards the boys.

"Run!" Rob cried, and the two boys sprinted up Lee's Field, a stubby road opposite the school. It ended abruptly with a high fence but led to a footpath which sprouted off. The car didn't pause at the junction with Nottingham Road, instead it lurched across, its headlights bouncing behind the two boys in the gloom. The whine of the engine grew louder, and the boys ran as fast as they could up the hill.

Rob risked a look behind. The car was gaining. Houses flanked their left, with lights on and cars in driveways. It was only a short distance to the alley ahead where the car couldn't follow them, but it seemed an impossible distance to cover. The car's horn blared. There was a thud when it hit a hole, and the suspension absorbed the shock.

Rob's art folder flapping clumsily at his side, slowing him down.

"Drop it," Jason shouted, but Rob couldn't let it go. Besides, if they got to the alley, Rob had an idea they might need it to throw at Danny or use it as a makeshift shield.

Rob's thighs burnt with the effort, and the fire seemed to have spread to his lungs. He willed himself to run faster. Where he found the energy, he didn't know. Jason took his turn to look behind, wide-eyed in terror. They had run out of road and went clattering into the high wooden fence at the end of Lee's field. As they did, Rob pushed Jason to the left, throwing himself in the same direction. There was a screech of brakes and a loud crunch as they tumbled to the ground. Rob didn't wait to marvel at their escape. He was up and dragging Jason to his feet after him. Without breaking his stride, he stooped to pick up his folder. The car door opened as they disappeared around the corner of the footpath. Danny's car blocked the entrance, its cracked lights glaring maniacally into the fence it had broken.

"That's it. Run away, you pussy. I'm going to fucking kill you, Rob."

Rob heard Danny hit the bonnet of his car in frustration. Then the boys were back on Main Street and hurried across to disappear into another alleyway, in case Danny was following on foot or had doubled backed up Nottingham Road in his car. He wouldn't catch up with them, not today at least.

53

22ND NOVEMBER 1820

SWADDLED like a newborn at her bosom, Amos was light, but her burden was heavy. She carried a shovel as well, wrapped in hessian. Mary stole away from the foundling house under the cover of a heavy mist that had settled like a shroud over the town as night fell. It smothered the noises of the mewling cats and clatters of domestic life. Raucous shouts issued from the public houses where men drank away their woes. Mary slipped through the mist, wisps curling in her wake, stopping to check she wasn't being followed.

Under the weeping willow, Mary laid Amos gently by the mossy trunk of the tree. Around the edge of the canopy where it brushed the ground, Mary dug Amos a hole to join his four friends and a new fifth friend, that of her own son Edward. They would all be together with Jack in the Green, in this old place of magic that didn't forsake its own because they were of the land and Jack *was* the land.

The spade was heavy, the earth saturated with sorrow. She wept quietly as she laboured, until she had the hole ready. Amos fitted perfectly. It would be a fine bed for him, and Jack would take care of him. Grief had piled on top of grief, and if it wasn't for the other lives that still needed her back at the foundling house, Mary could imagine lying here with her children and never leaving. But other children did need her, needed her badly.

Mary covered Amos carefully with his blanket of dirt.

It was as she patted down the last clod of earth on top of its little hillock that Mary heard the voices not far off. The night's mist had muffled their excitement and cloaked their torches. Now, too close to run away, she heard anger growling from the mob. Mary shook as a trapped animal shakes when caught in a snare and hears the dogs approaching.

Mary made to flee up the field toward the Windsor's farm, but Giles Brennan was already behind her, having sneaked behind the willow through the fields, anticipating the mob flushing her out. He caught Mary by the arm, squeezing her in the vice of his blacksmith's grip. From between the drooping branches slipped the Reverend Moseley. The lantern he held rocked, casting prostrating shadows around him. His eyes, looking from grave to grave and then to the dirt on Mary's hands, were as dark as a viper.

She made to strike Giles with the shovel in her free hand, but he caught her by the wrist, and she cried as much from her broken heart as from the pain.

The rest of the posse arrived, trampling in under the sacred canopy, standing on the graves of her children.

The Reverend sneered. The creases in his face cast shadows like fangs. "Bring the witch," he said, and the men jeered, rushing forward to grab hold of Mary, laying their hands on her as all of them had once dreamed they could.

54

RICHARD STOOD on the street looking up at the building. It wasn't what he expected. Knocking back another couple of paracetamol capsules he'd borrowed from John's medicine cabinet, he took a few mouthfuls of water. Since last night, the kidney pain had been excruciating, keeping him awake, which was its only blessing. The pain remained this morning as he dragged himself to Euston Station and walked on towards the Bloomsbury campus of University College London, until he reached Taviton Street and the Department for Anthropology. The building was a late 1970s box, utilitarian and as anodyne as daytime TV. Richard took hold of the handrail and hobbled like an old man up the short flight of steps.

Inside, swarms of undergraduates bustled around him, dressed in their chaotic array of clothing and hairstyles, all expressing their individuality so they became a swarming malaise of discordant colours and styles that blended into a Jackson Pollock of sameness.

Pushing his way through the doors to reception, Richard asked to see Professor Sandra Josephs. The receptionist looked Richard up and down, and he got the impression she was trying to judge if he was homeless. Something didn't quite ring true with him. He was reasonably smartly dressed, not dirty but dishevelled, and could have passed for an academic. Richard knew it was his face that let him down: two day's worth of stubble growing on his chin; deep black circles worn under his eyes; his hair in need of a wash; but more than that, the look of a haunted man more akin to the trauma of those who sleep rough on the streets of London.

"Professor Josephs' room is 351, up on the third floor. She says to go straight up." And to answer Richard's perplexed look at the scrimmage of undergraduates, she added, "You want to take the lift on your right. Third floor. Head down the corridor through another set of double doors. Professor Josephs' room is on the left-hand side. Her name is on the door; you can't miss it."

Richard said thanks and took a swig of water. He spilled it clumsily down his chin and ignored the strange look from the receptionist.

On the third floor, things were much quieter. It was sedate and office-like, bland in its institutional interior design. Utilitarian floor coverings. The habitual use of Magnolia paint and fire retardant squares checkered the false roof overhead.

Richard found the door he needed. He readjusted the satchel on the shoulder, which carried all his papers, and took another drink, unable to wash away the pain in his kidneys or the fatigue or his growing sense of desperation. He knocked.

"Come in."

Like the building she inhabited, Professor Sandra Josephs wasn't quite what Richard expected. There hadn't been a picture on the website and she was younger than he thought she would be, perhaps a similar age to him, born in the mid-to-late 1970s. She had short, brown hair, a roundish face with a distinctive nose: thin with a pronounced ski slope to it. She wore an enormous baggy woollen cardigan, unbuttoned over the top of a T-shirt, jeans, and canvas baseball trainers to finish the ensemble. She had risen as the door opened and rounded her desk to meet Richard in the middle of her office.

"Richard Peters, from *The Telegraph*, is that right?" She offered her hand. "Aren't you the Westminster correspondent? I've read some of your pieces, I'm sure."

Richard shook her hand. "That's right, well sort of. I've since moved paper. I'm now the editor in chief of a local paper up north,

The Newark Advertiser. I used to be on the staff at *The Telegraph,* and this could end up being a piece for them." There was a little truth mixed in with the lies. "Thanks for agreeing to see me, Professor Josephs."

The Professor took a seat on the other side of her desk from Richard. "Please, call me Sandra. My undergraduates do. I'm not big on all the hierarchy stuff. I understand from your colleague," Sandra glanced at her computer terminal, "Deborah... Keeley," she nodded to herself, "that you had some questions about curses, beliefs in them and such?"

Richard sat with his satchel resting on his knees, trying not to feel like a student about to ask a stupid question. "I'm wondering how they work? Curses, I mean."

Sandra leaned back in a chair and laced fingers together in front of her and looked up to the ceiling, pondering the question seriously. When she looked back to Richard she said, "It depends on the type of curse."

"Are there many types of curses?" Richard pulled his notepad and pen from the satchel.

"Gosh! Yes," Sandra said enthusiastically. "Curses are quite possibly as old as humankind. They could be even older. We don't know whether Neanderthals cursed one another, or if any of our other hominid ancestors, if they had the power of speech, did the same. But what we do know is that every recorded human society both in the written record and those indigenous populations who we have studied all have a curse system in their culture. But they all work differently. For example, my most recent paper was in fact about the Tupilak curses of the Inuits. Have you heard of it?"

Richard said he hadn't and took a long drink from the water bottle, finishing it.

"Tupilaks could be put in the category of malevolent curses or revenge curses. A shaman creates the Tupilak when they feel wronged. They put on their seal parka backwards and use sacred incantations, or a spell if you like, to call forth an avenging Tupilak. It's a kind of Frankenstein's monster, pulled together from the dead parts of animals which the Inuit hunt, and not uncommonly, parts of their dead children. It is a strange literary coincidence that Mary Shelley set much of the story of Frankenstein in the Arctic. But that's nothing but a footnote. The only way a Tupilak can be stopped is if a more powerful shaman calls another Tupilak."

"So if I understand this correctly," Richard said, "the only way to stop a curse is to conjure up a more powerful curse?"

Sandra smiled accommodatingly, but shook her head from side to side. "In that specific instance, or in many other types of curses of the same category, then yes. But as a general rule, no."

Richard visibly deflated, frowning as he sucked on the empty water bottle.

Sandra rose from her desk. "Could I get you a drink of water?" Richard said yes, and Sandra poured a glass of water from a jug she had sitting on a cabinet.

"Do you have a specific curse in mind?" Sandra asked, taking a seat again.

Richard pulled out the folder containing all the information he had on the Witchopper. He placed it on the desk in front of Sandra. With a look of intense curiosity, she carefully opened the file and leafed through the pages.

"I'm researching a local ghost story - local to me that is. It's kind of a detective case if you like. There is a ghost, the Witchopper, who for all intents and purposes seems to have been a real person by the name of Mary Hooper. There is a local playground game and nursery rhyme about her. There are numerous deaths associated with the Witchopper that have occurred at varying intervals since her death. I've been trying to discern a pattern or a reason for the deaths. Reading between the lines and taking the local folklore from the nursery rhyme and playground game, it fits the pattern of a curse. As the nursery rhyme says, if you see the Witchopper, then you wake up dead, at least some time later."

Sandra took a few more moments to skim through the material in front of her, while Richard waited pensively.

Sandra looked up from the pages. "It could be a curse in the nursery rhyme, originally at least. It's interesting. I've never really thought to look at British-based cases, outside of the Romani

335

community and, of course, the more Judeo-Christian institutionalisation of curses."

"I'm sorry, I don't understand."

"Which bit?" Sandra said cheerfully as Richard finished the water.

"Any of it, really. But the first bit, you said at least originally. What does that mean?"

"There may have been a curse in the original story of Mary Hooper. I would need to study it in more detail to be sure. But the deaths after that couldn't be because of a curse." Sandra offered Richard more water which he took gladly.

"I know this will sound like a stupid question," Richard said, "but why couldn't they?"

Sandra poured the water and spoke. "Well, firstly because a curse requires someone to make it. Mary Hooper is dead, and therefore, who is there to make the curse? And secondly, as you know curses are not real, at least not in the magical sense."

"Is there another sense?" Richard asked.

"Of course; the psychological. That is how curses work. It is something that connects the study of curses with things like the placebo and nocebo effects. There are many studies of voodoo for example, and the belief in it, that makes it so. The human mind is a powerful thing. For my part, I think there's ample evidence to suggest there is probably some evolutionary advantage from having a profound psycho-biomechanical link. That is to say, modern hominids had a strategic advantage from extreme forms of tight-knit, socially cohesive groups. It's plausible that there would be selective pressures for those people who could literally believe in something that wasn't real, either of God, or shamanistic practice to make you well again, or even on the flip side within that religious milieu, that your priests were powerful enough to kill other people."

"So it's all in my head?" Richard was thinking out loud before he was even aware of it.

"Excuse me? Your head?"

"I mean it's all in the head," Richard corrected quickly and took a drink of his water.

"Like I said, the mind is a very powerful thing. Nothing is just in the mind. It's only modern societies that have plagued themselves with this mind-body duality. It's a kind of material reductionism. Is that helpful?" There was a hint of doubt in Sandra's voice, as though she knew she was losing her seminar group.

"Definitely; very informative." Richard pretended to scribble something on his pad. "But you said something else earlier about the Christian institution of curses?"

Sandra laughed lightly. It wasn't an unpleasant laugh, rather it was like one of her undergraduates got the wrong end of the stick, and she was about to correct them.

"The Judeo-Christian institutionalisation of curses. It was actually the thesis of my monograph, the one before last. Essentially, my thesis is this: all curses are about justice from one perspective or another. A curse is a means to rebalance a wrongdoing. As such, one could argue that curses, even as part of pre-rational, magical thinking, are at the very heart of human reasoning about morality. In the Judeo-Christian tradition, sin has been institutionalised. Eve was the original sinner, tempted by the serpent in the garden, eating of the forbidden fruit of knowledge, and then corrupting Adam so easily. Catholicism turned this into the original sin, something with which we are all born with and ultimately to be controlled by the Church. It is only by observing the law of the Church, taking the sacraments, chanting the prayers - and what are they if not spells - and engaging in all the rhythms and rituals which are the foremost signs of magic, curses, and beliefs that we can break the curse. So pervasive were these rituals, that through the institutional evolution of the mediaeval period, and then on from the enlightenment, the religious structures of the church largely became the template upon which we built our legal system and our system of government. Our very notion of a just society is based on the prevention of wrongdoing on the one hand, and the balancing of that wrongdoing on the other."

Richard tried not to frown. This was getting nowhere. He finished the second glass of water as he thought.

"If someone believed they were cursed, what should they do?"

Sandra reopened the folder in front of her. "Just what is your story about exactly?"

"I think it's possible that people in this town, Southwell it's called, believe that they see the ghost of Mary Hooper, the Witchopper, and the curse has perpetuated down the generations."

"You mean they believe the ghost of Mary Hooper passes on the curse?" Sandra turned the pages once more with interest.

"Something like that, yes."

"And are there people today who believe they are cursed?" Sandra looked up at him, still bent over the pages of the dossier.

"Yes, there are."

"Fascinating! This would make an extremely interesting local case study," she said to herself.

"But what should they do?" Richard tried to hide the urgency in his voice.

"If what you're saying is true, that such a profound superstition still holds sway in the English countryside, then telling them it's all in the mind really won't help. For them the only way to break the curse is to find the solution contained within the common folklore. That should contain the key to how to right the wrong that was done."

Richard's face fell. "And what if there's no tracing the folklore of how to do that?"

Sandra sat up slowly, brows knitting together, examining Richard. "Then I would tell them, whoever they are, that there really aren't any such things as ghosts and curses."

Richard's voice tightened with worry. "But you just said that wouldn't make any difference."

"I know. But there is nothing else to say, and then all we have is the truth."

Richard stood suddenly, his chair toppling behind him. He righted it awkwardly and urgently gathered the papers of the dossier spread out in front of Sandra. "Thank you for your time, Professor Josephs. I must be going." Richard stuffed the papers back into a satchel.

Sandra stood, a look of concern on her face. Richard had opened the door when Sandra stopped him. "Mr Peters."

Richard paused.

"Please, I'd like to give you a copy of my monograph. Maybe reading it will help."

Richard forced a smile and looked down at the book which contained a frontispiece of an old wood block with a witch on a broomstick. A lunatic's laugh peeled through his mind but stifled it and dragged it back through the doors of Bedlam.

"Thank you." Richard took the gift with trembling hands.

"Call me if you have any further questions." Sandra placed a hand lightly on Richard's forearm.

"That's very kind of you. I will," Richard lied. He knew this woman couldn't help him. Perhaps no one could, but there was one other person he was willing to try.

55

THEY THREW her into the cell, and Mary tripped, landing heavily on her hands and knees, hair hanging around her face as she sobbed. She pulled her torn clothes around her, covering her modesty. The iron door slammed, and with the sound of a dislocating bone, the key turned in the lock.

The feel of their hands was still with her. They had dragged Mary from the willow, splashing through the stream and up past the mill. Pushing and pulling her along, their fingers like harsh vines twisting their way into the folds of her body. They cuffed her around the head, squeezed at her breasts, and roughly shoved hands between the cleft of her backside.

Mary had begged and pleaded and sobbed only to be jeered at and spat upon and yanked over the Burgage, passing under the Hanging Tree, as her garments ripped on the way to the jail.

She held herself now on the cell floor while the men argued outside.

"We should wait for the magistrate." It was Geoffrey Smith. Mary had helped him with his wife when they came to her about a rash that plagued his private parts. He had passed the rash onto his wife. They came again when their youngest child had the croup, and they had no money for the doctor.

"The witch should be hanged for what she has done," Giles Brennan said. A cheer of agreement went up from many of the men.

"She should be flogged first." That was Robert Ward, the wainwright. Mary's aunt had helped Robert and his wife with two unwanted pregnancies on top of delivering their six children. He had been a willing participant in the treatment and had insisted on fixing Aunt Jenny's cottage door come the winter.

"Aye!" agreed a chorus.

Mary thought of her children alone in the foundling house without her, the pestilence taking them one by one. With every fibre of her being she needed to be with them, and she flung herself at the cell door.

"Please, good sirs, I beg you let me go to my children." Mary stretched her arm through the bars beseechingly. A hard slap stung the back of her hand, and she withdrew it.

"Ha," Giles laughed cruelly, "so you may kill the rest of them?"

"That's if they are not already dead with the sickness *she* brought upon them," said Owen Fletcher, the mill's foreman and father to at least two of the bastards in Mary's care.

"No! They are my babies. I must go to them. They need me," Mary sobbed.

"They aren't yours, witch," Giles spat.

Mary looked from face to face, searching for an ally. She caught the gaze of Geoffrey Smith, who cast his eyes down as quickly as he could.

"Geoffrey Smith, please sir, you know me. Did I not help you when you were sick?" Desperation strained in Mary's voice.

"Do not listen to her, brothers. I know you are all men of good Christian character and would not fraternise with such a wretched wench as this."

Mary could have clawed at his lying flesh, if only she could reach him. She should have gelded him and then cut his throat. Only the love of her children stayed her hand. "I was good enough for you once, Giles Brennan. Did you not bed me when I was nothing but a girl and put a child in my belly? You thought well enough of me then."

Giles strode to the bars, and Mary glared at him in defiance. Then he hawked and spat a wad of mucus through the window on Mary's face.

"See how she lies, brothers? Do any of you good men remember this woman ever being with child?" Giles swept a finger across them. Mary could see the men dredging their memories of the many times they had looked at her covetously, or remembering her with their hands down their britches. And Mary knew in none of those memories or fantasies did she have a swollen belly.

Geoffrey Smith was the first to say, "No," quietly. Then several others together, and with greater conviction, jeered, "*No.*"

"The children are sick," she pleaded, hoping they still had some civility to appeal to. "The doctor would not help. I could do nothing for them. Oh, please sirs, let me go to them."

"You are going nowhere, witch. How is it you are not ill? It is because you made them sick. Why? I do not presume to know the ways of a wicked mind," Giles spoke with hands on his hips, puffed up before the crowd.

While she hoped for a chance to sway the others, Mary could stand no more from that man. "Even when you beat your wife?"

"What man does not discipline his wife when she needs it? Especially when they have been corrupted by the likes of you." Giles turned to the men, but pointed back at Mary who hung on the bars of the cell window. "She tricked my wife into taking a potion that killed our unborn baby. My poor Emily screamed as she bled our baby in clots of blood. She," he jabbed his finger, "is a child killer. And I would bet she has done it to you. You might not have even known, thought it an accident, while all the time it was *the witch.*"

"*Aye!*" the men jeered. "Hang her," one said. "Beat her." "She must pay for her sins," another shouted, any doubt in the group being trampled by the growing excitement.

Giles paced in front of them. "We should not wait for the magistrate, lest this evil escapes."

"But what should we do?" Geoffrey cried out.

"Hang her," Owen Fletcher shouted.

The Reverend Moseley stepped into Mary's view. Dressed all in black, a red leather bible held to his chest. "We used to know what to do with witches in times past, when Cromwell ruled the land. A witch is like a bee's sting: we must pull its stinger out, or it shall continue to pump its vile poison into our flesh."

"*Aye!*" jeered the men. "*How?*"

The weak always need a shepherd.

"She must be cleansed with pain, of course," the Reverend intoned solemnly, "to prepare her for the Hanging Tree."

The men bleated in agreement. There was a hurrying of feet. Mary fled to the back of the small cell, looking around frantically for anything that might help. She had nothing except herself, and there were so many of them. She was weak, the magic ebbing from her and impeded by the stone walls and floor. She knew what they wanted. Groping hands and a lifetime of covetous looks told her as much.

It would not be given willingly.

The key turned in the lock.

56

BUFFETED BY STUDENTS, Richard hurried from the University campus. They swirled around him like a mob. Their carefree manner, their seemingly ordinary lives, their futures stretching out ahead of them made him realise just how much he'd lost and how much more he was about to lose. He was a man walking to the gallows through a laughing crowd.

"Hey!" a young man said, as Richard bumped squarely into his chest. The boy ricocheted off, spinning on his heels. "What the fuck, man!" the boy shouted, but Richard didn't stop. He kept walking through the endless hive of people, skittering in all directions. The noises of the city crowded in on him. Helicopters and planes overhead. Choking traffic. Ten million lives pressed up against each other. A giant ecosystem of human life, consuming and being consumed.

Richard blundered his way to Waterloo Bridge and bought another bottle of water from a kiosk. He shakily handed over a twenty pound note and, white of face and blue of lips, Lesley Tibbits handed him his bottle and change with warmth and grace, asking Richard if he was alright. Richard staggered back and was tutted at by busy Londoners. The Nigerian kiosk owner looked genuinely worried for Richard.

"Sir, are you okay? Please, come. Sit." But Richard had already lurched away.

Gulping at the bottle, the water trickled down his chin, unable to quench the burning sickness. With trembling hands, Richard fetched his mobile phone from his jacket pocket. The numbers in his address book were a blur. He couldn't find what he needed. Contacts spun so fast he felt motion sick on top of his growing delirium and panic. At the other side of Waterloo Bridge, Richard threw the empty bottle of water in a black rubbish bin and clung to the railing trying to get his bearings, on his phone, on where he was, on the chaos of his life. Only one of those options solidified.

Typing R E V with his thumbs, the Reverend Lovegrove's number popped up immediately, and he stabbed at the screen with his index finger. Placing the phone to his ear, Richard thought he heard a child's playful giggle. He looked around, thinking of Rob laughing on a shoulder ride down Southend Pier. He joined the flow of people walking along the South Bank of the River Thames with the phone ringing in his ear.

A soft susurration, like autumn leaves crumbling underfoot, whispered in Richard's other ear. He pinwheeled in the flow of people. Londoners veered away from him, repelled by his look of instability.

The sun glistened from the rippling peaks undulating across Old Father Thames. There was hardly a breeze. The few trees planted at intervals barely moved. Richard quickened his step, the phone still ringing in his ear. He looked behind as the rustling grew louder.

The phone stopped ringing. "Hello?" Richard couldn't disguise the desperation in his voice. "Reverend Lovegrove..."

"You have reached the voicemail of..." The mechanical voice read out the digits of the Reverend's mobile phone number.

"Shit!" Richard turned on his heels and paced back the other way. Several people started at his outburst and the force field around him expanded.

Richard scanned the criss-crossing streams of people, searching for what he knew was coming. Had she really followed him here? He knew she had. He wasn't such a fool to think he could outrun fate. Closing his eyes, Richard pressed his knuckles to his ear, trying to block out the fermenting whisper of decay which Richard felt in every cell of his body. Mary Hooper loomed from the dark of his imagination, her broken mouth smiling behind strands of dirty hair. Her mutilated hands clawing for him as if to drag him down into the darkness with her.

"Please leave a message after the beep," the mechanical voice said.

Running invisibly across Richard's path, another child laughed. Richard hurried back the other way as he spoke.

"Reverend Lovegrove, it's Richard Peters here, editor at *The Newark Advertiser*. We met very briefly at my house a week or so ago." Was that right? It seemed longer. So much had happened since then. "I've been trying to reach you about a story I'm working on. It's actually very urgent. The story is about Mary Hooper. I understand you're something of an expert on her. I'm down in London at the moment, but please call me back as soon as you get this message, any time, day or night. I *really* need to hear from you." He added a final, "Please." The word came out as a plea, and he hung up the phone.

There was a swirl of a shadow that rushed past Richard, along with a powerful sweet and earthy odor. Children giggled as if he was in the middle of their playground game. Richard flinched as something tugged on his mobile phone. He held it in a firm grip as fear clutched at him.

The man who tried to snatch the phone tugged again, but Richard did not see him. The man had a dark beard and almond eyes; he was almost as skinny and gaunt as Richard, his mirror image. Richard, however, saw Mary Hooper, white as bone. Bile rose from his stomach. The blood drained from his face, and an involuntary scream wailed from his mouth. At that moment, his desire to live crystallised into an intense need, and he fought back, swinging his satchel of papers as hard as he could into the body of Mary Hooper. She laughed at him, her black mouth opening wide, exposing her grey tongue and broken teeth. Richard felt the cold seep into him. It was the cold of the grave. Then from the ground broke forth roots and tendrils. They slithered around his limbs, coiling around his ankles, lashing his wrists pulling him back and forth, as Mary

346

cackled maniacally. But still Richard fought, holding onto his mobile phone and thrashing at her ineffectually with his satchel.

Suddenly the roots tightened as if some unseen force had cranked a pulley and Richard's entire body stiffened. His legs and arms straightened. A pulse of energy ripped through his body, spasming every muscle. His jaw clenched. His back arched. His fingers splayed open and he dropped the mobile phone and satchel. A child tittered with joy as the rustling reached fever pitch. Contractions forced Richard to glare at the sky, trembling. Mary Hooper was gone, replaced with blue.

Richard collapsed to the ground, the tension released. Another man lay across from him, a gaunt face like his own. Richard could not move, but saw the two policemen move closer, holding what Richard at first thought were guns and then realised were Tasers.

57

LOVEGROVE WAS SEARCHING for inspiration and found himself pulling on a jacket to take a long walk. He walked away from the Minster, leaving behind the monolith that his new book had become. It wasn't the book's fault; it was his. He needed to connect with something. It had once been God. Serving the community was something he loved, but Lovegrove felt like a fraud, no better than the Bible-thumping hucksters asking for money. With the senior students at the high school now all on exam leave, he couldn't even fill his time with his pastoral duties there. He hoped the walk through the countryside, like when he was a boy, would clear his head. It was as a boy wandering through the beauty of the land that he first thought God had spoken to him through the surrounding wonder.

At the brow of the hill on Main Street, the Burgage looked lush and verdant. The green of the trees was almost iridescent except for the one solitary tree in the bottom corner of the common. He wondered when the council would come and remove the Hanging Tree. It had better be soon. It was as dead as Mr Nietzsche's God, and a strong autumn gale might bring the whole tree down, tearing up the roots, blocking the road. Or a bough could fall on someone. He turned left onto Lower Kirklington Road and decided to pop in to see how Brian and Millicent were managing. They were in his thoughts and prayers - whatever they were worth - a lot recently. He knocked and waited. He thought there was movement inside and knocked again. Nobody answered. Not everyone wanted to talk to the God-botherer. He didn't mind. Continuing his walk, he crossed the road and cut through a passageway onto the nature trail when he felt a buzzing in his pocket.

He'd missed a call from a number he didn't recognise. It was probably a call centre telling him that he had been in a recent road accident, or he was entitled to a refund on mis-sold insurances on a loan he'd taken out. He hadn't had an accident or owned any loans. Of course, it could be someone who wanted to speak to him. Perhaps there were still miracles. He tapped the screen and waited to listen to the message.

On hearing the voice of Richard Peters, Lovegrove slowed. There was something in the man's tone that worried him greatly. Richard Peters sounded anxious, yes, but also afraid. And that fear didn't tally with the subject matter: Mary Hooper. The Reverend shook his head in disbelief. Perhaps the Lord did move in mysterious ways. *If you even believe in God anymore*, he mocked himself. So urgent was Richard Peters' voice that the Reverend immediately hit the number to call him back, but now it was his turn to go straight to voicemail. He left a message as genially as he could and said to call back whenever Richard had a moment; he would love to chat about Mary Hooper. The Peters family had been on his mind as well. Such behaviour from the father rang worrying bells. In a world that no longer believed in souls, he often wondered if the clerical life had become like auxiliary social work. If it had, he was probably okay with that, and made a mental note to follow up not just with the father, but also the boy Rob and his mother Jane. Just in case.

Reaching a nature trail, the hedgerows and fields teemed with life. Swallows swooped. A flock of starlings pulsed like a shoal of fish swimming in the sky. Thrushes and blackbirds, even the crows, went merrily along their way, building nests and feeding chicks. A fat grey squirrel scampered across the path and disappeared into the bottom of the hedgerow. He lamented the greys, that invasive species that had pushed out the more delicate and elegant red squirrel, but nature was red in tooth and claw, as Tennyson wrote.

"And so are people," he said out loud, as the plight of poor Mary Hooper popped into his thoughts.

Lovegrove had studied the diaries of his counterpart two-hundred years previously, the self-important Reverend Moseley. Extended extracts populated the appendices of his thesis. People of that time wrote in euphemism, but it was easy enough to see that he and other men of the town had done something awful to Mary Hooper. Moseley died only three weeks after the unlawful hanging of Mary. They found him in the Minster's nave, slumped against the font. Perhaps there was a God. Lovegrove chided himself for being so judgmental.

He strolled on towards the village of Halam, letting his mind wander freely. He might even wander as far as Morton Wood. There was beauty in this countryside, but he still felt heavy and lost. No, not lost, but searching. He was searching for some meaning, something deeper that lay at the heart of it all. He once thought it was God, whoever he or she was. He chuckled, though it really wasn't funny. There was a melancholia underlying his problems. It was as if he could sense something was there, but it was just out of reach. It was why after university he'd decided to become a minister. And then, after that, why he came back to his hometown to minister to the parishioners here. It was why, still unsatisfied, he had pursued a PhD at the University of Nottingham to further his interest in folklore and religious belief and, ultimately, the local legend of the Witchopper and Mary Hooper. He still hadn't found what he was looking for. A small academic publishing house offered him a contract to turn his thesis into a monograph. He took it in the slim hope of finding his ultimate goal. And that is what delivered him to this briar of confusion, this thicket of doubt. He had in Jung's terms found himself deep within the dark wood of the soul and craved the light to find a way home.

Lovegrove remained lost in this reverie until he happened upon something. There, ahead of him, in the middle of the nature trail, were a couple. As he drew nearer, he realised the man was down on one knee. The woman, clasping a hand to her mouth. A few yards more, and he realised who they were. He had gone to school with them. The man was Alec Finn, who ran a most excellent building and carpentry business in the town. In fact, Lovegrove had engaged him to do some restoration work at the vicarage three years ago. And the woman he noted, happily, was Lucy Moore, Lovegrove's own first love. They had kissed when they were fifteen at a party and then stolen away to a bedroom upstairs, and then, well, things had taken their course. It was a thing he would never forget. But the next week Lucy dumped him and went out with a boy named Greg Williams, aged nineteen; by today's standards Greg would be a sex offender, dating and bedding girls under the age of sixteen.

"It appears I've come too early," Lovegrove said as Alex slipped a ring onto Lucy's finger. The Reverend became momentarily distracted, noticing Lucy held a poppet figure made of grass, some four inches long, and tied around the neck and waist, like the ones he often removed from the Chapter House.

Alec stood up. "The idea just came to me." He was a handsome man with a little extra beef around the waist and looked both happy and a touch bemused.

Lucy, now in her early forties, looked more beautiful than ever. She marvelled at the ring on her finger and stood up on tiptoes, wrapping Alec in her arms and placed a loving kiss on his rough cheek. Alec blushed like a schoolboy.

"Congratulations, this really is wonderful." The Reverend offered his hand to Alec, who shook it heartily. Then he did the same to Lucy. They both leaned in and pecked each other on the cheek, a little awkwardly.

"I know not everyone wants a church wedding, nowadays, but you know where I am if you need me."

Alec was about to say something when there came a great panicked shouting.

"Timmy! Timmy! Come back here, for God's sake!"

A large and enthusiastic Labrador came bounding along the nature trail, leaving its master far behind. The dog blundered into the three of them, wagging its tail, its tongue lolling ecstatically from its mouth. It focused its attention on Lucy, barking happily and jumping up at her. Lucy evidently loved dogs, and playfully wrestled with the animal for a moment, ruffling its head, and saying, "Down, boy. There's a good boy." And just as Timmy's owner was running up to them out of breath, a lead dangling limply from his hand, Timmy took off like a shot.

"Timmy, wait." But Timmy did not wait. He veered off to the right into the hedgerow, barking manically.

"He must have found a squirrel," the Reverend said.

"He hates squirrels. They're the only thing in the world he does hate. That and walking on lead," the man said forlornly.

Lovegrove was beginning to feel uncomfortable and was annoyed at himself for feeling so. The memory of Lucy's nails on the skin at the back of his neck rushed through time to greet him now, vivid and electric. "I'll help you find him," he said, and bid the lovebirds goodbye.

***

TIMMY HAD CAUGHT the scent of it, a strange musty smell, like meat, like one of those dead rabbits he sometimes sniffed when they lay lifeless on the road, their guts pushed out once the car had run over them. That silly but wonderful man of his would drag him away from the amazing smells.

Timmy bounded, barking through the undergrowth. It whipped against his fur as he pointed his nose, inhaling the scent thickly, and then came out on the other side and growled.

He'd not been in this place before. It was a feast of glorious, unknown aromas, but that one strange musty smell was strongest. There was a rock with a hole in it with pebbles placed around its edge. Timmy could tell humans had left them. There was also food: pieces of cake, dregs of tea and coffee, fizzing drinks, whiskey, even a trace of perfume and lipstick, and then behind it all that dirty musk. There was a sound constantly tickling his ears. He heard it all the time. All dogs did, like a wind continually blowing, or water running, only really quiet. Here, in the space within this hawthorn hedgerow, it was loud. Timmy had another sense, that preternatural knowing tingle down his spine. It raised his hackles and moved like electricity to his paws. He pulled back his whiskery lips, exposing his canines, and growled.

The sound grew. Churning. Turning. Crumbling.

The ground moved. Timmy's nose filled with a new, more disturbing scent. He pawed at the floor, priming for the fight. Saliva drooled from his snarling mouth, and the growl in his throat was uncannily like the noise of the wild wood.

"Timmy!" Lovegrove shouted.

"Timmy!" the man shouted. "He is forever running off, the silly dog. Still, someone is enjoying life." He nodded back to the couple behind them.

"Indeed. I went to school with them, as it happens."

"Really? How lovely. Maybe they'll ask you to do the wedding."

"Ha! That's what I said."

"I think he went through here." Timmy's owner started pushing through a gap in the hawthorn hedgerow.

Lovegrove followed him in. "Oh, this is where the Fairy Well is."

They came out in a small clearing at the edge of a field. The man shouted for Timmy, putting both hands to his mouth and facing different directions. The Reverend joined in, ambling around the corner of the field until he found himself next to the well. It was a large old piece of granite, with a gully hollowed out in its centre at the bottom of which was a drainage hole, rough and irregular. The whole thing was mottled with a pale green lichen and the dark greens of algae. All around the well were little trinkets and offerings. Smooth pebbles, a piece of Lego, a chunk of Mars bar, pieces of bread and cake.

Something else caught Lovegrove's eye. Lying at the side of the well, he could see just the edge, a curve of red, and a hint of chrome. He stepped a little closer, and the dog's collar came into view. It was a thick red collar, and it had been snapped. The

Reverend bent down to pick it up when he realised it was covered in blood.

"Have you found something?" the man said, hurrying up behind the Reverend. "That looks like Timmy's collar." He stepped around the vicar and picked it up. A puzzled look on his face changed to one of horror. He looked at his hands, opening them as if offering penance, scared incomprehension dawning on his face at the blood glistening on his fingers.

58

THE POLICE ARRESTED Richard and the mugger and put them in the back of separate police vans headed to the station in Walworth. They processed Richard, took his wallet and phone, his belt and shoes, and put him in a holding cell. Someone came along regularly to check in on him. He sat alone, recovering from the effects of the Taser. In the cell, the sounds of the police station rattled like a snare drum. Eventually, the cell door opened, and they took him to an interview room. They took a statement, which went through the details of his day. Once a story checked out along with the CCTV footage from the south bank and witness statements, it was clear Richard was the victim in all this.

"Mr Peters. If I can give you some advice," an officer said, "next time, just let him have it. We found a knife in his jacket. Things could have been a lot worse."

Tell me about it, Richard thought, but nodded in agreement.

They brought Richard's things, depositing them on the interview room table. He asked for a glass of water. It was in a small plastic cup from a water dispenser and looked like a proverbial drop in the ocean of his thirst. They left him to make a phone call for someone to come and pick him up. He argued that he was fine and they should just let him go. They insisted that it wasn't a good idea after what he'd been through. At the very least, surely he had some family who would like to know what happened to him. There was another story he didn't want to get into with them, and so he agreed. They left him to it.

The officer shut the door behind him. Richard jumped at how loud it seemed, as if the door was wrought iron. When he looked, it was the same reinforced, fire retardant door it had always been.

Richard wasn't sure who to call, but he noticed he had a missed voicemail. He listened to the Reverend Lovegrove telling him to call back at any time. *I'll phone once I get out of here*, he thought and caught the whiff of strong body odour and stale alcohol and of cold damp and grime. The fire retardant door stood impassively. Life beyond the door was a muffled percussion. His thumb hovered for a moment, and he hit the contact name. The phone rang; Jane didn't pick up. He tried again and got the same response. Rob was up next. But the phone didn't even ring. So it was that Richard settled on his final choice, and called Deborah Keeley. He half expected it to go straight to voicemail, but it didn't.

"Richard? How did the meeting go?"

Richard filled her in on the awful morning, redacting any mention of his hallucination during his attack, and asked her to come and pick him up. She was in *The Telegraph*'s office at Canary Wharf, across and downriver at the London Docklands.

"I'll be there as soon as I can. I was thinking."

"Yeah?" Richard was tired and his head pounded.

"Thought I'd order us a takeaway for dinner, get sushi from *Bonsai*, a bottle of Pinot Grigio, stream a movie. What do you think?"

Richard thought about Jane and Rob. Thought about how far away they were and how he'd ruined it all, smashed their family beyond repair, how impossible everything felt after today's spectacular failure with the Professor, and then his encounter with a mugger-cum-vengeful spirit. He just wanted something to be easy.

"Sounds nice. Your place or mine?"

"God! Mine. John's flat is the size of a wheelie bin."

As Richard hung up and put his phone down on the table, he froze when a child giggled behind him. He turned in his chair. The corner lay empty. Another giggle accompanied by hissing whispers of things snaking under the floor. Richard stood, knocking over his chair. He spun around in the empty room. The strip-light stuttered overhead as the whispers grew, like the angry rushing of blood. The footfalls of bare feet ran behind him. Richard ran for the door. It was locked. He pulled at it frantically and banged, calling out for them to open up. The whispers were an angry rattle right behind him. Several children snickered then; Richard wheeled to face them. They weren't there.

But she was.

The Witchopper, fixing Richard with her one dark green eye that glared through filthy, black hair. Death and decay pervaded, wafting before her as she glided across the floor, her head jerking in the stuttering light, reaching with her broken fingers.

Richard was trapped at the door, frozen to the spot, shaking. All roads had led here, to this final destination, and it was an unforgiving place.

Mary took his face in her cold hands and tilted her head like a lover returned from the grave, her fetid breath an icy breeze on his lips, and she kissed him. Richard balked, tasting death and decay. It enveloped him, and still he could not move. His eyes were wide with fear, glaring into the earthen green eyes of the Witchopper. Into them he fell, pitching into an abyss. The interview room dissolved away. Richard was no longer in the interview room at the Walworth police station. He fell back through time and into Mary Hooper. His end would be her end.

The cell door was flung open, and the mob along with their jeers piled through. They brought with them an overpowering smell of sweat and alcohol. They grabbed at Mary, a fevered mass with many hands, which dragged her to her feet and towards the door, silencing the words she tried to form to call forth her defence. Richard felt, as Mary, one side of his head sting so badly it felt as though Mary's skin fizzed with acid. Mary tasted blood, and the room rocked as she was pulled this way and that. The hands pawed at her breasts, buttocks, and groin. Someone took a fistful of long hair and yanked back her head just before she was lifted briefly off her feet and then bent double by a punch to the stomach.

357

Wheezing, Mary mouthed for air while a hand took its time wrapping her hair around its fist. The following yank forward tore hair out at the roots. Mary's head was snapped up to face the calloused knuckles of a hand. The fist shot forward and Richard, as Mary, felt her nose crunch, smearing across her face. She choked on the blood and felt something light but hard on her tongue, realising it was her front teeth. The world came back into focus through a haze of bright lights dancing in front of his eyes.

Giles Brennan pulled Mary from the jail cell, holding her by the hair and leading her like a lamb for slaughter. The others followed, punching her face and body with a frenzied cruelty. George threw a kick, his hobnail boot connecting squarely with her backside; her leg went. Mary buckled; they jeered, and she received another punch to the face for losing her feet, one eye closing with the swelling. Giles flung open the door to the Minster and they tumbled into the night. The mist had thickened, covering their sins from the polite eyes that might be watching from the townhouses and cottages. They crossed the narrow dirt road and hauled Mary up the bank onto the lush Burgage surrounded by trees.

They tore off her clothes and Mary felt the cold air seize her naked torso. Involuntarily, her skin goose-fleshed and her nipples hardened. Hands groped at Mary's breasts painfully. She tripped, falling on hands and knees into the muddy grass. No one pulled her up this time; instead, she descended deeper into a terrible world of pain and humiliation. An unseen man lifted her skirts from behind. There was a sound of snapping twigs when a boot landed on her ribs. Breathing became a desperate memory once more. More blows rained down on Mary's head, cauliflowering her ear like a bare knuckle boxer's. Another fist struck behind her other ear, and Mary's jaw dislocated and hung slack from her skull. Breathlessness, suffocation, choking and anguished pain became bedfellows for the last humiliation. They raped her.

Mary wept and tried to cry out, barely able to speak through her slack jaw.

The images of children, lying sick and dying in a dark house, came to Mary. Her little ducklings coughed and wheezed and wept for their mother, and Mary wept for them, knowing their fate was sealed with hers. The foundling house was a mausoleum for the unwanted, a tomb for the town's shame.

But in seeing those children something stirred inside Mary, something deep and powerful. She reached out, not with her mind. The susurrant rustling came with a feeling, a vibration. The sound was of family, and they were angry, hurrying to Mary's aid as her rage transformed into a raging burning wildfire. An affinity with all things coursed through her.

Mary tried to speak the old tongue. But it choked wetly from her mouth, and each utterance she made was met with another blow.

"Deop, digol wudufeorh, to cuman!"

Mary mustered all the will she had left, calling on her God.

The ground rumbled.

"Don't let her speak, brothers," Giles grunted from behind Mary.

The rustling had grown to a hissing crescendo. Beneath the men's feet the grass of the Burgage green shook, unsteadying them; cries of fear went up. Some swivelled their heads frantically, searching the mist. From the ground sprang roots and tendrils.

"Silence the witch!" Moseley's shrill voice commanded.

Coiling serpents of vegetation writhed from the ground and tried to ensnare the men. They cried out as brambles snapped like whips in the air, slashing and cutting. They thrashed against the bondage of the wild wood, the air thick with the musk of earthy decay. Those who had knives unsheathed them and cut at their lashings.

"Swine bewiscan, swa þes deofollufu ic acwellan."

The heel of a boot stamped down on Mary's head. The world pitched and rolled in an unforgiving storm of pain and disorientation. Only the vision of her dying children kept her conscious, but her concentration was broken, and the vines of the wildwood retreated to the earth.

"Kill her, kill her now," the cry went up.

Suddenly, Mary's defilement stopped. She was lifted to her knees and dragged under the armpits through the mud. Her senses swam back to her from the nightmare of the foundling house to the hell of men's desires.

"Deop, digol wudufeorh, to cuman!"

The earth came alive again. Briars snaked around the men, cutting them with thorns, until Giles Brennan, with the power of a blacksmith's hammer, struck Mary like a piece of iron to be bent to his will. She couldn't speak. Richard felt the blow as a bright flare of searing pain only stopped by the tightening of a rope around her neck.

They grunted and snarled with the effort, and Mary was hoisted from the ground. She clawed at the thick hemp rope constricting her throat. She kicked frantically, twisting and rocking. The world below swung from left to right, zooming in and out of focus. The angry mob below looked up not just with hate in their eyes, but lust and excitement. There, swinging with only moments left of life, and the thought of all the children dying alone in the foundling house, with every defilement and act of violence against her, the purity of Mary's rage found harmony, whose resonance was so powerful it would echo through generations. Mary's hands came away from the rope, accepting her inevitable death. She splayed her hands, touching the energy binding everything, and in that moment Mary's rage, her anger, her love for the children, her hate for every one of those men beneath her, crystallised. Jaw hanging slack, nose smeared across her face, teeth broken, Mary's final breath murmured the curse in the old tongue.

"By Jack in the Green, by water and land,
By the moon and the stars, by your own evil hand,
May your lust become thirst and my death see you damned."

Mary Hooper was dead, swinging by the neck from the Hanging Tree on the Burgage. With their hate, the men dispersed into the mist, all except the Reverend Moseley. He stood beneath her, the rope still creaking, and wet his lips. Her bulging eyes were already clouding with death's veil. The briefest of twitches kinked Moseley's cheek before he turned up his collar and followed the other men into the mirk.

The door to the interview room opened, and the police sergeant stepped in. His brows knitted together, wondering at first where Richard Peters had disappeared to. His things were still on the table.

The room was apparently empty. One step further into the room disabused of this opinion. He saw a foot sticking out from behind the table, and immediately feared the worst. He ran to the man, but it was evidently too late. Richard Peters lay slumped against the interview room wall, his head turned to the side, his eyes open and staring blankly at nothing. The sergeant quickly took a pulse and felt nothing.

59

Rob couldn't keep his mind on his revision. French conjugations felt like the least of his worries. Last night had been a turning point. His mother had grown too concerned when Rob had winced at his kidney pain. She called Dr Bishop, who did a house call. He checked Rob over: sticking a thermometer in his mouth; felt the glands under his chin; took his blood pressure with an inflatable cuff; and then pushed the skin of Rob's abdomen and lower back. Rob sucked in sharply.

"I want you to come in for some tests tomorrow as a precaution. Your mum says you're drinking a lot?"

Rob nodded, pulled down his T-shirt.

Dr Bishop smiled warmly. "It's more likely you're overstressed, with exams and everything else."

Rob knew what he meant by "everything else".

"Blood and urine tests will flag up diabetes or any kidney related things. But don't worry about it. Stress is the likely culprit. In the meantime, I'll give you a prescription for Dioralyte in case you are dehydrated. I know this will sound stupid, but sleep is a powerful medicine. It's important to shut down every night. No screen-time two hours before bed. Go for a walk and then do something relaxing, like listen to music before bed."

With Jane sitting across the room, looking anxious, Rob agreed. Since then, he'd existed in a mental limbo, feeling detached. His only tether to the world was the pain in his kidneys, which felt like Danny had finally caught up with him and pummelled his lower back. The acidic burn of dehydration went from the back of his throat to the pit of the stomach. In the mirror, he thought he looked like a ghoul, with sunken eyes and drawn cheeks. He asked Jason about it, but his friend said he looked normal.

Jason now monitored what was happening online for Rob, as Rob couldn't face it. His alleged accounts were still plastered with the video of him and Julie, accompanied by lurid comments apparently from Rob himself. Jason did his best to police the web, getting things taken down and lodging complaints, but the comments and videos were like zombies who didn't even die from a double tap to the cranium. The only bonus of it was neither the police nor the school believe that it was Rob who was responsible. Though they couldn't prove it was anyone else, either.

Je suis fatigué lined the paper in front of him, repeated over and over again in his handwriting, like 'Redrum' in that movie *The Shining*. There was a sound of wheels churning gravel and Rob looked up from the page to see the tall policeman, Constable Playfair, stop in their driveway. He looked as though he was gathering himself, and there was a suggestion of something in his manner that made Rob feel uncomfortable. The constable took off his hat and fixed it under his armpit and walked up to the door. There was a firm knock. Rob's heart was already sinking. He put down his pen and went to the top of the stairs. His mum looked up to him as she went to the front door.

"I wonder who it is?"

The Constable didn't smile as he stood there on their porch, but there was a kindness in his eyes. "Mrs Peters."

"Constable Playfair?" His mother's voice was tentative.

"Could I come in for a moment?"

"Of course." Jane stepped aside, and the Constable made eye contact with Rob before the two adults disappeared into the living room. Rob walked slowly down the stairs to the hall. Their voices weren't easy to make out, coming through as a broken melody. That was until his mother let out an anguished cry. Rob burst into the front room. His mother had sunk to her knees, and the officer looked down pitifully, a hand hovering above her in hesitation. Rob ran to her, joining her on the floor, throwing arms around her.

"What is it, Mum? What's wrong?"

She let out another wail that sliced into Rob, flaying him to the bone of his soul. The hackles stood up on the back of his neck, and his stomach dropped, as if a knife had opened his belly. Their world slipped away from under them, like offal from a slaughtered lamb.

His mind whirled with the possibilities, which his mother all too quickly confirmed.

"He's dead. He's dead." His mother wept, shrinking into his arms. His own grief was a hot bloom of pressure, forcing the tears from his eyes.

The rest was a blur. Rob wasn't sure how any of it happened. He stayed by his mother's side for much of it. The policeman must have contacted some people. Perhaps Rob or his mother had told him who. Eventually Dr Ken Bishop arrived, the Reverend Lovegrove, then Tim, the deputy editor from *The Newark Advertiser*, and others Rob couldn't remember. They were movable shadows. They brought things. They said things in soft consoling tones. They whispered in adjacent rooms and looked sympathetic. Jason came too. Rob was thankful. They sat in his room for a while, saying nothing, while Jason read through articles and message boards online, searching for clues. But this ritual of death was an adult world, and eventually his friend was busied away by the bustling shadows that attended their grief.

Night came and went, with Rob lying on the bed beside his mother, looking at the ceiling, ignoring the images that rushed in on him. Even the rustling sounds that before were so threatening now seemed insignificant, or maybe appropriate. They were the sounds of death. Rob knew the Witchopper had done it and that she would come for him soon. His own impending death now felt less important next to his mother's grief, and his own. Richard hadn't been a good dad, but he was a familiar fixture in their lives. Coming to Southwell had started to change things, and Rob felt a relationship growing between them. Now the emotions were an overdose of a drug coursing through his veins.

When the sun rose, Tim from the newspaper pulled up in a car. He drove Jane to fetch his father's body home from London. Dr Bishop stayed with Rob. He made tea and food, which Rob didn't want to eat. They spoke. Rob couldn't remember what about. He watched his mother's car go and wanted to cry again. With that hot bloom of pressure he felt like his head would explode. But then Rob realised he couldn't cry, not because he did not want to, but because his body did not have the water to spare. He acknowledged this understanding with detached acceptance, as the car disappeared.

He felt utterly alone, in a purgatory of grief.

60

THE THIRST and lethargy were indistinguishable from Rob's grief and the other thing that preceded them all. It had risen again through the days of preparing for the funeral: fear, squatting deeply like a toad at the bottom of a rotting stump. Worst still, the toad passed unnoticed by the outside world, burying itself deeper still inside the boy, as he stood at his father's graveside. If he could, Rob would have wept for his father, as he was lowered along with his half of their secret into the grave, never to return.

Rain accompanied the graveside liturgy. It painted everything a runny watercolour of greys and black, leeching all the vibrancy from the Spring, soaking the paper that was Rob's life until it tore. Rob heard the vicar's words, but not their meaning. They had never been a churchgoing family, even in this Minster town, but Richard Peters had been a short-lived pillar of the community. They were in the middle of England and its countryside, where gentle traditions contained a whisper of the fervent piety of the past.

They were doing the thing that was expected. However, Rob could feel through the fog of his grief and fear that even with close family, a few colleagues and community figures, and Jason at his side, that this wasn't private enough. Questions peered uncomfortably over mourners' shoulders and half-answers hid under the coattails of social niceties.

His mother's hand gripped him so tightly it hurt, but Rob said nothing. She was holding on to him as though he were a wet root protruding from a freshly cut grave wall and the only thing preventing her from falling into the grave as well. Not for the first time, Rob was an anchor point around which adults buffeted, thrown away and then pulled back around him. Their behaviour seemed to him as inexplicable as the weather, one moment clement, the next squalling tempests. And so it was a surprise when his mother's grip released his hand, but she did not follow his father into the cold, wet ground. Instead, she swore right in front of the Reverend Lovegrove, the town mayor, the staff of *The Newark Advertiser*, Rob's Headmaster, Mr Khan, Mr Bryce, his form tutor, and Miss Longman, his art teacher, who stopped dabbing at her eyes, just as the coffin came to rest.

"That bitch!"

Acrid, like a piece of festering meat placed in the mouth only to be spat out into a napkin at a dinner party. There was an awkward pause in the liturgy during which glances sought to confirm if this was nothing but the minor, understandable slip of a grieving widow or something that would develop into an altogether more socially awkward event, such as full hysterics.

"That bitch!" repeated Rob's mother, this time in a voice intended to cast beyond the assembled mourners, acridity now fully developed, chewed on and vomited forth without care for fellow diners. She was staring over the mourners on the other side of the grave. Miss Longman thought *she* was the object of his mother's ire at first, her face mixed with surprise and mild panic. Jason looked at Rob, but Rob was still in the opioid stupor of the bad trip his life had become.

"That fucking bitch!" Jane was shouting now. Still holding her black umbrella, Jane was on the move. She broke rank, stepping back and around Rob, leaving him in the rain. She was off, striding on mushy ground between granite gravestones, in a march that wobbled her at the knees each time a three-inch heel of her smart black shoes impaled the sodden grass. The mourners first looked at each other with wan horror, then at the wobbling spectacle, spitting fury and brandishing a fully opened umbrella, finally following the direction of the widow Peters' path to find, at its end, another woman. This other woman was quite similar in appearance to Mrs Peters, but not similar enough to be a sister. She was formally dressed but not all in black, as if she wanted to show her respects but pass unnoticed as a relative visiting another grave, and she was at least ten years younger than Rob's mother.

The shock of Jane's outburst had put the mourners on their heels. It wasn't until Tim, the now acting Editor-in-Chief of *The Advertiser*, said, "I think we should do something," that they made a move, by which time it was altogether too late. Jane's shoes had since been lost to the graveyard's sodden ground, and now unhobbled, she closed in on her target with a liberating fury. Every possible Anglo-Saxon expletive emanated from her mouth as a Boadicean war cry. The other woman held up her hands and was saying something in an apologetic tone that couldn't be heard above Jane's fricative venom and guttural consonants.

The two women were face-to-face now. Jane pitched the umbrella above her right shoulder and swung it down into the younger woman's side. It bounced off and broke two of the spokes. Jane swung again and again, backing her nemesis against the trunk of a sycamore. Each swing became more powerful, but still negligible, as the spokes broke, creating a flail of nylon and cheap metal.

Ken, Tim, Mr Khan, Mr Bryce, and Miss Longman were now at a run to intervene. Jason stared agape at the unfolding drama.

The other woman lost her footing on a slippery root and fell back. Jane showed no mercy, lashing the umbrella across the younger woman's face, cutting her cheek and bruising her ear. Cowering on the ground in a foetal position, arms shielding her pretty face, the younger woman cried out, "I'm sorry, I'm sorry." Jane whipped her and whipped her and whipped her, but it wasn't enough. In the hail of expletives and frustrated by the lack of damage her flail had inflicted, Jane reassessed its application.

The mourners were only ten yards from the women now.

Jane turned the flail on its end to become a pike, bent and

warped, which she thrust down like an ill-placed coup de grâce into the pretty blonde's hip. The other woman yelped as the umbrella point punched into her floating rib and again as it struck her shoulder. The next one was sure to hit its mark, right in her ear or throat or better yet her eyeball, to pop out one of those pretty green eyes, to make her not so pretty anymore. Then, on all fours, she would grope for it on the cemetery floor, snivelling with her face all tears and snot and blood and optic nerve.

But Ken tackled the shoeless Jane Peters and brought the assault to an end before any real damage was done.

"I'm sorry, I'm sorry," the younger woman snivelled.

Jane Peters had stopped swearing. Ken had broken the spell of her rage and held her now on the ground, muddy and weeping with an uncontrollable tide of grief.

"He's mine, he's mine," was all Jane could repeat.

But, of course, he wasn't, not anymore. Richard Peters, Editor-in-Chief of *The Newark Advertiser*, formerly of the Fleet Street *Daily Telegraph*, pillar of the community, father, husband, adulterer, was dead and buried along with a secret only Rob and his friend Jason would believe.

Through all this, Rob looked on, a bystander. Jason had put an arm around his shoulders. It did not hurt, nor did it comfort. Rob felt nothing toward it. What did any of it matter? He knew what would happen, how slow and painful it would be, how unbelievable yet inevitable it all was. He couldn't cry about it. He was too dehydrated to cry. All he had left was his grief, a terrible thirst, and that fear, squatting deeply like a toad at the bottom of a rotting stump.

61

ROB SPENT the long hours staring at the ceiling of his bedroom, trying to ignore his imagination as it concocted phantoms out of the dark. Her mouth was coal-black, lips pulled back in a rictus sneer of broken and missing teeth, lank black hair falling round a face, pale and gelatinous, opaque with decay. And her eyes. Dark and green as lichen, that smothered all the light. She had taken his father, and Rob could feel she would come for him at any time.

Rob heard the post hit the mat with an unusually loud thunk. He knew his mother would have heard it too. She hardly slept since the funeral. Footsteps and sobs reached him through the walls, a sound-track of grief. The post was their cue to get up and join the mindless rituals and rhythms of normal life, acting it out with the same conviction and believability as a primary school nativity. By the time he'd pulled his tired body from the bed, Jane was already at the top of the stairs tying her silk dressing gown in an aggressive knot, as if it was the only thing holding her together. She didn't acknowledge Rob. Perhaps she didn't realise he was there. Her head disappeared around the turn at the top of the staircase.

When Rob came around the same corner, he stopped, looking down on his mother. She was staring at a thick manila envelope in her hands, trying to decipher the handwriting. Flicking it over to look for the return address, the fingers suddenly gripped the packet, crumpling its edges. She turned, her face filled with rage, up to Rob. He could see the muscles at the side of her jaw rippling, and she shook. Rob thought his mother was about to explode. He lowered his eyes and thought about retreating to his room, but that was the last place apart from here he wanted to be, and so he stood where he was, unable to go forward or back, trapped by the unspoken emotions of adults once more. Jane didn't explode. Her eyes glistened. A rivulet of water fell first from one and then soon the other eye. She blinked at the tears, and bringing her forearm across her mouth to stifle her sobs, Jane rushed from the doormat, exiting stage left, unable to maintain the act of whoever she was supposed to be playing.

Rob wanted to go to his mother nearly as much as he wanted her to come to him. If only she would gather him up in her arms, rock him, kiss his head, let him cry into her shoulder, and tell him things would be okay. Since she dropped his hand at the funeral, they had barely spoken. Jane would infrequently remember to make food. It didn't matter, Rob told himself. He wasn't hungry anyway. He ate because it was the thing he was expected to do. People eat. Normal people chew food, fill their bellies, feel sated. Normal people, Rob thought wanly, following the sounds of his mother's weeping.

The lid of the bin closed with an angry metallic clank. Jane Peters, tears still rolling down her face from eyes bloodshot and puffy, turned on the kettle, punching the button with her index finger. The kettle rocked briefly on the countertop; the water sloshing inside, grumbling with the heating filament. From the doorway, Rob watched his mother get down one mug, not two, from the cupboard. It slipped from her fingers, falling to the countertop. It bounced and leapt from the edge, tumbling to its death, smashing at Jane's feet. She pounded the counter with the soft pad of her fist, letting out a sob and then screamed, hitting the counter with her fists over and over, until her scream broke into the cry of an inconsolable child. Jane slowly crumpled in on herself, folding to a crouch, and fell back against the counter. Rob ran to her. She sobbed, not returning the embrace, but clung on his arm. Again, like a child.

DR KEN BISHOP CAME QUICKLY, knocking at the front door and entering without waiting for a reply. He had his large, black leather doctor's case and a reusable shopping bag, covered in multicoloured polka dots.

"Hello," he called, guessing correctly the source of the sobbing. Rob had managed to get his mother to come to the comfort of a sofa, where she continued to cry hysterically. It had taken Ken only fifteen minutes to drop everything and get around to the house.

Ken put down the polka dot bag next to the armchair, leaving him with his doctor's case. He set the black leather block next to Jane's feet and bent down on one knee in front of her, holding out his hands, and gave Rob a look that said it was okay to let her go now. Rob felt a wave of relief. Ken knew what to do, and Jane fell sobbing into his arms, where he spoke words of solace into her hair. He didn't tell her that things would be all right, or that he understood, only that he was here and to let it out.

Rob got up to leave them to it.

Ken's warm hand found Rob's, half out of the seat.

"Well done, Rob." The doctor's face was serious but kind.

All Rob could do was nod to show he'd heard.

"I'll see to your mum. Then we can catch up, okay? Do you want to put the kettle on while I see to Mum?"

Twenty minutes later, Ken came into the kitchen, setting the polka dot shopping bag back on the table. Rob sat with an un-drunk cup of tea still weakly steaming in front of him. He went to pour the second mug for Ken.

"I'll get that, Rob. Thanks."

Rob looked at the bag.

"I brought you and your mum some food. The ladies from the WI had me in food for about six months after my wife died." The doctor smiled weakly at the memory. "Cooking is the last thing you and your mum should be thinking about. It's mostly bolognese, stew, chicken curry. I make a mean chicken curry."

"Thanks," Rob said, his throat hoarse and dry.

The doctor was looking at Rob with concern.

"I've given your mum a sedative to help her sleep, and I'll bring around a prescription for sleeping pills after work and explain to her how to use them."

The ghosts on the surface of Rob's tea had disappeared, and the milk had formed a membrane. Rob watched the wrinkles in the tea's skin slowly form.

Ken put down his mug. "Rob, I don't know what it's like to lose a father at such a young age. But I want you to know, I'm here for you and your mother, and if there is anything, anything at all you need, you just give me a ring. Any day, any time. Okay?

"Yeah, okay."

There was a brief silence in which Rob knew the doctor was looking at him again. The chair scraped across the floor, and Ken came around the table to Rob. He crouched down, just as he had done to help Jane. Rob felt his warm hand on his wrist, feeling his pulse, and the other laying its back across his forehead.

"Are you sleeping?"

Rob lied with another wordless nod, and he could sense the frown out of the corner of his vision.

"Rob, this is all going to be so painful, and it will hurt for a long time. I know you know that. I wish I could take the pain away and make it all better, but I can't. No one can. But I promise you, in time, maybe a very long time, things will get easier. You'll never forget him, and it'll always be painful, but you will come through this."

The doctor said some other things. They were nice and not patronising. Rob heard the words, the skin on his tea turning a dark necrotic brown. All he could think was how his dad was wrong; he'd lied. He didn't or couldn't sort this out, and time was something Rob knew he didn't have. But there was something new. The manila envelope. What was in it? Why had his mother reacted like that? As low as Rob felt, there was still a glint of curiosity, a spark of a fight, which the package in the bin kindled. That was, if he could make it through another day.

62

THE NIGHT HAD BEEN a slow torture of waiting for morning until the earth shook Rob from his bed.

The sun was seeping into Rob's room, overwhelming the glow of the bedroom's electric lightbulb, which had stood sentinel through the interminable night. Rob felt the vibration, like the stamping of a great foot upon the earth, and remembered that day in the shower at school when he ran through the endless fog. He sat up: listening, feeling. Faint noises of early morning floated in from the world outside. Traffic. A paperboy. Someone returning or leaving the night shift. A bicycle, and an insomniac dog walker.

Hesitating, fear held Rob in its tremulous hands. He'd spent the first half of the night with his feet tucked beneath the bedcovers, wrapped in a cocoon, only his face looking out into the menacing shadows. Until he risked getting out of bed, sweat dripping from his wasted body. A force of will pulled his feet over the edge of the bed, under which the blackest of black places lay, and from where he was sure a marble white hand with broken and missing nails would fix its corpse-cold fingers around his leg and pull him screaming into the void. Heart racing, his feet hit the carpet, still covered in the childish racing cars, and he ran to the door, switching on the light and banishing the shadows, at least from the room, if not his mind.

He'd made it to morning, and this was his last chance to break the curse. If that was possible. But still he sat frozen in the aftershock.

A second tremor, more insistent, shook the empty glass of water on his desk.

Rob jumped from the bed.

Birds sang.

Rob listened.

He had definitely felt the earth shake, but the melody of life waking up carried on as if nothing had happened.

Rob dressed quietly. The pain from his kidneys was excruciating now, and his limbs were as heavy as a dead tree. He pulled on his jeans, a T-shirt, and slipped on trainers, speckled with flecks of paint from his art coursework. The school and exam board had given Rob special circumstances, exempting him from exams, and they would use his coursework to calculate his grades. For art that was a good thing. It was the inevitable A star he would have got but now might never get to enjoy. None of that was important anymore. He'd found an old hoodie of his father's in a black bin bag his mother was about to give to charity. It was from an old band, *Nirvana*, with a smiling yellow emoji face gazing comically on the front. The irony of it felt right for what they would try to do today, and he wanted to have something of his father's with him at the end.

Despite May turning to June, there was a chill in the air. Rob's mother hadn't worked out the heating timer yet. That would have been one of his dad's jobs. It was still difficult to believe that his dad wasn't here, that they buried him in the ground and his body was decomposing. Rob banished the *Tales from the Crypt* pictures he could not help but draw in his mind. It was odd, Rob thought, for a man always absent, working late, missing birthday parties, never available for weekend football matches, school events, that his absence should be felt so deeply. They had spent more time together since moving from London. Things were maybe changing and then... the Witchopper. She occupied the rest of Rob's thoughts, and he knew there was another reason he missed his father so much. He still wanted an older, stronger man with the experience of life to sort this out, like he'd promised. But he hadn't; perhaps he couldn't.

The morning having banished the shadows under his bed, Rob crossed the floor of his bedroom. He could almost forget the hand lurking beneath the bed. Almost.

He crept to the bathroom and grunted, eyes closed with the effort, as he peed. A thin molten trickle of urine spattered into the pan below. He staggered back with shock. His urine was dark brown, almost the colour of coke, red mixed with the ammonia. With a sense of dread, he looked at his penis, still pinched between his thumb and forefinger. It was numb and shrivelled, and he couldn't feel anything through it. When Rob let go of it, it was with the feeling of it coming off in his hand. He flushed away the evidence, forgetting briefly that he didn't want to wake his mother. But that was unlikely, given the pills. Splashing cold water on his face, Rob looked at his gaunt features in the mirror. *Move, god damn it! Get going!*

When the hissing began, Rob ran.

He hurried back to his room. The sounds weren't loud, not yet, but they were there. She was coming. He knew it. Maybe he was out of time. Rob eased his cupboard door ajar. The ball-sprung latch hovered just before the point of no return and the door popped open. Rob grabbed the flimsy slatted panel, stifling the noise, and listened.

Blood pulsed in his ears; birds sang, and death approached, whispering quietly, but as real as the tremor that compelled him from his bed.

Kneeling on the floor, he pulled out a box. Placing it to the side, Rob reached into the dark, his skin crawling, warning him of the danger. Groping around, he remembered a scene in *Flash Gordon*. It was another of the all too few connections with his dad. They'd watched it together years ago when Rob was still too young for it. But because of that, the image had remained vivid in its technicolour terror. Prince Barin and Flash, in a test of manhood, stuck their hands through the holes of a rotting stump deep in the swamp. A mud-covered scorpion awaited the man who chose the wrong hole. Rob eased out his schoolbag, which he'd stowed in preparation. No scorpion stung him. Unzipping it slowly, Rob double checked to confirm that the Manila envelope posted by someone called Deborah Keeley was still there. Rob now realised she was his father's mistress and the reason they left London - or one reason at least. The letter accompanied Richard's notes. His mother hadn't found them once he saved them from the bin. And then Rob thought with sad longing, *How could she?* Rob had taken over the chores, cleaning, cooking, putting out the rubbish for collection. Dr Bishop popped around every day too and ran the vacuum cleaner around and helped keep things straight. Sometimes, one or the other medical secretaries came too, getting the washing through, doing a little ironing and straightening the downstairs. Rob's mother didn't nag him anymore to tidy his room, and she wouldn't be in there dropping off laundry. As far as she knew, the letter was in the bin where it belonged.

But that manilla envelope had been the final straw. Last night Rob saw her take twice the dose of sleeping pills with a glass of wine. He found her passed out on her bed with the TV talking to itself. He turned off the TV and laid a blanket over his mother. She was as present in Rob's life as his father.

Rob shouldered his rucksack and sneaked from his room, tiptoeing along the landing, avoiding any creaking floorboards, until he reached the head of the stairs. He paused and listened. The slow, rhythmical breaths of his mother sound asleep came from her room.

The stairs presented another obstacle, but he let the stairs creak under his feet. The house slept on.

In a side pocket of his backpack sat a full bottle of water, which he'd filled in preparation the night before. If the bottle had been empty, Rob would have had to navigate through the house and fill it up in the kitchen now. Water would rush through the pipes, and the house would stir as the network of tubes rumbled, waking his mother. She would rush to the top of the stairs and see his despair and help him. But that was a fantasy, only as real as a tableau he could compose in his mind and put on the sketchpad with the pencils he'd packed, like a comfort blanket.

Instead, Rob put his hand in his pocket and found the letter he prepared the night before. He unfolded it, reading the words telling his mum he'd gone out early to get milk, and that he might go round to see Jason. Both were lies: their fridge was full of milk and food provided by Ken. And Jason was in on their attempt to solve a puzzle with missing pieces. He would meet Rob at the Minster. He folded the letter, with 'MUM' in large black letters on both sides of the paper, to catch her attention no matter which side it landed.

His hand on the door handle, Rob gave a final, hopeful look upstairs. He turned and unlocked the front door. The latch clunked, but he knew now nothing would wake his mother, and something else was pulling him on, something that his father and he had started, and that he must see through to the end because the end would find him, regardless.

He stepped over the threshold into a fresh morning and closed the door. Inserting his fingers into the letterbox, he lifted the brass flap and posted his letter through. It fell without noise to the door-mat, lying unread in the house of mourning, while Rob left to face his fate.

63

IT WAS THERE, everywhere, in the darkness of the wild wood. What it was, Julie could not tell at first. She was being watched. No, not only watched. She knew what that felt like. Eyes were always on her, searching her out when they believed she wasn't looking. More than once she thought how her appearance had a power and that power was a curse, something she neither asked for nor wanted. No, she wasn't only being watched. Felt? Known? She couldn't explain it. The forest was alive in a mirk of overgrown vegetation. It hummed with life, and that was what Julie felt. The vibration of it. Energy coursing. Her skin prickled, fingers and toes tingling. Pulse *rattatatting* in her heaving chest, and the blood surging in her ears. There was a cacophony of crunching, skittering, snapping and snuffling, accompanying the deep ribbit of toads, chirps of frogs, and twittering of many species of bird.

Moving through the wood, the plants reached for her, seeking Julie out, wanting to touch her. They didn't grab and pull at her like Danny did, groping. They touched her tenderly, with love and adoration, with knowing. This should have been a frightening place, but it wasn't. It was *home*: with all its strangeness.

But then it changed.

There was a great rumbling that staggered her. With tender care, the plants held her up. The sounds of the wildwood fell silent. Beneath Julie's feet the earth transmuted to an undulating state neither liquid nor solid. The plants enveloped her, holding her safe and upright, but also they began to smother. Vines of ivy and mistletoe, branches of oak, sycamore, birch and chestnut, entwined around her limbs, slid around her naked body, coiled around her neck, growing verdantly around her head, framing her face with lush foliage instead of hair.

A god in this place grew from the ground before Julie. But she could not make out its features, because the faces of gods are not to be looked upon even by their priestesses. Julie felt the god growing within her, pushing out everything else. The deity was the harmonic of all the vibrations she had been feeling in the dark wood. Its leaves and branches coiled from her ears, squeezed from beneath her eyes, and forced open her mouth to spring forth life in a primal scream.

Once more the earth shook, and Julie woke.

She was in her bedroom. The sun yawned between the houses of the council estate. The light a tired blue. Not only had the electricity bill not been paid, but her parents kept the heating to a minimum. Julie sat up in freezing cold. The strangeness of the dream along with its details was already fading. A forest? Something? What? A feeling? A powerful one. Already it was beyond her grasp, and as it disappeared, only the realities of her life were left in the dismal light of her bedroom.

Pulling back the covers, Julie swung her legs over the side of the bed, and as had become a habit, she touched her belly. She felt happy, sad, terrified, as well as love for the life growing inside her. It was an impossible love that touched every part of her, like that power in the dream. What was it about? It was overwhelming to feel all these things at once and by herself. Sharing them with Sally and Effie had felt good, and Effie had been the one brazen enough to buy a pregnancy test from the chemist in town, bearing the look of concern from the pharmacist, who put it in a paper bag along with a handful of leaflets. But Julie still felt alone. She needed to tell Danny, to share this with him. But that was another source of fear. How would he react? Would he want her to get rid of it? Did she want to? No. She knew she should. That was what everyone would tell her, but that wasn't what she wanted. How could she, feeling what she felt? How could she kill that love? But could she do it alone? Effie and Sally said no matter what, she wouldn't be alone. But they would finish their A levels, go to university, get jobs, meet their husbands, and Julie would be left changing nappies, and nursing a baby in the middle of the night, and trying to raise a life. Julie looked at the cold truth of that and still the love she felt warmed her.

And then there was Rob. What was that thought? Nothing that she could do anything about. Julie was sure now that Rob was as much of a victim as she was in the cyber bullying, and Jason had been right when he spoke to her at the end of school. Rob was nice. God! And his dad just died. That was so awful. She'd cried when Effie texted her the news and wanted to message him. Instead she sent a message to Jason, who said he'd pass it along. There was a pang of regret that stuck to the thoughts of Rob, but Julie had made her bed with Danny. Ha! What a phrase. She touched her belly again.

So much whirled in her head and when she stood, blood rushed to her head. Steadying herself on the desk, she felt a twinge, a light cramp in the pit of her abdomen. It passed along with the head rush.

Julie pulled her curtains and her heart sank. The forget-me-not, which had sprouted in the middle of her window sill next to her indomitable family of cacti, lay limp and dying. Its delicate leaves withered, as if parched of water. Its once purple petals were pale, like ghosts of their former selves. The plant was dying. Julie reached for the forget-me-not, and even before she could touch it, it withered further, shrivelling and draining of all colour, until it was nothing more than a grey knot of threads. Julie pulled her hand away, and her stomach cramped again, harder this time, causing her to suck in the air through her teeth and sit back on the bed.

Tears sprang to her eyes, and Julie felt afraid. It was probably nothing.

The leaflets the chemist had put in the paper bag with the pregnancy test had been about all aspects of pregnancy, along with helplines and website addresses for further information and advice. Julie knew occasional cramps were a normal part of pregnancy. But still she reached for her phone. Time was up. She needed to tell Danny.

He had a dark side, Julie knew that, and it came out as anger, but there were reasons for that too. For all the money he had, Danny missed his mother, Julie was sure, and his dad seemed less than supportive. Danny had a good side too. He must have. He could just as easily be excited about this baby as she, and if not excited maybe he'd learn to be and in the meantime stick by her. Of that, Julie was less sure, but hope and love, they were things she clung to. Danny loved her, Julie told herself as she picked up her phone and sent the message.

LIKE MUCH IN HIS LIFE, the world had conspired against Ally, and he had to bring his plans to a head. A phone call the previous afternoon had been followed by the arrival of a car filled with serious looking men with shaved heads. One had a moustache, which confirmed to Ally they were from Belfast. Only in Belfast had the moustache lingered on without irony, still taken as seriously as the Reformation, and just as ridiculous to the modern world. Ally had been banished to his room, but nothing was unusual about that. Eventually, the news was relayed by his drunk uncle, who slurred even more than usual, panic dripping from him like sweat. His father was dead, tortured and stabbed twenty-seven times by rival drug-pushing freedom fighters, while in the safety of maximum security.

Ally was going nowhere, certainly not home to Belfast. Despite the panic, his uncle didn't look sad, and Ally knew why. He'd already tracked the transactions back to people his uncle shouldn't have been in league with. They were the kind of people who would torture and stab his father to death for control of his freedom-fighting prostitution rings and money laundering bookmakers.

Ally sat working at his desk all night, setting his plans in motion, unleashing his rage. Accounts were hacked. Money disappeared. Lots of money. Some were placed in his uncle's accounts with an easy to follow trail to ensure his throat would be slit by one side or another.

He leaked information to newspapers. But the blood letting of his father was bad enough to indicate they would not stop there. They would come for his uncle, and then, they would come for him. Ally was sixteen and old enough to be made an example of. Sins of the father and all that. Younger men than he had had their kneecaps shot off or railing spikes driven through their thighs or their brains beaten out in front of their families with baseball bats while their *mammies* screamed. And so Ally was going to bring as much down around him as possible. There would be a bloodbath in Belfast, Derry and Portadown, as each side blamed the other for the damage Ally inflicted upon them unseen.

Then there was his own prison to deal with. Ally couldn't break out of it, and a bit of him didn't want to. He'd face whatever came with a smile and cutting one-liner. And while he was waiting, he'd do what he did best. Manipulate. Undermine. Infect. They all thought they were so perfect in this fucking idyll, with their perfect fucking lives, and perfect fucking school, and over-priced houses and over-achieving kids in after-school clubs, with their gastro-pubs, and craft ales, and German cars, with humus colonics and baba ganoush facials before their Spring skiing holidays in France.

Their perfection was a lie.

Ally had dug beneath the surface, through the loam of zeros and ones, between the mycelium of fibre optics and bacterium of data to dig up the roots of their hypocritical souls, and secret them away. He unearthed the information from their virtual boxes and delivered it. Fetish browsing histories, digital correspondence confirming affairs, credit card payments to escorts while on business trips, collections of photographs teachers, nurses, car dealers, and all the other sanctimonious perverts shouldn't have: he emailed it all to the relevant parties. Spouses, newspapers, websites, social media accounts, and the police all received an enormous delivery of ripening horse crap.

But like any treasure, they would have to take their time to dig it up because Ally also unleashed a special virus of his own making to bury them in more shit. Their digital lives would crash around them, long enough to cause panic. Maybe he was freeing them, and he was an unseen god delivering them to a new life, reborn in the manure of truth. Maybe. Like a god, he didn't care. He never had, not about them, only about *her*, and she was the final piece of his plan.

Today Ally would take Julie. She was up early too. The software monitoring all her devices told Ally as much; she wanted to see that Neanderthal Danny. Ally leered. He'd sent a special little package to Danny's Chief Constable father early last night. A naughty boy was he, mixing with people he really shouldn't be. Eastern European gentlemen with connections to his younger wife. Tut tut. Danny must have had about as much fun as the night Ally nudged him into the house of mirrors. Stupid fool, so easily manipulated and clearly into Julie for all the wrong reasons. Deep down, Ally was sure Danny wouldn't care when he took Julie, certainly not if his search history was anything to go by. Not unless Julie was circumcised and hung like a donkey, which Ally had video footage proving she wasn't. No, she was all woman, and Danny just wasn't into that kind of thing, even if he couldn't admit it to everyone else.

Ally picked up his phone and watched the dot representing Julie. Everything was coming together. He could feel it. Today was the day to end all days. As he pocketed his phone, he could have sworn he felt the earth move.

64

Rob panted as he cycled up the Ropewalk. The gradual climb of the hill towards the centre of the town made him wheeze like an old man. His limbs were heavy and his throat burnt sickly, but he wouldn't stop. The hunting whispers followed, driving him on. The rustling came from the hedges and grass verges. He could hear them churning beneath the tarmac of the road and pavements. Tunnelling, squirming roots pursuing, playing with their prey.

When he turned at the crossroads onto Queen Street, Rob could free wheel, but he didn't. They were gaining, growing louder.

He pedalled hard.

A stitch stabbed hard enough in his kidneys to make him groan.

The parade of quaint Victorian redbrick shops flew by, and in the reflection of their windows, Rob caught glimpses of her. Mary Hooper, like in the house of mirrors at the fairground, flitting from antique shop to butchers' to shoe shop to bakery, cafe, hardware store to bookshop. Never seen clearly. Only the fleeting impression of a dirty hag with long lank hair in the gloom of shops still closed in the early morning.

Rob didn't even look as he skidded through a right turn onto King Street. He heard a row in one of the flats above the shops, raised voices followed by a scream and a crash of something against a wall.

He had no time to wonder about it or notice a woman hurry along with tears rolling down her face.

It was still early, and the town was quiet, and he had to meet Jason before he was caught. They were meeting at the Minster. It was holy ground, and he'd be safe there; he hoped. The small roundabout at the centre of the town was only feet away. Rob stood on his pedals and pumped them hard, hearing the whispers at his back. The Witchopper flashed by in the window of Gascoines' estate agents, her hand outstretched.

Rob turned his head looking back.

The bike wobbled.

He corrected, swerving hard left to head down Church Street.

The Land Rover loomed as a dark green shape. Its horn blared and tires scuffed the road as the brakes locked.

Rob's swerve took him away from the front of the Land Rover, but he collided with its side.

Everything came to an abrupt halt.

Sat in the middle of the road, with little more than grazed knees and elbows, Rob looked up. The front wheel of his bike turned slowly. The back wheel had buckled badly.

He looked back skittishly, already getting to his feet.

"Gosh, are you alright, young lad?" A man had alighted the dirty Land Rover and hurried around to Rob. He steadied Rob and followed his gaze back to the roundabout. "Are you running from something?" he asked, in an avuncular tone.

"What? Sorry. No." Rob turned back to the man who looked like a gentleman farmer, in Wellington boots and a Barbour jacket. The pursuing whispers had stopped. The farmer didn't look like he believed him.

"I'm afraid your bike's banged up." The farmer picked up the bike, examining the damage.

"What seems to be the trouble here then?" A new voice came from behind Rob.

"Constable Playfair, I'm afraid we had a little collision. The boy seems alright, but his bike, well better it than him."

"Rob Peters, is that you?" Constable Playfair said. "You are in the wars at the moment. How is your mother doing?"

Rob shrugged.

"That good, huh? And you?"

Rob rubbed the graze on his elbow. "Okay, I guess."

Constable Playfair answered the farmer's quizzical look, "Rob's father was the editor of *The Newark Advertiser*."

"Oh?" the farmer said, and then realisation dawned and he repeated it more emphatically, "Oh! I was sorry to hear about his passing. I used to read his column in *The Daily Telegraph*. He had a cutting wit."

This was a revelation to Rob. He'd never thought of his father as funny, but then there was so much left undiscovered about each other. As genial as this traffic accident was becoming, Rob wanted to get going. Jason was waiting.

From behind his smile, the farmer appraised Rob. "No harm done here, apart from your bike. I'll tell you what. I'll give it to my man, Eddie. He can fix anything. You come and get it on Wednesday. Have you got a job for the summer?"

Rob shook his head.

"Well, we've plenty of work for a strong young man. Good outdoor labour. A few hours here and there. Put a few pounds in your pocket."

"Now that's an offer. Mr Windsor owns the biggest farm around here. There isn't a thing he doesn't know about the land," Constable Playfair said.

"Thanks, that would be great," Rob agreed, knowing it was unlikely he'd ever get the chance to take him up on the offer.

"Fantastic. Mine is the farm up behind the old willow tree, on the other side of the River Greet. You probably call it the stream. It's never been much of a river."

"The willow!" Rob remembered something in his father's notes he was going to bring up with Jason.

"That's right where you lot have your parties on a Friday night," Mr Windsor nodded.

"I don't think we should be encouraging that," Constable Playfair offered, not without humour.

"You and I both had our nights down there. They all do. It's on my land, and I don't mind. Wish they'd tidy up a little after themselves. But young'uns will be young'uns. And we all need to make our offerings at the tree."

"Offerings?" Rob said.

"Rob's not long lived here," Constable Playfair explained.

"Come up on Wednesday and I'll tell you all about it." Mr Windsor was putting Rob's useless bike in the back of his Land Rover. He slammed the door shut, and Rob could have sworn he felt the earth shake again. Mr Windsor paused, along with Constable Playfair. They seemed to stop, not just to listen, but to pay attention to everything around them, sensing. But like a flash of Mary Hooper in the shop windows, they were back to normal the next instant. Mr Windsor climbed into the cab of his four-by-four. A shriek came from another of the flats above the shops. Constable Playfair tipped his cap and hurried off, and the rustling whispers sounded once more.

JASON STOOD WAITING at the north door of the Minster, clutching his own bike like an eager steed.

Rob checked behind, holding his side. The stitch, that was the less distressing term to use for it, stabbed again as soon as he started to run the short distance down Church Street to cut into the Minster's graveyard. He felt pursued.

"I thought you were bringing your bike?" Jason said.

His expression dropped when he saw Rob's face.

"Is it open?" Rob panted.

The susurrations hissed and crackled, reaching a menacing peak.

"I haven't checked." Jason couldn't see anything in the graveyard.

Rob bustled past him into the portico. The door gave under his effort, but it was heavy, and he had to lean his whole weight behind it to force it open. He held the door for Jason, who ran in after him. Rob looked back the other way, the whispers of things moving through the earth having become a wall of white noise. As he tried to close the door, it suddenly seemed to resist his attempts, as though an invisible force applied itself.

"Help me," Rob cried through gritted teeth. Jason added his weight to Rob's.

The door closed. Silence reigned. The boys leaned back against the door.

"You sure know how to get a boy excited." Jason peered through the latch. "What was following you?"

"The sounds." Rob bent, put his hands on his knees, swallowing the acid in his throat.

"I couldn't see anything."

"She was following me. I saw her in the windows, like that time in the house of mirrors."

"Saw who?"

Both boys spun to find the Reverend Lovegrove dressed in his long black cassock. His head was tilted, face sanguine but quizzical.

Rob could not think of what to say.

"Mary Hooper," Jason blurted.

Rob pictured an ambulance with the back doors flung open, and he and Jason in straitjackets raving in the back before they were carted off to the secure hospital at Rampton.

"Not Mary Hooper the Witchopper?" The Reverends' smile flared, and his voice crackled with warm laughter at the notion. The boys looked wearily into the graveyard. The smile guttered on the Reverend's lips.

"That's right. She cursed Rob and his dad when they went to The Witch's Brew to write a story. They've been tortured by her ever since, haunted by visions and dreams. Rob has even been attacked by killer brambles. His dad tried to find a way to break the curse, even talked to a professor in London. But..." Jason took a breath and the next thing was a sad consequence in his tale, "well, you know what happened. A man in the prime of his life just dropped dead in London. Heart failure, at his age, with no previous history. Come on!" The Reverend looked like he was about to say something, but Jason wasn't finished. "Now, she's coming for Rob. We think time is up and Rob has to break the curse, or we'll be burying him with his dad this time next week. But that's just a potted summary. We're kind of pressed for time. Desperate wouldn't be an overstatement. So, we came here to go through the notes in the quiet of the Chapter House, which has the Greenman carvings. Rob saw a reference to him last night in his father's file, from some old diary, and..." Jason finally seemed to have run out of things to say.

"The Reverend Moseley's diary?"

Rob straightened up. "Yes, I think so." If they were going to carry him off to the psych ward, he'd go with his head held high.

"You two had better come with me. I think a cup of tea and a little chat is in order." The Reverend turned and walked down the nave. He hadn't gone far when he stopped. "If things are as urgent as you say, you'd better hurry up." He continued on and the boys followed, exchanging puzzled looks.

JASON PERCHED ON A STOOL, Rob on a wobbly school chair in the vestry. Both nursed mugs of tea. The Reverend added milk to his and sat at his desk, swivelling his chair to face the boys.

"Oh!" His face lit up. "I almost forgot. Chocolate Hobnobs. I brought a new packet with me this morning." He fetched them from the pocket of his coat hung on the wall and insisted the boys take two each before having the same himself. "Down to business," he said, dunking the first of his biscuits with precision timing, then tapping it on the side of the cup and biting the disintegrating biscuit in a quick practised movement. The Reverend rolled his lips together, raising his eyebrows in a high arch at Rob and Jason in an expression of pure pleasure. Finally, he said, "Mary Hooper, I don't know if you are aware of this but I wrote my PhD thesis about her. Well, her and some local folk religion."

Jason and Rob looked at each other, stunned.

"In fact, your father wanted to speak to me, Rob. He phoned me on the day... well, on the day he died. Unfortunately, we kept getting each other's voicemails. He sounded very urgent that day, and now here is his son with that same urgency. There's no voicemail now, so I think you had better talk, and I had better listen. Start from the beginning and leave nothing out."

Jason inclined his head toward the vicar in encouragement to his friend, and Rob began. He filled the vicar in on everything he could remember, with Jason providing reminders along the way. He covered the first sighting of the Witchopper, details of his dreams and visions, full of dark images from a wild wood, writhing with plants and bugs. He covered the incident in the shower where children laughed in the mist and the floor became like quicksand he barely escaped, as something huge stamped unseen in the mirk. The menacing bramble that attacked him in the alley when the vicar had found Danny standing over him. The picture he'd drawn of Julie in the wood that came alive with the giant oak becoming the Greenman. The old woman who painted blood on their door. What he knew of his father's visions, and the night at the funfair when Mary came to him in the house of mirrors.

"And the thirst. Don't forget that!" Jason added.

"Thirst?" Lovegrove raised his eyebrows again, the first action he'd performed throughout Rob's account.

Rob explained about his and Richard's unquenchable need for water. As he did, the Reverend reached behind himself for a large black volume and began leafing to the back of the book.

Rob finished speaking, and they sat in silence for long seconds while the Reverend traced his finger down pages, his eyes darting, brow furrowed. "Aha! There it is." He stabbed the page with his digit. "The Reverend Moseley's diaries talk of the same thirst."

"Who's the Reverend Moseley," Jason asked.

"He's me, sort of. Well, me several hundred years ago at the time of Mary Hooper's demise."

The boys didn't understand.

"He was involved in whatever happened to poor Mary. A terribly self important man, by what's in his diary. Nothing was explicit in those days, particularly about things they were ashamed of. They cloaked it in euphemism. But reading between the lines of his diary and what the magistrates wrote, something terrible happened to Mary Hooper. The official report says she was hung without trial for killing four children. But their bodies were never found. Many more of the children died while unattended for several days in the foundling house after Mary's death. Anyway, I digress. Moseley wrote of a terrible, all consuming thirst, which he could never slake. He died three weeks after Mary was hanged, found dead in a pool of holy water at the great font in the nave." Lovergrove gestured to the door of the vestry.

"You believe us?" Jason said.

"About the curse," Rob added.

"I think you need someone to believe you, and so I do. I do not believe you are lying to me. So, let us proceed with this line of thinking. If curses can be made, they can be broken. I suspected that Mary Hooper may have been what they would have called in those days a *cunning woman*. It's one of those words that has changed its meaning over the years. In the 1800s it still would have meant sort of magical. It was used to describe the kind of people that in a pagan society would have been shaman or religious folk, I suppose like me. And even though the Christian Church swept away or, indeed, incorporated the symbols, dates and religious sites of much of the old beliefs, there was always a residual of that religion possibly right up to the period of the Great War. For all I know, there may still be lineages of people still practising the old ways. I don't know of any personally, but this is getting us away from my point. Shamans are often marginal people, most certainly when a more dominant religious force has taken over. I believe, reading between the lines of the primary sources, that Mary was one such person. For example, the magistrate from Nottingham noted many herbs and tinctures which were discovered in the foundling house after Mary's death. This was taken by people such as Moseley as proof of her witchcraft."

"My dad says in his notebook he believed that Mary was trying to help the children."

"I'd agree," Lovergrove said. "The children probably came down with a disease that neither she nor any medicine at the time could have been able to cure. She lived on the edge of society doing something for the town which dealt with a great moral shame: caring for their unwanted children. We know this because the Minster was the primary charitable source for the foundling house, and they kept excellent records. Sadly, through Moseley, they seem to have kept it in a state of complete destitution. I think it was probably common knowledge that Mary was a Wiccan or a cunning woman. As you know well, small towns like a whipping boy. I'm sure even at your age you know how things can get twisted." The Reverend sighed, and Rob knew he was referring to the trouble he and Julie had.

"I think they did something quite terrible to Mary, and it suited the town to believe that she was evil, rather than their own neglect being the true sin. I believe they punished her as a witch, something that was against the law at that time. The Reverend Moseley's diaries, while obtuse, hint at something quite dreadful occurring, suggesting more than death. Rather than facing up to this, the town turned Mary into the bogeyman, or rather the Witchopper."

"But the curse?" Rob asked in a dry whisper. He finished his tea.

The Reverend nodded gravely. "Let us assume that Mary cursed the town. We may assume that it was connected to the great wrong done to her and quite possibly the children in her care. What I've read about curses tells me they are born out of a sense of injustice. They are a kind of judgement. But I think the thing that we should focus on, Rob, is that curses can be broken. We all carry a sense of guilt around with us. In some sense we are all sinners that have things we feel we need to apologise for or give recompense. That is the human condition. So, Rob, maybe ask yourself is there something that you could give to Mary, or is there something that you feel deep inside you have done wrong?"

Rob hung his head, wiping his nose on his sleeve. He didn't answer the Reverend Lovegrove and thought of Julie.

"Rob's a good guy," Jason said, putting a hand on Rob's shoulder.

"Good people make mistakes all the time," the Reverend said.

"But how can Rob have to make amends for what an entire town did two-hundred years ago?" Jason protested.

"And how would we give it to her?" Rob's voice quavered.

The Reverend opened a drawer in his desk and picked something out. He held it in his palm for the boys to see. It was a tiny figure made of grass, a loop for a head, and knots to give it legs and arms.

"A poppet?" Jason said.

"Indeed. People, I don't know who, leave them in the Chapter House every few weeks."

"I don't understand." Rob rubbed his eyes, trying to clear his mind.

"It's an offering to the Greenman, I believe. I've lived in Southwell my whole life, and there are other places, too, that people leave things. The Fairy Well. The Devil's Heel..."

"My granny always said to sprinkle salt on the roots of the Hanging Tree," Jason butted in.

The Reverend smiled and nodded encouragingly, "... and the old willow."

"The willow?" Rob said. "That's mentioned in my dad's notes."

"Yes, that's where the mob arrested Mary and where they thought she was burying the children. It's always been very popular with the young folk of the town on Friday evenings."

"Mr Windsor mentioned it this morning too," Rob said, searching his mind for connections, wondering at the coincidences.

"Charles Windsor, the farmer?" the Reverend said.

"I think so. I ran into his Land Rover this morning. But that's not important. It's just that the willow keeps coming up."

"We could visit each of those places and make offerings, like salt at the Hanging Tree, food at the Fairy Well. You know, like a pilgrimage," Jason said as though trying to convince himself.

Rob looked doubtful.

"I think it's an excellent place to start," the Reverend Lovegrove said encouragingly. "Pilgrimage and offerings, both of which are forms of sacrificial offerings, are features of penance in most religions. It couldn't hurt. In fact, I think it would be just the ticket."

The boys stood, Jason shouldering his satchel, Rob his rucksack. The Reverend rose with them. Rob felt it made some sense, but had the feeling they were still missing something and that it was too easy.

"Let me know how you get on," the Reverend said, showing them to the door. "Oh, wait." He hurried off. "Take these." He handed over the rest of his prized packet of chocolate Hobnobs. "There couldn't be a better offering than these. Just let me take one more for later."

65

It was agonising how long she had to wait. Julie dressed, pulling on her jeans and T-shirt, slipping into a pair of trainers, and ducking into a hooded top to warm herself up, all the while keeping an eye on her phone.

Sitting on her bed cross-legged, cradling the phone, it finally lit up, pinging with the message. The room was a little brighter now, although it was still early Saturday morning, as Julie read Danny's reply. She said she really needed to see him. Danny had replied to come round at about ten. Julie said it couldn't wait, and Danny relented, saying to come now and that he'd be dressed by the time she arrived. It was eight.

Julie slipped silently from the house, with nothing but a mobile phone in her back pocket, hugging her elbows over her belly. She hadn't cramped again and felt relieved. The town was waking up, and twice she passed houses with full-blown arguments muffled, like someone screaming into a pillow.

Danny met her at the front door in his bare feet, hair still a mess, picking sleep from his eyes and looking like he'd hardly slept. He opened the door wide for her, and Julie ducked under his arm.

She stood in the expansive hallway. The large staircase rose to the first floor. The chandelier suspended above their heads was dull and unlit. A huge bouquet of fresh flowers was arranged in a crystal vase on a polished side table under a picture of Danny's father and his not-mother Karolina. Julie still held her elbows despite the warmth of the house. Danny closed the door and took her into his arms, layering his mouth to hers. She allowed his tongue to dart into her mouth for a few moments, then pulled away.

"I need to tell you something," Julie said.

Danny frowned and then shrugged. "Whatever. I need coffee and toast. Do you want some?" He seemed more sullen than usual.

"Are you okay? You looked tired."

"My dad is a prick is all. He and Karolina left late last night."

"Left?" It was the way Danny had said it. Julie could tell there was more to it.

"The police turned up and arrested him and her. The Chief Constable! Can you believe it?"

"Why?"

"Something to do with her. They took all our computers, files, books, records. Trashed the place."

Julie looked around. The hall had been unaffected, but here in the open-plan kitchen, the living area had been turned over and looked like a college dormitory. Drawers and cupboards all around the kitchen stood ajar, having been searched.

"That's awful. Are you okay?" She put a hand on his arm as the kettle grumbled to a boil. He tensed under her fingers.

"Yeah, I'm fine. Good riddance."

"You don't mean that."

"What the fuck would you know?"

Julie shrunk away, and Danny poured water into a French press, where the coffee grinds churned in boiling, black clouds. They stood in awkward silence until Danny forced the plunger down, squeezing the coffee under slow, increasing pressure.

"So what's so urgent?" Danny sipped at the black liquid. "That fucking Rob Peters video online again? I told you, people will get bored of it soon. That Rob is just some stalking pervert."

"It's not Rob."

"Are you defending him again? You haven't forgotten he gave me

396

this?" Danny pulled back his Ken doll hair. The stitches had dissolved, but the healing wound was still pink and raw.

Julie shook her head.

"Has your dad gone off on one again?"

"No," there was frustration in Julie's voice.

"All right. You don't need to get pissy with me. Then why did you wake me up this bloody early on a Saturday morning. I've hardly slept after my dad's colleagues got finished with the place."

Julie touched her belly. "It's nothing to do with Rob or home. It's about you and me." There was a huge lump in her throat. Danny looked confused, his annoyance growing.

"What about us? What's wrong?" And then he said, as if uttering something preposterous, "You're not breaking up with me are you?"

Julie shook her head, her eyes still brimming with tears. One overflowed and trickled down her cheek.

"Then what is it?"

Julie had thought about this hundreds of times, playing it over and over again in her head. All the different ways she would say it. How Danny might react. What he might say next. But here, in the reality of the situation, none of it tallied comfortingly with what she'd imagined. And so instead of saying it calmly, having laid out that she really liked Danny and that young people could do anything, she just blurted it out.

"I'm pregnant." Her tears overflowed.

Danny stopped blowing on his coffee and stared at her with a mix of horror and anger.

"What? You've got to be kidding me? We've only done it once. I thought you were on the pill?"

The tears kept rolling down Julie's face. "I thought you'd use a condom," which seemed entirely beside the point now.

"I can't believe you let me do it without saying anything," Danny almost shouted, his tone angry.

What could she say? That she felt pressured? But had he forced her? No, not in that moment. Although dumping her because she wouldn't and then getting back together with her when she felt so vulnerable had left her wanting to make him happy, because that might have made *her* happy. Now that all started to sound thin and naïve, and she didn't feel she could tell Danny any of it.

Instead Julie said, "But what do you think?"

"What do I think?" He slammed down his mug of coffee so hard that the black liquid sloshed onto his hand. Julie flinched; Danny winced as the coffee burnt his hand. "Shit!" he shouted, rubbing his scalded skin. He started to pace up and down the kitchen in short stretches in front of the counter. "What do I think?" Now Danny was shouting. Julie shrank away.

Coming to a hard stop, Danny pointed at her. "You did this on purpose. You're trying to trap me. Or maybe you're lying. How do I know you're telling the truth?"

"No," Julie sobbed.

But Danny wasn't listening. "Yeah," he said more to himself, "how do I even know it's mine?"

"Danny, stop." He wouldn't and neither would her tears. Julie found herself backed up to a dining chair, which poked sharply into her back.

"You didn't answer." Danny rounded the kitchen island between them. "Well, is it even mine, or is it that prick Rob Peters'?"

"You were my first time."

He barked a cruel laugh. "You're joking." And then realising there was no joke there, he said, "What do you expect me to do about it?"

"I don't know."

"You don't know?" Danny grabbed her by one of the elbows she still hugged tightly to herself. "What do you want from me, except to ruin my life?"

"Danny, I don't want anything. I just want..."

"What? To have it?" Danny was shouting now, pulling and pushing at Julie's elbow.

"Danny, please. I don't know. I just wanted to talk to you."

"What is there to talk about? Get rid of it, of course."

Her only answer was a piteous and anguished look.

"Jesus! You want to keep it, don't you?"

"I don't know."

"I don't know. I don't know," he mocked, marching her now,

tugging her along by the elbow, out of the kitchen and back into the hall. "The fact that you don't know means you're thinking about it. You're insane. I'm not being trapped with a fucking baby and some poor slut before we've even finished school. We're going to the doctor's right now, and they'll give you a pill or make an appointment or whatever it is to get that thing out of you now."

Every word hurt more than how hard he gripped her arm and yanked her along. But that pain paled in comparison to what hit Julie next. The sudden intensity of the cramping in her belly doubled her over, and she cried out in agony.

"What's the matter with you?" Danny let her go, the look on his face was as though he'd dropped something dangerous, and he stepped back.

Julie whimpered, shrinking in on herself, clutching at her stomach. The pain was all consuming in its power. She gritted her teeth, biting down on the excruciating cramping. Danny hesitated, as if she were an ember that might still be too hot, and if Julie could have opened her eyes, she would have seen that at least he didn't believe she was faking. However, the anger was still there, boiling beneath the surface, only tempered by Julie's obvious agony.

At last, the pain subsided. Julie took deep lungfuls of air. Something wasn't right. She knew it now. These weren't merely cramps. Something was very wrong, and that realisation had its own kind of pain. A yearning ache. The feeling of falling into an abyss and knowing the fall would last forever, because no one could catch her. The grief was deeper than anything she could have imagined, a limbo where lives that were wanted and loved, but had never lived, dwelt.

Julie tried to stand and found she had the strength, though she was unsteady, at least at first. Danny came to help her. He held her up, putting an arm around her waist.

"I'm okay," Julie told herself.

Danny thought she was talking to him. "You don't look it. Christ! This day couldn't get any worse."

"I think maybe I need to go to the doctor."

"No kidding. It's probably for the best." It was insensitive and cruel.

Even though she felt weak, Julie wanted to scream in his face. She even turned to him, ready to do so, and that's when she saw the look there. So out of place was it, that Julie followed his gaze to her crotch, and there, blooming like a dark flower on a time-lapse camera, a patch of scarlet staining her jeans. Over Danny's shoulder, the ostentatious arrangement of flowers that sat on the side table in the hall began to wither and die. Their once vivacious blooms turned to ash, flaking like dead skin to the wood below. She saw their stems shrivel, twisting to threads of grey and black. Death soured on her tongue and rustled like whispering ghosts in her ears.

66

THE SIGN HAD BARELY COME to rest on 'Open' when Jason and Rob burst in, the bell above the door announcing them.

"Gosh! You're early," the owner said, a sky-blue apron tied around her waist.

The boys hurried to the fridge and lifted out cans of coke and fizzy orange. They grabbed a few packets of crisps and piled their haul on the glass counter displaying hot baked goods.

"Two meat pasties..." Rob began.

"And a sausage roll," Jason pointed.

"Large or small," the owner said, picking up a pair of tongs.

"Large," the boys chorused.

"Better make it three, just in case." Jason held up as many fingers, and grabbed sachets of salt from a wicker basket on the counter with his other hand.

Rob nodded in agreement. "And one of those?" He pointed to a round, country loaf dusted with flour on the shelf behind the owner.

"This is quite a feast. You boys going on a picnic?"

Rob searched for his wallet in his backpack. "Something like that."

"That'll be eleven pounds and sixty six, duck."

"I've only got a tenner," Rob said.

Jason found the rest in his wallet, and Rob stuffed the lot into his backpack, struggling to zip it up.

"Thanks," they called, and the bell tolled again behind them.

The owner went back to humming a tune the boys had interrupted. She put a hand in the pocket at the front of her apron and idly played with a straw poppet lying hidden there. Her humming ceased for a moment as she listened; cans of fizzy drinks in the fridge rattled together like gossiping pensioners. When they stopped, she sniffed in acknowledgement. Crossing the shop floor, humming as she went, she turned the sign from open to closed and locked the door.

THE DEAD TREE creaked above them.

"Here." Jason handed Rob half of the tiny sachets of salt. They tore them open and sprinkled the white grains over the roots of the Hanging Tree. "There," Jason dusted off his hands, "that's a start."

Rob looked up into the tangle of branches. "Is that it? Are we supposed to do something else?"

"We could pour out some Tango too. It's usually the salt people do here." Jason rooted through the bottom of the backpack on Rob's back, pulling out a can of fizzy, as well as the notebook and file, and handing the latter to Rob. "Got it!" Jason zipped up the backpack and cracked the pull on the can. It gave an angry, serpentine hiss.

"What now?"

"Guess we pour it over the roots like the salt and move on to the next place and repeat."

"Don't I need to say something?"

"What would you say?"

"Sorry?" Rob sounded doubtful.

"Hmm! You don't sound it?"

"Does that matter?"

"Probably, you know, if we're taking this whole pagan pilgrimage seriously. And as you're about to die an agonising death at the hands of a pissed off ghost who was hanged two-hundred years ago on this very tree by a bunch of yokel idiots, I'm guessing, yes."

"But what have I got to be sorry about?" Rob thought about his dad and all the crap he'd had to put up with since moving here. He thought about how scared he'd been the whole time and how tired and thirsty he was and how ill he felt. He didn't feel sorry. He felt mad, and he sounded mad.

Jason put up his hands, the can of fizzy orange still in one of them. "Hey! I'm on your side."

Unseen leaves rustled in the bare branches of the hanging tree.

"I know; I'm sorry."

"That's great, but you don't need to say it to me."

"Very funny."

"I try."

There was a screech of car brakes.

"Oh shit! Let's run." Jason tried to pull Rob away, but Rob had no intention of running, not anymore. Not from Mary Hooper and not from Danny. All things, it seemed, were being drawn together today.

"Peters, you fag, what are you doing here?"

"Rob, come on. We've got other things to do." Jason tugged at his shoulder again.

With Danny bearing down on him with a look of rage, Rob thought about capitulating. There were things scarier than Danny afoot. But when he saw Julie get out of the car, eyes puffy with tears, Rob's resolve hardened.

"Danny, don't." Julie was holding a hand on her belly and looked in pain. Rob immediately thought Danny had hurt her.

"You talk a lot about fags, Danny. Ever wondered why?" Rob was clenching his fists, scrunching up the file and notebook in one of them. Julie bent double, turning Rob's anger to concern, but also breaking his focus.

Danny grabbed a handful of Rob's *Nirvana* hoodie, twisting the smiley emoji, and planted his forehead in Rob's face. The nose bone crunched. Bright pinpricks of light flared like sparklers on Bonfire Night.

Rob found himself sitting on the grass, observing with perplexed disconnection. Sheets of paper from his dad's notes floated around him like giant butterflies, torn from their binding. Julie was shouting, pulling at Danny, who threw her off. She landed in a heap and clutched her stomach. Rob thought she looked so sad.

A can of Tango spun through the air, spraying a Catherine Wheel of bright orange jets. It hit Danny in the chest and bounced off. He flung the tattered notes aside and punched Jason in the stomach, who doubled over like Julie.

A boom came up through the ground as if a giant was stomping its foot impatiently, and Rob felt thick coppery liquid trickle down his throat.

The Hanging Tree moaned, and the sun disappeared.

Rob looked up into the face of a dark angel who'd returned to finish what he'd started in an alley several weeks ago. This time he looked more vengeful and out of control, as if he'd been cast from heaven and now had nothing to lose.

A fist created another galaxy of stars before Rob's eyes, snapping back his head and tottering him to his back. The world pitched away to a cotton-spotted sky.

A weight settled astride Rob, mounting his hips. Danny's eyes were phosphorus flares of fevered rage. Strangely, he pawed at Rob's face, dragging his fingers over Rob's lips. Then Danny hit him with the back of his hand, spinning his head the other way. Jason was trying to stand, still mawing for air.

His senses still out of sync, Rob looked back up to Danny. Julie was at his shoulder. He now backhanded her too. Her head whipped to the side, but when it came back, hair messed across her face, Rob could have swore Mary Hooper had taken her place. It must have been so, because in his disconnected world things became stranger.

Large and powerful, Danny's hand settled around Rob's throat, but no sooner had he begun to squeeze, he stopped.

The echoes of the world bounced together like a penny spinning to rest, stopping sharply and normality, whatever that now was, rushed back into sync. There wasn't any screaming or shouting. Rob struggled to make sense of the situation. Jason looked as confused as he felt but with an edge of wan horror. Julie stood upright glaring at Danny, her hair still covering her face. And there was someone else with them. It took a second for Rob to place her. It was Millicent, the mad old lady who'd painted blood on their door. Her hands were outstretched and she was saying something. Rob's senses couldn't have been completely back because he couldn't understand anything she was saying. It not only sounded like gibberish but as though two people were speaking at once. Then he saw Danny, clutching at his throat. Spittle slobbered from his puce face. His eyes bulged before they rolled back in his head. Moments later his arms became weak, as if only gradually forgetting their purposes, and fell away to hang limply at his sides. The ligature around his neck suddenly uncoiled, snaking behind Danny's body, which fell heavily to the grass of the Burgage.

Still struggling to stand himself, Jason staggered to pick up the torn sheets of notes, and then hauled Rob up. Blood dripped down his front, staining the emoji, which smiled idiotically. Jason tentatively reached a hand to Julie, who stood rigid, her arms spasmed straight, fingers splayed. Rob could still not see her face, turned as she was to Danny's unconscious body, hair hiding her features. When Jason touched her, they both jumped. Her face spun to them, and for a split second Rob thought he'd see Mary Hooper, but it was Julie, frightened and confused.

"Alright, Jack. I got here as quickly as I could. Stop fussing," the mad old lady, Millicent, said to herself as she tottered over to them. Rob could have sworn something changed in her eyes, like the whites had momentarily flashed dark.

"Come quick, my ducks. Before he wakes up. There's no time. Oh, you've been in the wars," Millicent said to Rob, looking him over with soft warm hands. She gave Jason a nudge. "That way. To my house. It's not far. I'll get you sorted. Give you what you need. Go on. I'll get Julie."

How did she know her name, Rob thought? Jason was already leading him down the Burgage towards Lower Kirklington Road.

"That's it, my duck. I know it's a lot to take in. Bit of a shock, isn't it?" Rob heard Millicent say to Julie. He looked behind to see the old lady put a comforting arm around Julie's shoulders. "I'll explain everything, if you'll just come with me. That's it. Don't worry about him. He'll wake up in a minute. You didn't kill him."

67

THEY CROSSED the road from the Burgage, and as they did Millicent hurried by them to lead the way. She didn't live far, in fact, it was only a few doors down from Rob's, he remembered, thinking back to the night Millicent had come knocking on his door, scaring the life out of them, a dead rat in hand, blood on her fingers, painting symbols on their door. Nothing strange there. And now here she was, right when they were trying to put an end to the weirdness. In a normal world, he would get Jason and Julie to run away with him as fast as he could. But Rob hadn't lived in a normal world for a month now. He felt they had to follow Millicent. Perhaps this was all the pieces falling in together. Perhaps the mad old lady was connected to the madness of his own life. Perhaps.

Rob's mind stopped wandering when Julie threaded her arm under his, taking his weight on the other side from Jason. He felt something tremendous then, as Millicent crossed back over the road and scurried up her drive. Julie and Jason diligently looked left and right, and the three of them crossed the road, and Rob felt the strength of his two friends beneath his arms. Jason, implacable and loyal, despite their friendship only being a few weeks old. And Julie, somehow, in this mad universe, was actually here with him, helping. Why? Rob's vision in one eye was bad, puffed up from Danny's backhand and the broken nose. The skin was already feeling taut and stretched, like it might split open. Rob smiled and his face stung and throbbed.

"Thanks," he said to both of them. Julie had looked so serious, but suddenly her features lightened, as if a weight momentarily lifted. They made eye contact, and Rob's heart skipped. She smiled too. Not the boyish, half-concussed grin Rob displayed, but a smile that quirked perfectly at the corners of her mouth, and seemed so unfathomable that Rob wanted to draw it, to capture its beautiful complexity forever. But then it was gone, like a flock of starlings startled into flight.

Millicent turned the key in her front door. "Tea," she announced. "You kids, take a seat in the front room with my husband, Brian. Don't worry, you won't disturb him. I'll put the kettle on and make us a special brew, and bring you something for those cuts and bruises, young Rob." The old woman hurried off through a door to the right.

Rob wasn't sure that he'd ever mentioned his name to her, but then again, someone must have said it either during the fight, or on the walk to Millicent's. His brain was still a little fuzzy.

Feeling Rob had his strength, Jason let him go and led the way into the living room. Julie didn't leave Rob's side, and they walked, still holding each other, into the living room. It was full of plants placed on sideboards, in the corners, around the fireplace, some hanging from baskets, or perched on frames like tea-stands. The three teenagers set themselves down on a large patterned sofa. Millicent's husband sat with his eyes closed, reclining in a wing-back chair, his head slightly to one side, mouth closed in a deep sleep.

"Anyone else feel like we've gone down the rabbit hole?" Jason broke the silence.

"I've been down the rabbit hole for weeks," Rob said, touching his face, which twisted, only making it worse.

Julie's voice quavered. "I could have killed him."

Rob sat between his friends, and now there was no need to hold on to her, though he wished he could. Julie looked terrified.

"What? No. That's stupid," Rob said as lightly as he could, looking from Julie to Jason, whose face only confirmed Julie's terror. Which didn't make any sense. They were in a fight. Danny was beating Rob. Jason was on the floor hurt and then... and then what? How exactly did it end? How did Danny end up on the ground unconscious? In Rob's befuddled mind, he'd just assumed Jason had... no, that didn't make sense either.

"What happened back there?" Rob looked between the two of them.

"I..." Julie raised her hands, half-miming the recent memory, as if replaying it would make sense of it all.

"You're a witch," Jason said, but he wasn't joking or throwing out one of his quick insults.

"But I... That isn't possible." Julie didn't sound as though she believed herself.

The tea tray rattled. "Did someone say *witch*? That's a bit rude. I prefer *cunning woman*, from the old tongue. Or you young 'uns seem to like *Wiccan*. Both are nicer." Millicent set down the tea tray on the coffee table before them. "I need a few other things. You three carry on your chat."

"See, rabbit hole," Jason said.

"Witch?" Rob stared at Julie, who still searched her hands for an explanation.

"Yeah, unless you've got another reason Julie can speak elvish and call forth roots from the ground to choke Danny unconscious."

The blur of images Rob could remember from the fight started to make some sense. But this, Julie, a witch, with powers? It left him even more stunned, and his head hadn't yet cleared from Danny's fists.

"Don't say witch," Millicent called through, "and it's not Elvish. That bloody Tolkien."

"But I didn't. I couldn't." Julie's eyes were glassy.

"You did and, apparently, you can. Look, this is going to be a lot to take in on top of, well," Jason twirled his hands like a stage magician, "your superpower, but Rob has been cursed by the Witchopper. Any relation?"

"None of us are blood relations; it doesn't work like that." Millicent called through, still rummaging for something out in the hall.

"She's got good hearing," Jason whispered.

"I heard that too, and it's the plants who are telling me what you're saying. Now hurry up and tell her about the curse."

Jason looked suspiciously at the many plants but went on, summarising everything that had happened to Rob and his dad, just as Rob had earlier told the Reverend Lovegrove. Julie sat and listened until Jason finished with Julie's dramatic intervention at the Hanging Tree.

Julie paused and then said, "I was sorry to hear about your dad." She took Rob's hand and his heart all at once stung with the loss and skipped with elation. "I wanted to text; I messaged Jason."

"You did?" Rob shot Jason a look.

Jason rolled his eyes. "I thought you had more important things to worry about. I was going to get around to it." He tutted at himself. "You two are insufferable. Can we get focused? Julie is clearly part of this. I don't know how or why, but it'd be too much of a coincidence that another wi... person of supernatural abilities turns up at the very moment you're on a pilgrimage to break the curse."

Millicent bustled into the room carrying a pile of old notebooks, some of which looked dogeared, others like stacks of ancient parchments roughly bound in tatty leather covers. She handed them all to Julie, who was more bewildered than ever.

"These were all mine. Now they're yours, my duck. I'm sorry we didn't find you earlier," Millicent said, squatting in front of Rob and picking up a poultice, he'd not noticed, from the tea tray. "You're a late bloomer, but powerful by the looks of it. I had a time countering your spell. It often comes out in times of stress. I suspected Jack might have been holding you back for this. Not that the silly old fool would admit as much to me." Rob hissed as the poultice touched his black eye. "Don't be a crybaby. Hold that there. It'll take down the swelling in no time and numb the pain." Millicent stood, poured the tea, handed it out, and took her own cup, which was already full with a yellowish liquid. She eased herself in another winged chair next to her sleeping husband, who hadn't stirred at all.

"Now, I haven't got much time. I shouldn't really be here anymore.

I'm a silly old lady, but Jack in the Green gave me one more thing to do, so I agreed to stay a little longer. Lucky for you, I did."

"Jack in the Green, the Greenman?" Rob said.

"Yes, Rob, but we really don't have enough time for ecumenical matters. Everything is coming together. I can tell what I know, but then I must leave. So, please hold on to your questions and listen. Poor Julie is playing catch up, and she is the key," Millicent raised a finger, silencing Jason and Rob. "Yes, *the key*. She is one piece of the puzzle that you boys have been missing. What you didn't realise - how could you? - was that this was never just about you, Rob, or your father. You are part of it, but only along with Julie." Millicent lent forward sipping her tea, her nose wrinkling as though it was too bitter. "I know you have lots of questions as well, Julie, and troubles of your own. And I'll get to those too. Julie is special. She knows that now, but it's obviously a shock. And that is because she is like me. There have been many of us through time, especially in this place. Jack was always strong here, going back to when the wild wood covered all the land, back before we slunk down from the trees. More of that is in my notebooks. Far more than I can say now is in there for you, Julie. Study them. They have everything you need to learn. I'm only sorry that I could not have met you a few years ago when I had my full wits about me."

Millicent seemed very sad then and drank a little more of her tea.

"Rob and Julie, you must go to the old willow. That is where Mary buried her children. That is where they caught her on the night they defiled and killed her, bringing this curse upon the town. The curse has gone on for far too long. Too much blood has been spilled. More than enough to satisfy Jack. It must be broken. You, Rob, are the lock. Julie is the key. Your curse, Rob, is something of a mistake. Although, it has a whiff of Jack's hand to it, if you ask me. You are caught in your father's wake. He committed the sin, the adultery, didn't he?"

Rob nodded. All three teenagers sat with their mouths agape, listening.

"But, so the plants tell me, at the same moment that your father was dishonouring your mother, you were with Julie. And because she is a Wiccan and because of the strength of feeling, the shame and embarrassment and the injustice that she felt, my guess is that caught you up in the curse. There are always grey areas in these things. Anyway, the only hope you have to break it is for you both to go to Jack in the Green. You must go to his last church, the old willow. I hope that will be enough. I don't know how the curse will be broken, only that Jack wants you to go there. But know this, Mary will not give you up easily, Rob. She is an angry spirit, not just for what they did to her, but what they did to her child. She's coming for you, as she came for your father."

Millicent let the information sink in. She laboured to say her final words, tiredness having swept over her. Taking her husband's hand, she finished her tea with a gulp.

"Can I use the bathroom?" Julie said.

"Of course you can. It's down the hall, on the left."

"Now boys, remember those books are for Julie. It's important that she has them. And you, Rob, must go with her to the willow immediately. It will not be easy to understand." Her words had begun to slur, and her eyes drooped. Rob said that he didn't understand. He wanted to ask so many questions.

"I've told you everything I know." Her eyelids almost closed, Millicent sounded drunk now.

Julie appeared at the door, one hand on her belly, pain on her face. Rob and Jason stood quickly, noticing the dark patch at the crotch of her jeans for the first time.

"What's wrong?" Rob said.

"I think we need to go now," Julie said from the door.

"You're bleeding." Rob went to her.

Millicent slurred from her seat, "The likes of us can never have children, my duck. The baby would never have been born." The boy's eyes grew in realisation as Millicent's eyes closed and her head lolled to the side. The teacup fell from her grip and smashed on the floor.

Jason moved to the old woman, shaking her arm and then her shoulder. Nothing would rouse her. Finally, he put two fingers to her neck and felt for a pulse. "She's dead," he said with cold realisation. A darker thought appeared in his eyes and he moved over to Millicent's husband. He put his fingers to the old man's neck and recoiled quickly. "He's dead too, ice cold."

"The tea," Rob gasped, scared for Julie, whose hand he'd taken. "Do you think she poisoned us?"

Julie shook her head. "I don't think so. Just hers."

Jason examined the leaves scattered amongst the shards of Millicent's cup, sniffing them and then checking their own tea. "Julie's right. I don't think this was the same as what we were drinking. Ours was normal black tea."

"What are we going to do?" Rob said. "We can't go to the willow now. What are we going to do about them and you?" He said to Julie. He could see the police in his future, just like at the end of his father's life.

"You two go," Jason said. "I'll sort this out."

"But..." Rob began, but Jason was ahead of him.

"Go. No one needs to know you were here. I'll make up a story. I'm good at that, remember? We started the day looking for answers. Well, now we've got them. How many more signs do you need? Finish this."

68

"ARE YOU OKAY?" Rob asked as they walked side by side down Lower Kirklington Road, back towards the Burgage where they would turn and head towards the Mill. It was a simple question, but he knew he was asking more than that. *Are you okay being here with me? Are you okay with the craziness of what you have landed up in after your mental boyfriend, or ex-boyfriend, wanted to beat me to death? Are you okay with the baby you have lost, and that some crazy old woman who committed suicide in front of us told you you can never have children? And oh, yeah, you are a witch, and you didn't even know it, and you're the key to breaking a two hundred-year-old curse? Are you okay with all that, Julie?* He meant all of that and none of it, but wanted to say something.

"I don't know."

That was a fair answer in the circumstance.

"We should go to the doctors?" They were walking the other way.

"But with everything you and the old woman said, we need to go to the willow."

"You're bleeding," Rob stopped walking.

Julie stopped, and they faced each other.

"You're hurt too," she said. Their eyes met.

And then there, after everything that had gone on between them, Rob said, "I'm sorry."

"What for?"

"For everything. The video. The comments. For," and his eyes flicked down to the red on Julie's jeans.

"None of it was your fault. I know that now. Maybe I always knew that, but I was mad and then Danny..." She trailed off.

Rob couldn't know what she was thinking, although he wished he could. That would have prevented so much misunderstanding. He couldn't know, but maybe he could have guessed, in the same way that his artist's pencil could say more than he could ever possibly hope to, that she was thinking about Danny. That she felt stupid, a ridiculous little girl who played at being a woman, who "needed" to have an older boyfriend. The girl who didn't want to have sex, not really, not yet, but went along with it to please an older boy she hardly knew. She'd played at being an adult, and now there were adult consequences. Maybe that's what she was thinking.

"Did he hurt you?"

"No, not deliberately, not..." and the tears fell.

Rob put his arms around Julie. He hoped that was okay. She let him and put her head on his shoulder as the tears flowed silently. He held her, and she let him comfort her. When she was ready, she raised her head. They were so close, Julie's breath was a warm breeze on Rob's cracked lips that almost blew away the thirst and the pain. She planted a soft kiss on Rob's lips, lingering for a second.

"Ow!" He winced. "Don't make me smile. It hurts."

"I'm sorry." She reached for his face, taking it in her hands tenderly, but she was still smiling, a giggle popping effervescently.

Rob laughed too and winced again, putting a hand to his mouth. Their foreheads touched, and then Julie took his hand in hers and eased it from his mouth. Their laughing had stopped, their smiles relaxed, and their lips touched again, parting. It stung, but Rob ignored it because it was a good thing. A kiss without pretensions or expectations, and if it was the last kiss they ever had, Rob would be sad but also happy that they'd had it.

"We should get going?" Julie said, and Rob had to rouse himself from the spell of their kiss.

414

They set off to face whatever awaited them at the old willow tree, their fingers entwined like their fates.

———————

REVISION COULD WAIT AS FAR as Henry and Chris were concerned. They didn't need much persuading, and met Ally at the top of the Ropewalk on their bikes thirty minutes after he'd messaged them. It was a great road to cycle down, being all downhill. They had the sun in their faces and the breeze brushed their skin. A backpack had all Ally needed: a length of rope, some plastic ties, and a switchblade borrowed from his uncle. Ally left the cut-throat razor from the box under his uncle's bed on the bathroom shelf, in case his uncle was the pussy Ally suspected him to be. Now free, Ally itched with excitement. He could barely conceal his erection, even riding his bike. His phone mounted on his handlebars, he led them toward the dot on the screen which had come to a rest for a while, but was on the go again, drifting down Lower Kirklington Road. She'd been to Danny's, then left, getting as far as the Burgage. After that, she'd stopped at a house Ally had no intel on. It didn't even have an internet connection as far as he could tell. She was there for around thirty minutes, which is when he called Henry and Chris. Ally thought maybe she'd seen Danny and now was on her own. If not, they'd follow until she was. Soon he'd have what he wanted before it all ended for him. Chris and Henry could have a go too if they liked.

They reached the bottom of the Ropewalk and stopped at the junction, checking for traffic, and then turned onto Lower Kirklington Road. Ally's itch prickled. The town was eerily quiet for a Saturday morning. Dads were usually out mowing lawns, kids being taken to Saturday morning clubs. But today was different, and Ally knew why. As the houses rolled by, arguments squawked from doorways and windows. Others were in stone silence, as if in mourning. It felt good, knowing how he'd improved their lives by delivering a dose of truth.

Ally's itch became a clawing talon when he saw them: Rob and

415

Julie, hand in hand. They were still a long way off, but he could tell it was them.

"Look at that!" Ally called over his shoulder.

"Is that Julie?" Chris said.

"Yep, and who else?"

Chris squinted, peddling side-by-side with Ally. "That's Rob. What are they doing together?"

"My thoughts exactly!" Ally said. He'd worked so hard to mess things up between them to his own advantage, but still he couldn't get her on her own. Rob kept coming back from whatever Ally threw at him. And even more unbelievable, they were back together. But as the talon squeezed and Ally throbbed, another opportunity had presented itself, and Ally meant to capitalise on it. A scapegoat had emerged from the thorny woods, someone with a history of perving on Julie Brennan.

There was the rattling of a chain, and Henry called out. "Wait up, guys. My chain has come off."

Chris applied his brakes, hearing that, and Ally did too. He'd need both of them, especially for a face-to-face encounter, but also Ally felt that Chris and Henry deserved to help him scratch his itch.

"For Christ's sake, Henry, hurry up will you. They're getting away." Ally sat astride his bike, watching Rob and Julie, who had stopped. Henry fumbled, tinkering with his chain. Rob and Julie kissed and kissed again. Ally's anger grew, squeezing the throat of his desire without a safe word.

"Come on," he shouted at Henry.

"I'm nearly there," but the chain slipped off the gear when Henry tested the peddle.

Rob and Julie walked hand-in-hand and turned off Lower Kirklington Road, heading down towards the old Mill. *Returning to the scene of the crime, eh, Robbo?* He thought with cool relish.

Muffled shouts came from a house behind them.

The boys eventually pushed off, pumping at their pedals, unaware of the imperceptible vibration that shook the road, nor of the hissing in the grass and hedgerows as the world rolled by.

69

THE TEENAGERS APPROACHED the Hanging Tree, riding abreast like three horsemen. In the distance, a siren from an emergency vehicle wailed a discordant harmony with the birds' spring chorus. At Ally's house, men with shaved heads were already pulling up. A man with a mustache retrieved a baseball bat from the boot. His uncle held and then put down the cut-throat razor. Ally was right: he was a pussy, and because of that he, his wife, and two girls would be the unwilling participants in a game of Belfast Baseball, in which there was no ball, the batter had as many swings as he wished, and the crowd always screamed. Ally would have loved to see the carnage he was recording in his house and across the town in secret. But it would have to wait, if he got to see it at all. None of it mattered. Only Julie Brennan did, and in minutes he'd be getting what he wanted, and she'd be getting what she deserved, and so would Rob.

Without warning, a car bolted from the road, crossing their path. It saw them late and hit the brakes, sounding its horn as it came to a sudden halt, tyres skidding. All three boys slammed on their brakes too. Their forearms chorded and their own wheels locked, grating across the asphalt to a halt, inches from the car's side door. The car idled, parked in the middle of the junction. Ally should have felt shocked or afraid, but he didn't. He felt alive. The itch of his excitement almost tickled him into an unhinged giggle, which if he started he might never stop, and he could have laughed all the way to Hell. That sounded fun.

The door opened and out jumped Danny. His face was a look of pure fury. When wasn't it?

"What the fuck do you pricks think you're doing?"

Ah, Danny, a poet for his generation. All that misdirected anger. A dead mummy. A daddy who doesn't wuv him. And trying just a little too hard to prove to himself he's not gay. So sad, it was funny. The itch tickled the giggle, but Ally caught it in time. Chris and Henry were flicking up their pedals in preparation to bolt. Ye of little faith!

Danny was almost on them. Ally noticed his injuries from the house of mirrors had largely healed. Cuts had granulated. The black eye was little more than a yellowish brown tinge to the side of his face. He wore only jeans and a T-shirt. The muscles of his large arms bulged beneath. And there was something new, Ally noticed. Perhaps a present from the Chief Constable? An angry red welt around Danny's neck. Ally had to wipe the smirk from his mouth.

"Crap, let's leg it," Chris whispered, his gears ticking, tick, tick, tick.

"The very man we've been looking for," Ally said, confidence ringing through his voice.

Danny wasn't expecting this. It was off script. The boys were supposed to be cowering away from him. Chris and Henry were, but not Ally. No, not Ally. He would never cower. Danny looked puzzled at this confident and diminutive Irish boy greeting him like a best friend.

Danny stopped in his tracks. "What?"

"We've been looking for you."

"Have we?" poor, slow Henry muttered.

Ally ignored the slowness of Henry. He knew Chris would be sharper and noticed him take his foot from his pedal.

"I was just saying to Henry and Chris, here, that I bet Danny Broad would like to know what we've just seen."

"Why would I give a toss?" Danny took another step forward to intimidate Ally.

Ally gave a nonchalant shrug. "We were just minding our own business, taking a break from revision, cycling down this road here, when we saw a strange thing. Do you want to know what it was?"

Danny looked to the sky incredulously. "No, not really, you little shit. I'm more concerned you nearly drove into the side of my car."

"Fair enough, we clearly weren't paying attention," Ally said, which wasn't true, as Danny cut across their right of way, but Ally wasn't about to start an argument with this particular psycho. "But like I said, we were a bit distracted. You see, we just saw your favourite boy, Rob Peters, walking hand-in-hand with your favourite girl, the lovely Julie."

Danny's incredulous look vanished. An intense anger made his jaw ripple. "You're lying. You're just a wind-up merchant."

I am indeed a wind-up merchant, Danny. But I'm not a liar, I'm the fucking giver of truth. How did you like my little delivery to your daddy last night, you big fruit? Who's the bigger liar: the policeman dad who's taking money from the mob; or his gay son trying to bang a pretty little girl instead of watching Cock Jocks 17? I guess lying runs in the family. Ally sidled up to Danny. "Like I said, big man, it was a bit out of the ordinary. One doesn't expect to see those two together after everything, now does one? But there they were, bolder than brass, walking hand-in-hand in the lovely spring sunshine. They even stopped for a snog as if they didn't have a care in the world. Isn't that right, lads?"

Even Henry had caught on, and both he and Chris nodded vigorously, "Yeah."

"Where are they then?" Danny looked around.

"We were way back there, when they were here. Kissing on this very spot. Hands all over each other. Julie feeling Rob's arse like a... well, I won't say. I know you've a soft spot for her. Anyway, they headed down there." Ally pointed towards the Mill.

Danny spun around, looking down the road. "I don't see them."

Give me strength, you fecking idiot. "This was a few minutes ago. But I have a good idea where they're headed." Why exactly Ally knew this, he couldn't tell. His itch was pulling him on. He felt destiny lay down that road, left behind the Mill and along the stream to the old willow tree. He didn't understand why, but he knew everything was coming together, and that Danny was the final piece of the puzzle. Rob, Danny, and Julie together. A love tryst gone wrong. Very messy. Very useful to Ally's purposes. Very chaotic. Perfect.

70

Rob pulled back the branches of the willow, and they entered Jack's church together. It was as if they had travelled through time. It could have been the night before, or the weekend before that, or the one where they had last been here together, talking before the police came. That felt like yesterday and a lifetime ago. The floor was still littered with cans, butts of cigarettes and joints, stray bottles of cheap wine and cider from the revelry the night before. More would be back tonight to do the same, drawn to this place as they had been for generations, never understanding why. They just came, celebrating life, being together, playing music, singing songs, being young.

Now Rob and Julie were back there together, Rob expected something dramatic to happen, but nothing did. But regardless, there was a big part of Rob that felt happy just to be here with Julie, their fingers laced together, no expectation, no awkwardness, no desire, just here, being themselves. Maybe that was it. Maybe that was how the curse would be broken. And yet Rob was still so thirsty. Kidney pain stabbed in his lower back. He felt as weak as ever, and though the poultice Millicent had given him had helped, his head pounded and his face hurt, and he was sure he had a concussion.

"What do we do?" Julie said.

"I don't know. I've got the offerings in here." Rob unshouldered his backpack.

"Should we have brought the books, or your dad's notes?"

Now they were here on a mad woman's instructions, following clues that seemed anything but, Rob had a twinge of doubt. "I don't know. Maybe you could..." He fluttered his fingers as though he was about to produce a coin from thin air.

Julie laughed. "It's not like that. I don't know what it's like. It just happened when Danny attacked you. I was angry. Maybe that's got something to do with it. But I'm not angry now."

"You're not?"

She laughed again. "No, I'm not." But she didn't explain further. "Maybe we should wait a while and see what happens?" Julie gave Rob's hand a reassuring squeeze.

"I guess so."

Julie considered the mess on the floor. "Let's tidy the place up while we wait? I never thought this was some important place before. We come here every week and mess it up."

Rob longed to keep holding Julie's hand. It was a tether, something real to hold on to, something connecting to this world, something that told him he was still alive. But she was right. Tidying up felt like the right thing to do, so they gathered up the cans and bottles, and scraping along the floor with their shoes, sweeping the butts of cigarettes and joint roaches into piles.

"Someone must come and tidy this up at some point," Rob said.

"How come?"

"Otherwise, we'd be waist deep in empty bottles of Liebfraumilch and White Lightning cider," he said, inspecting the giant blue bottle and dropping it with other empties in a growing pile.

"I never thought about it that way. I wonder who? Probably the Council."

There was a familiar domesticity between them as they worked. At one point Rob looked across the clearing and saw Julie bending over with a grimace, soldiering through her own pain. He really loved her. He knew it could be a teenage infatuation brought on by almost anaphylactically shocking levels of hormones. Still, it felt so powerful and pure; he hoped that maybe one day she would love him like that. *If you've got that long*, he thought.

"I'm sorry, about the baby."

Julie had heavy sadness in her eyes and gave a small nod of recognition. Rob realised that was maybe one of the reasons Julie was here helping him and not going to the doctor. It gave her something else to think about. He couldn't imagine what it felt like. He knew what it was like to lose a parent. The feeling that all the facade of order and control in the world was just that, a projection of the Great and Powerful Oz, a lie, no more real than the pouting duck face of an Instagram model who cuts herself all alone at night only to airbrush the scars away in the morning. Julie's avoidance of the reality of what happened to the life inside her was no different from Rob avoiding dealing with his father's death.

"If nothing happens here soon, we should head up to the doctors' surgery, what do you think?"

Julie made a small noise of half-hearted commitment. Knowing she was holding back the tears, Rob left the subject. The last thing he wanted was for her to feel any pain.

But for both of them, that was a wish that would never come true.

The three horsemen, now completed and made four, had kept their voices in check and crossed the stream further up, cutting into the field behind the willow, avoiding the usual route where branches would have brushed against their bodies and twigs snapped underfoot. Danny was the first to enter the sacred space under the willow canopy. With him came an angry saturation, low like a lisping growl, as if the wind was shaking the shaggy branches of the willow tree to the sound of distant thunder from an approaching storm.

"Now this is a surprise," Danny sneered, his eyes darting angrily between Julie and Rob. "Seems both of you think you can just make me look like a total dickhead." Danny spat every word as Ally, Chris, and Henry filed in behind him. Ally and Chris wore dark grins, while Henry looked like he was about to take a test he hadn't revised for. Rob saw them as a pack of wolves. The willow had become their den, and Rob and Julie were the little pigs in a house made of leaves, fag ends, and plastic cider bottles. Chris pushed Henry in front of him, and the wolves circled.

Rob backed up protectively to Julie. She did the same coming to him, until they bumped together, searching for the other's hand.

Ally turned the screw. "How sweet. Do you think Robbo has been shagging Julie all along?"

"Shut your face, Ally. You're such a complete prick," Rob said, through gritted teeth.

Julie was tugging on his hand, whispering in his ear, "We should go."

"You're not going anywhere." Danny broke ranks from the pack.

Ally had taken off his backpack and produced the switchblade from its depths. The knife made a satisfying snap as it flicked open. Madness glinted in the blade, and with it he severed any way back to their normal lives. (Little pigs, little pigs, let me come in.)

Rob tried to shield Julie, but Danny was on them, one hand reaching over Rob's shoulder. He caught Julie by the hair and brought his other elbow crashing down on Rob's head.

Rob staggered back, hearing Julie scream as Danny held her by her ponytail, her feet skidding through the dry leaf litter. Julie's hand slipped from Rob's in his daze. He groped for it, finding thin air as she was ripped away.

Discarding something he had no more use for, Danny flung Julie in an arc. She stumbled, one hand touching the ground. Feet faltering in uncontrollable strides, she came crashing into Ally and Chris, who caught her by the arms as her head struck the trunk of the willow tree, and she went limp.

The rustling was now a screaming wind, tearing through Rob's mind. He covered his ears, but it made no difference. Danny was there grabbing the material of his hoodie, fist cocked behind his head. He wasted no time, thundered a fist into Rob's face. The world wobbled on unpredictable axes: left to right, up and down, around in circles.

Life, it seemed, was on repeat: they were back in the house of mirrors, or on the Burgage, or down an alley, and maybe countless other times in the past and future, like Mary reflected over and over in an infinity of mirrors. Rob saw her flash in the whirl of his mind, and a child's laughter cut through the white noise raging in his head.

Even through his spinning world, Rob's only thought was to get to Julie. She lay on her front, dazed, a trickle of blood running down her forehead. Ally gestured with the knife in his hand for Henry and Chris to hold her arms.

Rob cried out, "Julie!" but Danny stepped astride his body and pulled Rob flat to his back.

"I said, you're not going anywhere, pretty boy." Settling his heavy weight on Rob's belly, like the school ground bully he was, Danny hocked and spat in Rob's face.

Julie was coming to her senses. The trickle of blood from her forehead fell onto the roots of the willow tree. The gently rocking boughs rustled like a snake's furious hiss in the long grass. Julie only saw the dirt and rough bark pressed up against her face, but she felt Ally behind her, and the press of the blade into the material of her jeans. It ripped with a harsh tug of the blade on the thicker material of her waistband.

"Grab her arms," Ally shouted, as if calling over a fierce gale he could not hear.

Chris pinned one of Julie's hands to the dirt, and shouted at Henry, "Grab hold. You'll get your turn." Wavering between two choices, Henry capitulated. Ally's madness had infected them all, and Julie's other arm became immobile. The blade in one hand dancing beside her flesh, Ally yanked at the waist of Julie's jeans and cool air touched her skin.

"No!" Rob screamed, reaching, trying to squirm from beneath Danny.

"No, you don't." Danny rained down punches, hitting Rob in the neck and side of the head, sending a blinding ache through his throat and constricting his breathing, strangling his cries.

"She's just a local tart. We both had a go. Why shouldn't these boys? Besides, me and you have a date, Peters." Danny pinned one of Rob's hands to the floor. "I don't know how your queer mate jumped me on the Burgage. But he's not here to save you this time." And with his free hand, Danny buried his fist in Rob's face. His already broken nose crunched again, and Rob choked a spray of blood into the air. The tiny droplets fell to the ground, nourishing it, providing the necessary blood offering.

A child giggled, playing unseen in the clearing. The ground shook like a tolling bell.

Julie struggled with all her strength, but the boys overpowered her. She still felt woozy from hitting her head on the tree. Ally had pulled her jeans and underwear to her knees.

"Look," Henry cried, struggling to hold her. "She's bleeding."

Julie's underwear were soaked with blood.

"Good," Chris said with a shrug. "It wasn't us."

"Just shut up and hold her," Ally said struggling because Julie was bucking frantically. Ally took a fist full of Julie's hair and jerked back her head. The whites of Julie's eyes darkened, moss green furring across them in a velveteen patina. Her arms stiffened in Henry and Chris's grip, and her fingers splayed as Ally brought the blade to her throat.

Min sweostorum...

Chris punched the words from her mouth, whipping Julie's head to the side. Ally pulled the blade away, nicking her throat.

"Careful, you wanker. Do you want to fuck a corpse?"

The cut wasn't deep on Julie's neck, but the blood dripped in fat droplets onto the roots of the willow tree.

Consciousness was leaving Rob. He had one hand free to protect his head, and Danny's easily avoided the flimsy defence. He'd huffed and he'd puffed and he'd blown Rob's house in. Rob knew now this would end only one way: Mary's curse would be broken, but only because someone else stepped in to take his life. That, it seemed, was the answer. Why Julie had to pay the price as well, he couldn't understand. It was cruel and unfair.

Rob wanted the last thing he saw to be Julie, but when he turned his head the horror was unbearable, though he would not look away. Danny's fists slammed into his skull over and over. Ally had put down the knife. He held Julie at the hip with one hand while the other

426

hand wrenched open his fly so he could take what he had always wanted.

Rob croaked, blood pouring from his nose, mouth, and a cut around his eye. But now he couldn't even hear his own voice over the raging life around them, skittering beetles, churning worms, the liquid rot. The ground beneath them began to move.

Ally and Chris were so entranced by their act they didn't notice at first when Henry cried out. Ally had managed to get his trousers down. With eyes as focused and dull as the brushed steel of the switchblade, he was readying himself, when Chris cried out as well. His concentration was broken and he was ready to snatch up the blade resting in the dirt and gut his friends. But when he saw both of them lashed with roots around their wrists and snaking around their necks, Ally's calculating brain surfaced and found itself bewildered. More roots were coiling around Chris and Henry's legs, binding them, pulling them to the ground. With her hands free, Julie tried to crawl away, but her legs were fettered by her own clothing. Ally, trousers also around his knees, lurched after her, seemingly at home in the melee. The ground was now as alive as a pit of snakes. Roots slithered from the soil and ensnared Ally too. They bound the struggling boys like Egyptian mummies, enveloping them in fold on fold of root. Julie initially felt relief before she realised she was being bound as well.

The world was nothing now to Rob, even the rustle was a distant whisper. Punches rocked his limp body like waves lapping at the hull of a boat. There was a blur above him. Breathing was a struggle after Danny had broken three of his ribs, cracking them like dry branches. Both Rob's eyes were closing. Blood choked him, but inexplicably the punches had stopped. The blur that was Danny had frozen for a moment, then rose and tilted, floating in the air. Rob felt it too, his weight suddenly taken. The earth was a porous, moving thing. The tendrils and roots wound around his limbs. They did not hurt. There was a comfort in it, as if he were a swaddled child. They bound his legs and body in a cocoon. And as the roots of the wild wood slid over his face, the light of the world succumbed to the dark.

Under the canopy of the willow, the violence ceased.

All was still.

Six bodies, bound in the roots and tendrils of Jack in the Green, lay between the discarded remnants of teenage frivolity. The ground gently shook. The soil loosened, and slowly the six bodies were dragged into the earth, pulled to another world entirely.

71

DOWN, down, down through the earth they were pulled, dragged by the roots. Each of them screamed. No one heard, muffled as their cries were by blinding earth and gagging vine. An endless fall, head over heel until all sense of themselves was spun from them. Up became down; down became up. The light was a distant land from which they were exiled. Their new home, through which they descended, was a mouldering place where life begat death and death birthed all the future from the rank mulch of decay. On and on they tumbled, deeper and deeper into the womb of the Earth, to its very root, to the forgotten place of the wild wood.

SENSES CAME BACK one by one to Rob. First there was feeling. His unquenchable thirst. The acid burn in his throat. Bruises ached; cuts stung; his kidneys stabbed. Then there was sound, strange and unfamiliar, distant at first, dampened by the fog of his returning consciousness. Like countless unanswered telephones, frogs chirruped. There were the deep, burping croaks of toads. Birds called, some sweet and twittering, others harsh, forbidding caws, some wild hoots and others frantic siren calls. Snap of twig, groan of trunk and rustle of leaves. The feet of a doe and her fawn whispered through leaf litter. Then smell. The earthy loam of life; the musk of animals in heat; the sweetness of flowers and sour of rotting carrion, finished with by the largest of predators to be consumed by the smallest of organisms; the fermentation of bacteria and fungi. And last of all, sight returned. Rob's eyes pried open in the depths of a dark and wild wood.

Forcing his aching body to sit, Rob blinked. A bright cleft of pain split his head in two. He looked around and found himself in the middle of a clearing. What time of day it might be was difficult to judge, if time held any sway here. The forest around him seemed ancient and ominously thick. Moss drooped from branches like unkempt beards on a craggy, old man. Overhead, the canopy let in a little light. It could just as easily have been light from the moon as from the sun. What illumination found its way through came in weak twinkling fragments, as if it only dared enter with meek deference. Thick undergrowth and dead falls surrounded the clearing; dense forest stretched out beyond in all directions.

There was something above Rob. The cleft of pain in his head when he craned up to see what it was seared through his brain, causing him to cry out, momentarily silencing the forest's chorus. Above him were the branches of a tree. Not a willow but a great oak. Its boughs were long and gnarled, like the fingers of a gypsy fortune teller. It was gigantic, seeming without end in any direction, merging into blackness above the rest of the forest all around. Rob tried to ignore the pain in his head and followed the course of its boughs to its trunk, as thick as a house, and at its centre a fathomless hollow into which the meek light of the forest dared not enter. Turning on his knees to face the tree and with the fluidity of an old man, he creaked to his feet.

Rob hesitated, but was compelled to investigate. Perhaps he was spat out of the hole in the tree, but then where was Julie? And where were Danny, Ally, Chris, and Henry? These were all more reasons to check. In his daze he'd initially forgotten about them. Now the moments before they were pulled into the ground flooded back, along with the fear, and he moved with even more trepidation towards the giant of a tree. But he couldn't see anyone else. Maybe he was dead and this was... what? Heaven? It didn't feel like heaven. He felt no inner peace. In fact, he felt the same: physically spent but alive, and with that new glimmer of hope that shone in the form of Julie. Where was she?

The huge roots of the oak pushed up the ground beneath Rob's feet, making it uneven the closer he got, and he was still at least twenty feet away. Now the cave was a black eye staring at him. No matter how frightening it might be, this could be their way out, his and Julie's. He should take a closer look and then go and find her. But that wasn't the only thing pulling him on. There was something he needed to see. Something, which as he looked at the tree drew his artist's eye. It was the way the hole seemed not just to be dark but to be totally devoid of light. Light was the artist's tool and Rob was always curious about it, how it could competently change an image. The way the bark knotted wasn't right either, probably because of the hole. The mix of curiosity and fear made his footsteps tentative and slow. In the low light, the detail of the trunk was about to come into focus when the snapping of a branch echoed in the clearing. Rob whipped around and froze. The frogs and toads had stopped. The birds didn't sing. An uncanny silence pervaded. Then the ribbit of a single frog broke the stillness and the chorus of life started up once more.

Taking another step, he turned back to the giant oak. The bark came into view and Rob's mind reeled. His eyes darted all over the great trunk, checking and rechecking, unbelieving at first. He started to trust his eyes and needed to see more, not knowing that he would regret it soon enough.

The bark was thick, more like petrified stone than wood, or perhaps more like the thick hide of a rhinoceros, greys and browns, flecked with dirt, moss and lichen, ossified with layers of ancient growth. But it wasn't the texture of the bark that was so curious. Like the carvings of the Greenman in the Minster's Chapter House, the bark was covered with *faces*, most with anguished expressions, eyes wide, mouths gaping. Rob was only a few feet away. The dark hole in the middle of the trunk yawned to his left. And the faces, how many he couldn't tell, were packed together, each different, wrapping around the impossibly wide trunk and stretching up, up and up into the canopy of the tree and along the thickest of the boughs overhead.

Slowly, Rob circled the tree. He reached out and touched it. It was not cold, like stone; nor did it feel like wood. The faces felt like what they were: hardened flesh. He shuddered.

The circumference threw him in a wide arc, stumbling over the roots. The more he looked, the more he had the feeling that these faces were neither carvings nor natural growths. The hints of haircuts and the facial hair on some of the faces suggested they were from many different times, and Rob began to suspect they were trapped here. It reminded him of the tormented pictures produced by William Blake, or the images of Dante's *The Nine Circles of Hell*, festooned with tortured souls.

He was almost back to the other side of the tree, when a face caught his eye. Many of the other faces were an artist's dream, riven with emotion, their lives having weathered character into their features. But that was not what caught Rob's attention, rather it was familiarity. A face he would know anywhere. A face he could pick out in a crowd, or which he might have looked for when he was small and holding his mother's hand as they bustled through the throngs of people on Southend Pier.

It was his father.

The face of Richard Peters, open mouthed, tongue bulging and protruding from his mouth, eyes popping grotesquely from their sockets as if he had been hanged, was trapped in the bark of the great oak. Rob reached for him, just able to touch him. Tears producing bright stings from the split in his eyes, which were almost swollen shut. Richard looked dead, and he felt it too. There was no life there. Rob pulled at the bark, trying to get his fingers in to see if he could pull him free, but it was no use. His father was trapped in the tree, held in purgatory, never to be freed.

"No," Rob whimpered, digging his fingers to the grooves of the unforgiving bark. "Please, no." He pulled and pulled with all he had. But it made no difference to the fate of his father, who remained trapped in the skin of the great tree.

WHEREVER SHE WAS, it was soft and warm and smelled of sweet blossoms over a rich scent of dark humus. Julie stretched out, the bed beneath her moving to accommodate her. She felt rested, drowsy even, but then, like a twist of Ally's switchblade, the memories of her attack, of the attempted rape by Ally and his friends, came back. She sat up as though jolted with an electric current. Julie scanned her surroundings and pulled up her jeans and the twisted, stained knickers within. The blood had dried and was starting to crust. In the circumstances, that didn't matter. She tried to get her bearings. She remembered the enveloping roots of the willow tree. And now she was in a forest or wood, and a thick, dark one at that. Not like any wood she'd been in, not even like Sherwood Forest where they had taken school trips and played at being Robin Hood and Maid Marian when they were small children. It was loud too, but on reflection she liked it. This wood wasn't a place in which she felt afraid, even as she looked out for Ally, Danny, and the rest. With the thought of Rob, she had the growing sense of being at home, that nothing here would hurt her. In fact it was better than home.

Something touched her hand, like a small child tugging at her for attention. It was the frond of a fern slowly unfurling, followed by ivy, mistletoe coiling down from the trees, bluebells, foxgloves, primroses, snowdrops and forget-me-nots, all blossoming around the bed of moss on which she lay. They had all come to see her, she knew that. She felt them, every one of them, the trees too, and the animals, more timid but there, watching. Red squirrels in the trees, rabbits and hares among the bushes and ferns. Badgers from their dens. Deer: does, stags, and fauns. A brown bear, somewhere padding on broad paws, and a pack of grey wolves, aloof but aware, great as phantoms in the mist.

Julie could not help but grin with the joy and wonder of it.

"Hello," she said to the fern, petting its green blades as if she were ruffling the hair of a child.

Two grey squirrels ventured down the trunk of the nearest tree, next to her bed of moss. She reached out to them, and they were

433

about to walk on to the palm of her hand, when shouts issuing from the mist scared them back to the safety of the canopy. The shouts persisted, growing shrill and terrified, but they were muffled by the fog. There was more than one person, from more than one direction. Although, that could have been a trick of the forest, throwing the sound this way and that.

"Rob?" Julie called. It could be one of the others, Chris or Henry, or worse Danny or Ally. She didn't want to meet them. But what if Rob was hurt or scared or they had found him first? They needed each other, she and Rob. That was why they had gone to the willow together. She should go to him. But which voice? Which direction? A shrill scream sounded through the fog beyond thick undergrowth and a fallen elm.

"Rob!" Julie shouted, and headed toward the scream.

72

"GET OFF ME." Ally yanked his arm free, followed by his leg, to the sound of snapping vines. The plants reached for him again, searching for his limbs, attempting to wrap around his body. He tore and ripped them. The pungent woodiness from their chaff and weeping stems hung in the air. He stumbled away from the hollow, rotting trunk, he had been slumped against.

Free of the plants and getting his wits about him, Ally took in his surroundings, reconciling the new information with his last memory when he nearly had Julie. He'd been so close. She was right there, in his hands ready for the taking. Even the memory aroused him, and he ached with furious desire. None of it made sense. The coiling roots. The tumbling dark. And now this place, this new reality. Was he dead? It was a possibility. Was he alone? Maybe, but then the others, Chris, Henry and... and *Julie* too, they were all bound with the roots and pulled into the earth. So it was a logical deduction that they were in this place as well. That itch of his could still be scratched. With that realisation, Ally knew in this world his life's purpose was the same as in the last.

Cobwebs of mist wrapped around the dense tangle of woodland and undergrowth. Ally checked the impenetrable canopy above, unable to deduce if it was day or night. It wasn't pitch black, therefore, it could be daytime, but as he could see no evidence of a sun, and the plants in this place were moving and treacherous things, he wouldn't assume that there was a sun at all. Nor indeed could any of the physical laws of his world be taken for granted. If he could find a clearing, or some high ground, he'd be able to get a better sense of where he was by locating north or identifying a landmark to navigate by. Ally slapped away another vine as he got moving. Chris and Henry could be somewhere near, and if they were that meant he could finish what they had started. And here, wherever here was (because it certainly wasn't Middle England), appeared an excellent choice for disposing of bodies.

Ally's itch told him his whole life had led to here. To be sure, he was wary. The experience of being dragged into the earth by God knew what made sure of that. But Ally was pragmatic. He'd always played whatever life put in front of him. At this moment he only had limited options, but that was nothing new. A forbidding forest or a house with a padlock on the fridge, it was all the same to him. The strategy remained the same: gather information; find friends, or better yet, Julie; and peel away the skin of civility for a nasty and brutish end.

He set off quietly, picking his way through the undergrowth. Without a path it was about tracing the course of least resistance between trees and bushes, some of which quivered as he passed or sent out fronds and stems to grab at him. Occasionally, Ally would have to clamber over a dead fall, watching his footing, not wanting to slip and impale himself on the branches that jutted upwards like bone spears. In other places, the foliage thinned, and the forest floor was soft with leaf litter. The mist was a sluggish apparition, moving in slow wheezing undulations. Ally liked its cover. It limited his vision, but it would limit others' sight too. It cloaked him like a graphical interface while he navigated through the source code, the base of zeros and ones, to the root of it all.

"Rob?"

Ally stopped, listening. That was Julie. Not far off. To his left. Ally moved carefully, watching his footsteps, being sure not to snap a twig or trip in the looping root of a tree. He was stealthy. He could have

436

been at his keyboard, searching, probing, trying to find a way through someone's firewall, if they had one at all. The plants pawed at him. But they were weak, and Ally was strong with the itch, with the urge of the hunt.

He found himself by an ivy-covered tree, cloaked in mist. He hid behind it, swatting away the ivy. Julie stood in a small clearing, flowers blooming all around her, covering the woodland in a carpet of bright colours.

"Rob!" Julie shouted, hearing more screams.

Ally heard them too, screeching like an old dial-up modem, pathetic and obsolete. He followed, gathering information. He'd found Julie. Now for the nasty end.

CHRIS LET OUT AN AGONISING CRY. "No! Get off."

Leathery tendrils of a bramble, as thick as Chris's own wrists, had snaked out from its hulking briar and ensnared his leg. It tightened, thorns puncturing his skin. Small jets of blood spurted from the wounds, followed by the hot drips of crimson, glinting dully on the plant's leaves. Feet skidding, Chris was unable to resist as the bramble dragged him slowly along the forest floor. He pawed frantically at the vines, cutting open his palms, until a second thorny tendril snapped through the air and coiled around Chris's wrist, slicing deeply into his flesh, tapping a healthy flow of blood that watered the hungry plant.

"Help me, Henry."

The whites of Henry's eyes were blazing lamps of fear as he stood paralysed. He shook, mouth quivering, short stuttering breaths wracking his chest, and a discoloured patch bloomed and spread at the crotch of his jeans, turning them from light to dark blue, a yellow trickle running over his trainer.

More tendrils shot from the briar as Chris was pulled closer. Barbs like nails drove into his thigh, and it tightened with tremendous force, sawing through flesh with a spiralling constriction. Chris screamed as the thorns flayed through the meat of his leg, peeling back skin, exposing yellowish fat, and then the red of muscle and white of ligaments and fascia. It continued to drag Chris forward, stripping the flesh from mid-thigh to the knee, skinning him alive. He would have continued to scream, to call for his mummy, but for another tendril that wrapped around his throat. It cut off the air and sliced open both jugular veins, spraying Henry with hot geysers of scarlet.

Each of Chris's limbs, his head, neck and torso were lashed with thorny ropes, hauling him to the quivering threshold of the briar. Tugging, cutting, squeezing, Chris's skin was shucked from the bone on his arms, his scalp torn off to the sound of tearing paper. Two branches paused before his belly like rearing cobras and then struck, burrowing into his belly button, which was too small for them to share. It stretched wider and wider as the branches bored deeper. When they pulled back, they split open his stomach from groin to ribs. Out tumbled Chris's offal with a wet slap before the hungry plant fell upon it. Finally, Chris's mutilated corpse disappeared into the mass of writhing branches.

Henry stood quaking as the briar consumed his friend. He closed his eyes tight shut.

"It's just a bad dream. It's just a bad dream. It's just a bad dream." But when he opened his eyes again to check the nightmare hadn't vanished.

Bones snapped. Something slurped and squelched in the moving tangle. Henry trembled. When it had finished, a barbed coil unfurled, creeping toward Henry. He silently shook his head, fighting an internal battle between seeing and believing. Finally, he moved, in a shaky stride, first one leg and then another and then reconnecting his body and mind. Each step added to his conviction in the terror of his reality and soon he was running, running for all he was worth, tearing through the undergrowth, branches whipping at him, fine spider webs catching his face, undergrowth tangling his feet. Almost hyperventilating, he risked a look behind and tripped over a root, coming down hard. Leaf litter puffed up, desiccated brown flecks sticking to his sweat. He scrambled to his feet and pushed on, delirious, not knowing where he was going and then finally stumbled from the heavy growth of the forest.

The sudden lack of resistance catapulted Henry. He found firm ground in the small clearing before the forest floor changed texture. It was no longer solid, nor liquid, but something in between. His foot sank up to the calf but his momentum pitched him forward onto a knee, and he was sinking. For a moment, Henry couldn't comprehend what was happening, but it vanished as the cold mud touched his genitals and he realised he was going to be sucked under. He groped for solid ground and found nothing to grip. Handfuls of soft earth squished through his clenching fists. Panic became frantic terror, and the more he struggled, the more he sank. He needed to be calm, but he couldn't.

"Help! Please, God, someone help! I don't want to die. Please!" Henry made frantic tugs with his whole body. His muscles burned with fatigue. His pleas were squeals. "Help! Please." He was up to his navel and still descending.

"Rob."

Henry stopped shouting. He heard a voice; he was sure of it. "Over here, please hurry. Hurry, over here. Over here."

Julie rushed from between the bushes. She saw Henry in the quick-mud up to the bottom of his rib cage. She came to a halt just in time, as the ground softened underfoot, and putting the pieces together she scrambled back to the edge of the clearing.

"Julie, please, help me." Henry reached forward with a beseeching hand, as he sank to his chest.

Henry saw her standing at the edge of the clearing, looking at him. She wasn't coming forward. She wasn't helping. She was thinking. *Oh God, she was thinking.* But even simple Henry, whose mind moved as slowly as the sucking mud that held him, knew what she must be thinking about, what she was remembering.

"Please, Julie. It wasn't my idea. Help me. I... I was just there. I went along with it. I'm sorry. Please, I wouldn't do anything to you."

Still Julie stood motionless, thinking, looking as though she was trying to decide as Henry sank up to his armpits.

73

ALL SHE HAD to do was nothing, which wasn't doing anything at all. Julie could let him die for what he did, for all the awful things he had been party to. She knew Ally was the brains, and Henry and Chris were the stooges. The humiliation, the shame, the anger rushed up. The whisper of the wild wood underneath the woodland chorus, beneath the earth, from within every living thing grew in her mind until she felt the tingling vibration of each life. The image of the video played in her mind. The stream of comments on every app. The looks and smirks. Then, into the arms of Danny. A life inside her, there and then not there. Followed by the truth. Danny's confused rage added to Ally's manipulation, magnifying everything until it was out of control, and Rob was being beaten to death, and she was about to be raped. And then what? Ally would cut her throat, Julie felt sure of that. Julie felt it come over her as it had at the Burgage. The whisper became an angry hiss of white noise. The life-force connecting everything hummed like a tuning orchestra finding its pitch.

Henry blubbered, fat tears rolled down his cheeks as a bubble of snot popped from one nostril. "Please... I... don't... want... to die."

The mud was up to his throat, and he had to crane his chin to keep his mouth above the surface. One arm still broke the pool, slapping ineffectually. He was pathetic. He might be awful, cowardly, and stupid, but Julie couldn't let him die.

The white noise faded back to a whisper.

Quickly but carefully, Julie edged her way forward, feeling the ground with her toes, until it became soft and didn't feel like it would take her weight. She dropped, her knees sinking a few inches, but settled on firm ground. She reached for Henry. He wasn't too far away and Julie could take his hand. On her first pull, their hands slipped, wet with sweat and mud. Julie fell back. Henry let out a pitiful whimper and closed his mouth tight shut. His panicked glare looked sideways at Julie and his arm reached. Julie hurried back to the indentations her knees had left, and planted her feet for more leverage. Bending over she caught hold of Henry's hand, his nose now barely above the surface. She was setting her feet, but Henry pulled too hard before Julie could get a proper grounding. She fell belly down on the mud. Henry held on.

"Let go, please Henry."

Henry shook his head. Julie kept her weight spread. She wasn't sinking, not yet, but she would if she stayed much longer.

"Let go, Henry," Julie said softly. "I'll get something to help. A branch. I'll be able to heave you out then. If you don't let go, you'll pull me in with you."

Julie saw a glint of understanding in Henry's eyes, and a second later he let go. Julie crawled backwards on her belly, the thick membrane feeling as though it would give way at any time.

Henry's nose slipped beneath the mud, and he let out a muffled cry.

Julie searched the ground trying to find anything that would help, but the ground was bare. She didn't want to run and find another patch of quick-mud, so she moved with haste but not speed. Henry's arm still broke the surface above the elbow, but his eyes were about to be submerged.

"Hold on. I'll find something. I promise," Julie shouted, circling around the mud, undergrowth brushing against her. A branch scuffed the side of her trainer and she stopped. Grabbing hold of it, Julie expecting it to be stuck, but it dragged free. It must have been nearly as long as she was tall, but not too heavy. A little weathered, its bark was damp and slimy. Not ideal, but it was the only thing to hand, and she needed to act now. The crown of Henry's head was sucked under, only his hand remained, flexing.

Julie hurried back to her safe spot and lowered the branch, missing Henry's hand on the first attempt. Like a fisherman, she recast. Henry closed his fist just at the wrong moment and the branch struck the knuckles of his fist. Grunting with the effort, Julie tried again, risking putting her foot a little closer to widen her base and give her more control. It worked. The branch lowered more slowly, and she delivered it into Henry's palm, which clamped around it. He clung on, and Julie heaved with everything that she had. Her feet slipped in the mud. She took another small step forward so that she could put the branch under her armpit for a better grip. Bending her knees, she pulled again, crying out, every muscle in her body tensing, the thin muscles in her neck strained and her face reddened. But the more she pulled the less effect she had. Henry's hand disappeared.

"No," Julie shouted defiantly, and redoubled her efforts. Gasping for air, she heaved again, crying out with the exertion. It was everything she had, everything and more, but it didn't work. The resistance suddenly eased, and the branch sprung out of the mud. Julie toppled backwards.

She grabbed the branch again, scrabbling forward on her knees. She poked under the surface of the mud where Henry had been.

"Henry, come on. Grab it, grab it, please grab it."

Julie stood and pushed the tip of the branch deeper into the mud, wiggling it around, hoping Henry would grab hold. He didn't. With the mud sucking at the branch, she withdrew it with effort and thrust it in again, feeling, probing and finding nothing. Her head fell to her chest.

"I'm sorry," Julie said in a low murmur.

The push between her shoulder blades was hard and unexpected. The force of it propelled Julie into the middle of the quick-mud, and she immediately sunk up to the knees.

Julie struggled, but the mud had her. She was sinking, sucked down by gravity. She couldn't turn, stuck as she was, and tried to look behind but only saw a shadow. Twisting back the other way, she saw her assailant: Ally. He prodded and probed with his foot, as she had done. Taking note of where her footsteps had gone before him, he edged his way around the quick-mud, a smirk of satisfaction on his face, and she knew he had been watching her. Some things never changed, even after being dragged into the underworld, or whatever this place was.

Julie said nothing. She wasn't going to give him the satisfaction. Instead, she glared at him, hearing the whispers once more grow angry along with her. Hatred seeped through every part of her body, like oozing mud, powerful and irresistible.

Ally prowled the edge of the clearing. The long branch had fallen in with her and lay on the surface. She could use that, fight him off. It might also be something that could help her get out, although she doubted that.

"Nothing to say to me, Julie? No? Get you, the great Julie Brennan. So perfect, so beautiful. Everybody wants Julie. She's so special. But not for the likes of me. Now, Danny. That's a different matter. Thick as shit but oh those big muscles and perfect hair!" Ally touched himself with mock ecstasy. "Still, maybe he's not the stupid one. You do know he's gayer than a Bishop in a bathhouse? You think I'm lying?"

Julie scowled and said nothing, but the mention of Danny being gay caused a flicker in her resolve.

"It's making sense now, isn't it? Well, Julie, as it's just you and me, I can tell you, as a friend, you know? Danny's internet search history was enough to make a hooker blush. In that respect I suppose you do share something in common, only I think he is a bit more partial to cock." Ally twitched his eyebrows suggestively. "Beats me what he'd do with a whole college football team. Ha, beats me, get it Julie? Like he'd beat off the entire team. Ouch! You're no fun."

"You're just not funny," Julie spat back.

"The goddess speaks!"

"Fuck off, you pig."

"Now, now that's a dirty little mouth on one as special as you, your majesty. I like the idea of you having a dirty mouth."

"You're sick." Julie's anger grew. The whisper had become the crackle of white noise.

"Me sick? You've got me there. But you'd be surprised; I'm far from alone, only I'm not a hypocrite about it."

"Rob's not." Julie had found a hook to distract him and bide what little time she had while she searched for a way out.

"Ah, Robbo! I liked him. Did you see what Danny was doing to him? A lot of pent up rage was being vented there. Issues, like I said. A little too repressed. To be honest, I think he needed to shag Robbo. They're both handsome devils. They'd make a cute couple, don't you think? No, ouch, well, you're biased. Rob might have protested, mind you." Ally shrugged.

Julie had an odd thought. She remembered watching a movie at Sally's. They bought *Dora The Explorer* to stream as a laugh because they'd all had a Dora phase in primary school. Effie even still had her Dora backpack in the bottom of her wardrobe. The movie turned out to be surprisingly good, written for teenagers like them, who'd grown up with Dora. But the odd thought was Dora had a strategy for getting out of quicksand in the jungle. Julie remembered it now, and started to lean back in the mud, attempting to let the pitch of her body gradually float her legs to the surface as she distributed her weight. It might work. When she'd fallen flat on the mud helping Henry, she hadn't sunk in immediately. She just needed some time.

"But why did you pick on Rob? He was your friend."

Ally squatted on his haunches and leered. "Pussy magnet. Nice guy. Talented artist and a new boy, which made him exotic. And it worked, didn't it? Even the great Julie Brennan was drawn to our Robbo. I thought he'd be a bit young for you, but I saw how his pictures caught your eye. If you think some twat from London is exotic, then I'm a bird of paradise, and I have talents Julie, real talents. If you understood how talented I am, if you'd been to the places I can go, if you knew the things that I found, would you open your legs for me, Julie Brennan?"

"Never. You make me want to puke." Julie saw the dark flash in Ally's eyes, and something else. She thought she felt it, too, in the angry rustle in her mind. It was part of the cacophony, but she picked out the individual note. A silent scream of anger, like all the world's computers shrieking with a virus before crashing, and she knew it was Ally. It was his note in the great vibration of life.

The darkness in Ally's eyes disappeared as quickly as it came. "Never is a very long time, and it looks like you're sinking pretty fast. Already up to your waist. I could help you. Would you like that Julie? I'd be your hero. I don't see Robbo or Danny rushing to your rescue. Let's make a deal. I help you; you show your appreciation. Show me how eternally grateful you are for saving your life. It's not much to ask, is it? Danny and Rob had a little taste, Danny the full mail. You could give me a bit more, to say thanks to your knight in shining armour. Show a poor Belfast boy a little compassion. Sometimes videos aren't enough."

"Everyone knows it was you," Julie snapped. Her legs had risen a little. She'd slowed the rate, but she was still sinking.

"The video with Rob? Of course it was me. Proof is the thing there, Julie. No one can prove it, and that's only a hint of my talents."

"Why did you do it? We never did anything to you." Julie's panic was growing, and she could feel the fizz of the background white noise in the tips of her fingers.

Ally nodded. "Not directly, no. But sometimes not doing something is as bad as doing something. You know that, Julie? Like neglect, like being ignored. And then again, why not do it? You know, you're not so special. You're not the only one. I've the video of all of you, in your bedrooms, prancing around in your underwear, stripping off and getting into your pyjamas, some of you playing with yourselves, or with your *boyfriends*." Ally fluttered his fingers in front of his groin and bit his lip.

"You're a sick bastard," Julie said, the quicksand now reaching her chest. She reached for the bank in front of her, groping for a handhold. There was nothing there, only viscous cold mud squelched through her fingers.

Ally barked a laugh. "Time is running out, Jules. Here's the deal. I save your life; you show some appreciation. If not, maybe I just let you sink a little further, like you did with Henry."

"I tried to save him."

Ally shrugged. "You keep telling yourself that. Seems to me, you wasted a few precious seconds. Like you've been doing trying to distract me. Maybe I'll let you drown a little bit, then pull you out."

The anger inside Julie was like a hot coal flare in the oxygen of panic and hate. Julie closed her eyes, covering their turn from white to solid orbs of green. With Julie reaching out, seeking a grip on something that wasn't physically there, the vibrations of life had come to her, like in her bedroom when the forget-me-not had bent towards her, and at Danny's house when she cramped with pain and the flowers wilted, and on the Burgage, where her anger had burnt hot from Danny's attack on Rob. She was connected, connected to the plants and the animals of this place. She could feel them, and they could feel her. Maybe it was the magic of this place. Whatever power Millicent believed that she had, in this place it was growing. She sensed all life, including the malevolence in Ally. Julie sensed the desire of the organisms around her, to act for her, to bring her vengeance, and she called them to her. But as they came, Julie felt Rob, too, and the angry spirit that hunted him, moving quickly through the wild wood.

"It's no use, Julie. You need my help. Beg. Ask me nicely. Tell me you'll do anything for me. Tell me you'll open that pretty mouth and let me..." Ally started to recount what he wanted Julie to do to him in lurid detail.

As she slowly slipped deeper into the mud, Julie wasn't listening. She was tuning in, feeling and calling the forest around her to her. Julie sought the right plant, one close enough and strong enough to do the job. She linked with it, finding it near and hungry.

"... And then when you've done that, and you're grinding slowly..."

Ally never got to see his fantasy become a reality.

The briar lashed across his cheek. Three of its thorns cutting deeply into his flesh, raking parallel lines across his face, slashing it to the bone. He fell to his side, bringing a hand to his cheek, blood pouring through his fingers. More and more briars lashed out, hooking into him. A shrill scream tore from his mouth as tendrils lashed like whips through the air and coiled around Ally's limbs. The scream was silenced by the thick branch of the monstrous bramble as it wrapped around his gaping maw. It coiled tight, ripping the flesh of his mouth open to his ears and dislocating his jaw so that it fell open. His blood gushed from his mouth like black vomit, over a lolling tongue the jaw slack, hinged open to the throat. A choking gurgle came from the struggling boy as he was lifted into the air. More tendrils spiralled through the air. Two reared and struck at Ally's eyes, which popped, oozing gelatinous gore down his cheeks. He was still alive, his head shaking in futile resistance, until two more branches struck. One came low, across the ground beneath him, and thrust straight up, its thorny length impaling Ally between the legs, lifting him higher into the air. The last branch buried into an ear hole, wiggling like a grotesquely large and barbed worm. With these, Ally's whole body convulsed in a twitching climax, as the forest parted. A giant white flower, at the heart of the briar, it's petals moist and glistening lay open. The tendrils drew Ally's dead body toward the heart of the plant. Its velveteen petals closed around the corpse, the flesh already dissolving in the putrefying enzymes. The tendrils withdrew, the forest closed, and the whisper sighed.

Ally was dead, but Julie took no pleasure in it. She had felt his anger and his pain, and tears brimmed in her eyes, still moss green.

She saw *her* then, standing in the mist between two elm trees, a fleeting glimpse of Mary Hooper, lank hair over her face. Julie knew it was her because she felt her presence along with all the other life, along with Rob. But with that thought, Mary was gone, gone to complete the curse and take Rob as her prize.

This above everything else put urgency into Julie's efforts. She found the humming vibration of the life around her, she reached out to it. It wasn't hard now. The bramble came back to her, soaked in blood, crawling over the surface of the mud. Julie took hold, careful to avoid the enormous thorns. It dragged her from the mire, depositing Julie on the safe edge of the clearing, before retreating into the depths of the dark wood.

Julie closed her eyes to look for Rob and found him in pain and with his heart broken. Mary was close and getting closer, and with dread throwing her into a run, Julie wondered if she could get to him in time.

74

IN THE BLACK of the unconscious, Danny was still screaming with rage, still in the fight with Rob, sitting astride him, consumed entirely by the need to destroy. With smatterings of blood, each blow that found its mark fuelled his anger. He did not mean to stop. He would pound Rob until there was nothing left, because he was the whipping boy for all Danny's frustrations. He was the cancer that took away a young boy's mother. He was an absent yet domineering Chief Constable father. He was Karolina not-mother and her fake tits and screaming orgasms and snide comments. He was the difficulties at school, not being able to fit in and make friends, which were the manifestation of something much deeper, something that had twisted into a thicket of self-loathing in the crucible of repression. Pretty-boy Rob was the personification of that. And because Danny could not kiss him, hold him in his arms, lay with him or someone like him and make love to them and be loved in return, he had to destroy it.

So, when the scream woke him, lying in a babbling stream, Danny sat bolt upright in the confusion of his new world. The strangeness of his situation scared him. He was in a dark wood cloaked in mist, a hostile place like a little boy lost without his mother. Fear quickly became anger.

He drew up to his hands and knees. Cold water had numbed his legs. Large stones felt smooth and hard beneath his hands. Another scream, one of torment and sorrow, drifted through the wild wood. Danny's hand instinctively closed around one of those smooth stones, the size of a house brick. He rose from the stream, turning to the sound, meaning to finish what he'd started.

UNABLE TO FREE HIS FATHER, Rob let out a tortured cry. He caressed the hard features of Richard's frozen face, and wept, staggering back, drunk with trauma. It was too much: the burdens he'd carried; the visions he'd endured; the growing realisation of his impending death only cemented by his father's actual demise; and now this, face-to-face with his everlasting fate. To be trapped in... where? The flesh of Jack in the Green? It would end here for him too. Rob sank to his knees and wept. He wept for his father, for his mother, for the life he left behind, and he wept for himself, but most of all he wept for Julie. He was responsible for dragging her here with him, and now she was lost and afraid within the wild wood.

Resigned to his fate, Rob did not react when he heard the rustling which had become so familiar. He knew that Mary was near. He smelled the woodland decay, felt the preternatural prickle on his skin. This was it, then. The end. He raised his head from its penitent slump. The laughter of children playing unseen was swallowed by the mist. Mary stood on the far side of the clearing, shrouded in the blanket of grey-white vapour. There she regarded him with skittish jerks of her head, as if hesitant to approach. One dark eye narrowed. A leer grew on her broken mouth. She began to move forward and halted, twitching. Mary's leer turned to a silent, broken toothed hiss, and she retreated into the mist.

Someone was blundering through the undergrowth towards the clearing. Rob thought of Julie. He had to get her away from the Witchopper. He owed her so much more than that, but this was the only thing he could do.

"Julie, no!" The words sounded blunted and felt foolish. Surprise mixed with a sense of deja vu, that his life was on tragic repeat. Rob didn't have the energy to translate what he was seeing into a picture. Danny ran across the clearing, under the boughs of the giant oak. Rob watched him in slow motion. The stone swept down. It would crack open Rob's head and dash out his brains. But there was an unexpected second movement. A whip of motion through the air. The rock's descent was arrested, preventing it from connecting fully on Rob's skull. Rob fell heavily on his side, a bright red gash opened, pumping a hot flow of blood. Wasting no time, Danny fell on him, picking up where they had left off. With an animal scream, Danny brought the stone down to the side of Rob's face. There was an audible wet *snap*. Danny raised the rock in both hands. Rob's eye socket was destroyed. The flesh peeled away, exposing the full orb of his eyeball, brighter amongst the scarlet and pink of excoriated flesh. It bulged, almost completely out of its socket, and somehow Rob was still conscious.

Groaning, Rob choked on his own blood. He coughed a gout of blood into the air, which was followed by a wailing siren of pain. Danny raised the rock, smeared red, above his head and brought it down again, smashing Rob's nose and mouth. Rob's nose was spread across his face in a smudge of pulped flesh. The rock destroyed skin, bone and teeth, opening a cleft in the middle of his mouth. The teeth of his upper jaw had disintegrated. The gums were torn, flooding his throat with blood. The next blow was sure to relieve Rob of life, and his suffering would be at an end. Though Danny would continue until there was nothing left, on top of Rob's twitching body. But the *coup de grâce* never came, and Rob would have to live with the excruciating pain for a while longer.

"No." It was an order, booming like thunder.

Julie had run through the forest, drawn by Rob's screams. She moved with impossible speed. Thick brush and undergrowth parted before her. She floated over dead falls, borne by the plants around her, which lifted her, gliding her through the maze of this otherworldly domain. Julie did not run into the clearing, but descended, having leapt over the upended roots of a chestnut tree. Like a stone skimming over the water, her feet barely touched the top of the obstacle, and she floated down slower than gravity would insist, with her arms outstretched; her words still reverberated. As Julie touched down, the vines and tangled roots of forest receded.

Rock raised above his head, Danny stopped. The look of pure anger barely changed as he noticed Julie alighting from her descent.

She was a mess, filthy with dirt and blood. But inside she felt confident and powerful. Both sure of herself and clear in what she meant to do. Her presence only angered Danny further, who disregarded her as callously as he'd thrown her to wolves in the guise of Ally and his friends. He returned his attention to Rob, lifting the rock even higher.

"I said *no*," Julie screamed, projecting both hands forward, fingers splaying towards Danny. She felt at one with the forest now, she knew that it would do her bidding. It came, an even greater power in this place, with the great oak tree standing sentinel behind Rob and Danny. In two straight lines between Julie and the boys, the ground exploded. Roots tore up from the soil, showering dirt and leaves. One root reared up like a snake and slapped the rock from Danny's hand. Another lashed across his torso, knocking him powerfully away from Rob.

Danny held his stomach, winded.

Julie ran to Rob, collapsing beside him, tentatively laying hands on his wounds, but afraid that she might hurt him. He was barely recognisable. His protruding eye glared wildly, and he was choking on his own blood. She didn't know what to do. Moments ago she found tremendous power coursing through her. Could it be used to save him? But Julie hardly understood it. She wielded the power naively and with a lack of knowledge. She knew she couldn't help. Rob was dying.

"I'm sorry," Julie sobbed and bent to kiss Rob's mutilated face, to leave him with one final kiss. She held him, tears mixing with his blood. Emotions surged through her, powerful and uncontrolled. The forest began to rustle softly. From her hands sprang forget-me-nots. Around Rob's body grew snowdrops, sprouting and unfurling from green shoots. Crocuses, primroses, foxgloves, dandelions, daisies and buttercups bloomed in a bed beneath them. The vines came.

Mistletoe sprouted, weaving itself into a pillow under Rob's head as he wheezed. Ivy burgeoned into a blanket, enveloping his body, preparing him for the final journey.

He had become Julie's entire focus in this place. She knew now, she cared for him, perhaps even more than that, much more. In his ruined state, she saw him now as he had seen her that day in the Chapter House - something beyond physical beauty. That they sat now in the picture he had etched with lines of pencil, another world beneath an ancient oak in a magical forest, only confirmed they had a powerful connection, drawn together by forces they could not fathom. But for all that, on the day Julie lost her baby, she would lose Rob too. The sadness far heavier than a stone whetted with blood. A crushing and powerful thing.

Danny hefted his stone, enjoying its deadly weight. He moved slowly and deliberately towards his quarry consumed by the allure of death. Its simplicity and finality had gifted him solutions to all his anger. His feet crushed the flowers around Rob's deathbed and an ivy stem snapped, shocking Julie from her reverie. When she looked up, with eyes as green as moss, he should have cowered before her. With all the uncontrolled instinct of her newfound power, energised by panic and anger and above all love, the ground exploded around them. Danny staggered, dropping his stone. Julie threw herself over Rob as great geysers of dirt erupted into the air. The cracks from the snapping roots of the tree at the centre of the world rang like thunder. And with a tremendous groaning, the oak tree behind them rose from the earth.

Danny gaped, petrified. Julie shielded Rob, seeing from the corner of her eye the monstrous rearing form of a tree that was no longer a tree but a God in the form of a giant man. Its gigantic trunk of a body was textured with the faces of countless damned souls. Mighty roots spiralled together to form colossal legs. Boughs became corded arms, and branches knitted together forming Jack in the Green's craggy features. Leaves were his hair, sprouting not only on his head but also from his ears, and the corners of his eyes and mouth, like tusks.

Jack towered above them, higher and more imposing than any

domineering father, gazing impassively down high above the canopy, backed by a starless night sky. Danny screamed in defiance, and with the action of a petulant child picked up the stone he'd dropped. He flung it as hard as he could at Jack in the Green, and it bounced ineffectually off the giant's knee. Jack tilted his giant head, leaves swaying. Birds settled on his shoulders. Danny bunched his fists, his face contorted. Jack blinked, raised one of his gigantic legs and stamped down. Danny was obliterated in a stamp of Jack's foot, which shook the wild wood to its root.

Julie opened her eyes. Danny was nothing but a red smear in the dirt. Jack in the Green gazed back, waiting, and the birds settled back on his shoulders

Through pearls of tears, Julie looked into the face of the god of the wild wood. "Please help him," she begged. "I'll do anything. Please save him. What must I do?"

Jack said nothing. His implacable face waited. And from the edge of the clearing came Mary Hooper to claim Rob's soul.

75

JULIE FELT the Witchopper before she saw her, that same feeling from the mud, like a blade of ice drawn down her back. It was a visceral reaction to Mary's intent, which Julie sensed in the scream of her vibration.

The wild wood fell silent. All watched; all waited.

Julie had only seen Mary fleetingly in the wood before she rushed to Rob, not even thinking about Danny. The Witchopper had only ever been a vague monster from her childhood, filled in with the standard caricature of a witch. Green-skinned, large hooked and warty nose, finished off with a pointy black hat. But the Witchopper was not like that at all. As scared as Julie was watching Mary Hooper glide across the clearing, borne by the plants of the forest, she felt pity too. Just like Rob, dying on the ground next to her, she was broken and mutilated.

Mary twitched and jerked as she came on. Through the shredded curtains of hair over her face, she glared at Rob with her one dark eye. Julie still covered Rob with her body below Jack. The giant remained unmoving, surveying the specks of mortal life.

"Stop," Julie called. "Leave him alone. He's dying anyway."

But Mary did not stop. She kept coming, clothed in the dirty rags of her death, filthy with mud, blood, and excrement from when her bowels gave way at the Hanging Tree. Julie could see the angry purple band of bruising around her neck from the rope. Mary said nothing in reply. The cloyingly sweet smell of decay hitched in Julie's throat. Mary was only feet away and bent forward, reaching with twisted fingers, white as bone, nails broken and missing, meaning to have Rob's soul. Julie knew she meant to draw it from him and place his face upon the body of Jack in the Green.

"Get away from him," Julie snarled, standing to face the Witchopper, putting herself between Rob and the vengeful spirit.

Mary drew back, a hiss contorting on her purple lips. Her grey tongue flicked from her black mouth, with a flicker of confusion soon replaced by fury. Julie could feel her power and rage, and knew Mary could feel hers in return. A fellow witch denying what was hers by right, with the powers given to her by Jack in the Green. Mary looked up to the god above them, her mouth working wordlessly, fidgeting and twisting.

Jack did nothing. There was only gentle creaking of wooden limbs, like settling beams of an old manor house.

This did not please Mary. Julie felt it in her mind as a rattle of a snake rearing up to strike, venom burning in its glands, swelling and expanding ready to plunge in Julie's neck. She felt the intent before it happened, a great mumbling and rushing, the rustling surge of life through the bowels of the earth, building and gathering force. But Julie was a girl who had just discovered her powers. She could meet it only with inexperience.

From beyond the clearing, monstrous briars rushed through the wood, snaking through the mist. Thick and leathery tendrils burst into the clearing from behind Mary, slithering past her through the air, her arms rigid and aimed at Julie. It's gigantic thorns would eviscerate her, pull her to pieces as it had done to Ally.

With a grunt of effort, Julie reacted on instinct at the last moment. She called to what was closest at hand and threw up a wall of ivy between them. She knew already that it was too weak. The briars shredded the wall, lashing through like the tentacles of a kraken from the depths. She yelped as one of the tendrils knocked her aside, cutting deeply across the forearm protecting her face. It carved a deep laceration, drawing blood which the hungry plant tasted.

She scrambled back to her feet quickly, ignoring the pain in her arm. The blood dripped down her forearm, over her fingers onto the soil below. Mary was already on Rob, straddling him like a possessive lover. He wheezed and coughed up a clot of blood, moaning in torment. The churning grew in Julie's mind. Mary reached out a hand, splayed like a talon, inches from Rob's mouth. A wind picked up and began to rush through the trees, shaking the boughs of the ancient forest.

"I said, *get away from him.*" Power surged through her and Julie raised her arms, her body as rigid as a lightning conductor, and returned fire. A barrier of flowers grew around Rob, and yanked him back towards Jack in the Green, slipping away from Mary's grasp. She gave another hiss at being denied once more, and turned her angry face to the young witch.

He's mine, Julie heard Mary screeching in her mind. Another wave of rage, one that stretched over two hundred years. Fuelled by the death of a dozen of her children, by her humiliation, betrayal, rape and brutal murder at the hands of lecherous and covetous men.

"No," Julie screamed back, "he's *mine.*" And she meant it. She meant it with every part of her being. Julie's was a scream of care and compassion. A scream of motherly protection and nurturing. It was the scream of Mother Earth and of the womb of life. It was a scream of love. Julie and Mary's passions were the negative image of each other, clashing in the sacred centre of the wild wood. Dark and light. Vengeance and forgiveness. That clash became an explosion, a shock wave that Julie thought for a moment would sweep away her mind. But it didn't. What had been taken was paid for. What had been sinned against was absolved. What had been trapped in hate was set free in love.

The thorny tentacles of the briar slunk back into the depths of the dark wood. The silent wind died, and the trees settled. Mary's twisted face softened and she withdrew from Rob, clasping her broken hands in front of her.

Julie ran to Rob, falling to her knees. His chest struggled to rise and fall. Each breath was ragged and wet, and his eyes were no longer open. Julie didn't know what to do.

"Please," she said to Jack. Tears tumbled down her face. Far above, Jack stared down and his ancient boughs creaked.

Julie turned to Mary. "Please." Her voice cracked like a broken heart, but Mary shook her head sadly and lowered it.

Placing one hand on his chest, Julie felt Rob's life becoming weaker and weaker, and with it she laid a final kiss on his ruined lips. It was then she felt the constriction, and with it believed she had been tricked. The ivy and pillow of mistletoe twisted and grew, binding them together, covering them. Julie panicked, already unable to move. She looked towards Mary, whose face was changing. Her broken features smoothed. Her lips grew full and smiled once more, with teeth no longer shattered but straight and white. Her hair was black and curly, hanging loosely around her shoulders. She had been made whole and smiled with warmth at Julie. But Julie still didn't understand. The plants were going to smother their heads.

"Wait, what's wrong? I thought it was over?" Julie shouted, not comprehending. Was this part of the twisted curse? Could it never be broken? Would it claim even what little solace she and Rob had in the moments left? The ivy entwined around their necks, pressing them cheek to cheek. She felt Rob's final breath leave his body, and heard the words in her mind from Mary: *Thank you.*

With her last glimpse of the wild wood, Julie saw Jack in the Green sink back into the earth, becoming the ancient oak. In the middle of his trunk was a cleft forming a deep cave, which the plants were dragging them towards. Darkness enveloped them. They were covered completely, a chrysalis of root and leaf, pulled into the dark cave at the heart of all things.

IN THE HALF-LIGHT OF DREAMS, fine shafts of light dappled their faces under the canopy of the weeping willow. Birds twittered in the trees and hedgerows that ran along the stream at the edge of Southwell. In those first moments of consciousness, they heard a song, sung slowly

457

by a woman with her back to them, dressed in a shawl and long skirt, covering petticoats. She was hunched over, covering her eyes, waiting to spring around. Six children crept closer, sniggering behind their hands.

"If you see the Witchopper
Then you'll come a cropper
No matter how hard you try
If you look in her cold black eyes
When it's time to go to bed.
You will be sure to wake up..."

Mary Hooper sprang around. She was young, beautiful, surrounded by her many children, who squealed with delight as she gathered them in her arms. It was a dream, lilting in the haze of semi-consciousness and evaporating as they woke.

Julie opened her eyes; Rob lay on his side next to her. He was groggy, slowly coming around like her. She snapped awake, sitting up, urgently checking him for wounds that were no longer there. She caressed his cheek and then lowered her face to his, kissing his forehead, nose, and finally his mouth. They pressed tenderly into each other, a feeling so intense that it seemed endless. Only the joy of their smiles broke the kiss, like a new dawn splitting night.

They sat up, looking at themselves and each other, made whole.

"I'm okay," Rob said in disbelief.

Their clothes were filthy with dirt and dried blood, but their bodies were replenished. Their hands found each other's, and they raced from that old sacred place into the bright, clear sunshine of an early summer's afternoon. Treading along the bank of the stream, they crossed the uncertain stepping stones. At the Mill, they found three discarded bicycles, which would wait forever for their owners to return.

Danny's car was parked at the side of the road. Slowly baking inside, an air freshener in the shape of a fir tree dangled from the rearview mirror.

Julie and Rob walked up to the Burgage and turned right onto Lower Kirklington Road. A police car raced past with blues and twos. Rob and Julie stopped, but the police did not. Three men in high visibility vests and hardhats had turned up at the Burgage in a Council flatbed truck. One of them slapped down a visor on his hardhat and yanked a chainsaw to life, as another finished spray-painting cut marks on the Hanging Tree. A third drank tea from a flask and read the sports pages in the paper.

They set to harvesting the tree for firewood and stock for a local carpentry business. The timber would find its way into homes as handmade mirrors and coffee tables. Some would even become a wardrobe in a child's bedroom, the spirits of many hanged souls worn into its grain.

The chainsaw felled the dead tree, bringing it to an end.

Rob and Julie left it behind and walked home together.

76

IT WAS GOING TO RAIN. The air tasted of ozone and there was an oppressive heat as though a fever was about to break. There was a flash of lightning over Brackenhurst, and a rumble of thunder a few seconds later. It felt like the summer storm would wash everything away and leave the town of Southwell feeling clean again after a summer fraught with drama. A police chief with East European mafia connections arrested and his son disappeared. Sex and financial fraud revelations for individuals all over the town, with no seeming connection between them, and no trace of the anonymous hacker who dumped the information on *The Newark Advertiser* and Nottinghamshire's Serious Crime Unit. A family slaughtered in their home by Irish republican paramilitaries, apparently because the father, a local lawyer, double crossed them while laundering money. Their nephew, orphan of a Scottish mother and notorious IRA commander, was missing along with two other boys, whose bicycles were found near the abandoned car of the disgraced Chief Constable's missing son. There appeared to be connections between it all, but as yet the police were unable to evidence anything.

Rob and Julie stood holding hands at Richard Peters' grave.

"I should have brought flowers," Rob said.

Julie leaned in and pecked him on the cheek. "No problem." She looked around sheepishly, checking they weren't being watched, and squatted, touching her fingers to the grass. Forget-me-nots, small and purple, bloomed. Their tiny heads unfurled, as if they were waking up, until the entire grave was matted with them.

She stood up, opening her palm to Rob, and picked one remaining forget-me-not and gave it to him. They kissed like teenagers in love, because that's what they were.

"Thanks," Rob said, nodding to the grave. "But aren't they spring flowers?"

Julie wrinkled her nose. "It's the best I can do at the moment. There's so much in Millicent's books, but it's a bit slow going."

"That reminds me," Rob said. "When are we meeting the guys?"

Julie inspected her watch. "Sally said she'd meet us at the coffee shop in about twenty minutes, and we can all check at the same time. And Effie and Jason should be here any time. They were stopping by the chemist to get some make-up."

"Which one?" Rob grinned.

"Both of them, I think. Jason said Effie could vamp him up if he got straight As," Julie said, taking Rob's hand to move off from the graveside. They walked back towards the flagstones of the central path that led from the west door of the Minster up to Main Street. They walked slowly, savouring a long summer with no school.

"Is your mum any better?"

"She has good days and bad. The pills help her sleep, and she gets up in the day. It might only be for Ken's house visits."

"He seems to be around most days."

"He brings food. We have a chat over tea and he goes."

"I like him."

"Me too." Rob changed the subject. "How do you think you did?"

"Probably, not good. Hopefully enough to get to A-levels."

"You'll do great. I know it." Rob kicked a small stone, clearing the path ahead.

"We both will."

End

461

ALSO BY DAN SOULE

NEOLITHICA

Some things should stay buried...

The discovery of a young boy's body, brutally murdered and preserved for thousands of years in a Scottish peat bog, brings with it more than a find of a lifetime for archaeologist Mirin Hassan. After the death of her husband, Mirin wants life to get back to normal for her and her young son. But media attention and professional rivalries become the least of her worries. Something other than cameras followed the corpse back to the university. A malevolent force grows unseen. The weather turns biblical. Violence and death spread beyond the university. Could it be connected with the strange discovery? The city grasps for a rational explanation, but time is up. Chaos has arrived, as Mirin realises some things should stay buried.

Book 1 in the **FRIGHT NIGHT** series of bone chillers, Neolithica is the breakout novel from horror author Dan Soule. A mix of Dean Koontz and James Herbert, with a dash of Lovecraft. **Buy it now** if you're a fan of bestsellers like *Phantoms*, *Darkfall* and *The Rats*. Get it here.

NIGHT TERRORS

SWEET DREAMS AREN'T MADE **of these.** Something more than ghosts pursues a family through a desert war zone. A slaughterman says goodbye to his job, but a place of death opens many doorways to darkness. From a father with a dark past, a young woman's inheritance passes on more than she thinks. And a mother's coffee shop daydream could unleash her worst nightmare. These are just some of the dark imaginings that will infect your dreams and rip you from sleep with a cold sweat because you've got NIGHT TERRORS.

Editor of *The Ghost Story*, Paul Guernesy, says: "Dan is a cinematic writer... he steadily builds the mood of his narrative from a whisper of uneasiness to a crescendo of full-blown cosmic horror."

So, grab this collection today from the pen of breakthrough horror author Dan Soule. Join the growing horde of insomniacs who've said goodbye to sleep and hello to NIGHT TERRORS. Download it for free at www.dansoule.com

IN TOOTH AND CLAW

If dreams come true, then so do nightmares. Especially when demons hide - and devour - in plain sight, or the wrong psychopath is recruited for their dream job. When a telephone rings for a forgotten boy in an old red telephone box, or when the sinister origin of a curse is locked within a children's nursery rhyme, then the horror will follow you darkly into your dreams. And it will still be there when you wake.

Download it for free today on Amazon and join the growing

zombie horde of readers spellbound by horror author Dan Soule's storytelling. Let the eight stories fester in your putrefying claw as they worm into your mind. Click here if you are reading on Kindle.

ACKNOWLEDGMENTS

There are a number of people who make any book possible. Witchopper was no exception. I'm indebted to my editor Joe Sale for his comments and revisions.

My wife, Jenny, is always one of my first readers. Her encouragement and tolerance for my sometimes obsessiveness to writing time remains so central to making my stories happen. A number of beta-readers gave me invaluable feedback: Sandra Would, Niall Anderson, Alex Green, Billie Wichkan, Beaulah McLean, and James Klabunde.

Their keen eyes helped clean up the draft and spot small inconsistencies which often get away from the author in such a large writing project. A big thanks also goes to Sherie O'Neil for her proof-read. As a dyslexic writer, I am greatly indebted to all these wonderful folk.

Two police officers need a special mention too. Graham Lees and Michelle Downes who helped with some of the details of police procedure and London police stations.

The cover design was done by Stuart McMillan, a former martial arts friend, from when we used to train in Brazilian Jiujitsu together in Coatbridge, Scotland. Stuart has illustrated a number of my stories over the years as well as doing the cover for Neolithica. You can see the illustrations in my collection of short fiction IN TOOTH AND CLAW.

❀ Created with Vellum